Breakthrough

Michael C. Grumley

ISBN:
ISBN-13: 978-1475031904
ISBN-10: 1475031904

xxix

BOOKS BY MICHAEL C GRUMLEY

BREAKTHROUGH

LEAP

CATALYST

AMID THE SHADOWS

THROUGH THE FOG

THE UNEXPECTED HERO

DEDICATION

To Autumn and Andrea, two of the most wonderful
women to bless this Earth.

ACKNOWLEDGMENTS

Special thanks to Kelly Foster, my number one fan.
Without her, this book would never have been written.
Thanks also to Andrea, Mom, Steve, Richele, Jennifer,
Dan and Don, for their proofreading and expert feedback.

1

SOMETHING OUT THERE sounded strange. He pressed the headphones in tighter against his ears.

Sonar operators were a special breed. Few people could sit in front of a computer screen, fighting monotony day after day, listening to the faintest of sounds through lonely ocean waters. But for the few who could, it was surprising how attuned a human sense could become. Eugene Walker would rather be a *Ping Jockey* than do any other job in the Navy. Here, he could *hear* everything. Even on a boring night like this, he knew exactly what surrounded them as they slid silently through the dark waters.

What he was listening to tonight was odd though. He had heard it for some time but couldn't pin it down. He shifted in his seat and studied the computer screen in front of him, listening to the strange sound picked up by his computer. He played it again and again, and still could not place it. Some jockeys were rumored to be so good that they could identify the current moving through the coral, but those guys had spent their entire lives on their boats. He couldn't hear currents, though he had identified some natural occurrences that the computers could not. But this one was strange; a steady hum at a very low frequency and just barely within the range of human hearing.

Not more than ten feet behind Walker stood Commander Sykes, reading through yet another fascinating maintenance report. Sykes was a stickler for detail, as most were, but even the best commanders eventually fell prey to the unrelenting boredom of perfect routine. He picked up his warm coffee and sipped, letting his mind wander to his wife and girls at home, wondering if they were in bed yet.

He glanced at his watch absently and turned the page, now just scanning for anything that stuck out.

By pure instinct, from the corner of his eye, he noticed his Navigation Officer repeatedly looking at the instruments and then back to the table and his digital map.

"Something wrong, Willie?"

Willie Mendez didn't reply for a long moment. Reporting a problem to the XO wasn't something you did without triple checking. "Mmm…"

Sykes turned slowly, still reluctant to take his eye off the report which was now blurring into a jumble of words.

The officer looked closer at the large illuminated, three square foot map between them. "I'm getting something strange here, sir."

Sykes looked at the table and back up to another monitor, seeing the problem immediately. He took the clear rule and recalculated himself. He frowned and looked back at the young navigator.

"How many times have you checked this?"

"Four times."

Sykes scratched his chin while Mendez spoke. "Plotting from our last verifiable had us here, two minutes ago." He zoomed in on the screen, enlarging the area. A small circle appeared next to his index finger, joined by small GPS coordinates hovering beside it. He then moved his finger further up the chart in the same direction. "Now it's reporting us here."

"In two minutes?" Sykes' response was rhetorical. He shook his head and sighed. 380 knots was a bit optimistic for a nuclear class submarine. Was it a glitch? This wasn't the first computer malfunction they'd had, far from it. He knew that software written by some geek hyped up on Jolt was far more fallible than traditional mechanical or electrical systems. Hell, even the cooks knew that by now. "Anything else acting buggy?"

"No, sir."

"Run integrity checks on both systems."

"Already started, sir." All eyes turned to the monitor now displaying the results. "Systems report no consistency errors."

Great, broken software that doesn't even know it's broken. Sykes looked closely at the orange GPS display. "Try re-synching the satellites."

Willie complied and waited. He began to slowly shake his head. "Birds look good. I've got five…now six. Pinpointed to one meter and reporting the same coordinates."

The Commander didn't respond. He remained focused on the GPS screen, thinking.

Eugene stuck his head out of the tiny radio area and dropped his headset around his neck. "Sir, I've been picking up something for the last few minutes on sonar. It might be related."

Sykes' eyes trained on Eugene. "What is it?"

"Not a vessel, sir. Nothin' I've ever heard before."

Sykes put the second headset on and listened as Eugene played it for him. "What the hell is that?"

Frowning, Eugene switched back to the live feed and closed his eyes. "…it's gone now."

"Any ideas?"

Eugene sighed. "I'm not sure. At first I thought it may have been thermal vents, but that wasn't it." He watched Sykes look back at Willie and return to the table. After a long silence and with forced control, he put his mug down. Stepping from the room over the lip of the hatch, he continued down the long gray, metal corridor. "Of all the damn timing."

*****

Captain Ashman replied to the knock on his door with a simple "Enter". Sykes stepped in, his head barely an inch from the piping overhead.

"What it is?" he hardly needed to look up from his own

reading to know who it was.

"Sir, we seem to be encountering some problems with our navigation system. It's put our position off by about fifteen miles."

Ashman looked up. "Fifteen miles?"

"Yes, sir".

"Did you run diagnostics?"

Sykes nodded. "Yes sir, by the book but cannot find any problems."

Ashman tapped his finger gently against pursed lips. "Could our speed be off?"

"No, sir. The propulsion systems are in perfect sync. It's just our position that's incorrect. I suspect it's a misread somewhere in GPS, but we can't verify unless..."

"If we surface, the mission is aborted." Ashman's tone was sharp. "Did someone upgrade our systems before we left?"

"Not that I'm aware of, sir."

"If I find out that someone was stupid enough to upgrade anything before a four-month mission, I'll personally escort them to the brig!"

"Yes, sir!"

He took a deep breath. It didn't matter whether someone upgraded the system or not, it was still broken and probably could not be fixed from here. Even if it could, it would leave enough doubt to abort the mission anyway. No one would risk continuing on and having a problem crop up at deeper depths. Down there you can't just pop up to the surface.

"Talk with the engineers and make sure no one made any changes." Sykes nodded. He'd expected this order before he knocked on the Captain's door. Ashman retracted his legs and stood up. "Take us up. Tell them we're coming back."

By the time Sykes made it back to the bridge, he was developing a bad feeling.

2

THE CAYMAN ISLANDS were first discovered by Christopher Columbus in 1503. Named Las Tortugas after the many sea turtles, the islands were governed as a single colony for centuries, until they became an official British territory in the late 1960's. Like many Caribbean islands, the majority of business in the Caymans was tourism, flocked to regularly by thousands of sunburned, overweight Americans with too much money and a penchant for cat naps. Arriving in Georgetown and setting out for adventure in their sparkling rental cars and air conditioning, most visitors would be hard pressed to spot remains of the devastation inflicted by the hurricane just a few years earlier. Progress could be simply astounding when it came to the anticipation of more money.

While undetectable from the island, Georgetown was in fact still visible, albeit barely, from the 38 foot catamaran across the stretch of ocean. Anchored much closer to Little Cayman, the boat sat listless in the gentle ocean swell, swaying side to side just enough to allow the lazy halyard an occasional slap against the aluminum mast. The warm winter breeze flowed gently through the lines and over the sails, which were rolled up tight. If close enough, an observer might mistake it for abandoned with no one in sight. Though at this distance the only neighbors were seagulls, two of which sat comfortably on the port hull.

A disturbance in the crystal blue water slowly appeared nearby and a ring of bubbles surfaced as a gentle turbulence. A moment later, a dark head emerged and looked around. Spotting the aft of the boat, a mask was quickly lifted over the short hair and the man swam forward. Upon reaching the small ladder, he gently tossed the mask and snorkel aboard and with surprising ease, pulled his upper body quickly out of the water, allowing his legs to find the rungs. He reached back and unbuckled each fin, tossing them up and grabbing his towel in the same motion.

He retrieved a bottle of orange juice from the small refrigerator and went forward to relax on the trampoline. Peering at the larger island, he could make out the faint image of a jet ski skirting across the water. It amazed him how many people loved noise. Insistent that they need a break from the grind, they travel to a remote area to unwind, only to shop with a thousand other tourists, or zip across the bay on a rocket running at 80 decibels. He smiled to himself and tipped his orange juice in their direction.

To each his own, he thought. He should, in fact, be thankful. If they were not over there, they would probably be here next to him. With that, he stood up and squinted at the glimmering horizon. Having to decide what to do every day was just the type of problem he wanted.

His body suddenly stiffened. The sound was extremely faint but unmistakable and he felt a flutter of grim acceptance before reaching for the binoculars. He wiped the water from his face and peered through the lenses. He stood, watching stoically as the tiny black dot in the distance slowly grew into the recognizable shape of a helicopter.

3

IT HAD ALWAYS surprised Chris Ramirez how busy

Fridays were. He would have guessed a Saturday or Sunday, but the last day of the school week was always the busiest. This was thanks to all the nearby schools and their field trips, which meant playing host for four exhausting hours. An obligation Chris had finally been freed from just three weeks earlier with the hiring of a new tour guide. Of course, now he had to admit that giving the tours to the kids was not all bad. It was the fact that their retention levels dropped to zero once they were through the front door that bothered him. From there, they could see the aquarium's star attractions, dolphins Dirk and Sally. Not that he would have been any different at their age.

He strolled through the empty lobby sipping his coffee. As he approached, he smiled at Betty behind the information desk and his replacement, Al, who was looking over his schedule and straightening his tie. What a beautiful day these new Fridays were, now that it allowed him to return to his real work.

Chris glanced at his watch; thirty minutes until the doors opened. He headed downstairs to the bottom level of the main aquarium. There, he stood before the giant wall of glass, holding back more than a million gallons of water. On the other side, the gentle rays of sun were already illuminating the water with a soft shade of blue from the tank's open top. He watched both shadows dart back and forth effortlessly through the rays of sunlight. The dolphins were swimming about with a grace of which only they were capable. He looked higher at the third shape. It waved to him, at which point he smiled and waved back with a gentle swipe of his coffee cup. The figure turned and swam back toward Dirk and Sally. With that, Chris walked down the hall to the aquarium's private rooms and dropped his backpack onto the desk.

Swimming with dolphins was beyond what most could imagine, and she should know, she did it as often as possible. She rarely missed a Friday, as it was the one day that the aquarium opened late, leaving a forty-five minute window between feeding time and opening time. Over the last five years, Dirk and Sally had especially come to enjoy their swims together, it was more than obvious. They constantly swirled around her, letting her run her hands over their slick bodies, and in turn, would playfully bump her as they passed beneath. She looked at her watch, gave them one last pat, and headed for the ladder.

Alison Shaw surfaced and held onto the ladder while she cleared her mask. She noticed a distorted shape quickly approach and looked up, removing her foggy goggles to see Chris smiling down at her.

"Weren't you just downstairs?" she asked, brushing hair out of her eyes.

He did not answer.

Alison looked up again with a squint. "Something wrong?" He continued to beam. "Why are you smiling?"

He bent down. "I think you're going to want to see this."

Her eyes shot open. "IMIS?"

Chris grabbed her hand, pulling her out of the water with one hand, and handing her a towel with the other. She stepped out, quickly dried off and pulled a long sleeve shirt and shorts out of her bag. She and Chris had been friends for years, but he still snuck a glance now and then at her trim figure. A few inches shorter than average, she was still far from the norm when it came to female marine biologists. Hurrying to get her sandals on, they ran across the viewing area and into the building.

They burst into the research area to find Lee Kenwood in his usual spot, at a large desk crammed with monitors and keyboards with cables snaking all over the floor, something Alison always imagined the bowels of a phone company to look like. Behind Lee and against the wall were several tall metal racks holding dozens of computer servers each. In the middle section of one of the center racks stood a monitor, keyboard, and mouse, used for

11

manually controlling any of the one-inch thick machines, even though it was something Lee rarely had to do anymore. With the myriad of systems on his own desk, he could now just as easily connect to the servers remotely.

The wall opposite the servers was part of the dolphin's tank, constructed in clear glass to allow optimal visibility for study. Before the thick glass stood six mechanical apparatuses of varying height and complexity, with a digital video camera perched on top of each. Around the room were several dozen books and journals on topics ranging from marine biology, to language analysis, to writing code in various computer languages.

Alison made it to Lee's desk before her wet bag even hit the carpeted floor. "What is it?"

He looked through his rectangular glasses at Chris. "Didn't you tell her?"

She pushed her way in front of the screen. "Tell me what? What is it?!"

He gently pushed himself away from his desk, rolling out of the way and allowing her a closer view. "Looks like it's done."

"Are you sure?!" she asked looking back at the tank. She could see Dirk and Sally on the far side anticipating the first wave of children.

Kenwood grinned "Pretty sure." He rolled closer again and clicked the mouse, bringing columns of various numbers and results onto the screen. "See…Frequencies…Octave Ranges…Inflection Points-"

"What about Inter-click Interval and Repetition Rates?" She scanned the large monitor excitedly.

"Right here. And we have multiple video positions for each of them."

Behind them, Frank Dubois burst into the room. "Just got your message. What's up?" By the time the last word rolled off his tongue, he realized he did not need an answer. He knew simply from the look on their faces. "Tell me it's done."

"Oh, it be done, Captain." Lee grinned. He pointed to the screen as Dubois leaned in behind Chris and Alison. "All the variables have been identified. Look, if you add them up you get almost the exact same number listed with the video positions, divided by three." He clicked another button and brought up the system log. "And look at this; it says the last variable was found almost two months ago, so there hasn't been anything new in terms of behavior or sounds." He leaned back with a cocky nod. "This envelope has been licked and stamped!"

Alison smiled. Lee always had a creative way with words. "I trust you've already made the call to IBM?"

Lee nodded. "I did. They're coming down to verify."

Now Chris turned and looked at the dolphins. "Who's coming?"

Lee smiled. "Uh…everyone."

"Fantastic." Dubois turned and headed for the door. "I've got to make a call. You busy today Ali?"

She laughed. "Are you kidding?"

"Well, when you come down off of cloud nine, maybe you can spare a few minutes…we'll need someone to write us up a press release." With that, he let the door close behind him.

4

THE SILVER DOORS opened and John Clay stepped out of the oversized elevator. With a sharp right, he made his way down the long white hallway of the Pentagon's D ring. From the far end of the hall, Admiral Langford spotted Clay and broke off his conversation with another officer. He walked to meet him and handed Clay a thick folder.

"Sorry, Clay." The admiral was shorter by a couple inches but moved erect and with a sharpness that always made Clay feel he was looking up. They met several years prior when Admiral Langford took over the department. He'd been under Langford ever since.

Clay fell into step with Langford as he opened the folder and scanned the first page. "A computer glitch, sir?"

"Apparently there's more to it," Langford responded calmly. "It was originally filed as a glitch but we can't replicate it." He nodded to a woman walking past them. "Navigation system was working perfectly since the sub left port and then, all of the sudden, they're fifteen miles off course."

Clay tried to keep up while flipping through several pages of what most would consider random computer code. "Any changes in direction?"

"No change in direction. Same course but fifteen miles further out." Langford could see the problem taking hold in Clay's head. Clay was one of the best analysts he'd ever had, with a mind like a steel trap. Langford never had to repeat anything to him.

"Sounds like that would rule out drift or cross currents. Might be something with the engines if it were one of the older subs, but the new class measures speed by GPS too. How about a satellite problem?"

They turned and continued down another hallway adorned with pictures of past military officers. "That's what I thought, but so far we haven't had anything else reported."

Clay spoke without realizing it. "Those sats are all semi synchronous. A GPS receiver is never locked onto the same six signals. Which means by now-".

"They're all part of other sets." Langford pulled out a security card and swiped it through the reader next to a metal door that read DNI in large blue letters. "We identified all the sets that the Alabama was using for that entire week and ran checks on them individually. Nothing." Langford swung the large door open. "How was the trip?"

"Short, sir."

"I'll make it up to you."

The Department of Naval Investigations was a large department and took a large part of the Pentagon's second floor, rings A through E, on the west side. Consisting of several hundred staff, most specializing in legal and personnel issues, the department was growing as a result of the softening of military policies. Personnel issues such as harassment had skyrocketed over the last several years as the military struggled to adapt to twenty-first century expectations. Next to legal and HR, the Navy's technology group was small by comparison. Clay's team was smaller still. *Electronics and Signaling* was a specialty that very few understood, let alone were interested in. Even the brass, who were often technology's strongest advocates, did not really want to know *how*. They just wanted it to work. Clay's E&S team often had to find out why a technology was *not* working, where the failure occurred and why. It required expert level knowledge in a wide variety of technologies including computer chip design, networking, signaling and a thorough understanding of the electromagnetic spectrum.

Clay turned a corner and passed a number of offices. His aide, Jennifer, was clearly expecting him when he opened the door and walked through.

"Hi John." She said, hanging up the phone. "How were the Caymans?"

"You would have hated it," he smiled and moved past her into his office. "No reality TV."

She grinned and followed him with a folder of her own. "I'll be sure to cross it off my list." Jennifer laid the folder out and set aside his stack of messages, which Clay eyed with dismay.

"All of these in just three days?"

"You're a popular guy." She flipped through the folder for his benefit. She pulled out a number of documents from the back. "And these need your signature."

"What would I do without you?"

"Oh stop. You're going to give her a big head." They both looked up to see Steve Caesare in the doorway, smiling. At six foot, with matching dark hair and mustache, he was one hundred percent Italian but without the ties to the mob, or so he said. Caesare and Clay had been friends since the beginning, meeting in the earliest days of their now twenty-two years of service, and working through most of those years and several departments together.

Jennifer smiled and left the room, flicking him on the arm as she passed.

Steve entered and sat down in a chair across from John's desk. "Our leaves are getting shorter and shorter. Pretty soon they'll be shorter than our lunches."

Clay dropped Langford's folder onto his desk and fell into his chair, turning it toward Caesare. "You're lucky you didn't come. The shorter it is, the more depressing the return." He took a deep breath. "Tell me why we do this again, for love of country or something?"

"It's the chicks."

"Langford talk to you already about the Alabama?"

"Yeah, I gave him that same folder this morning." Caesare stretched out his legs and leaned back. "It's strange. I haven't seen anything like it. Probably not earth-shattering, but they want to put back out quickly before the crew gets lethargic. We've been working with their technicians, going through everything with a fine tooth comb."

"Find anything?"

"Not yet. We're about to start tracing out cables."

Clay sighed and leaned forward, opening the Alabama's

16

folder. "Were there any other vessels nearby using the same satellites?"

Caesare shook his head. "No, the closest ship was only using four of the same birds, not enough for a true comparison-". He was interrupted by his cell phone. He looked at the number before answering. "Hey, any news? Okay, be right there." He ended the call and stood up. "Borger may have something."

*****

Will Borger was a true throwback from the hippy generation, though technically a few years too young to actually qualify. He wore his hair long in a ponytail, likely trying to make up for the top of his head which was losing ground. He routinely wore round glasses and loose fitting Hawaiian shirts. He was the epitome of the old computer geek and Clay and Caesare liked him immensely.

The two walked into the lab, filled with computer and satellite equipment, some so complex that it was almost unrecognizable even to them. Most of the shelves were a tangle of wires and cables, connecting dozens of monitors, computers, oscilloscopes, and amplifiers. Clay estimated that Borger had enough coax cable in his office to start a television company. A wooden desk sat in the corner under an old lamp with almost a dozen keyboards, some stacked on top of each other.

Borger stood nearby hunched over a table covered with a giant red and white map. He looked up with raised eyebrows. "Hey Clay, I didn't know you were back."

"Yeah, almost like it never happened."

"Ah, you must have gotten called back for the Alabama. I hear they want to get this zipped up and back out to sea next week."

Caesare glanced down at the map. "What's this?"

"The Earth. At least part of it. I finished stress testing the sats and didn't find anything so I decided to take a look at the coordinates using the new Jason-2 satellite."

Clay was familiar with the Jason-2. Replacing its predecessor, the Jason-1, which itself replaced the TOPEX/Poseidon, the first satellite designed to study the planet's magnetic field. Those early missions had changed how satellite computer chips were designed and significantly increased their ability to withstand high doses of solar radiation, resulting in a boon for the satellite industry. Yet, while the first two returned a wealth of information, the Jason-2 was the first craft sensitive enough to detect fields closer to the surface. He recalled the launch creating quite a bit of excitement among the scientific community.

Borger continued. "The maps won't be completed for a few more years, but because of its launch orbit, the equator was the first area to be mapped, including the Caribbean where the Alabama reported the problem."

They moved in closer. "And?"

"Well, here's the rest of the equator and here's the area around Bimini," he said, pointing to a large darkened circle. "According to the J-2, there appears to be a very high level of magnetism here."

"Any chance of a fluke? Maybe the instruments aren't calibrated yet."

Borger shook his head and ran his hand over the rest of the map to straighten it. "I don't think so. As you can see, the rest of the measurements are accurate. Pretty coincidental that we'd see a glitch happen right here. If I had to guess, I would say the sea floor has an unusually dense iron composition."

Clay looked up. "But that shouldn't affect GPS."

"Well, maybe not by itself, but we've been having small solar flares all month, and those have been known to throw off all kinds of things especially satellites. The flares we had on the day the Alabama experienced this problem were pretty small but with the area having a high iron concentration, the ionization may have rendered the satellites unable to accurately pinpoint their position."

"How long did the flares last on that day?"

"Six or seven hours, I think. I'd have to check."

Clay stood up and tapped his finger on his chin, thinking. "So if the flares were the cause we could expect to see inconsistencies in the sub's data for up to six or seven hours prior?"

"Probably," nodded Borger. "They may be *very* subtle inconsistencies though, depending on how close they were to the area and their heading."

Clay looked back to Borger. "Can you find out exactly how long the flares lasted?" He then turned to Caesare. "Let's pull all the sub data for that entire day."

*****

Four hours later, Caesare walked in and dropped a thick stack of paper on Clay's desk.

"The Alabama's complete log from the 31st. Communications, navigation, propulsion…everything except the ship's menu."

"And?"

Caesare shook his head. "Nothing. Not a single discrepancy. And let me tell you, that is one boring read."

Clay flipped through the pile. "Borger says the flares lasted almost eight hours, off and on. Anything else from the tech team on board?"

"Nope. They're still tracing and testing cables, but I don't expect to find anything."

They both knew that the cabling was more of a formality than anything else. A last act of diligence for the sake of being thorough. Wiring and insulation in these subs were meticulous. Rarely was the cabling ever found to be responsible. He pushed his chair back, finally shaking his head after a long moment. "Well, whatever it was, it wasn't a solar flare, or a systems problem."

"Or *wiring*," Caesare added, leaning against the door frame. "We going out?"

Clay nodded.

5

ALISON SIPPED HER tea and stared intently at the screen. It was about to start, and she could almost hear her heart beating. *What's with the anxiety?* She thought to herself. *You'd think you were the one on television.* She was rarely nervous, if you could even call this nervousness. It was more excitement than anything else. Her press release had been picked up by dozens of papers and news broadcasts, all wanting an interview. She would never have imagined that kind of response, but with the progress they had made recently, maybe it was not so surprising.

What was surprising, was that they managed to make it on television and quickly. NBC called and wanted Dubois to be part of their Monday show, just three days after their press release went out. Previous announcements, albeit less exciting, had only been picked up by local papers. Something about their latest news sure got somebody excited. It made Alison wonder who got bumped. Hopefully some corporate executive lined up to hype a new product line or brag about how much richer they were.

Chris Ramirez approached with his own mug and looked at his watch. "Didn't start yet, did it?"

She shook her head and bobbed her tea bag a couple times.

"You know you should have gone with him," he said,

taking a tentative sip.

Alison shook her head. "Nah. He's better at this kind of stuff."

"True," Chris said, with a shrug. "Definitely doesn't have anything to do with him loving the spotlight."

She raised her cup to hide the grin.

Suddenly Matt Lewis's face filled the screen, his words barely audible until Lee turned up the volume. "Here we go!"

"...at the Miami City Aquarium where a team of marine biologists have been trying to do the unthinkable. Talk to another species. With me today is Frank Dubois, the director of the center and the research being done there. Welcome, Dr. Dubois."

"Thank you, Matt." Frank's face filled the screen and both Chris and Lee let out a whoop. He looked good, comfortable on camera, much better than she would have.

"Doctor, I have to say, this is really exciting. I never knew there was such research being done at the aquarium. How did this all get started?"

Frank flashed his perfect smile and shrugged graciously. He was a natural. "Well the idea is not all that new, but the technology required for this approach was not available until very recently. We started with a small grant and eventually garnered enough interest to pay some salaries. In fact, much of the first two years of research was done on a volunteer basis by our senior researcher, Alison Shaw."

Lee Kenwood leaned over and gave her a friendly bump. "All right, Ali."

"It's a miracle," Chris mumbled under his breath.

"Stop it!" She blushed and stared back at the screen. Accepting compliments was not her strong point.

Lewis continued on screen. "So tell me about this IMIS system."

"Well, it's a distributed computing system which means we divvy up the load to a lot of smaller individual computers, over a hundred in this case. This gives us processing power much greater than what we could achieve even with a super computer, and at a fraction of the cost."

"And what does IMIS mean?

"IMIS is short for InterMammal Interpretive System."

"And this IMIS translates the language?" asked Lewis.

Frank smiled. "Well not yet. But basically yes. IMIS works by recording all of the recognizable sounds from our dolphins; all of their clicks, whistles, even postures. Once all of those have been captured in multiple scenarios, we then start the translation process using an advanced artificial intelligence program." He smiled again. "Or at least we attempt a translation."

Lewis frowned. "So is this going to work? I mean, how long will it take to make this kind of breakthrough?"

"Well, the recording phase, or what we call *phase one*, has been completed. Now we've begun phase two, which is Translation, and that's all computer. Unfortunately, since this has never been done before we really don't have an estimate on how long it will take. But the intelligence program is designed to learn as it goes, so every day it should get a little bit smarter."

Lewis shook his head incredulously. "How on earth do you write a program that talks to dolphins?"

"You get IBM's help." They both laughed. "IBM is actually one of our sponsors. They have donated most of the hardware and a lot of programming brainpower. The software is really quite impressive."

"I bet it is," Lewis continued, looking down at his notes. "It says here that NASA is also one of your sponsors."

"That's right."

Lewis shook his head. "Okay, IBM I understand, but why NASA? What interest would they have in something like this?"

"That's a common question. NASA is more interested

in the technology that we're using than us actually making contact. They are hoping to build on the technology and one day use it to communicate with an alien intelligence. If they find one, that is."

"Really?" Lewis was genuinely surprised.

Frank took a sip of water and nodded. "Yes. Their thinking is that our hopes of communicating with aliens are pretty remote if we haven't even learned to communicate with another species on the same planet." He shrugged. "The fundamental approaches should be very similar."

"And here you are on the verge of doing just that."

Frank smiled again and raised his hand in a cautionary gesture. "Well, I don't know if I would say on the verge. We're *closer*, a lot closer than say we were six years ago, but there is still a lot of work to do. In all honesty, we may still be in for a very long wait. Like I said, it's up to the computers now."

"So, if you are able to translate, what will you say? Obviously, you're not going to ask them what it's like to be a fish." The audience laughed.

"Well, we might still ask them that," Frank said with a smile. "But no, it's going to depend on what we can translate, if anything. Dolphins are the second smartest animal on the planet and they are the only species besides humans that are self-aware. For example, when you put a mirror in the tank, dolphins will actually look at themselves and even examine their bodies. They understand the connection and the fact that there is a world around them, so the depth of exchange possible here is staggering."

Lewis scooted forward slightly with genuine interest. "Let me ask you this, without knowing what level of translation *might* be possible, what at this stage are you *hoping* for? In other words what are you hoping to learn if all goes well, even if it takes years?"

Frank tilted his head, momentarily considering the question. "Well, first and foremost, we would want to know who they are as a species. And by *we*, I mean us humans, would want to know, as one sentient being to another, as one civilization to another."

"Civilization?"

"Yes," he continued. "We define a civilization as an advanced state of society. Obviously they have no technology or industry but government and culture are huge components of what we consider a civilization. Like humans, dolphins are social creatures. We know they live and operate in large groups, sometimes in the tens of thousands. But what is really exciting is the idea of culture. Again, dolphins are extremely intelligent, compared to the rest of the animal kingdom. They even have a sense of humor."

Alison watched the salesman emerge in Frank. This was how he got their funding year over year. He was a god.

"We know dolphins have a complex language. But imagine…if they have the ability to pass information, not just to each other, but from *generation to generation*. We could be talking about a lineage, about a progressive cognition. That is culture!"

The idea had not been lost on Lewis. He sat motionless for a moment before speaking. "Wow. That is really exciting." He reached out his hand. "We wish you the best of luck and can't wait to have you back."

"Thank you." Frank smiled and shook.

"Dr. Frank Dubois," Lewis said, closing. "Director at the Miami City Aquarium."

"Alright!" Ken reached forward and turned the volume back down. "Maybe now we'll get some real funding."

Alison smiled, her fingernail still between her teeth. *Not bad*, she thought, *not bad at all*.

6

THE PATHFINDER WAS an oceanic research and survey ship. At just under three thousand tons she was capable of an impressive sixteen knots fully loaded. Commissioned in 1994, the Pathfinder was one of the Navy's most modern and capable science vessels, performing experiments throughout the Atlantic Ocean. Clay could see the ship's unmistakable white hull from the window of the Sikorsky Seahawk helicopter, even at altitude. And at two hundred feet long, the Pathfinder was large, though still one of the smaller ships in the research fleet. He knew landing a helicopter of this size was going to be tight.

The helicopter banked slightly and began a gradual descent. Clay relaxed and laid his head against the headrest. Next to him, Steve Caesare slept soundly, almost in a catatonic state. A trick many learned in their early days of service was "sleep when you can", and Caesare had taken the lesson to heart. Clay often joked that had he been there; Caesare would have slept through the bombing of Pearl Harbor.

Clay watched through the window as the helicopter dropped closer to sea level. After a few minutes, the pilot leveled off and skimmed the last mile at just under a hundred feet, low enough to see schools of colorful fish below the clear blue water. He slapped Caesare awake and fastened his seat belt.

The helicopter slowed and hovered as it positioned itself over the ship's black landing pad. It floated close to the deck until the pilot could match the rising and falling of the ship on the ocean swells. Reaching the last few feet, the craft dropped suddenly and bounced onto the pad. An ensign trotted out beneath the slowing blades and pulled the door open. With a quick salute, he unfolded the small set of stairs outward and motioned for Clay and Caesare to follow him.

They grabbed their bags and made their way off the pad and across the deck. After climbing two flights of stairs, they opened a white steel door and stepped onto the bridge.

Captain Emerson looked up as the two men stepped inside.

Emerson grinned and extended his hand to Clay. "Clay, how the hell are you?"

"Good, Rudy. How are things in paradise?"

"Not bad. I don't think I've worn long sleeves in two years," he said smiling. He turned to Caesare. "And, who do we have here?"

"Rudy, this is Commander Steve Caesare. He's in E&S too."

Emerson shook Caesare's hand and eyed the small trident pin on his collar. "Pleased to meet you. You were a SEAL too, were you?"

"A pleasure, sir. Yes, some time back. Was in Somalia in '93. Got transferred out a year after that."

"Somalia." Emerson sighed. "That was a real mess."

"Yes, sir, it sure was. Lost some friends."

Emerson frowned and nodded. "So, what is it that has us racing across the whole damn Atlantic to meet you fellas?"

Clay smiled. Like Caesare, Emerson was another old Navy friend. And though he took great pleasure maintaining his gruff exterior, much like the old sea dogs, he was never able to fully pull it off. Nevertheless, Emerson had fun playing the part. He was a good friend to have, being skipper of one of the leading research vessels in the Navy's Military Sealift Command. A large part of the MSC's primary mission was to provide a wide range of support operations including fueling, vehicles, ammunition, and supplies.   Being part of the support system for the entire U.S Navy gave Emerson a deep insight into many things in which the military arm was involved.

Clay shrugged.   "Just some signal interference.   We need to put it to bed so the Alabama can go back out.   We lucked out that you were closest and have the new ROV onboard."

"Well, we're certainly one of the more comfortable ships."   He signaled to a subordinate to take over the bridge.   "You'll like the rover called Triton II; no tether and uses ultra-low frequency which gives it a damn impressive range."

"How deep have you taken her?" asked Caesare.

"Four thousand feet, maybe more.   We'll have to ask Tay.   He's the lead engineer."

Clay and Caesare were impressed.   Almost a mile without a tether was nothing short of astounding.

Emerson led the men outside and back down the way they came.   At the bottom of the stairs, a female officer stopped and saluted.   The captain returned it quickly without slowing.   He saw the men exchange looks from the corner of his eye and replied without being asked. "We have six female officers on board.   Bit of a pain to set up separate quarters and all, but it's worth it.   Having them aboard raises the level of professionalism, contrary to popular belief."   He ducked and stepped through a doorway and after a left turn, stepped into the galley. "Coffee?" he asked, picking up a pot and selecting a mug from a neatly stacked pile.

Nodding, they both accepted a cup in turn.

"So, what kind of interference you guys having down here?"

Clay shrugged.   "Not entirely sure.   Nothing too serious, probably just interference based on high iron in the soil.   We need to get some samples for analysis."   He sipped from his mug.   "We may have to come back out with an old sub and spot check if we don't find something obvious."

Caesare looked at Emerson. "Incidentally Captain, we'd like to get some system logs from the Pathfinder too and compare them with the sub's. It's likely an issue with depth or proximity to pockets of mineral concentrations, so we should eliminate surface ships from the list while we're here."

"Of course," Emerson nodded. He looked at his watch. "We should head aft. Tay and the team should be about ready to launch the Triton. We'll be at your coordinates within a few minutes."

Reaching the stern of the ship, Clay and Caesare found several of the team slowly lifting the Triton II up and off the deck. The craft was a noticeable change from most of the Navy's previous remote operated vehicles. Unlike the older tubular designs, the Triton was closer to U-shaped with most of the craft built around a clear sphere. A number of motors and fins were attached to what was considered the back, though the entire craft was still more round than anything else. Unlike the traditional designs of submarines, a sphere or globe maintained perfect pressure on all sides as it descended, in essence making the craft stronger the deeper it went. By designing the Triton around such a shape, it was able to reach deeper depths without special efforts to increase body strength required in older tube shapes. The tradeoff, of course, was speed. With more surface area meeting the water while it moved, Clay guessed that the Triton was likely twenty-five percent slower than older models. Nevertheless, with the benefit of a deeper limit without a ship having to carry thousands of feet of thick cable to use as an umbilical cord, he could see why the Triton II was so popular.

Edwin Tay was of Chinese descent and looked to be in his late thirties. He was shorter than the rest of the team but was clearly in charge. He was giving a steady stream of instructions as they smoothly moved the rover out and over the water, suspended by a long, thick articulating arm. He finally turned and motioned for one of his team to lock it in place just moments before the drone of the engines disappeared and the ship began slowing to a stop. Emerson caught his attention and waved him over.

"Mr. Tay, meet commanders John Clay and Steve Caesare. Our friends from the E&S team in D.C."

Tay shook their hands. "Welcome aboard. I hear you've come to have some fun with our new rover."

Clay laughed. "I'm afraid it's a bit more boring than that. We just need some soil samples to take home. We were fortunate that you were in the area, especially with the new rover."

Tay looked back at the craft, hanging suspended in the air and swinging slightly from side to side. "Yeah, she's a beauty. Battery life is a little limited, but I suspect that will be improved in future versions. Even with that, we've had her down to forty-three hundred feet without a glitch. Pictures as clear as cable TV," he said with a wink.

"She's a nice looking sub," Caesare replied.

Tay quickly wiped his forehead. "We still need to run some checks, but we should be ready to launch within about fifteen minutes or so. In the meantime, we have a pretty decent galley if you guys are hungry."

Clay put a hand on his stomach. "Sounds good to me."

"Let's go round something up then," said Emerson, nodding his head back the way they came. "It's almost lunch time anyway."

*****

Captain Emerson removed his hat and scratched the base of his hairline. His gray hair was cut short, a style many in the military never outgrew. He dropped his hat on the seat next to him and picked up his second cup of coffee for a drink before continuing. "Getting a bit of pressure to resolve this, are ya? I'm sure Washington isn't happy with that large a crew and sub sitting idle dockside. What's it costing them, a million a day?"

"One point four, actually." Clay frowned.

Emerson grimaced. "I hope Langford is backing you guys up."

"He's pretty good about that," Clay said, watching Caesare take a bite of his pork chop with raised eyebrows. The food was excellent. "Still he's got Miller breathing down his neck with the cost, but he can only stand on procedure for so long. He made sure to mention the number a couple of times." Clay reached for his own mug. "I suspect we're looking at an anomaly here, but we have to go by the book. We haven't found anything wrong with the sub or the satellites which means a site survey. If we find the soil rich in iron or other minerals, we'll need to file a report with a theory which means scientific testing and peer reviews. We may not have an answer for years."

Emerson nodded. "If it comes down to a theory, they'll ship out the next day. Nothing more that can be done until more testing bears something out."

Clay took a bite of his salad. "So, anything interesting on the research front?"

Emerson shook his head. "Only on how we are becoming more and more commercial with each project. Corporations are driving it all with their friends in Washington beating their 'in the interest of national security' drums which means that anything connected to energy these days, especially the black liquid kind, is considered national security. Most of our projects in the last few years have been soil and drilling samples thinly disguised as marine research which really means looking for new oil reserves for the conglomerates." He leaned back in his chair unable to hide his irritation. "I'll tell you this, corporations have become the puppet masters behind the government." Emerson exhaled heavily. "This is not the same Navy we started with, gentlemen."

"Agreed," Caesare said with his final swallow. "It's not an adventure anymore, it's just a job."

Emerson laughed. "Maybe it's time we reversed our motto." He leaned forward again and picked up his fork. "Don't get me wrong though, there are still some interesting things happening in the research area. Hell, just our ability to probe deeper with better systems like this new Triton generates a fair amount of excitement. The level of detail we're able to track has the Navy talking about fields of underwater sensors and the idea of developing a living map, all live data and changing as it happens...pretty amazing stuff."

"Sounds interesting." Caesare emptied his water glass. "I wonder how much we'll spend trying to weaponize it."

Emerson laughed again, harder. "I like you, Caesare. A fellow cynic. How'd you ever get mixed up with Clay?"

He smiled at Clay before replying. "Ah. We met in SEAL training, back in '89. Clay got thrown out a while later. What was it again?" he asked jokingly, "wearing dresses or something?"

Clay grinned. "Bad knees."

"Right. Anyway, he ended up in intelligence working with some of the old members of SEAL Teams One and Two, so we worked together on and off for a couple years until he went off to Investigations. We stayed in touch and one day he said he was looking for someone to join his team."

"So you moved to Washington." Emerson was clearly enjoying this.

"I had no choice," he shrugged. "He had too much dirt on me."

"Sadly," added Clay, "everyone has dirt on Steve."

"So, from SEAL team to an electronics expert. That's quite a jump," Emerson said.

"Well, like Clay, I had a science background before joining the SEALs."

The Captain nodded. "Well, I'm surprised we haven't

met before. This isn't the first time Clay has hijacked one of my ships in the name of E&S."

"Yeah, well, the last time," Clay mused, nodding at Caesare, "he was getting married...again."

"A girl in every port, I'm sure." Emerson looked at his watch. "The team should be about ready. I'll drop you off at the comms room before I head back up to the bridge."

The communications room served as the headquarters where most of the Pathfinder's research was done. Packed with wall to wall instruments, it was roomier than they were expecting, and clean as a whistle; a reminder that Emerson ran a tight ship. They ducked slightly as they stepped into the room. Several of the team members were there with one seated at what looked to be the control panel for their remote wonder. Tay stood behind his seated comrade, looking over some instruments. He stood up quickly, just as Emerson nodded, and headed back up to the bridge.

"You guys ready? We're done checking out." He looked out the small window. "Should have plenty of daylight depending on how many samples you need." He motioned to one of the men next to him. "Grab them a couple seats, Pete."

Clay and Caesare sat down and scooted forward, close enough to see the monitors clearly. Two were displaying a video feed, one of the rover swinging from the metal arm outside, and the other showing the view looking out from the Triton's bubble. The gentle waves, distorted through the craft's reinforced Plexiglas, could be seen slapping against a small section of the ship's hull.

"All right, all systems go?" Tay asked, looking around the room. Most of the members turned from their instruments and nodded with an "aye".

"All right, let 'er drop," he called out.

The crew member in the seat reached forward, grasped a chrome handle and pulled back firmly. All eyes went to the first monitor and watched it fall from the steel arm into the water a few feet below. Tay smiled and looked back at his visitors. "That was always the worst part with the tethered rovers."

The second monitor showed water sloshing across the Triton's bubbled window, with roughly half beneath the water line.

"Everything up on screen, please." A moment later the other monitors came to life displaying a variety of statistics and graphs. The largest monitor reported information on battery charge and graphs for each of the rover's nine motors. Each graph listed the current and RPM of its individual motor, giving an impressive level of granularity. "Looking good."

In the chair, Jim Lightfoot grasped a large joystick and gave it a gentle twist. The rover banked right and began moving away from the ship.

"Okay," Tay said standing up straight. "How deep was your sub when it had the problem?"

"Five hundred and seventy meters."

"Alright Lighty," he said patting his teammate on the shoulder. "Let's take her down."

With a gentle push forward, the Triton's view became clear as it slipped below the surface. The water was crystal clear with the colors becoming dark blue as the craft descended into the ocean's depths.

"Full steam ahead."

Lightfoot continued to push forward on the joystick and the small specks floating in the water suddenly raced past as the rover accelerated. Clay looked up and watched the RPM's of the motors jump.

"Lights on," called Tay. Instantly, the increasingly dark water became a tunnel of white light as the LED's ringing the front of the Triton came to life.

Caesare looked at Clay, clearly impressed.

"Passing thirty meters," called out a crew member.

"So, you guys think metal deposits in the soil are what

threw off the sub's instruments?"

"That's the theory. The area seems to be highly magnetized. If the soil is rich enough, it could be influential."

"Have to be damn rich, I would think," Tay said looking back at the screens. "Maybe we should stake a claim and start mining." He said with a grin.

Clay smiled in response. He hadn't considered the possible commercial aspects of such a discovery. The soil would have to be surprisingly rich to interfere with the sub's signaling, and any soil with that level of density might prove very attractive to mining companies.

"Who knows," said Tay. "You guys might just solve the old triangle mystery."

And litter the Caribbean with thousands of mining rigs, thought Clay.

"Passing one hundred meters."

The video feed now showed nothing but the white light in front of the Triton's window, surrounded by a ring of black water. The specks in the water zipped by now, looking more like strings than dots. It reminded Clay a little of the special effects of stars speeding past in the old science fiction movies.

"How much physical range does the Triton have in those batteries?" Caesare asked.

"Depends on our speed," replied Tay. "With our planned speed and depth, we should be able cover a few square miles and still have enough to get her back to the ship."

"Passing two hundred meters."

"You guys realize that we'll only be able to scoop the soil down to six or seven inches deep right? We only have-" Tay stopped speaking as he noticed some interference in the video monitor. "That's strange. We've never seen interference at this depth before." He turned his head slightly without taking his eyes away. "Let's record this," he called. Behind, him a crew member typed a few strokes on his keyboard and another monitor began displaying a copy of the Triton's video feed. A red circle appeared in the upper right hand corner, indicating a recording in progress.

"Passing three hundred meters."

The interference was getting noticeably worse now, reminiscent of the old TV antennae reception that Clay had used as a boy. The snow was quickly taking over the screen.

"Alright, let's slow her down," Tay cautioned.

Lightfoot pulled back slowly on the joystick.

"Passing four hundred meters."

"Slow her down! Slow her down!" barked Tay.

"I'm trying," replied Lightfoot. He pulled back harder on the stick. There was no noticeable change in speed. The specks were still flying past and becoming very hard to see with so much interference. They were almost invisible now.

"Turn us out!"

Lightfoot twisted the joystick trying to bank the Triton out of its steep dive. The picture shifted only slightly.

"We're losing her!" Lightfoot shouted.

He gave it everything and pushed the stick hard to the right. The rover continued its path downward. He jammed it left. "I'm getting no response!"

Tay jumped past Lightfoot and slammed his hand down on one of the buttons on the control panel. "Blow the tanks before we lose signal!"

A moment later, the video screen faded to black. The interference was gone, along with the signal.

There was a long silence before Tay spoke. "Shit." He sighed and rubbed his forehead. "Let's try and track it with sonar and see where it lands. With any luck, it emptied its tanks and will float to the top." He backed up and leaned against a metal desk along the opposite wall, thinking a moment before turning to Clay. "If it doesn't come up, we're going to have to call in another ship with a tethered rover."

"How long will that take?"

"Depends on how far away they are. Probably a few days. We have more than enough room for you two, if you'd like to stay."

"Thanks." Clay looked around the room. "Do you have a phone I can use for a ship to shore?"

"Yeah," replied Lightfoot, standing up. "I'll show you."

Caesare frowned and watched them leave. Three more days. That was one call Admiral Langford would not be happy to get.

Tay turned back to Caesare. "Well, you sure have something down there." He looked back at the blank monitor. "Triton uses ultra-low frequency at 3 hertz, which should be immune from damn near everything. Whatever your problem is, it's not mineral deposits."

7

ALISON WALKED DOWN the darkened hall with a cold Coke in her hand. She didn't care for sodas but she needed the caffeine. She looked at her watch. It was almost midnight and she was thinking about home, especially after sleeping in her office the last few nights. As Alison entered the lab, she saw Lee still sitting at his desk, looking at the racks of servers and their countless green lights flashing and illuminating the dark walls with a soft glow.

"I didn't know you were still here," she said, pulling up a chair and sitting down next to him.

He smiled without looking over. "I really should go home. I'm beat."

"Why don't you?"

He looked at her, with a smirk. "Why don't *you*?"

"I guess I just want to see what your servers can do," she said playfully.

"It could be a long time, Ali," he said, looking back to the servers. "It could be years before they spit something out. Hell, they may never spit out anything at all." He opened his eyes wide trying to fight off the exhaustion. "But I'm just like you, too excited to go home, and sitting here watching it work is…I don't know…addictive."

By *it*, he meant the large flat panel monitor on his desk. On it the screen displayed the collective results from over a hundred servers, which were constantly processing. On the top half of the screen, dozens of jagged lines stretched from one side to the other, like the line graphs found in spreadsheet programs. The lines represented various streams of raw data recorded twenty-four hours a day for the past four years; frequencies, interval clicks, pitches, video, everything. The lines jumped up and down vertically, weaving in and out while the system looked for relationships between the streams and their trillions of bytes.

Lee looked at the last rack along the wall. The systems there had a noticeably different look, with far fewer lights. Unlike the servers, these lights all blinked at exactly the same time. It was the rack that held the data itself, thousands of terabytes and a seemingly infinite number of variables, all of which IMIS was diligently sifting through.

Alison knew that Lee had a special place in his heart for the equipment. He worked hand in hand with IBM in setting things up and was part of the programming team which designed the artificial intelligence software that was now working through all of the data. He was also the expert on all of the digital camera and recording systems located strategically around the giant tank, recording every conceivable angle of Dirk and Sally's movements and body angles. The system was now going over those shots frame by frame, along with everything else. As a marine biologist, how the intelligence of the machines worked was beyond her. But Lee was as sharp as they came, and he had spent thousands of hours testing the algorithms. If it failed, she knew it would not be due to lack of effort on anyone's part. Her worst fear, in fact, all of their worst fears, was that they would be long retired, or even dead, before IMIS found anything.

She looked at the screen with Lee and watched the pictures of the dolphins flash across, frame by frame, beneath the dancing, jagged streams of data.

"Do you think we'll ever see anything?" she asked, lowering her chin onto her crossed arms.

After a few moments, he sighed. "I don't know. I sure hope so." He turned and gave her a wink. "If not, it's sure been a great ride, eh?"

"It sure has." She patted his arm softly. "Let's go home. It's about time we slept in our own beds. Besides, we don't want your wife down here chewing us out."

Lee laughed and stood up. "Yeah, you don't want that. Trust me."

*****

Alison sat in her car and watched Lee drive away. The lamppost overhead showered her small Chevy with yellow light as she stared past the building and out at the dark ocean behind it. She had dreamt of this day for years and now that it was here, she was scared to death. The tens of thousands of hours she'd spent studying and planning and documenting, was all done in an effort to get to this point; Phase Two. She knew that of all of the work they would do, Phase Two was the biggest unknown. Not gathering information, but actually being able to translate it. Lee was right. It was a long shot. There was no way to know whether any of it would be decipherable using something so potentially limiting as human logic.

Alison realized that she had been afraid of this phase from the very beginning, and had simply ignored it, suppressing her fear by focusing on all the work that was still ahead of them. What if it didn't work? What if the last six years had been a complete waste, getting this far only to find a brick wall and a powerful computer system that couldn't make heads or tails out of their data? What if the data was collected wrong? What if they had left a major piece out, something that never occurred to them?

Alison leaned back against the vinyl seat and closed her eyes. *God, please let this work. Please don't let me die without ever knowing.*

8

THE ANTARCTIC WAS unforgiving in November. At two full miles above sea level the interior of the continent could reach temperatures of -130 degrees. The Halley research station was located near the south end of the Ronne Ice Shelf and served as a research outpost for some of the most intense climate studies on the planet. Shared and co-funded by the United States and Europe, the station was used year round by various teams conducting research, the bulk of which was measuring climate warming changes over the last several thousand years. Using ice samples drilled from the frozen ground, the evidence was overwhelming; the planet was warming quickly, faster than any natural cycle recorded. Whatever the arguments and theories back home regarding cause and effect, the result was indisputable. The atmosphere was warming and the ice continent was melting.

Leo Torbin and Gale Preece were staffed at the Halley remote field camp for another three weeks. They had completed their studies and spent most of their remaining time compiling data, while huddled together in the outpost's small concrete framed structure, and habitually monitoring their diesel fuel level. At two o'clock in the morning, they lay in their cots, long since accustomed to sleeping through noise that would have had most people wondering if they were going to live to see the next day. Specially designed blankets covered them to their necks. Leo's wool-capped head stuck out from under his blankets while Gale's remained completely concealed below the thick fabric. A slow rise and fall of the blanket was the only evidence that Gale was even there.

On the plain gray walls hung a variety of tools, clothing, pots and pans; necessities of a humble and tenuous residence. In the furthest corner from the door, next to the large propane heater, sat a metal desk covered with stacks of handwritten papers along with two Toughbook laptops, specially designed to work in extreme conditions. A second door with a sign reading "Toilet" remained shut, providing a small amount of additional insulation from the howling winds outside and their constant onslaught against the concrete walls.

At first, the sound of a strange rumble was drowned out by the winds outside, but as it grew, the rattling equipment throughout the room grew louder. The walls of the shelter began to shake violently, causing some of the pans to leap from their hooks and fall onto the floor. One of the laptops vibrated across the desk and fell off, crashing into a metal bucket and sending it sliding across the floor. The thunderous rumble became deafening.

Leo jumped from his cot while half awake, and tried to grasp something for support. He turned just in time to see the shape of Gale tumble from her bed and onto the floor.

He reached and grabbed her arm, trying to pull her to him as she struggled to get the blanket off. It was an earthquake!

Holding onto each other, they managed to pull themselves into the nearest corner and covered their heads. Everything seemed to be falling around them now as the small building swayed eerily from side to side. Leo grabbed the rest of Gale's thick blanket and wrapped it around them. Under the blanket, they quickly found themselves praying that the structure would hold. He dropped his head and squeezed Gale tight.

*****

The earthquake lasted less than two minutes but the wind took five hours to die out. By seven a.m., conditions had receded to a gentle ten miles per hour when the thick metal door of the still-standing Halley outpost swung open. Leo and Gale both stepped out, clothed in full protective suits and never so happy to see the sun. In all of their time spent in Antarctica, it was the closest they had come to dying. All it would have taken was even a small hole in the wall and the wind would have done the rest.

They looked around at the icy desert, stretching out as far as they could see. Leo looked up at the transmission tower and frowned. The tower was in perfect shape but the shortwave transmitter inside was smashed. Thankfully, their backup line of communication was unharmed. He pulled the brick sized satellite phone out of his large jacket pocket and flipped up the oversized antennae.

As Leo removed his glove to dial, Gale walked over to the snowmobiles. One sat on its side, yet both vehicles appeared undamaged. The small shack housing the giant diesel tank looked like it held up, as well as the larger building. She turned and did a full scan. Aside from the mess inside the main station, everything looked oddly normal.

"McMurdo, this is Torbin at Halley camp. Can you hear me?" he yelled into the phone while looking at Gale. "Yes, we're alright. Looks like we had an earthquake last night." He paused, looking around. "Critical systems seem to be in working order but we've lost the shortwave. Repeat, we have lost shortwave communications. We're going to finish a sweep of the base and have a wider look around on the bikes." He listened again. "Yes, right. Will do."

Leo hung up and stuffed the phone back into his pocket. "They want us to call back after we have a look around. If there are any immediate problems, they will move the delivery up. If not, they'll bring another shortwave unit with them next week."

Gale nodded. "Well, the generator works, so we have heat and electricity, and we're certainly not short of food and water."

Together, they grabbed the overturned snowmobile and pushed it back up onto its treads. "Could have been a whole lot worse." Leo checked the vehicle's gas tank for any leaks.

Gale checked the ignition, turning the key back and forth.

"Wow, look at that!" Gale turned and followed the direction of Leo's arm and gasped. In the distance, the blue sky above suddenly ended on the horizon with an enormous wall of *white*.

"What the hell is that?"

Leo shook his head. "I don't know. It's not a storm." He climbed onto one of the snowmobiles. "Let's take a ride and have a look."

*****

The Halley camp was over a hundred miles from the Amundsen-Scott South Pole station and over a thousand miles from the supply station at McMurdo. With help so far away, they kept to a slow pace on the snowmobiles, taking almost an hour to get close enough. It looked like many of the "white outs" seen in the Antarctic but this one was not moving. Instead, it seemed to linger in the air for as far as the eye could see.

Side by side, Leo and Gale entered what looked like a white fog and visibility quickly dropped down to a few dozen feet. They slowed the machines even further to a crawl, carefully scanning the ground for any sudden rifts exposed by the storm. They had been to this area many times, as their camp was the primary station of study for the ice shelf, but they couldn't tell exactly where they were.

Leo stopped, raised his darkened glasses, and looked up. The sun was completely blocked out which made it harder to see any detail on the white ground. Gale put her snowmobile in neutral and pulled out a hand held GPS unit.

She raised her goggles up over her hood. "We're still about 5 miles from the first ridge. How much further do you want to go?"

Leo watched the white fog carefully. "I think it's starting to clear. Don't know how far out it extends though. Let's go up a little further and see if it thins out more."

Gale nodded and put the device back in the pocket of her oversized parka. They continued creeping forward.

After several more minutes, the visibility slowly started to improve and the sun began to make some limited progress getting through. They both watched the ground carefully as they slowly sped up.

"Look out!" Suddenly, Leo stopped his snowmobile with a tight clench of the brakes. His bike quickly started to tilt forward as he stood and pushed himself backward up and over the back of the seat. He landed head first on the snow and barely crawled out of the way before his snowmobile lifted its end into the air and disappeared.

Gale twisted her handlebars tight to avoid hitting him and nearly pitched into a sideways roll. With gritted teeth, she was just able to stay on and avoid following his tracks which abruptly disappeared less than a foot away. "Jesus!"

She jumped off and backed away. Gale and Leo retreated several more steps to assure themselves that they were safe.

"What the hell is that?" He said, slowly stepping forward while Gale unconsciously tugged him backwards.

Leo gradually inched toward the end of his tracks to see how far the drop was. Near the edge, he tested the strength of the snow with a few heavy steps. Gale instinctively took his other arm to let him lean forward and peer over the edge. He could see his bike lying on its side below.

"How deep is it?" She asked from behind him, reaffirming her grip.

Leo shook his head. "It's only about 15 feet down. But…this is no hole." He waved her forward. "Come here, carefully."

She took several small steps forward until she was able to look over the edge. She looked to the side where the air continued to clear and began to reveal how far the cliff extended.

"Oh my god."

"Oh my god is right. This thing goes on for a long way." He pulled her back away from the edge with him. "What does the GPS say?"

Gale pulled the GPS out and checked their coordinates. She looked at him with a worried look on her face.

"Where are we?" he asked.

She shook her head. Worry was turning to fear. "We're nowhere *near* the Shelf."

9

THE FRONT DOORS of the aquarium were locked and would not be opened again for eight hours. All displays were off and only a few overhead lights lit the long tiled floor. Darkened posters lined the walls, barely legible in the shadows, displaying some of the aquarium's upcoming events.

With all the lights off in the lab, the tiny blinking lights from the servers now gave the room an eerie glow. The hum of the machines was much louder without the white noise from the building's air conditioning system. In fact, without the servers, there would have been no sound at all.

The colorful data streams continued to dance across the top of the monitor on Lee Kenwood's desk. The IMIS system never stopped. It continued relentlessly processing the data.

Suddenly all of the lines came together for a single moment, the point of intersection instantly highlighted by a large green circle. A note sounded and letters appeared in the lower left hand corner. *Words Translated: 1 - Estimated Accuracy: 77%*

As suddenly as they had stopped, the streams began dancing again.

10

ALISON RODE UP to the back door of the aquarium and jumped off her mountain bike. It was almost noon and she had promised herself she would only stop to get the mail she'd left the night before. Her bills were just one of the casualties of working seventy hours a week for the last two years. It was a miracle they hadn't turned off her electricity yet. She leaned her bike against the wall and retrieved her keys from the small pouch under the seat. She unlocked both dead bolts and swung the door open with a squeak. After a quick trot down the darkened hallway, she unlocked a second door and walked into the lab, now brightly lit from sunlight coming through the glass walls from the top of Dirk and Sally's open tank. She could see the dolphins on the far side, swimming back and forth before a large pack of children, all pushing their noses against the cold glass.

Alison smiled and walked into her office, a small nondescript room housing little more than a desk, computer, phone, and a foldup cot in the corner. The books and paper were carefully stacked and organized, a reflection of her sometimes irritating attention to detail. She pressed the button on her phone next to a blinking light and typed in her code. The messages started playing aloud while she looked around her desk.

"Hi, Ms. Shaw. My name is Jay Sunderland and I'm a reporter for the Miami Independent. I wanted to come in and interview-"

Alison moaned and cut it off. The next message wasn't any better. She continued scouring her desk for the envelopes. Frowning, she looked up and thought for a moment, then leaned and looked out through the doorway. They were sitting on Lee's desk with her cell phone on top.

She walked briskly by and picked them up when something suddenly caught her eye. She looked at the screen and her eyes shot wide open. "Oh my god!"

In a panic, she reached for the phone, knocking it and most of the paper off the desk along with the mail. She quickly picked up her phone and began typing a text message with her shaking hands.

*****

The late morning sun shone through the slatted blinds and across a figure in a large queen bed. The room was simply decorated with a large dresser and desk, on top of which sat a laptop computer and a pile of papers. Around the room were several pictures of group events, most with friends packing into the shot. The settings of the pictures varied widely with some on the beach, some in mountains, and more in what appeared to be small and remote villages.

A professed over-sleeper, Chris Ramirez was still face down in bed when his phone chimed. Barely more awake than asleep, he sighed and felt absently for it on top of his headboard. He rolled over and pushed the comforter off his head. He rubbed his eyes held his phone up about a foot from his face, and read the message.

"Oh my god!" he yelled. He quickly tried to get up but tumbled out and onto the floor along with his sheets. He desperately tried to kick them off and ran into the bathroom, dragging the top half of his bed behind him. He stopped and read the phone again before dousing his face with cold water and running his wet hands through his messy brown hair.

*****

In his small apartment, Lee sat in the living room and stared at a wide computer monitor. With his hair sticking up and a fresh layer of stubble, it was clear that he had been in the chair for quite a while. He wore a lightweight headset and watched the screen intently as his onscreen character moved in and out of large rooms, carrying a fearsome weapon. In the video game, his avatar scanned from side to side looking for enemies. Seeing none, Lee relaxed and reached for a can of Mountain Dew. He raised the can to his lips and quickly emptied it just as his phone burst out playing Bob Segar's *Old Time Rock and Roll.* He reached for it, keeping his eyes on the screen. When he held it up and peered at the tiny LCD screen, he froze. "Hooooly cow!" He jumped out of the chair, tearing his headset off and grabbing a pair of pants from an open dresser drawer. He hopped and stumbled through the bedroom doorway with only one leg in.

Lee passed the doorway to the bedroom where his wife was sleeping. He quickly ran back in and yanked a t-shirt out of a large drawer. "I gotta go honey!"

*****

Frank Dubois and his wife sat at a small table on the patio of a small French café. A tall shade protected them from the already blazing sun. He was reading the Wall Street Journal on a tablet computer, while his wife nibbled on the last of her croissant and flipped through her Martha Stewart magazine. She felt a tiny vibration against her hip and looked down at her purse hanging over the back of the chair. "Ooh honey, your phone is buzzing," she said, reaching in.

Frank lowered the tablet and reached out for the phone. He turned it around and looked at the screen. He instantly jumped out of his seat, knocking over the entire table.

"What, what is it?!" she cried, looking down to see if she was now wearing part of her breakfast.

He bent down and quickly picked up their things. "We have to go!"

*****

Lee's old Volkswagen beetle and Frank's BMW raced into the aquarium's rear parking lot at the same time, both screeching to a halt next to each other. Lee leapt out and ran in front of the BMW's silver hood as Frank kissed his wife. "I'll call you later!" With that, he chased after Lee and disappeared into the dark hallway, with the large steel door closing behind them. They both sprinted down the hall and arrived to find Alison and Chris standing behind Lee's desk looking at the screen.

"What have we got?!" Frank asked excitedly.

Alison didn't reply. She simply smiled and watched their expressions as they reached the desk and saw for themselves.

"Right on!" Lee exclaimed, thrusting a clenched fist in the air. "Three words!" He grabbed the mouse and clicked on a button labeled *vocabulary* which brought up a small window with the three words listed within it; *Hello*, *Yes*, *No*.

Everyone shouted in excitement and pressed into a clumsy group hug. Alison took a deep breath and covered her mouth with her hands, trying to keep calm.

Lee looked at the details of each word. "Look at the accuracy, seventy-seven, seventy-eight, eighty-one!" He smiled broadly. "Can you believe it? The damn thing actually works!"

"We don't know that yet," Alison said. They tried to remain calm but couldn't seem to wipe the excitement off their faces. "This may very well be an error." They all turned toward the tank. Dirk and Sally were watching them from the other side of the glass, slowly moving back and forth.

"They're watching us," Chris said.

Alison smiled and approached the tank, placing her palm gently on the glass. "They've probably never seen us this excited before."

Lee looked at Alison. "So…what do we do now?"

Everyone turned back to Frank, and he knew why. Part of the project's planning naturally covered what they would do in the event that the system actually translated something. The protocol they agreed upon called for a series of data checks and careful documentation. Of course, those procedures left out one big factor, which was the sheer excitement and elation of the thing actually working.

Frank looked serious for a moment, but was finally unable to suppress his smile. "Let's at least try to maintain *some* protocol. Chris, grab a video camera and we'll document later."

Chris ran across the room and picked up a small camcorder while Lee slid into his chair. He powered the camcorder on and pointed it at Lee's monitor.

Lee took a deep breath and typed out the word *Hello*. He looked at them over his shoulder and clicked the large button labeled *Translate*.

Nothing happened.

Chris began to speak when Lee held up a hand and stopped him. Finally, from the underwater speaker submerged within the dolphin's tank, a high-pitched sound emerged followed by two distinct clicks.

Dirk and Sally suddenly turned and looked at the speaker. They swam over and examined it closely. They looked from the speaker back to the team on the other side of the glass, then back to the speaker again. Dirk bumped it gently with his nose. Sally swam closer to the side of the tank, briefly opening her mouth and returning the same sound with two clicks.

Suddenly the word *Hello* appeared again on the monitor just below the word Lee had typed.

11

ALISON FELT A LUMP in her throat. She was so overcome with emotion and excitement at the same time that she could barely move. Still grinning, she watched Chris and Lee trying to quickly verify the camera had recorded correctly. Frank was sitting on the edge of a desk behind Lee's chair, staring at the screen in a daze. She knew what he was thinking. Beneath the initial excitement lay a blanket of doubt. After all, they had only exchanged one word. This could still be a fluke, a computer error, or sheer luck although Sally had clearly spoken something *back* to them. *Was it an actual exchange, or were they simply repeating what they heard?*

"No problems with the camera. We're good." Chris swung the camera back around to Lee's monitor.

Lee looked over his shoulder. "What next?"

"Try it again. Let's make sure we're not hallucinating here."

Lee nodded and for the second time typed *Hello*. This time, clicking the translate button without hesitation. Again, the sounds were repeated through the underwater speaker. Chris swung the camera to Dirk and Sally.

Sally swam in a tight circle excitedly and came back to the glass. She repeated the same sounds. The word *Hello* appeared again on the Lee's screen. He repeated the exchange a third time, and again, Sally replied.

"There was no delay through the speaker this time," Lee was thinking out loud. "Which means that when IMIS translates a word for the first time, it becomes permanent. It *is* learning."

Alison took a deep breath. Lee was right. This was not a fluke. But, it didn't mean that the word actually meant "hello" either. It could still be gibberish and Sally simply repeated it for them. Even some human languages were so complex that the slightest variations in tone or inflection could make the language nearly impossible to learn. The Navajo language was a perfect example. Their system was so complicated that unless you were born into the language, you would never be able to fully grasp it as an adult. This was the reason it was so successful when used in World War II against the Japanese. *Could the dolphin's language be the same way? Could IMIS think it was translating something that it actually wasn't?*

Chris pulled back from the camera's eyepiece. "Now what?"

Alison leaned forward. "The question is whether we have enough words for actual context. Send another word."

Lee typed the word *Yes* and slowly clicked the translate button.

After several long seconds, the speaker finally emitted a slightly different sound. This time Dirk swam over and joined Sally at the glass. No longer interested in the speaker, this time he spoke first, repeating the pattern. The word *Yes* appeared on the screen as the second incoming word.

"Unbelievable," said Frank, running his hand through his hair.

Alison walked over to the tank and looked through the glass, just a few feet from Dirk and Sally. *Were they talking?* She wasn't so sure.

Suddenly Sally made several long screeches and clicks. She swam again in a circle and repeated it.

The four looked at each other, then turned back towards the screen as Chris swiveled the camera back over Lee's shoulder. They all held their breath.

Finally, after a long pause, the computer beeped with large red letters appearing in the translated window. *Unable to Translate.*

"I figured as much," said Lee. "Until IMIS has identified them, it won't recognize new words." He turned back to the others. "It appears we're a little limited with three words."

"Do we know for sure that it's working?" asked Frank.

Lee forced himself to remain objective. "I think so, but it's too early to tell."

"Let's at least try the last word," he said.

Lee nodded and typed the word *No*. Clicking the translate button got the same response, again from Dirk.

After a long silence, Alison frowned and folded her arms. "We need to wait for more words."

*****

Alison rubbed her eyes and looked up at Chris' silhouette. "What time is it?" she asked, looking around her darkened office.

"Almost five. The sun will be up soon."

She nodded. "What's up? Did something happen?"

"We got another word."

"Really?! What?" She rolled off the cot and jumped up.

"Come and see."

She passed him and raced to the desk. "Food." she said, with a smile. "Have you tried it yet?"

"Nope, we were waiting for you," Lee said, approaching from behind with a can of Coke. Frank followed, looking as though he'd just been woken up as well. "Ready?" Lee asked, sitting down.

Alison looked at the tank. Dirk and Sally were already awake and looking at them expectantly.

"How about 'Food Yes'?" she offered.

They all gave her a strange look. "Food yes?"

Lee raised his eyebrows. "Ah I see. Very clever." He looked at Chris. "Ready to roll?"

Chris quickly stepped behind the camera and started recording. "Hit it."

With that, Lee quickly turned and typed *Food Yes* and clicked the translate button.

After hearing it Dirk, suddenly very excited, replied with a single familiar response and the word *Yes* appeared on the screen.

Lee smiled at Alison, but spoke to Chris and Frank. "By asking that, she provided an option for a single word

53

response, differentiating between what was asked and also eliminating it as a simple repeat. That, gentlemen, is a bonafide translation!"

Oh my god!

Frank jumped up and suddenly turned to leave the room. "Wait right here."

"Where are you going?"

He stopped in the doorway and looked back at her. "To get some champagne." He looked past them to the dolphins. "And someone get Dirk and Sally some food!"

12

CLAY AND CAESARE walked into Admiral Langford's office and silently closed the door behind them. He motioned for them to sit as he held the phone to his ear with the other hand. They sat relaxed, having been in the office many times. Langford's office was actually where most of their discussions took place, both formal and informal. While officially a bureaucrat, Langford still tried to remain involved in many of the details of his department, particularly on the technical side. He was adamant that any leader who did not or could not understand the fundamentals of what their teams did should not be leading those teams in the first place. He insisted it made for better decision making and created a more efficiently run department and his department's achievements were hard to argue with.

It had been two weeks since their trip to Emerson's ship. After three days of searching for the lost Triton rover with an older submersible they were forced to return to Washington and file a formal requisition to go back out and finish the job. Judging from Langford's expression, they knew what was coming.

Finishing the call, he hung up with a sigh. "Well, the sub is out," Langford said.

"They know that we can't hope to find the Triton or replicate the problem without taking a sub down," Clay replied.

Langford nodded. "They know. I made that abundantly clear. It's just too damn expensive. With these democrats cutting our budgets, we just can't justify spending a couple million dollars to steam out there and run some tests."

"What about Emerson's submersible?" Caesare asked. "They still haven't found it and that's going to be one expensive piece of equipment to write off. We could be looking for that at the same time."

Langford shook his head. "Let's not give up on the Triton."

Clay was not surprised. It was not the first time they were held up because of funding. Sooner or later, everything came down to money. What bothered him the most was that in all likelihood the decision was based on a spreadsheet rather than a death certificate. If the Alabama had been in the Mariana Trench when it had the error, it could have smashed into one of the trench walls and turned that submarine into a giant tomb. Clearly, someone had decided that this was an isolated system malfunction. Something he could not deny without more testing. Of course, he could not confirm it without testing either. Another shining example of naval bureaucracy.

"Well, if the Navy wants the Triton but we don't have access to a sub," Caesare started, "how exactly are we supposed to recover it?"

Langford smiled. "Funny you should ask."

*****

The United States Geological Survey was created in 1879 when President Rutherford B. Hays signed the bill appropriating the designated funds. Based in Reston, Virginia, the USGS had the task of providing detailed data on the planet's myriad environments and ecosystems. With a budget of just over one billion dollars, nearly 400 locations, and a network of over 10,000 scientists, technicians, and support staff, the scientific reach of the USGS was enormous. This was also the reason why the department's Director, Kathryn Lokke, routinely got very little sleep. With a tumultuous rise to the head of the organization, and with the previous director being caught in a scandal of fraud and extramarital affairs, Lokke had her hands full trying to run things and repair the damage to their image.

The irony was that the USGS was one of the better run organizations in the public sector; something Lokke thought about often. She could not help but take it personally, since she had spent the better part of her career at the USGS. In fact, Lokke was not only one of the first female directors of the department, but arguably the most scientifically capable as well, when compared to her predecessors. She had been a lead scientist for years and headed some of the organization's most difficult projects, which was why she found the job of running it all the more frustrating. She was not a bureaucrat and loathed having to play one, something else she thought of often. Especially as she exited the room after her 10 a.m. conference call.

Lokke walked quickly back to her office on the top floor and almost made it past her assistant without being stopped.

"Ms. Lokke!" said Richele, as she put down the phone. "Mr. Haines just called and said he needed to talk to you urgently."

Lokke frowned. "About what?"

"He didn't say. But he's on his way up. I thought perhaps you would like me to bump some other...perhaps more annoying meeting instead".

Lokke could not keep from smiling, even after being stuck on the phone all morning. Richele was obviously talking about Albert Petriono, the head of Energy and Minerals. Someone everyone tried to avoid. "Thanks Richele. That would be great."

She winked. "Already done."

Haines burst into the office two minutes later and quickly closed the door.

"We have a problem."

Lokke was startled. This was very unlike him. She pushed her laptop away and gave him her full attention. "What kind of problem?"

"Have you been told about the earthquake in the Antarctic?"

"Briefly. This morning."

Haines took a deep breath. "It was near the Ronne."

"Did we get another break off?" Lokke asked, thinking about the giant, island-sized piece of ice that had broken off the Ronne Ice Shelf a few years earlier.

"Well, for starters, it was no ice quake."

Lokke's expression became concerned. "Go on."

"We've got a couple researchers there in the Halley camp; got thrown out of bed in the middle of the night. The next morning they went out to take a look. They found a crack, a big crack."

Lokke held her breath. "How big?"

"Miles. "

Her next question was very deliberate. "Where?"

Haines inhaled slowly. "Beyond the shelf, on land. About ten miles in."

She stared at him for a long time, then finally leaned back in her chair. "Jesus." Haines sat silently while it sank in. Lokke looked at a large map on the wall of the Earth's southern hemisphere. "How bad is the slide?" she asked.

"Fourteen feet."

"Oh my god!" She shook her head in disbelief. "Has this been verified?"

"Yes. We had a plane fly down from McMurdo. They ran the length and measured 43 miles, most of it on land. The ground team verified the slide depth nearest the camp. It looks pretty consistent from the air. It was strong enough to set off all the seismic instruments on the continent."

Lokke knew what that meant. Even though the Antarctic was a rather small land mass, all of the earthquake sensors being triggered meant the shift was powerful, very powerful. "Let's get a large team and some equipment out there right away. We need to get all the measurements and verify with a ground penetrating scan before we communicate this out."

Haines nodded.

"In the meantime, I'll start getting people together."

13

CHRIS REPLACED THE camcorder's tape with a new one and handed the old tape to Alison, who applied a small label on its back displaying a tiny barcode. She then passed it under an optical scanner which recorded the number and brought up a small field on the computer's monitor to add notes. She typed a short summary of the exercise they had just completed and hit enter, adding the entry to the database.

"Ready for the next one?" Chris asked.

"Let's give them a break," she said looking at Dirk and Sally. She glanced down at her watch. "It's almost feeding time and I'm sure we've got a-"

Food now. Sally's words came over the speakers.

Alison smiled. She leaned over and typed *Yes, food now* and clicked the translate button. She turned around and picked up the phone to call the aquarium's feeding team.

Thank Alison, came the mechanical reply.

Alison suddenly froze. She dropped the phone and turned around to look at the tank. Both Chris and Lee had done the same. After a long silence, they all turned toward each other.

"What did she say?" asked Alison.

Chris leaned past Lee and looked at the monitor screen. "Did Sally just say *ALISON*?"

Lee scooted forward and studied the screen. "Uh…she sure did." He raised one of his eyebrows. "How the hell did she do that?" Lee typed several words on his computer and hit the enter key. Another window opened, displaying the transaction log files and hundreds of lines of cryptic text. He identified the last line translated and looked at the attribute signature of the word *Alison*. He then scrolled down examining the log details for all translations over the last two days. "Aha!" he said triumphantly, but suddenly leaned back in his seat with another thought. "Oh wow!"

"What is it?" Alison pressed.

He did not answer immediately. "Wow. That is really something else."

"What already?!"

"Context. IMIS translated for context." He almost seemed to be talking to himself. He quickly snapped out of it and looked at Alison and Chris. "You see, the design of IMIS' artificial intelligence, part of what allows it to learn, is trying to identify context. This is basically the relationship between multiple variables to achieve what it believes to be the best accuracy."

Chris frowned. "This is starting to sound Greek."

"Look," Lee said, starting to get excited. "Let's say IMIS is trying to figure out the word *hello*. If it thought it identified the right dolphin sound for *hello*, but that sound was emitted when the dolphins were moving away, the context of that interaction would show that translation to be wrong."

Alison nodded. "Of course."

"Obviously that's an over simplified example. What IMIS just did was apply that context on BOTH sides of the translation. Look at this!" He pointed to the translation logs on the screen. "What Sally said was not *Thank Alison*. She actually said *Thank girl*. But, IMIS not only identified and translated *girl* successfully, it also used its context algorithm to recognize that Alison is the only female among us; probably based on her computer account, since she has been typing some of the words to Dirk and Sally. Therefore, IMIS recognized that the message was meant for the only girl and substituted Alison's name. Hell, it even capitalized her name."

"Holy cow."

"Holy cow is right," Lee replied, "IMIS is even smarter than I thought." He looked at all the servers on the far wall with their hundreds of blinking lights continually churning through the data. "No wonder it's making such fast progress."

The phone rang, interrupting them. Alison quickly picked up the receiver. "Ali here."

"Hi Ali, it's Frank. Can you come up to my office please?"

"Uh, sure," she said, nodding. "Can it wait twenty minutes? We're right in the middle-"

"Actually it can't," he broke in. "I need you up here right away."

"Okaaay... I guess I'll be right up."

Chris gave a disappointed frown. "What, he can't wait

twenty minutes?"

"Evidently not."

"What's up?"

"No idea. He just said he wants to see me." She let the phone drop back into its cradle. "Check on their lunch, will you?"

"Will do."

With one last glance at the dolphins, she turned and headed for the stairs. She was in a good mood. They were making excellent progress with the project in the last couple of weeks, and as much as she knew Frank liked to grandstand, she was thankful that he agreed not to issue another press release after that initial translation. The attention they got from the morning show alone overwhelmed them with everyone wanting to come see Dirk and Sally. It was great for ticket sales, but with a host of people, including the mayor, all coming down for public appearances and photo ops, it slowed their work considerably. Frank enjoyed the attention but the rest of the team was frustrated with the delays and hobnobbing. *Okay, that wasn't totally true*, she thought. *She was the one frustrated.* The other guys enjoyed it too. She had often considered why she avoided attention but never came up with a concrete answer. Maybe it was all the looks in school, the luck of getting her mother's features and constantly being hit on. Maybe it was her determination in academics and always being singled out by the teachers. She had resigned herself to the fact that she would never really know what started it, but even if she did, would it change anything? Probably not. She would always be a bookworm at heart.

Alison reached the top of the stairs a little winded and realized that she really needed to get back to the gym. She walked down the short hallway and gave a polite knock as she opened the door.

"You won't believe what we just-" she began, as she stepped inside but her smile abruptly disappeared. Inside was Frank and two men dressed in shirt and tie. They all stood as she entered.

"Ah, here she is," said Frank, coming around his desk. "Alison, I'd like you to meet John Clay and Steve Caesare. They're with the-"

"Let me guess," she feigned politeness. "From the government. You're dressed too nice for the Army. CIA?"

Clay and Caesare were moving toward her with hands extended but stopped abruptly. "Uh, the Navy, actually."

She crossed her arms in front of her. "What a surprise."

The men looked at Frank with a trace of confusion. "Ali," Frank started. "These men came to talk to us about the project."

Alison raised her eyebrows sarcastically. "Wow, really?!"

"Uh, yes," Clay said, apprehensively. "We were just explaining to Dr. Dubois that we heard about your project and thought we might be able to help in the research with your dolphins."

"The government is here to help. And what kind of help would that be? Teaching them to attach mines to enemy ships?"

Again, Clay looked at Frank with more confusion, who was now looking sternly at his project lead.

"No, no, nothing like that. We may be able to help your progress with an opportunity to work hand-in-hand with your dolphins."

Alison's posture did not change. She gave Frank a long stare. "What kind of *opportunity*?"

Caesare gave her his trademark smile. "Recovering one of our small research submersibles in the Caribbean Sea."

Alison looked at him, then back to Clay. She was having none of it. "You can't do that yourself?"

"Well, we could," Clay said, ignoring the sarcasm. "But we thought it might provide an opportunity for you and your team; a real world interaction that might further your translation efforts, and perhaps even-"

"The dolphins haven't been out in the open ocean for years. They're not accustomed and we can't exactly put a leash on them. Besides, transporting them would be a major production."

"We're prepared to accommodate any requirements you have."

"I don't think so," Alison replied. "Besides, our translation capabilities are still much too-"

"Gentlemen," Frank interrupted, with a raised, yet professional tone. "Could you give us a moment please?"

Clay and Caesare nodded and turned toward the door. They stepped politely around Alison and closed it quietly behind them.

Outside they crossed the hall and leaned against the white wall with hands in their pockets.

"I don't think she likes you," Caesare said.

Clay laughed. "She certainly seems to have some strong feelings about the military."

"Kinda cute though," said Caesare. He took a few steps and studied a framed picture. It was an old black and white photograph of the aquarium's groundbreaking ceremony. He guessed the number of people in the small crowd to be about eighty, dressed in suits and gowns, forming a half arc around a few people in the middle with one of them holding a shiny shovel. The tiny plaque below the picture read *1925*. "This place has been around a long time."

Clay nodded, coming over to see the picture. "I've been here before," he said. "I was a boy, maybe seven or eight. My dad brought me when I was visiting him in Miami." He leaned in for a closer look at the picture. "It was a lot smaller then." Clay stared silently at the picture. He still remembered that trip clearly. It was the same weekend that his father told him of his parent's pending divorce.

Caesare looked back at the door. A small plate in the middle read *Dr. Frank Dubois, Director*. "So what do we do if they say no?"

Clay shrugged. "Break out our snorkel and fins, I guess."

Frank stepped forward and sat on the edge of his large oak desk. His face appeared tired. He hunched his shoulders for a moment and then dropped them with a sigh. He looked up at Alison.

"I think we should do this."

"What?" she scoffed. "You're not buying this are you? This is the Navy, Frank! They're not here to help us. They're here to find out how they can leverage the technology!"

"Look, Ali. I know how you feel about these guys and I know what happened before-"

"And you think it's different now? I guarantee you they're outside right now talking about how they can turn this into a military advantage. All they want-"

"Who do you think is funding this, Alison?" Frank suddenly blurted, with a wave around the room. "Santa Claus?! It doesn't matter whether it's NASA, the Navy, or the goddamn IRS! Government money is the only reason we're here! Do you have any idea how hard it is to raise this money?" He took a deep breath and dropped his tone. "Look, we're losing money. You know that. The ticket sales are still declining, even with the surge we got after that press release. The plain fact is that we need more time. We have so much more to do, but without our grants, we'll be lucky to keep the aquarium open until the end of the year."

Alison unfolded her arms and frowned. He was right. Without the money, all of this would come to an abrupt end sooner or later.

"Listen," Frank went on. "I know how you feel about these guys, I do. I know what happened." He watched

Alison tense up, knew he touched a soft spot, but he had to. He had always known that someday, it would eventually come down to this. "We have to play the game. At least for now. We have no choice. We have a big lead in this field, but if we get closed down, all of our information will be made available to everyone. And they'll be where we are in a matter of months."

Her shoulders relaxed slightly. "You think they would cut us off just like that?" He made no effort to answer. He didn't have to. Alison could not believe that she'd even uttered the words.

She walked slowly to the window and stared out at the palm trees jutting into the air from the next street like a row of towers. It was amazing how mad she still was. It was more than five years ago and she still hated to think about it. Her first serious research project, her first *meaningful* project was in Costa Rica. It was the world's first serious attempt to map and document the complete breeding and migration patterns of sea turtles. They had spent three years tagging, tracking, and caring for thousands of turtles while sleeping in tents with virtually no money. And in the end, they had accomplished something that no other ocean biology team had been able to do. God, they were so idealistic. At the time, they considered the Navy, and the US government, for that matter, a godsend. They provided the equipment, the computers, and the tracking devices. Without their grants, Alison's team would not have been able to track the reptiles off the damn beach, let alone across the Atlantic and Pacific oceans.

They knew beyond a doubt that if the program was extended, it would allow them to study not just the routes, but eventually their turtle's entire life span from birth to death. They were finishing their papers, some, including Alison, were finishing their doctorates when the hammer fell. In one coordinated effort, the Navy confiscated the majority of their work. Anything that was deemed in the interest of national security was permanently moved to government research teams in various fields. She and the team were stunned, unable to imagine how on earth a population of turtles qualified as a security threat. It never made any sense and they were all sure it was just some monumental misunderstanding. Through a friend, she had found out that the Navy had another agenda from the start. Their intention was to learn how they could use the turtles affixed with small, but powerful, transmitters to obstruct communications to and from enemy vessels, based on proximity of an agent turtle. *Agent turtle.* It still sounded as absurd today as it did then. Absurd or not, it was a shock to find out that the Navy's support was a sham from the beginning. They never cared about the biology. They simply wanted to deem whether it had a viable military application.

Of course, it didn't. The migration routes were helpful, but the logistical complications around the geographic management, the speed of migration, and the power needed to adequately block a signal, were simply insurmountable. In the end, the Navy dropped the idea and after two full years of legal arguments. They finally relented and made the whole of the data available to the scientific community. But by then, the idea of a longer, more comprehensive study was too difficult to fund and was as good as dead. The results were well received eventually, but a complete behavioral understanding from birth to death would have blown the doors off anything that was known about the species. By the time they could have picked up the pieces, the excitement was gone and most of the researchers had found other projects. It was less than a year after giving up that she met Frank, and his crazy idea about the science of language translation.

She turned from the window and stared at him.

He shrugged. "Besides, these guys could just be genuinely interested in helping."

She rolled her eyes and shook her head. "The Navy

has money and resources that we could only dream about. Why on earth would they come to us? I mean, really. How hard could it be for them to find a little submarine?"

"Fine." With a look of dejection, she unfolded her arms and walked toward the door. Before opening it, she turned back to Frank. "Do you realize, Frank, that we never sent out another press release when we made contact?"

He shrugged. "I know. Remember we were going to schedule another press release when we were ready to show the translation in action?"

She shook her head. "That's not what I mean. If we haven't formally announced the translation yet, how did the Navy know about it?"

*****

Clay and Caesare followed Alison down the hall toward the stairs. The conversation in Dubois' office appeared to be a significant one since Alison emerged with slightly less disdain for them. At Dubois' request, she offered to show them their lab and a demonstration of the technology used.

Silently, as they walked behind her, Clay acknowledged that Caesare was right. She was cute. She was also extremely intelligent and clearly not someone to be trifled with. At least not if you worked for the government. He didn't know what it was that had soured her, but he'd seen enough firsthand to feel sympathetic.

At the bottom of the stairs, they followed Alison through the new wing. Clay guessed it had doubled the size of the aquarium since his boyhood trip. The structural design was more modern, but was cleverly decorated to match the original building. This made the extension almost indiscernible to the casual visitor. They passed a horde of children all peering and waving at the dolphins through the enormous glass tank. The hall stopped abruptly at a large secured door where they found the tank continued on the other side, forming one of the walls of their lab. As they entered, Clay noticed another smaller set of stairs and realized that Alison had taken them along the scenic route. Maybe she didn't entirely hate them.

The lab was much larger than he had expected, with the far wall almost ten feet tall and largely covered with racks of servers. In the center of the room were three tables and four large desks, along with two young men who appeared to be in the middle of eating lunch.

Chris and Lee both turned when the door slammed shut. They quickly wiped their mouths as Alison approached with the two visitors.

"Guys," she said, crossing the room. "These gentlemen are from the Navy. They've come to learn about our project."

Chris and Lee suddenly stiffened.

"This is Chris Ramirez, another of our lead researchers, and Lee Kenwood, our expert computer engineer. I'm sorry," Alison said. "Your names again?"

"John Clay," he answered, stepping forward and shaking Chris' hand, then Lee's. "This is my associate, Steve Caesare."

"Pleased to meet you," added Caesare, with a shake to each.

"Ms. Shaw was nice enough to give us a walk through the aquarium. A very nice place you have here."

Lee relaxed, however, Clay noticed that Chris seemed to maintain a defensive composure similar to Alison's.

"Frank asked that we give them a demonstration," Alison said.

Chris said nothing but Lee eagerly sat down and brought the IMIS system back up on screen.

"Frank and I started the program six years ago," she started. "It wasn't long before we realized that we were going to need a lot more money and help. Chris and I worked together on a project in Central America, so we brought him on about a year later after Frank and I got our first grant." Alison came around the other side of Lee's desk and looked over his shoulder while he got things ready. "We brought Lee on after the second one. He's an ex-IBM'er." She motioned to the wall of computers. "They donated the servers and helped design the translation software and algorithm, called IMIS. It's the system that is actually translating our dolphin-ese."

Caesare raised an eyebrow. "Dolphin-ese?"

She shrugged. "That's what we call it. Who knows what the language will actually be called. When it's-"

"Excuse me," Clay interrupted. "I was under the impression that the translation was just beginning. Are you saying that you have a vocabulary?"

Alison smiled. "Well, *vocabulary* may be a bit of a stretch."

Clay was genuinely surprised. After a moment, he replied. "So...exactly how far along are you?"

Alison was still grinning when she nodded to Lee. "Let's show 'em."

Lee quickly typed *Hello* in the translate window.

Clay and Caesare, not knowing what to expect, turned toward the large tank when they heard the sounds emanate from the underwater speaker. They watched as the two dolphins, playing for the children on the other side, suddenly stopped and swam over toward them. Clay noted an odd feeling at seeing the dolphin's eyes actually seem to focus directly at them from the other side of the glass.

One of the dolphins repeated the sound and they watched the reply appear on the screen.

"Wow." Clay exclaimed. He looked at Caesare who also had his eyebrows raised. "That is amazing."

The other three seemed almost giddy. Alison leaned in closer to Lee's shoulder, her eyes fixed on the monitor. "Ask them how they are."

Lee quickly typed out *How you today?* and clicked his

mouse.

After hearing the sounds, Dirk quickly replied. *Good. How you.*

Lee responded. *Good. Thank.*

Alison straightened and looked at Clay. "Lee is working on adding voice recognition so we won't even have to type. That may take a while."

Clay and Caesare stood motionless. Their eyes wide open and mouths gaping. They were utterly stunned.

It took several seconds for Clay to recover. "What...what else can they-"

Dirk interrupted from the other side of the glass. *How long food.*

Alison smiled again. "They're always hungry." She leaned in and typed the reply herself. *Food soon.*

Clay looked at Caesare who was still speechless. "Wow," he said, looking back at the dolphins.

Lee swung his chair around and beamed at them both. "Gentlemen, meet Dirk and Sally."

Who them, asked Sally.

Lee offered the chair to Alison, who promptly sat down and replied. *Friends. They want help.*

Even in his dazed state, Clay suspected Alison wasn't thrilled about calling them friends.

Dirk and Sally suddenly burst into movement, swimming in tight circles, displaying what Clay assumed to be excitement.

Yes. Like help, Sally responded. *Dirk hungry.*

Food soon, Alison typed back.

Caesare could not take his eyes off Dirk and Sally. "This is unbelievable."

Lee gave a broad smile. "You should see them do tricks now!"

14

ALISON STOOD ON the mid-deck looking down at the large tank constructed on the stern of the Pathfinder. Two of the ship's cranes had been disassembled to create enough space to house the 10,000 gallon salt water tank, which left only a quarter of the space on the stern's open platform. On the third remaining crane hung a heavy sling made of fabric used to hoist Dirk and Sally in and out. Having them both confined to such a tiny space, with precious little room for movement during the five hour trip, made Alison extremely anxious. The fact that it did not have any windows didn't help matters. Nevertheless, both dolphins seemed relatively calm as their water gently sloshed back and forth with the rise and fall of the ocean swells.

Luckily, the weather provided them an ideal window with calm seas and blue skies, conditions not uncommon during the Caribbean's winter months. Alison scanned the horizon behind them and seeing no sign of shore, looked at her watch. She would be happy when this whole charade was over. She watched some of the others mill around the ship, enjoying the fresh air and smell of the open sea. Almost two dozen passengers were reporters or journalists invited along for the Navy's photo op. As far as Alison was concerned, they needed all the positive press they could get. One of the reporters below was examining the tank. He stood back and took what seemed like dozens of pictures which made Alison wonder if he was paid by the picture. She also could not help but wonder whether he knew that his hat was on backwards.

Alison tried to shake herself out of her slump. She did not want to be here, but it was not going to do any good to piss and moan about it the whole time. She took a deep breath and tried to appreciate the view. No one else seemed worse for the wear.

Clay approached from behind. "Are you alright?"

She turned abruptly. "Yes, yes. I'm fine. Thank you."

"Are you feeling seasick at all? If so, we can give you something for it if we catch it early enough."

She smirked at the comment but forced herself to turn it into a polite grin. "Sea sickness makes for a short career as a marine biologist."

He nodded. "Of course. Good point." He motioned back toward the bridge. "We'll be there soon. Mr. Kenwood is almost done setting things up."

She followed Clay back toward the front and climbed the third flight of stairs. She mumbled a thank you as he held the door open to the bridge. Stepping into the air conditioning, she was instantly reminded how warm it was outside.

On the far side of the small room sat Lee adjusting his equipment on a small table the crew had set up for them. Beneath were two large portable computer servers surrounded by a tangle of cables and wires. On top of the table sat Lee's keyboard, monitor, mouse and a couple other pieces of equipment she did not recognize. Chris stood behind him, peering out the window at the outline of Bimini Island, and trying to remain calm as a few reporters tried to squeeze by and snap pictures of Lee and his hardware.

"Are we ready?" Alison asked Lee.

"Almost," he replied. "I'm just running some test commands to make sure the system is ready."

"So what kind of a vocabulary will we have?"

He shrugged as he continued typing. "Everything that IMIS had successfully translated until we left. We obviously don't have the power to translate anything new, but," he motioned to the two servers underneath, "these babies are at least strong enough to handle the words we already have. Next, I'll run some test translations without piping it through the speakers and we should be all set."

*****

The ship's engines finally began to wind down as they neared their destination, and Captain Emerson returned to the bridge to verify all was well at the helm. After speaking with his first officer, he turned to Alison and her team.

"Ms. Shaw, is there anything else you need? We should be stopping in just a few minutes."

"No, I think we have everything we need. Thank you."

"My pleasure. As soon as we turn off the engines, we will begin readying the sling to get your friends out of the tank. I'm sure they are looking forward to a little elbow room, so to speak."

"Thank you," she replied. "Chris and I will come down to assist."

"Very well." With that, the captain nodded at the others and turned to speak quietly with Clay.

As the ship continued to slow, Alison and Chris looked at each other nervously. They shared a worry that they had not spoken to anyone about, except Frank, before leaving. Dirk and Sally were as much a part of the aquarium as they were, and Alison felt a deep love for the animals. But they were still in captivity, which means they were captives to the aquarium. Alison and Chris were worried, terrified in fact, that even though the dolphins demonstrated a strong connection with them too, there was no guarantee that once back in the ocean they would not simply make off for open waters. It had taken almost two weeks to arrange their leave from the aquarium and the construction of the tanks to transport them in, not to mention dozens of other details. During that time, their relationship with Dirk and Sally had gotten even stronger. With the startling progress that IMIS provided them, the dolphins seemed as excited to speak to the team as they were to them. However, they were still being kept from their natural habitat, from their home. Once out of the tank and back into open water, Alison was scared to death that she would never see them again.

The engines finally fell silent and the ship slowly coasted to a stop. A few minutes later, the giant anchor was released and it punched through the water with an enormous splash. Alison and Chris joined the crew members on the rear platform to ready the sling. They slowly rotated the mechanical arm over the tank and lowered it into the water. Although dangerous for such a small tank, Alison insisted on climbing inside and keeping a hand on Sally as the large fabric was slipped around her. Sally showed no sign of resistance. She quickly wiggled herself into place so the sling could be fastened securely. The reporters filled the deck above the tank and photographed the entire process.

Alison could feel the lump in her throat as she nervously watched the crew swing Sally across the deck and lowered her into the warm ocean water. They did the same for Dirk and had them both in the water in less than five minutes. Alison stood on the back of the ship in clear view and watched the two dolphins swim around excitedly. When they moved around the side of the ship, Alison bolted up the three flights of stairs back to the bridge with Chris hot on her heels. She sprinted through the door and over to Lee.

"Okay, let's say something!"

Lee nodded and pressed a button to engage the underwater microphone and speakers. He quickly typed out *Hello* and hit the enter key.

There was a long silence as they waited for a reply. Alison's eyes slowly widened with concern and she laid her hand on Lee's shoulder. They continued to wait.

"Should we try it aga-" Alison asked, but was

interrupted by Sally.

Hello Alison.

Lee gave her the keyboard and she typed. *Hello Sally. Are you ready to help?*

Yes we like help, came the dolphin's reply.

Alison looked at Chris. They both breathed a sigh of relief.

Where you Alison?

Alison typed back. *I am on the boat.* An error message flashed on the screen that said *Unable to translate.* She looked at Lee. "How do I bring up the list of vocabulary words?"

Lee pressed a few keystrokes and the list appeared, displaying all of the identified words to date.

Alison typed her reply again. *I am on the metal.*

Big metal, replied Sally.

Alison smiled. *Yes, the metal is big.* She looked up at Clay who had just joined them. "Are we about ready?"

He nodded. "Ready when you are."

"Okay. Let me make sure they're okay being out here."

Alison typed again. *Are you and Dirk afraid?*

No afraid, Sally said. *Dirk hungry.*

Alison laughed out loud. "That boy is always hungry." She typed back playfully. *Dirk is always hungry.*

Sally made a strange sound that the computer could not translate.

Alison suddenly looked at Chris. "Did she just laugh?"

He smiled excitedly.

Alison relaxed for a moment and straightened up. "Okay. Mr. Clay, what exactly are we looking for here?"

"A small white submersible, roughly three feet cubed in size." He handed her a picture of the Triton. "We estimate that it's somewhere within a three mile radius."

She looked at the picture. "Jeez, how are we going to describe this?"

Lee brought up the vocabulary list again.

Alison studied the list and then began typing. *Ready*

Sally? Ready Dirk?

Ready, Sally responded.

Ready, Dirk followed.

It looks like a metal bubble, she typed. *Please look and come back.*

We look, answered Sally.

The team listened for anything more, but the speakers fell silent. "They must be off."

Alison turned to Clay again. "Just to remind you, Mr. Clay, I don't know how far or deep they will be able to search. Dolphins don't go much deeper than 150 to 200 feet, so even if they can find it with their echolocation, they may only be able to point us to it."

"I understand," Clay replied. "We're not sure how deep it ended up since the submersible's buoyancy tanks were partially filled. There are also a number of reefs around here, so we may get lucky." He ended with a friendly smile. "And call me John."

15

CAESARE WALKED INTO Will Borger's lab and found him at his desk going over the map Caesare had seen last time he was there. Borger looked up and nodded. "Hi, Steve."

"Hey. Will. Thanks for making time for me," Caesare replied. He walked over and handed a small storage drive to Borger.

"No problem." Borger gave the drive a quick once over and turned to his computer to insert it. "Where's

Clay?" he asked, while typing.

"He's out playing with dolphins."

Borger smiled. "I'm not even going to ask." A window opened on his screen showing the contents of the drive. "Okay, so what do we have here?"

"This is the video file our friend Tay sent over from the Pathfinder. It's a recording the Triton submersible made during the dive...before we lost it for them. It's not very long, but Clay and I thought we should show it to you in case there was anything helpful on it. We're actually hoping it might give some indication of which direction it headed after after we lost contact."

"Okay." Borger started the video in half speed. He reached behind himself for another can of Jolt cola without looking away. He appeared to be constructing a small tower of empty Jolt cans on his shelf. Judging from the number of cans, Caesare wondered if Borger was a shareholder.

Borger popped the can open and watched as the Triton descended through the deep blue water. There was no sound but the video quality was crystal clear. At just over three minutes in, the first signs of interference appeared, with just a few tiny white dots that were barely noticeable. As the timeline increased, the dots became larger and more frequent, but were still nothing more than a minor distraction.

Suddenly, the interference became noticeably worse and Borger leaned forward. He stopped the video and rewound. He played the same several seconds over and over repeatedly, stopping on a specific frame.

"What is this?" he asked, mostly to himself.

Caesare leaned in. "What?"

Borger went back and forth between the series of frames. He pointed to the screen in the upper right hand corner. "This right here."

Caesare looked closer. A subtle but lightly colored shape appeared out of the blue. As each frame was played, the shape sharpened ever so slightly and began to resemble a line with a gentle curve. "Hmm… a reflection of light from the sub's interior light, maybe as it hits the front Plexiglas?"

"Maybe," Borger said, pursing his lips. He continued watching the frames again and again. The shape grew more and more distinct until the interference finally became so bad that it overwhelmed the rest of the picture. He backed the frames up again. "I don't think it's a reflection." He pointed to a small speck on the screen. "Ocean water is loaded with small pieces of debris and organic material. Look closely here…we can see a small piece of it moving past the window in this upward direction. And here it passes over the white shape. If the shape were a reflection, this small speck would have disappeared in the glare."

Caesare nodded. "Right."

"It's possible that it could be some other video anomaly, but I doubt it." He played the video forward again. "Unfortunately, right here the interference gets so strong that we lose it."

Caesare straightened himself up. "So we'll never know."

"Well, not necessarily," Borger replied, closing the window on the computer. He opened a program and typed a number of commands too fast for Caesare to follow.

"What do you mean?"

"What I mean," Borger said, as he now moved in and out of windows and programs. "Is that we may be able to remove some of that interference."

"How do we do that?" Caesare pulled up a chair and sat down.

"If we can identify the rate and degree of interference, the computer may be able to calculate for it and remove the interference from the screen. This is a technique that astronomers use with ground based telescopes called 'adaptive optics'. The earth's atmosphere distorts the light passing through it, so scientists have come up with a way to use a laser to measure this distortion and allow the computer to correct for that distortion. The results are images almost as clear as the Hubble telescope produces, orbiting far outside of our atmosphere."

"Of course, we don't have a laser to measure with." Caesare pointed out.

"That's true," replied Borger. "But we have the next best thing."

"Which is what?"

Borger smiled. "Mathematics."

*****

Clay leaned against the back wall of the bridge and waited with Alison and her team to hear back from Sally or Dirk. Lee Kenwood sat in front of the computer and looked through some of the system's logs. He looked up at Clay.

"You know, Mr. Clay. I mean John. I can record this session if you like."

Alison spoke before Clay could answer. "I'm sure they've been recording this from the moment we started."

Clay looked at Alison and then at Lee with a shrug. "She's right."

Lee smiled nervously. "Ah."

"I'm going to get some air." said Alison, as she opened an outside door not far from where they were standing. Chris followed her out.

Alison grabbed the rail to steady herself and looked over the side of the ship into the blue water. "I swear, these guys are all the same."

Chris frowned, looking uncertain. "I don't know. I'm not sure if this guy fits the mold that we've come to hate." He looked at her, trying to get her to grin.

She was not biting. "Didn't you hear what he just said?

He admitted to recording this whole thing without us even knowing."

"Yeah, but he didn't deny it. Did he?" Chris pointed out. "He could have just kept quiet and said 'sure Lee. That would be great if you could record it for us'. I mean, Christ Ali, this is the military. They pretty much record everything!"

She shook her head. "I don't trust him."

Chris dropped his head. "Ali, you don't trust anyone."

Her eyes widened in surprise. "That's not true!"

"Oh yes. It is true and you know it! Look, we've been friends a long time, but admit it, you keep your cards close to the vest on pretty much everything."

Alison squinted at Chris with a look of indignation. "Not everything!"

"Ali, you're great," he said. "But you've got to let some of this stuff go. I don't like the military either, and you know what, maybe they end up screwing us again, somehow. But I don't want to go through life being pissed off all the time." Chris looked back out on the water. "Look, I don't know this guy Clay. But, it seems like he genuinely appreciates our help with this. Okay, are they getting some PR out of it with the press? Sure, but who cares? They can't get some attention without us getting it too."

Alison stared at him for a long time and finally exhaled. "Fine. I'll give him a chance."

"That a girl," Chris said. He put his arm around her and gave her a quick squeeze. "Now, let's enjoy the view and try not to think about the fact that he's probably going through your purse right now."

Inside, Lee looked up from his monitor again at Clay. He was leaning against the wall to steady himself against the rolling of the ship, and watching the crew members at the helm.

"So, John. What is it exactly that you do for the Navy, if you don't mind my asking?"

Clay raised his eyebrows. "Not at all. I work for a department in the Navy called Special Investigations."

"That isn't one of those 'I'd have to kill you' type of groups, is it?"

Clay laughed. "No. Our investigations are unique issues, usually outside of normal naval operations."

"What kind of things do you investigate?" Lee was curious.

"Most of it is classified, but it typically has to do with system malfunctions or communication problems. An example might be two systems using overlapping frequencies and causing problems. Pretty boring stuff."

Lee smiled. "That sounds about as boring at a cocktail party as what I do."

Clay laughed again. "Well, if we run into each other at a party, I'll listen to your stories if you listen to mine."

"You're on," Lee said, laughing along. "Well, for what it's worth, it nice to be around another tech head for a change. I think I bore the team a lot with my geek speak."

"That's understandable," he nodded. "It's a hell of a project you're working on."

"That, it is," Lee agreed. "Things have gotten really exciting since the translations started. We didn't expect things to happen so quickly, but we're certainly happy about it. We were afraid it would be just the opposite, especially Alison."

Clay nodded and looked out the window at Chris and Alison talking to each other.

"Listen," Lee continued. "About Alison, she's a great girl. She's just very protective over this whole thing, especially Dirk and Sally. She had a bad experience with the Navy in the past, and kinda got screwed career-wise, so she's not too excited to go down that route again."

"I can understand that."

"She's smart as a whip too," Lee added, with a wink.

"So be careful."

Clay smiled. "I'll watch myself."

Captain Emerson approached and looked at Clay. "We're starting to see some chop." He then looked down at Lee. "Any idea, son, on how long we might be waiting here?"

"No, sir," Lee replied. "That would probably be a question for Ali and Chris."

Alison checked her watch and looked at Chris. "They *are* coming back, right?"

"I sure as hell hope so," he said, squinting.

The door opened behind them and they both turned around to see Emerson and Clay step outside. Emerson glanced at the water again and approached Alison. "Ma'am, any word from your dolphins?"

"Not yet."

"Well, it looks as though we're seeing some chop building. If the swells increase too much, we won't be able to stay here."

She raised her eyebrows. "You mean leave?"

"I'm afraid so."

"We can't leave without them!"

"Ma'am, I understand your dilemma, but if things get too rough, I have no choice but to weigh anchor. I cannot risk the safety of the other passengers."

"How much longer do we have?" she asked.

"It's hard to say. If conditions continue as they are, I would estimate we have one, maybe two hours."

Alison was clearly starting to worry. She nodded to the captain and turned back to the water looking for signs of Dirk and Sally.

As they stepped back into the bridge, Clay gave Emerson a curious look. "Have you noticed anything strange about the weather?"

"What do you mean?" Emerson asked, peering back

outside.

"Well, the current is getting rougher, but there is no wind and not a cloud in the sky."

16

SITTING ON TWENTY-NINE acres of land and housing over seventeen miles of corridor, the Pentagon was one of the world's largest and most efficient office buildings. On the bottom floor, tucked away in a tiny lab, Will Borger sat toiling over a program to try to remove some of the static from the Triton's video. It started with a long call with one of the programmers at U.C. Berkeley who spent an hour sending over computer code and walking Borger through the logistics, including the mathematical algorithms necessary. Since Borger was not looking for planets he had to rewrite several large sections of the program.

Behind him, Caesare walked back in with an extra-large pizza and two six packs of Jolt; his payment for commandeering the afternoon of the smartest guy in the building. Borger had been typing nonstop from the time Caesare left. Upon returning, Caesare was beginning to worry that this might take even longer, in which case he was on the hook for dinner as well.

"How are we looking?" Caesare asked, sitting back down next to him.

Borger took a break and ran carefully through the syntax of the text he had just added. "Had a couple of bugs I've been trying to work out. I think we may have it." He switched to another window and typed a command to compile all the pieces again. "Good. No errors this time." He typed one last command and slapped the enter key. "Let's give it a whirl."

Borger turned around and popped open the top of the pizza box. He grabbed a big piece and a napkin then turned back to the monitor. The screen filled with the video footage and advanced the frames again, in slow motion. Caesare bit into his own slice and leaned back watching.

The frames advanced quickly until the computer reached the point in which the first dots of interference became visible in the video. Suddenly, the video slowed considerably and the computer could be seen scanning the frozen picture pixel by pixel, and eliminating the extra dots before moving to the next. The two men watched silently as each picture became clearer and clearer. By the time the program finished, both Borger and Caesare were leaning forward trying to understand what they were looking at in the final frame. The Triton had changed direction, as the object on the screen was no longer visible in the corner. It was now stretching across most of the window.

"What in the world is that?"

Borger shook his head. "No idea. It looks like...an arc of some kind."

"Is that," Caesare asked, getting even closer, "on the bottom?"

"I think so. See some of this darker material around the outsides? That's coral." He thought a moment. "This reminds me of the bundles of fiber optic cable that the telecommunications companies lay underwater, but this is much bigger."

Caesare frowned. "It's not cable. The ocean is not that deep here, but even at that depth, we should not be able to see it. There's not enough light that far down. And there is no way the Triton's lights are strong enough."

"True," Borger agreed. "But that means that whatever it is, it's emitting its own *light*."

"This is bizarre. Can we determine how big it is?"

"We can do better than that." He began typing again. "If we invert the color..." the object suddenly turned black while the rest of the screen inverted to white. "...and we tell the computer to zoom out...we can have it use the current dimension to estimate what the overall shape is." He hit the return key again and watched the object shrink in size. Then, the computer began to add in pieces to complete what it calculated the shape to be. When it finished they were both shocked.

"Are you seeing what I'm seeing?"

Borger nodded. "It looks like...a giant ring."

*****

Lee sat at his small table and tried repeatedly to summon the dolphins. Every few minutes he typed *Hello Dirk*, *Hello Sally* and waited. No reply came. Alison stumbled in and grabbed for the wall behind him.

"Anything?"

Lee shook his head dejectedly. One of the small devices on the table abruptly slid with the pitch of the ship and he quickly grabbed it before it fell off.

Alison turned around and looked at Chris, who shared her worried expression. "We may have lost them," he offered gently.

Alison shook her head. "No." She looked down at Lee again who took the hint and typed another message to them.

Clay stepped into the room from the other side of the bridge. He nodded to Captain Emerson. "All of the passengers are in the lounge. It's a little tight but they should be fine, although several have gotten sick. They're sitting close to the door."

Emerson nodded and they both looked over at Alison and her team. They crossed the rest of the room before Emerson spoke. "I'm afraid we're out of time."

Alison held on, bracing herself against the wall. "Just ten more minutes. Please! We can't leave without them."

"Young lady, we can't wait any longer. If things get worse, we're going to be in some serious trouble. We have to leave!"

"Please!" she begged. "You don't know what losing them would do to us!"

Clay leaned slightly toward Emerson. "It will take us at least five minutes to get the anchor up."

Emerson stared at him, then at Alison. He exhaled and looked over this shoulder. "Officer Harris."

The first officer quickly turned around. "Yes, sir!"

"Let's get the anchor up."

"Yes, sir." He turned back to his console and picked up a phone.

A grim Emerson turned back to Alison. "It's going to take five or six minutes to raise that anchor. You have until then. But when it's up, we're leaving! Understood?"

Alison gave a meek nod. "Thank you."

In the bow of the ship, a giant motor slowly began turning and reeling in the enormous anchor chain. The ship was beginning to pitch wildly as huge swells rolled in under the Pathfinder. With each swell, the bow shot high into the air and crashed down on the other side. The dolphin tank on the stern had lost almost of third of its water to the violent up and down movements of the ship.

In the lounge, purses and camera bags fell off the shelves and tumbled across the floor. Everyone tried to find something to hold onto and a few became frightened when they lost their hold and fell on top of the person next to them.

Suddenly, the ascending anchor chain stopped with a loud clang.

Two crewmen below deck examined the anchor windlass and tried the motor again. Nothing moved. They tried again with more power. This time the motor remained frozen and started releasing a small cloud of gray smoke. The two men quickly adjusted the controls and reversed the direction trying to unwind the chain again; still nothing. The massive anchor was clearly wedged on the bottom.

With phone in hand, First Officer Harris looked at the captain. Emerson, like everyone aboard heard the loud noise and felt the sudden jolt of the ship. "The anchor windlass is jammed."

Emerson's eyes widened. "Well, get it cleared!"

"We can't sir! We've tried."

Emerson and everyone else in the bridge were struggling to maintain a solid hold on something. He looked out the window again. The skies were still clear, but the ocean was continuing to worsen, and quickly. He looked at Clay, who gave him an almost imperceptible nod.

"Cut it!" he told Harris.

"Aye sir," the first officer replied.

Below deck, one of the two crewmen dropped a dark mask over his face and fired up a large torch. He looped one arm over the large notched wheel. The second stood behind him and tried to provide support. The torch flame touched one of the huge chain links and slowly began cutting the thick metal.

In the bridge, the communication officer picked up another handset. He listened for a moment, then turned to Clay.

"Mr. Clay, you have a ship to shore call."

Clay stumbled forward, reaching for the end of the bridge's massive console. "Who the hell is it?"

The young man spoke into the phone and listened. "Caller is a Steve Caesare."

"For Christ sake," Clay growled. "Tell him I'll call him back."

He relayed the message, listened for a moment, and looked back at Clay. "He says it's urgent."

Clay snatched the phone and almost yelled into the mouthpiece. "Not a good time, Steve!"

"Are you okay?" asked Caesare.

"Yeah. Got our hands full. Make it fast."

Caesare's tone was serious. "John, listen. We found something on the video from Triton."

"Go."

"There is something big on the ocean floor," Caesare said. "Something *really* big."

Clay looked at Emerson while he listened. "What is it?"

"We don't know. It looks like a giant ring. Borger puts it at about twenty-five kilometers across."

Clay's eyes widened. "Did you say two five?"

"Yes, two five kilometers across," Caesare confirmed.

"Good god!"

"And you're sitting right on top of it. You need to get out of there!"

"We're working on that." Clay tossed the handset back to the communication officer and turned to Emerson. "We need to leave right now!"

Two decks down, the sailors stumbled back and forth trying to keep the torch focused on the chain. The bow rose up again and both grasped at the enormous windlass wheel to keep their footing. Tiny pieces of steel fell to the floor as the white hot torch slowly ate its way through the section of metal. Suddenly the ship rolled to port. Both the crewmen fell and tumbled into the metal wall, smashing the head of the torch and extinguishing the flame.

Officer Harris turned to Emerson again. "Sir, we lost the torch."

Emerson stared at him, thinking. "How far are we

through that chain?"

Harris was not sure what the captain meant but then realized. "Far enough!"

"Do it!"

Harris turned to the other men on the bridge. "Engines up, gentlemen!"

"They're here!" Lee interrupted. "Dirk and Sally are back!"

Alison lunged to his table and checked the screen. She immediately turned back to Emerson. "Wait! Wait!"

Emerson gave her a hard look and held up his index finger. "*One* minute!"

Alison typed as quickly as she could. "*Sally are you and Dirk okay?*"

Yes, answered Sally.

We have trouble. We have to leave. Follow us! Alison clicked the Translate button and looked around the bridge. Everyone was holding on to a piece of the room and watching her.

An error message appeared on the screen. "Unable to Translate."

"Oh, god," she groaned.

Lee looked over her shoulder. "Take out the exclamation mark."

Alison typed it again.

After a long wait, both dolphins finally responded with *Okay*.

"Go!" shouted Alison to the crew.

The Pathfinder's giant engines roared to life and the ship pushed forward. The chain became taut as the Pathfinder pulled hard against it. A shudder ran through the entire hull. Both crew and passengers held tight as the ship strained under the pull of the chain and anchor.

"Full power!" barked Emerson.

The engines roared louder. The chain scraped loudly on the side of the ship. Very slowly and below deck, the half-cut link near the windlass began to twist under the stress. Inch by inch, it continued to stretch and pull, until the chain finally exploded sending the broken end smashing through the hull as the ship lurched forward.

Nearly everyone on the bridge lost their hold and fell to the floor. The Pathfinder sailed across the immense swell and smashed bow first into the next wave. In the lounge, passengers bounced off the bulkhead and over tables, grasping for each other as they fell.

17

THE PRESIDENT'S VH-3 helicopter, Marine One, slowly approached the back lawn of the White House and stopped in a hover just a few feet above the grass. It gently touched down with little more than a bump as the giant shocks absorbed the weight of the heavy craft. The marine on board waited for the rotors to begin winding down before opening the door and deploying the step ladder. He held Kathryn Lokke's hand and helped her down the first steps and into the hand of a second marine waiting at the bottom.

She instinctively clutched her satchel tight as she reached the ground and was quickly escorted away from the helicopter. An older man with gray hair approached with a quick short stride that almost made it look as though he were stumbling. Bill Mason was the White House Chief of Staff and known for his no-nonsense approach to all things security. Kathryn had only met him a few times before. He always seemed impatient and in a hurry, though relatively polite.

"Nice to see you again, Ms. Lokke," he said, motioning

up a small manicured path that headed toward the back entrance of the White House. "Please follow me."

They reached a set of thick double doors and stepped inside, where Kathryn was asked to put her things on a conveyor belt to be scanned. She was then patted down by a female Secret Service agent and escorted forward. Kathryn quickly grabbed her bag from the far end of the belt and continued following Mason.

"Your flight was a few minutes late, so the President should be waiting." Mason turned a corner and led her down a flight of stairs into the basement. Two additional turns left them at the doors to the infamous Situation Room. "Is there anything you need?"

Kathryn shook her head. She had gone over the material and the presentation several times.

President John Carr was standing when she entered the room. He turned to meet them as Mason stepped in behind her. "Mr. President, may I introduce Dr. Kathryn Lokke, from the USGS."

President Carr seemed to tower over her with his six foot, four inch frame. "Pleased to meet you, Dr. Lokke."

She smiled nervously. "It's my pleasure, Mr. President. Thank you for meeting with me."

"Not at all," he replied, as he stepped back and grabbed a chair. "Please forgive me for being curt. I have a call with Israel in about twenty minutes. Shall we get started?"

"Yes, yes, of course," Kathryn answered and quickly fumbled to get her laptop out of her bag. Several other men were already sitting around the table. She recognized the Vice President, Secretary of Defense, and the National Security Advisor. Most of the others wore decorated uniforms and looked to be high ranking officers from the military.

She started speaking as she opened up her laptop and connected the cable to the large monitor behind her. "Mr. President," she looked at the others, "gentlemen, the USGS has been closely tracking some accelerating changes in the Earth's north and south poles for the last couple of decades, and more specifically the last several years." She pressed a button and the large screen lit up with the map she was displaying on her laptop screen.

"These are four pictures, two of the Arctic and two of the Antarctic. The pictures in each set are separated by two years." She turned around to point to the screen. "From this high a level you can easily see the changes occurring, and in fact these changes are accelerating. You may have heard a few years ago that a huge section of the Ronne Ice Shelf separated and fell into the ocean, floating north. The separation of the shelf happened due to the growing weight and pressure of the ice pack as measured over the years, at which point the pressure surpasses the strength of the frozen ice and a collapse occurs." Kathryn hit a button on her laptop and a larger screen of the Antarctic was displayed. A satellite image from earlier in the year showed where a piece had broken off the giant Ronne Shelf. It could already be seen a few hundred miles away in the photo. "This break was a surprise, but fortunately the impact was not serious." She paused and looked around the room again. "The reason I am here is because a few days ago we received a very large wake up call."

"An earthquake, or more specifically, a geological shift, has occurred along the shelf, and this time not in the ice." She advanced to the next slide, which showed the large ice portion of the shelf. Further south, a red line traced the shift that just occurred. It was clear the recent shift was on land and near the first large mountain range, heading into the heart of the continent. "When the huge part of that ice shelf broke off years ago, it floated away. It floated because it was ice and its overall mass was less dense than the water below it." The screen now zoomed in on the red line. "This latest shift occurred at the base of a glacier, which is a far heavier section of land mass than just ice. This land mass has now dropped by almost fifteen feet."

President Carr looked around the table and back at Lokke. "What does this mean?"

Kathryn paused. Her heart was beating fast, but she wanted to be careful how she phrased this. "It means a high level of risk for an impending natural disaster."

Mason spoke up from the left side of the table. "How high a risk are we talking about?"

"We don't know exactly," Kathryn sighed. She noticed a couple of the men frown. "We cannot determine how high without a more accurate timeline. Measured in likelihood and impact, the risk is...very high."

One of the men started to speak but the President held up a hand. "Ms. Lokke, when you say 'impact' what do you mean?"

"Well," she started, "there are a number of scenarios escalating in severity. The scenario we must consider is a massive slide of that glacial base into the ocean which would send a gigantic tsunami up through the Atlantic. The size would be something modern history has never seen."

"As big as the one in Indonesia?" asked Mason.

"Bigger. Much bigger. This could have the energy to destroy every major city or seaport on either side of the Atlantic, all the way up to London. The surge could reach many miles inland, which means several orders of magnitude larger than Indonesia."

There was a long silence in the room.

"So," the National Security Advisor took off his glasses and held them between his two fingers, "what do we do?"

Hank Stevas was a highly political figure. Short and in his late sixties, he had attracted criticism from both sides of the aisle. Stevas was known for being confrontational and overly brash, or 'rude' as others would politely call him. Someone Kathryn was hoping would not be in this meeting.

Kathryn took a deep breath. "Well, the best step would be to take a proactive approach and try to avoid what could turn out to be a global panic. This would mean purposely finding a way to relieve some of the strain being created. There are a few possibilities that require a certain amount of time and resource-"

"I see," replied Stevas, cutting her off. "And does everyone at the USGS agree with your assessment?"

Kathryn was expecting this. Hank Stevas had not so subtly attacked her a year earlier during one of her environmental reports. She was amazed at his total disregard for empirical facts, even his lack of interest in *learning* the facts. Instead, he attacked politically, by going after a person's character or reputation. After her run in with him last year, she later learned that he was friends with her predecessor. It seemed he was not going to let sleeping dogs lie.

Kathryn hesitated, only because of the satisfaction he was about to get, even though the answer was far from simple. "No."

"No," Stevas repeated nodding his head and frowning. "So, how many other scientists *do* agree with you?"

His accusing tone lingered in the air as she stared at him. How convenient that he said 'agree with *you*' instead of 'this conclusion'. "It's not that easy-"

Stevas spread his hands in a mocking gesture. "How many agree with you? Half? Less than half? Does anyone agree with your view? Being the head of the largest scientific department on the planet, I would hope that at least *some* of your subordinates would agree."

Kathryn had to force herself not to glare at the man. "Some, yes."

"Some," he nodded sarcastically. "Some." Stevas looked around the room, addressing everyone at the table. "So we have a minority *scientific* opinion here regarding a geological event that may or may not be a serious risk, and that could cost who knows how much. Might I remind everyone that last year you gave a presentation claiming that the ocean levels worldwide were actually falling, in contradiction to everyone else in the scientific community? They suggested the exact opposite. Even, in fact *calculating* the opposite."

Kathryn did not want to respond, but would not let it go unaddressed in front of everyone in the room. "My suggestion was that the widely accepted calculations were flawed based on failure to account for a number of variables such as lunar gravitational patterns, the Earth's equatorial bulge, and-"

"You claimed," Stevas cut her off again, "that the water level was falling, but could not explain where the disappearing water was supposedly going! Tell me, Ms. Lokke, does anyone agree with your claim now, a full year later?"

If Kathryn did not want to respond to his last question, she really did not want to respond to this one. Stevas had clearly known what the subject of this meeting was about and decided to dig up some dirt. Reluctantly, she answered. "Not to my knowledge. But you have to understand this isn't like walking down to the nearest beach with a measuring stick. There are many calculations involved."

"Not to your knowledge," he repeated.

"Look," she said, ignoring Stevas and addressing the others, "this is a grave situation. If we don't do something, and soon, to release some of the pressure along that shelf, we may be talking about the greatest disaster we have ever seen. If that piece of the continent collapses, we could have just a matter of hours to evacuate 50 million people." Now she glared at Stevas. "How smoothly do you think a last minute evacuation plan would go?"

Kathryn looked to the President, who had been watching the rest of the table with his hands folded in front of his mouth. "Ms. Lokke, do we have actual proof that this collapse is imminent?"

Out of the corner of her eye, she noticed Stevas putting his glasses back on. "No," she answered.

"Well, I'm afraid I'm not ready to go around warning half the countries on the planet, potentially starting a panic, over something that we cannot provide real proof of." He stood up and the rest of the table abruptly followed. "I'd like you to have your team conduct more research and return when you have something more concrete." He shook her hand. "Thank you for coming in."

Kathryn watched in stunned silence as all of the men shuffled out of the room, some shaking her hand on the way out. Stevas was not one of them.

She slowly gathered up her things and put them back into her bag while Mason waited for her in the hall. She could not believe what had just happened. The President sat there and completely bought Stevas' argument, which in the end was that she was incompetent.

She began to feel slightly sick to her stomach. She had been completely dismissed for nothing more than some political strutting. If she was right, then Stevas and the President of the United States had just condemned millions of people to death.

She walked out of the conference room and followed Mason back upstairs. Knowing they would do nothing until it was too late made her now hope that she was wrong, really wrong.

18

AFTER NEARLY AN hour of twenty foot swells, the conditions slowly calmed and the Pathfinder continued plowing north. The ship's crew and guests, thoroughly battered, began nursing their wounds. Several of the journalists had sustained injuries after being flung around the lounge, requiring treatment and some bandaging by the ship's medical staff.

On the bridge, Alison had made her way out to the side of the ship to make sure Dirk and Sally were still with them. The two dolphins remained near the bow, swimming and jumping effortlessly through the waves. Alison turned and stepped back inside just as Emerson returned to the bridge from the other side.

"Alright, Clay. I've got a ship full of sick and injured people and my lounge has been turned into a clinic. We've damn near run out of bandages and splints. What the hell is going on?"

"I don't know, Rudy. I'm still trying to figure it out myself."

Emerson shook his head. "I've never seen anything like that before. A storm out of nowhere with perfect skies, nearly sinking my ship; something awfully strange is happening here."

"I wish I knew," Clay replied.

"Well, what the hell was that call about? Sounds like you learned something."

Clay turned toward Alison and her team. "I don't suppose you have a security clearance?"

They all shook their heads in unison.

He sighed. Clay turned back to Emerson. "They're all going to need to be read on. Caesare and one of our experts at the Pentagon seem to have found something on the Triton video, recorded by your team."

Emerson looked at him expectantly.

"It looks like there may be an unidentified object on the ocean floor, something very big."

"How big?" Emerson asked.

"Upwards of twenty five kilometers."

"Jesus Christ!" choked Emerson. "Are they kidding?"

"I don't think so. They said it was in the shape of a ring."

Emerson furrowed his brow. "A twenty five kilometer *ring*. What the hell does that mean?"

Clay shrugged helplessly. "You know as much as I do. I'll call him back and see if we can get more information. In the meantime, Ms. Shaw, shall we find out what your dolphins have to say?"

Alison nodded. "We'll need to shut down the engines first."

Emerson looked at his first officer. "Give them a rest."

"Yes sir," Harris responded and gradually reduced the engines, finally shutting them down. The ship slowly coasted to a stop.

Lee sat down at the table and typed *Hello Sally Hello Dirk* and clicked the translate button.

Hello Lee.

Are you okay? Lee asked.

Yes.

Did you find the metal bubble?

Yes. Very far. Follow us.

Wait. Lee frowned at the captain. "I'm guessing you are not interested in going back."

"I think I'd rather chew broken glass," Emerson scoffed.

"I think we should-" Clay suddenly stopped and stared over Chris Ramirez's shoulder. A person was watching them from outside the window. Alison and the others turned around as Clay took a step between them to get a better look when the person suddenly raised something up and pointed in their direction. "Get down!" Clay shouted and stepped in front of Alison.

Alison grabbed Clay and peered around his shoulder. She instantly recognized the person in the window. It was the journalist she saw earlier with the dumb hat. The man was focused, not on them but on Lee Kenwood's monitor screen. When he realized the others were looking at him, he quickly put the object down and darted away.

"Hey!" Clay yelled and ran after him. He burst through the door and chased the stranger along the long catwalk, his feet banging the thick metal grate with every step.

The stranger ran quickly to the stairs and half slid, half jumped to the level below. He bolted past the lounge and headed for the stern of the ship.

"Stop him!" Clay yelled and cursed the fact that there was no one else outside. Most of the crew was inside helping the ship's doctor tend to the rest of the passengers. Clay reached the end of the second level catwalk and turned the corner to find the observation deck empty. He crossed over to the port side and looked forward. Emerson was running down the other side, toward him. Clay looked around again, just in time to see the man sprint past behind him. He reached the railing of the deck, above the stern's platform and the dolphin's makeshift tank. He looked around and then back at Clay. With Clay now just a few feet away, the stranger swung over the rail looking for something to land on, but at the last moment the man's sleeve caught a protruding bolt. The sudden change in motion caused his legs to pitch inward and his head and shoulders to turn out. He tried to correct his orientation as he fell, but could not correct in time. He hit hard, head first, making a sickening crunch.

Clay, followed by Emerson and now another crew member from the bridge, scrambled down the last flight of metal stairs and ran to the motionless figure. Clay put his fingers against the man's neck and felt for a pulse. "He's still alive."

Two more crewmen arrived. "Get the doc down here!" Emerson shouted. One of the officers ran back up the stairs. The remaining two knelt next to Clay and helped slowly turn the man on his back. They cut his clothes open, looking for other obvious injuries.

Clay and Emerson stood up and stepped back as the ship's doctor came running down the stairs and started checking his vitals. After a few minutes, the doctor looked up at the crewman. "Get him on a stretcher *gently* and get him to medical!"

Even against the rocking of the ship, Emerson's crew managed to get the injured man up the stairs without losing him or the stretcher. Clay and Emerson watched as the men made it to the second deck and took him forward of the lounge, to the medical area, located just below and back from the bridge.

Emerson shook his head. "This day is getting stranger by the minute." He started for the stairs when Clay reached out and grabbed his arm.

"Before we head back," he said, reaching into his pocket, "take a look at this." Clay pulled out a small silver object and showed it to the captain.

"What is this?" Emerson took it and turned it over in his hand. It was a small, flat rectangular piece of metal about an inch thick.

"I don't know," Clay replied. "But that is what he was holding up when we saw him through the window."

"Where did you get it?" Emerson asked.

"It was in his pocket."

"Hmm…looks like a silver brick. Or, maybe a digital camera, except there is nothing on it. No lens, no button, no anything." He handed it back to Clay.

Clay ran his fingers up and down the smooth sides. "Why would he be holding this up?"

"No idea."

Clay frowned. "The funny thing is that when I saw him, he looked like he was pointing it."

"Like a weapon?"

"I doubt it," Clay said. "Besides, he wasn't pointing it at us. He was pointing it at that kid, Lee Kenwood, and his monitor."

*****

Clay was standing outside the door to the medical lab

watching Doctor Kanna, the ship's doctor, examine the man who lay unconscious on his table. They had run a check on his fingerprints, which came up empty, as did his identification and press credentials. They were not sure how he managed to get aboard with the others, and assumed it was a mistake or some kind of forgery during check-in at the dock. After some questioning, they also found that none of the other journalists had any idea who he was.

As the doctor examined the motionless figure, he spoke into a small microphone to record the details of his examination. The injury was significant, and they had already sent for an airlift to the nearest hospital. Clay was watching Kanna take an x-ray when Alison walked up behind him.

"Any news?" she asked.

Clay shook his head. "Not yet. He seems to be a bit of a mystery."

"I hear a helicopter is coming out to get him."

He nodded. "The doctor thinks it's pretty bad."

After a long silence watching the doctor, she turned to Clay. "Listen…I wanted to thank you."

Clay turned away from the window. "For what?"

"You shielded me from whatever he was doing." She motioned to the figure on the table.

"Oh," Clay gave her a casual shrug. "It was nothing, just instinct." He began to turn away when he noticed she was staring at him. "What?"

Alison said nothing. Instead, she glared at him.

Clay finally got the message and smiled. "You're welcome."

Alison relaxed. "Can I ask you something?"

"Sure."

"Were you really just in this to find your probe?"

He smiled again. "Yes."

"No hidden agenda?" she said, with a skeptical tone.

"Just the probe."

Alison nodded at that. "I guess I owe you an apology."

"For what?"

She rolled her eyes. "Well, in case you haven't noticed, I've been kind of a bitch."

Clay laughed. "I hadn't noticed."

"Then you're blind."

"Is this the bitchy side?" he asked, motioning to their little exchange.

"Oh shut up," she said, shaking her head.

"Don't worry about it. For what it's worth, I don't blame you."

"What do you mean?"

"I read up on you a little, on what the Navy did with your project in Central America."

"What?" she said. "You read my file?"

Clay smirked. "File? What *file*? I 'Googled' you."

This time Alison laughed. "You found out about *that* from Google?"

"You'd be surprised. A lot of times we use it instead of the Navy's system."

Alison nodded her head while still grinning. "So…" she said, holding out her hand. "No hard feelings?"

Clay took her hand and gave it a gentle shake. "No hard feelings." He glanced back at the doctor who was continuing his examination. "So how are Dirk and Sally doing?"

"They're fine. A little hungry, but good."

Clay turned back to her. "I have to tell you, Alison, I've seen some amazing things, but what you've done with those dolphins is nothing short of earth shattering."

"Thanks," she said, with a shrug. "But it wasn't all me."

"I know. But it was a lot you." He looked seriously at her. "I think you're about to change the world, Alison Shaw."

Alison smiled. "I hope so."

Clay thought for a moment. "Can I ask you a

question?"

"Sure."

He spoke slowly, choosing his words carefully. "Is there anyone who would not…want you to succeed?"

"What do you mean?" she asked.

"I mean do you have competitors? Maybe other teams working toward the same goal?"

"Of course. There are several other teams. A few in the States and a couple in Europe. Why?"

Clay looked back to the man unconscious on the other side of the glass. "That guy seemed awfully interested in what you three were doing upstairs."

Alison looked confused. "I thought that was the whole point of being on the ship in the first place, to cover this. I just assumed he was trying to sneak a shot of the screen, you know, something to 'up' his story."

Clay turned back to Alison. "Then why would he run?"

Alison gave him a perplexed look. The thought had not occurred to her. "I don't know, maybe he thought he was going to get in trouble for leaving the lounge or something. The conditions were getting awfully dangerous."

"Hmm," Clay said to himself. "How much trouble would someone be in for that?"

"Are you kidding? This is the Navy." She gave him a sarcastic look. "You know the military! You guys are pretty obsessive about things."

"That's true." He nodded, still thinking to himself. He reached into his pocket and took out the small rectangular object he retrieved from the man's clothing. "Do you have any idea what this is?"

She looked at it. "A camera?"

"That's what I thought too." He turned it over and showed her the various sides of it. "But there's no lens, screen, or even lines, for that matter."

Alison reached out and took it. She examined it closer,

bobbing it up and down in her hand. "It's not heavy though. If it was solid metal, it would be heavy, right?"

"It depends on the metal, but yes. Generally, it would be much heavier."

"Then what is it?" she asked.

"I don't know," Clay said, as Alison dropped it back into his hand. "But if it's not a camera, why would he be holding it up to the window?" He looked at Alison. "I was assuming he was trying to steal your information."

She shrugged. "I suppose it's possible, but researchers usually tend to be more collaborative than competitive. I mean, don't get me wrong. There are definitely people who try to keep their research quiet, but that's usually in things like physics or electronics, something with commercial potential. When we keep things quiet, it's just because we want to get a big jump on everyone else, not for material gain. Let's put it this way, not a lot of people get rich over marine biology. Sure, we can write a book and get tenure at some expensive college, but it's not the kind of lifestyle that would cause you to keep things secret in hopes of becoming rich."

"Besides," she continued, "the other groups working with dolphins have taken much different approaches. More manual, and there's not as much technology involved. In fact, two groups are not trying to communicate as much as measure kinetic and energy influences."

"So, not much reason to be after your data," Clay finished.

"Not really."

Clay nodded, accepting her explanation. "You know, there is something else I need to tell you."

"Okay."

Clay took a deep breath. "I don't think I did you any favors upstairs when I asked if you had a security clearance."

"I thought you were joking," she smiled. "Why would

we have a security clearance?"

"Well, I suppose I was, but after talking to Captain Emerson and my superiors, it was agreed that whatever we experienced back there has to be treated as a security matter."

"What does that mean?"

"Well," he continued. "It means that everyone on board, including your team, will need to be debriefed when we get back to port."

"Okay." Alison seemed unconcerned. "How long does that take?"

"It's hard to say, maybe a couple hours each." Clay said. "Remember, this is the military. We tend to be obsessive about things."

Alison was surprised. "A couple of hours *each*?!"

"I'm afraid so."

"Well, that's not going to work. What are we going to do with Dirk and Sally? We just got them back into the tanks. We can't keep them in there overnight while you guys are asking us questions under a bright light."

"Bright light?"

"Well, I don't know how you do it!" she exclaimed.

"Relax. They've agreed to let you get the dolphins home before they put the big light on you. They will have to escort you back though."

"What do you mean *agreed*?"

"It took a little convincing," he admitted.

"From who? You?"

"The important thing is that you will have time to get Dirk and Sally settled first."

"Thank you." Alison said, with genuine sincerity. He was not turning out anything like she assumed.

"Don't thank me yet. The debriefing can be extensive."

Alison nodded and looked around the small room. She watched Doctor Kanna stare at a set of digital x-rays on a large screen. He stepped back with his hand on his chin.

"I guess we'd better start getting things packed up," she said. "Are you heading back upstairs?"

Clay shook his head. "Not yet. I have some questions for the doctor." He pulled the silver object back out of his pocket. "And I think I might borrow his x-ray machine."

"Okay," Alison said. She paused and then quickly held out her hand. "It was nice working with you."

Clay smiled and shook it again. "The pleasure was mine."

With that, Alison turned and left the room, closing the door behind her.

Doctor Kanna was still looking at the x-rays when Clay entered. About the size of a large clinic, the room was filled with stainless steel instruments and furniture. A small bookshelf on the far wall was filled with a number of medical journals and textbooks. Kanna looked at him momentarily, then turned back to the display.

"Dr. Kanna," he said, quietly.

"Hello, John."

"Any changes?" Clay asked.

"Yes, but not for the better. His condition is deteriorating quickly. I hope the helicopter gets here soon. I'm worried there may not be enough time," he motioned around the room, "and I don't have the equipment to do much here."

Clay nodded. There were only a few wires on the patient, monitoring his heart rate and blood pressure. Both of which looked unusually low, even with what little he knew about medicine.

"It's strange though," Kanna went on, "the worst of it is the blow he took to the head, and I think the brain is swelling. But, the rest of him appears relatively undamaged. Yet his respiration, blood pressure, and most everything else is depressed. Even his heartbeat looks to be irregular. Very odd and a little alarming."

Clay took a closer look at the man. "Could it all be a

result of the brain trauma?"

Kanna shrugged. "It's possible. He also looks like he's had some plastic surgery, which may indicate other health problems. We've got to get him to a trauma center where they can find out more." He looked at the x-rays closer. "This is also weird."

"What's that?" Clay stepped around the table and closer to the display.

Kanna pointed to one on the left. "He's missing a large area of bone around the right side of his rib cage." He pointed to another. "And here, he has a strange shape to his femurs. He may have a birth defect or some kind of deficiency. I wonder if it's given him a weaker bone structure, which might explain why his injury is as severe as it-"

The doctor was interrupted by a piercing alarm. The monitor showed the man's heartbeat slowing dramatically. A moment later, a second alarm sounded, and the graph showed the blood pressure dropping. Kanna quickly checked the monitor and the sensors strapped to the patient's chest and arm. "We're losing him! Where is that damn chopper?!"

Suddenly, the monitor's display became a solid green and went black with a loud pop. Overhead, the fluorescent lights burst. The room went dark with only small rays of sunlight seeping in around the window blinds. A strange blue sheen passed over the room's stainless steel table and shelves, and the air became warm. Behind Clay, a small white circle appeared in the middle of the room and slowly grew in size. As it reached a circumference of almost two feet, the ring began to stretch vertically into an oval. The room began to glow. Clay and Kanna whipped around in time to see the oval reach full length and touch the floor.

The pitch black center of the oval suddenly became a blinding white light, forcing Clay and Kanna to shield their eyes. After a few moments, the light subsided to a soft glow and turned dark. The table holding the patient began to vibrate and some of Kanna's tools rattled to the side and fell off on to the floor. The patient's table slowly started to slide toward the light. Kanna instinctively grabbed the table trying to stop the slide, but was pulled forward along with the table. It was not until one of the legs stopped against a lip in the floor that it stopped. The pull continued causing the table to shake harder, but the leg remained stuck. Kanna let go of the table and grabbed the unconscious patient as the shaking caused his body to vibrate toward the edge. In the next instant, the shaking stopped and everything fell silent. After several seconds, the stunned doctor opened his eyes wide as a figure appeared and stepped out from the large oval. He was dressed in light clothing and looked only briefly at the doctor. He gently lifted the end of the table over the lip and began pulling it toward the light himself, stopping only when he heard the loud slide action of John Clay's semi-automatic pistol being chambered.

The figure turned around to find Clay's gun just inches from his head. "What in the *hell* did you just do?" Clay said.

The man did not move. Instead, he looked down at the patient still on the table. He was no longer breathing.

There was not the slightest waver in Clay's gun as his finger moved onto the trigger. "Who are you?" He motioned to the light. "And how did you do that?!"

The man remained silent. He looked at the light and then back at the patient as if deciding something. When he spoke, it seemed reluctant. "Please, he is dying."

Clay momentarily glanced down at the unconscious figure on the table and back to the person before him. "Answer my questions."

"There is no time. I have only minutes to save him."

Clay brought his other hand up and wrapped it around the bottom of the gun, strengthening his grip. "Who *are* you?"

The man before Clay looked at the light again, emanating from the middle of the room. "Let me save him and I will answer your questions."

Clay shook his head slowly.

"Please. Let me save him and I will stay."

Clay hesitated, squinting at him.

"Please. I must save him!" he pleaded. His voice was beginning to sound desperate. "You have nothing to gain by keeping him here. He will die and you will still only have me."

After a long moment, Clay agreed. "Okay, but if you try to leave, I'll end it for both of you."

The man nodded. He lifted the table slightly, freeing the leg. Very slowly, the man took a step back and out of the way of the table, which continued sliding toward the light, unassisted. Clay watched the man on the other side of the table who, in turn, watched the table until it disappeared into the soft glow. He continued watching until the light finally blinked out and disappeared.

Clay turned his head so he could see the doctor from the corner of his eye. "Doc." Kanna did not respond. He just stared, stunned at the man in front of Clay.

"Doc!" Clay shouted, shaking Kanna out of his daze. "Call the bridge. Get some backup down here now!"

The doctor jumped for the phone and picked it up.

"Tell them to come armed."

Kanna nodded. As he spoke into the phone, Clay examined the man in front of him.

"So who are you?" Clay asked again.

The man stood motionless, staring at Clay. The gun did not appear to frighten him at all. Finally, he answered. "My name is Palin."

"Where are you from?" Clay asked.

The man slowly looked around the room. "Not far."

Clay squinted. "I'm going to need some better answers than this."

The man called "Palin" looked back at Clay. "I'll

answer what you ask. That was our agreement."

No sooner had Kanna replaced the receiver than several running feet could be heard on the loud catwalk above. Clay motioned behind Palin. "Back up against that wall and keep your hands in front of you."

Palin complied, slowly stepping back until his back brushed the wall. Moments later, Harris and Tay burst into the room behind Clay, with guns drawn.

"What happened?" asked Harris.

Clay did not take his eyes off Palin. "That's a good question. Let's start by having you handcuff Mr. Copperfield here."

19

CAPTAIN EMERSON APPROACHED Alison and her team who were in the process of dismantling their computer equipment.

"Ms. Shaw," he started, then looked at Chris and Lee. "Gentlemen. We have a change of plans."

Alison stood up. "What do you mean?"

"We need to offload you and the other passengers from this ship immediately."

They were confused. "What?"

"For your safety and the sake of national security, I need to get you off the Pathfinder," Emerson said.

"I don't understand. You were taking us back to Miami. Did something happen?"

Emerson shook his head. "I can only say that there has been a security incident. Believe me when I tell you that this is for your protection."

"An incident? When?" She scanned the bridge and did not find who she was looking for. "Did something happen to Mr. Clay?"

"John Clay is fine," he assured them. "There will be a Coast Guard cutter arriving in a few minutes. It is important that you and your team be ready to transfer as quickly as possible."

"Wait," she said. "What about Dirk and Sally?"

"I'm afraid the Coast Guard ship is not equipped to accept them. They will have to remain with us until we have the situation addressed and can return them to you. I'm sorry. Rest assured that delivering them will be our top priority and they will be well cared for until we bring them to you."

Alison would have normally protested, but she suspected something dangerous had just occurred. She decided this was not a good time to pick a fight with the Navy.

She looked at Emerson. "I have your word, Captain?"

"You most certainly do. Do you need any assistance?"

She looked at Lee who shook his head. "No, we'll be ready."

The Coast Guard cutter was half the length and much faster, judging by its sudden arrival making a half circle around the Pathfinder. It slowed and finished its circle, coming up alongside. Both ships lowered their giant fenders to protect their hulls from mutual damage as they pulled themselves together and placed a large walkway from one railing to the other.

All of the reporters were lined up with their belongings. Once they were motioned forward, they began stepping across one at a time. Alison, Chris and Lee paid a quick visit to Dirk and Sally. They then made their way back toward the bow. By the time they arrived, the last of the passengers were crossing over with the help of two sailors on either side.

Alison stepped up onto the walkway and turned back. Clay was nowhere to be seen, nor could she see the dolphin's tank, far back on the stern. She took a deep breath and walked quickly across. Chris and Lee followed.

When all passengers were seated and counted, the plank was quickly removed. The engines roared to life, and the cutter pulled away. As they charged forward, the Pathfinder slowly shrank in the distance behind them. Alison leaned forward and caught sight of the helicopters approaching the Pathfinder's bow. One large helicopter was accompanied by two smaller Apache attack choppers on each side.

20

KATHRYN LOKKE WAS sitting at her desk, but quickly stood up when she saw Phillip LeBlanc walk in. At nearly six feet tall and in his sixties, LeBlanc was the Secretary of the Interior and, in Kathryn's opinion, one of the few honorable politicians left at his level. He was also her boss. Having run the USGS a few administrations prior, just before the wave of scandals, LeBlanc noticed Kathryn early in her scientific career and became a mentor. He was instrumental in her becoming the director of the USGS as the person who encouraged her, or pushed, as she recalled, to go for it.

"How was your presentation?" he asked, sitting down on a leather couch which lined the wall near her desk.

She exhaled dramatically. "Which half?"

"Not good, eh?" LeBlanc asked, rhetorically.

"My good friend Stevas was there."

"Crap."

Kathryn sat back down. "Yeah, I wasn't expecting that. And now, as far as I can tell, both he *and* the President think I'm a loon."

"Stevas is a sleaze but he doesn't think you're crazy. Or stupid, for that matter. He's just playing nasty politics. You do know he's thinking about running next year, right?"

Kathryn's eyes shot open. "For President? Are you kidding me?!"

"That's the rumor."

Kathryn leaned back in her chair and covered her mouth with her hands. "Jesus, can you imagine what he would do to this department?!"

"Yes, I can."

Lokke shook her head and opened her bag, withdrawing her laptop. She plugged it in and pressed the power button before looking back at LeBlanc.

"So," he said, "I'm assuming they didn't react the way you were expecting."

"The way *we* were expecting," she corrected him. "And, no. Evidently, the idea of unpredictable risk is lost on them. The President said he wants more proof before going out to other countries and risking a panic." She spied him suspiciously. "You should have come with me."

LeBranc frowned. "No, you run the department now, Kathryn. I had nothing to add anyway." He leaned back into the couch and crossed his legs. "So he wants more proof."

"Yes. Hopefully, something slightly less compelling than an approaching tsunami."

He laughed. "Let's hope so."

Kathryn shrugged sarcastically. "Fortunately, I think they just want the day and time that it's supposed to collapse."

"So what's the plan?"

Kathryn logged into her computer. "We need more

evidence. And evidence that does not rely on my calculations of shrinking ocean volumes. Stevas really played me the fool on that one." She sat back again in her large chair. "I'm thinking that if we can get more exact measurements, use early indicators from the previous Ronne break off, and the speed with which it actually separated, we may be able to present a more realistic risk level. As long as we have a lot more facts than the other global agencies, they won't be in much of a position to argue. The only arguments left should be what we do about it and how much it will cost."

"Who else was there and, more importantly, did anyone *else* believe you?"

"Well 'believe' may be a strong word, but yes, I think there were a few who understood the risk I was trying to impart. Not surprisingly, it was the military officers and not the politicians. They seem to have a pretty solid grasp on risk and consequences. And Miller, the Secretary of Defense, seemed to be listening."

"No surprise there." LeBlanc replied. "After all, they have to fight wars. Politicians just start them." He went on. "If you don't know it by now, Stevas has the President's ear, and that's the polite version. Your best bet is to get as much data as is possible, and convince Mason to let you present it to the President while Stevas is not around. He'd probably be a bit more receptive."

"And how exactly do I convince Mason?" she asked.

He shrugged. "You're a good looking woman. Sweet talk him."

Kathryn pretended to be offended. "Did you really just say that?"

"Of course I didn't. You're hearing things."

Kathryn smiled and looked at her laptop, thinking. "I'm going to need to assemble a strong investigation team, starting with the group that documented the slide. We're going to need more people."

LeBlanc could see that she had just entered planning

mode. He stood up and straightened his tie. "You're also going to have to convince some of those people to get off their warm duffs and walk around in subzero temperatures for a while."

She suddenly stopped typing and gave him a concerned look. He was right. She was going to have to yank people off other projects. This was not going to make her popular.

He watched her expression change, with the full scope of what she had to do dawning on her. "This might be a good time to practice that sweet talking." And with a wink, he walked out.

21

THE TWO APACHE attack helicopters hovered just off the Pathfinder's bow, while the larger Seahawk lowered itself onto the ship's landing pad. Immediately upon touchdown, the door slid open and four marines jumped onto the platform dressed in combat gear and carrying M4 carbine assault rifles. They ran quickly out from under the turning blades to the base of the stairs, where several of the ship's crew, still armed, stood around John Clay and the smaller Palin. Clay stood close to Palin, who was handcuffed with his arms behind his back. He showed no expression as he watched the marines approach.

The first marine stopped in front of them and saluted to Captain Emerson, who also stood next to Clay. The other three, just a step behind, did the same.

"Sir!" the marine said, turning to Clay. "We have orders to bring you back to base. Are you ready?"

Clay nodded.

The marines grabbed Palin by the arms and walked him briskly back to the helicopters, the blades still spinning at full speed. Clay grabbed his duffle bag and pulled it up over his shoulder. He turned to Emerson.

"Thanks Rudy," he said, shaking hands.

Emerson nodded. "Keep me posted."

Clay gave an informal salute to the rest of Emerson's crew, then turned and trotted after the marines. He reached the chopper just as they hauled Palin aboard, and crawled in after him. The marines sat on all sides with their rifles pointed at Palin. Clay tossed his bag into the rear, climbed in next to them, and slammed the metal door shut. One of the men handed him a headset. He put it on and adjusted the microphone.

The pilot adjusted the rotors on the Seahawk, and the helicopter lightened until it lifted off the pad. It quickly rose into the air, flanked by both Apaches. They headed north, slightly away from the setting sun. Behind and far below, the giant engines of the Pathfinder roared back to life. It swung to port and began steaming north.

Under the sound of the helicopter's powerful thumping blades, Clay finished his conversation and removed his headset. He leaned against the door watching Palin. The man sat uncomfortably, with his hands still behind his back, eyes lowered at the floor. The marines watched him intently, with grips tight on their weapons. Palin looked smaller than before. He sat quietly and did not struggle. To Clay, he looked almost despondent.

Palin slowly lifted his head to look around the small cabin and the marines sitting around them. Their faces looked like chiseled stone. He looked at Clay and their eyes met. They maintained eye contact for a long time.

Clay could not help but notice something in Palin's gaze. Outwardly, he looked small and helpless but, at the same time, his eyes revealed no fear. When Palin looked away, Clay turned his head away too and looked out the window. After a few minutes, the blue ocean ended and was quickly replaced by white sand beaches as the helicopters raced north along Florida's Atlantic coastline.

*****

The Naval Air Station in Jacksonville was the largest Navy base in the southeast region and third largest in the United States. Referred to as "NAS JAX", the base was the largest in the region and specialized in antisubmarine warfare and some of the best aviator training on the planet.

The three helicopters arrived in just under two hours. They landed at a remote area of the base on the southwest corner to avoid attention. Several Humvee vehicles surrounded the landing area with their headlights on, and two dozen armed marines stood waiting. As soon as the Seahawk touched down, they rushed and yanked open the door. Clay quickly jumped down and watched the four marines climb out and strong arm Palin, as he stumbled down the steps.

"Easy!" Clay yelled above the sound of the rotors.

The marines paid no attention as they escorted Palin off the pad and over to one of the vehicles. The rest of the marines fell in around them. Clay ran to keep up, but was suddenly pulled aside by an officer.

"Mr. Clay?" he asked.

"Yes."

"Come with me please." The officer directed Clay to a different vehicle and opened the door for him. After he climbed in, the officer ran to the other side and slid behind the wheel.

Clay tried to find Palin in the glare of the bright headlights, but could not determine which vehicle they had put him in. The Humvees pulled out in unison and headed in a different direction, toward a small section of dimly lit buildings.

Clay's driver turned left and, instead, drove to a small two-story building at the edge of a dark, thick forest which extended for many miles. Had it not been for a single bright light and two marines standing guard in front of the metal door, Clay would have thought the structure was no longer in use. The officer brought the Humvee to a stop and they both got out. The driver noticed Clay instinctively looking into the back seat. "Someone will bring your things shortly."

Clay nodded and followed him to the entrance, where the officer waved an ID at the guards. The guard on the right turned around and punched a code into an unseen console. The huge metal door slid to the side with a loud hissing sound.

They both stepped inside into a brightly lit entryway, where they were met by four more marines. Two of the marines held their rifles, while the other two each held up a long cylindrical Geiger counter. One scanned Clay and the other scanned his officer escort. Clay produced his military ID and both were run under a computerized scanner. While he waited, Clay looked around the large room. There were four cameras, each in different locations. A large single hallway extended to a door at the far end. Both men retrieved their identification cards and walked to the end of the hall. The door was an elevator door, which opened as they approached. They stepped in and joined another armed marine, who maintained a hold on his weapon with one hand, and pushed the down button with the other. The tiny room jerked slightly and began its descent.

Clay stood calmly behind the marine, examining his outfit and gear. All of his previous visits to NAS JAX had been to some of the base's larger facilities, where he had made a number of friends. In fact, his last visit was just five weeks prior, where he spent the day in discussions with submarine engineers on another communication problem. He had never before seen the building he was now in, and it was quite clear that was by design. In fact, Clay wondered how many of the other 23,000 base personnel knew about it.

They descended for what Clay assumed to be three or four levels. When the doors opened, it was clear that the building's real heart was underground. In the background, several people hurried past back and forth. In front of them, a female officer waited while they stepped off. She turned to lead them without a word. Both men followed.

After two right turns, they arrived at a large conference room. To Clay's surprise, Admiral Langford was waiting, along with Captain Foster, the commander of NAS JAX. They crossed the room as both of Clay's escorts saluted and disappeared.

"Here he is," Langford said, extending his hand. "John, meet Captain James Foster. He runs the base here."

"Hello, Commander."

Clay saluted and then accepted Foster's handshake. "It's a pleasure to meet you, sir. I've been here many times but have never had the pleasure."

Langford got right to business, gesturing toward the large conference table in the middle of the room. At the far end was a flat monitor mounted to the wall. "Clay, we're about to have a call with the Joint Chiefs of Staff, the Secretary of Defense and the National Security Advisor. We are also going to include a few experts in various fields. Obviously, we need you to recount exactly what happened this morning on the Pathfinder, so we can understand what we are dealing with here."

Clay nodded. "Yes, sir."

"Do you need anything before we start?" asked Langford. "We have a few minutes yet."

"No, sir," replied Clay. "I'm fine."

"Excellent. Why don't we have a seat?" They walked over and sat down. "I hear you have a fix on the Triton

II?"

"Yes, sir, though it's probably a lead more than a fix. We don't know precisely where it is yet. We did not have time to investigate before all of the excitement."

"Understandable," Langford said. "Were those dolphins any help?"

"Yes," said Clay. "They claim to have found it, but that's the part we still need to follow up on. I suspect that it's going to be a difficult recover-". Clay was suddenly cut off by his cell phone ringing. It was Will Borger's number. He looked at Langford. "Do I have time to take this, sir?"

Langford looked at this watch. "You have four minutes. Make it fast."

Clay stood up and walked to the back of the room while Langford and Foster continued their earlier conversation. He accepted the call and held the phone to his ear.

"This is Clay."

"Hi Clay. It's Will," came Borger's voice on the other end.

"Hey, Will. What is it? Do you have something?"

"Yeah, more on our giant hula hoop at the bottom of the ocean."

Clay looked at Langford and Foster, who were still talking. "Let's hear it."

"We've been able to improve the video quality pretty significantly after fine tuning the program."

"Okay," said Clay. "And?"

Borger looked at Caesare, who was sitting next to him. "Well," he continued, "the thing looks to be moving."

"Moving?!" asked Clay. "Moving how?"

"Moving as in *spinning*," said Borger. "The thing is spinning. If my calculations are correct, I'd say this thing is making a complete rotation about every three minutes, maybe less."

"Jeez!" Clay exclaimed. "Are you kidding?"

"Nope."

Clay lowered his phone and looked at Langford and Foster, who were now watching him. "We've got to get Borger on this call, sir!"

The call started when the giant screen came to life. On the other end, it showed a large conference room, which Clay surmised was somewhere in the Pentagon. Around that table sat Secretary of Defense Miller and National Security Advisor Stevas. Several other military personnel, including the Joint Chiefs Chairman, the Vice Chairman and the chiefs for each of the five military branches; the Air Force, Navy, Army, Marines and Coast Guard.

A moment later, four other images appeared along the bottom of the screen, which Clay assumed were the experts that Langford had mentioned. Finally, in another small window, appeared Borger and Caesare. Borger was out of breath from running a quarter mile to the nearest video enabled conference room. Caesare did not look the least bit winded.

"Gentlemen," Langford began, "I'd like to dispense with introductions for reasons of expediency. John Clay has just arrived here in JAX and is ready to debrief us on exactly what happened on Emerson's ship today." He turned and nodded to Clay. "Go ahead, Clay."

"Thank you, sir." Clay stood up and faced the camera. He started from the beginning and explained the loss of the Triton submersible, the enlisting of the marine biology team in an attempt to find it, and everything that occurred on the Pathfinder from the time they left port. When he finished, he remained standing for questions. He thought to himself that if anyone were shocked by the story, almost no one on the screen showed it.

Miller, the Secretary of Defense, jumped in first. "So Commander Clay, you're saying that the air in the Med Lab just opened up and this man whom you call 'Palin' stepped right through?"

"Yes, sir," answered Clay. "That is what I believe

happened."

Stevas leaned forward in the video feed. "That is what you *believe* happened? What the hell does that mean? Did it or didn't it?"

"Sir," replied Clay. "I do not know exactly what happened, or how something like that is even possible. What I am explaining to everyone here is what I experienced, to the best of my understanding."

Langford interjected. "Might I suggest that before we get into a debate, we find out if something like that is possible? And if not, what else it could have been?" Langford called on one of the experts on the screen. "Professor Harding is on this call, who leads the physics department at MIT. Dr. Harding, can you please speak to what we may be looking at here?"

"Well," Harding started, clearing his throat. "To be honest, it sounds hard to believe." Harding's video grew larger on the screen as he spoke to the group. "The kind of technology required to accomplish this sort of feat...well, just isn't available today." He thought a moment. "Mr. Clay, is it possible that this Palin person was already onboard the ship?"

"It is," nodded Clay. "However, we checked with every crewmember and passenger. No one had seen him during boarding or any time on the trip."

"What about this patient?" asked Langford. "The one who was injured. Could they have had some trick up their sleeve, something coordinated?"

"It's possible," acknowledged Clay. "But I don't think this was a trick."

"And why is that?" Stevas shot back, from the Pentagon. "Why are you so sure this was not some deception? Mr. Harding himself said that it's not even possible, so it seems to me that some form of deception is the most logical conclusion here."

"Well, that's true, sir," Clay replied, "except for a couple of problems."

"Which are?" Stevas insisted.

"The disappearance of the examination table, not to mention the body that was lying on top of it."

Stevas did not appreciate the sarcasm. "Well, can we be sure that the table is in fact missing? You also said from your description that the man on the table and this Palin person looked very similar in appearance."

"That is correct."

"Isn't it possible that some kind of illusion or trick might make it *seem* as though there were two people when, in fact, there was only one?"

"I don't see what that would accomplish," Langford said. "If someone were in trouble, getting off the ship as an injured reporter would have been far easier than becoming a prisoner. Besides, why would someone go to so much trouble to get onboard a research vessel? To learn about some of our newly discovered oil deposits?"

"I agree," added Leonard Bullman, the Army Chief. Bullman was slender and had a quiet, thoughtful look about him. "Why the elaborate deception or risk of life and limb just to get on a science vessel?" He turned to look at Bruce Bishop, the Naval Chief sitting next to him. "Is there anything else on Emerson's ship of any serious value?

Bishop shook his head. "I spoke with Emerson an hour ago. There is nothing with that kind of value aboard. In fact, the majority of their data has not even been analyzed yet."

"Which means," said Langford, "that the only thing that changed on that ship by the time it left port..." he trailed off and looked at Clay.

"...was the dolphins," Clay finished.

"What's this little piece of translation software worth?" asked Defense Secretary Miller.

Clay shook his head. "Not much. According to the team, bragging rights primarily. Something worth winning a prize over, but certainly not a lifetime in prison."

Will Borger raised his hand on the screen and spoke. "Uh, excuse me."

Clay spoke up. "Gentlemen, this is Will Borger and my colleague, Steve Caesare. They discovered the ring on the ocean bottom. I asked them to join the call, as they have come up with more information on it. Go ahead, Will."

The video window showing Borger and Caesare grew larger and moved to the middle of the screen. "We, uh, have analyzed this quite a bit more and it looks like this ring is…moving."

Most of the participants on the call looked confused. Harding, however, looked intrigued. "What do you mean?" He asked, leaning forward.

"Well, when we say moving, we actually mean spinning. From my calculations, it looks to be making a full rotation every three minutes. Given that this thing has a total circumference of about 47 miles, that means it is spinning at a speed of nearly 700 miles per hour."

Everyone on the monitors were suddenly speechless. Harding's mouth fell wide open.

22

"WHAT DID YOU just say?" said Miller.

Borger continued. "The ring appears to be generating energy." He typed a few commands and his laptop screen appeared on the large monitors for everyone to see. The picture showed an area of the ring. "If we measure the light waves emanating from it, we can see a subtle shift in the Doppler which shows movement. The change in wavelengths allows us to measure the speed."

Nearly everyone on the call was still stunned.

"Will," said Clay. "What do you think this is?"

Borger shook his head. "We're really not sure. My guess is some kind of power plant."

"A power plant for what?" asked Stevas.

"I don't know," answered Borger. "There are too many unknowns. For instance, why is it underwater? Why is it located so remotely? How much power could it generate? It would help if we could see whether something was situated in the middle, but the resolution is not clear enough." He shook his head. "If it is a power plant, I've sure never seen one that spins like this."

"Let's back up here," Miller interrupted. "Obviously this thing is enormous. What country is even capable of building something like this, and undetected?"

No one answered, so Miller continued. "What would it take if we built it?"

"Thousands of men and a decade, at the minimum," Borger answered. "And that's assuming we weren't trying to keep it a secret."

"And that's probably conservative," added Harding.

"Okay, so we have some secret group that's been working on this for decades," Stevas said.

Miller raised an eyebrow. "Like who?"

"How the hell should I know? From where I'm sitting, the bigger question is not who built a massive power plant, but what is it for?"

"Maybe it's supposed to change the water temperature, and affect the weather or something," Mason offered.

Stevas raised his hand in agreement. "Right. Maybe they want to cause a hurricane or an earthquake. Or sap our national power grid and shut us down." He folded his arms across his chest. "I think we need to figure out what this thing does first."

Miller looked at the screen. "Dr. Harding?"

Harding frowned. "Almost anything is theoretically possible, given enough energy, but even if someone figured out how to create a hurricane or earthquake, there would be no way to control it. Your hurricane could go south instead of north, or east instead of west." He stared at the picture again. "I cannot imagine this being intended for weather manipulation."

"Fine!" Stevas barked. "Then you tell us!"

Borger blinked a few times. He swallowed hard. "This…" he started shaking his head. "This may sound crazy, but it reminds me of something a team of scientists are working on in Switzerland." He stared at his picture. "They have been able to establish a space-time relationship between two small objects. This was also done using rings, but they were very small, and the relationship only existed for a fraction of a second. It's a long shot, but there are several aspects that fit here."

"What do you mean when you say 'relationship'?" asked Langford.

Borger did not answer. He just stared at the screen, wondering if he should go on. This was almost too crazy.

"I think he means a tunnel," answered Harding.

Langford was confused. "A tunnel?"

"A wormhole," said Borger.

"What the hell is a wormhole?"

"A wormhole is a tunnel through time and space," Harding explained. "A theory from modern physics."

"And the Swiss have done this?" asked Stevas.

"Not this," Harding answered, shaking his head. "What Mr. Borger is referring to is a series of experiments carried out by the Swiss. However, they did it only for a moment and it was less than a millionth of a millimeter long. It also required an incredible amount of energy, equal to all of the electricity used by Switzerland in a year, compressed into less than a second."

"And you think we're looking at a giant version of this?"

"It's conceivable," Harding said slowly. "In their experiment, the Swiss team found a harmonic relationship between the rings. With enough energy and by spinning the rings, they connected at a harmonic level and made the tunnel possible." He scooted his chair closer to his monitor. "Mr. Borger, can you enlarge this image?" A moment later, the picture zoomed in. "One of the unique aspects of the experiment was that they had to spin the rings above the speed of sound to establish the harmonic connection."

Langford looked at Borger. "How fast did you say this thing underwater is spinning?"

"Just under the speed of sound."

"But the speed of sound is different in water than in air," Harding pointed out. He spoke as if he did not believe what he was saying, but could not stop himself from working though the theorem. "Sound travels over four times faster in water. But then again, if sound is a variable, then it's possible that a wormhole would require less energy under the water, and therefore be the preferred place to have it. But we would still be talking about a required level of energy that is far beyond anything we could manage."

"You mean 'we' as in the United States?" asked Stevas.

"No," said Harding. "I mean 'we' as in human beings."

A few people lowered their heads and mumbled an expletive.

Defense Secretary Miller took a deep breath. "Are you telling us that this was not built by humans?"

"It's a consideration."

Miller could not believe what he was hearing. "And you're telling us we may have a wormhole under the ocean?"

"Maybe," Borger said. "But even if we knew how to create that much energy, it doesn't sound like we have the means of doing it."

Harding nodded in agreement. "He's right. Not even combining all of the power plants in the world could do it. Which brings us back to the question, if we are not able to power this thing, let alone build it, then who is?"

"Or…if the power required is not here, where is it getting its power from?" Borger finished.

The men at the table looked back and forth at each other.

"Okay, hold on," said Miller. "Let's back up. Is there another explanation for this ring? What else could it be?"

Harding cleared his throat. "Well, if *we* made it, then its purpose should be limited to a few possibilities. If we did not make it, then it could be damn near anything."

"Mr. Borger," Miller continued. "How sure are you about your data?"

"Pretty sure," Borger replied. "I can certainly be wrong but I have gone over these numbers several times. Of course, there could be something else happening here that we can't see. In fact, it would almost have to be. For example, maybe there is something inside. Maybe this is not what it appears to be from our limited picture resolution. Some of the basic assumptions I'm working off here could be wrong. It's just a matter of likelihood at this point."

Clay spoke up and turned to Langford. "Sir, we need to get a better look at that thing. At the very least, we need to find the Triton and see what else it recorded."

Langford nodded. "Agreed."

"Okay," Stevas said. "Until we get a closer look at this ring, we need to consider the worst case scenario here. If it turns out to be something else, then all the better. If on the other hand this is some kind of wormhole, what the hell are we going to do about it?"

"Well," said Langford. "That should depend on what it's for."

"What it's for?" said Stevas, incredulously. "It's a goddamn tunnel. What do *you* use tunnels for?" He looked at Harding. "Doctor, is it just me or is the whole purpose of a tunnel to send something through it? Could whoever built this bring something through?"

Harding nodded with a raised eyebrow. "It's possible. We don't know enough about its characteristics, but yes I would have to agree, that is a possibility."

"Thank you," Stevas said with satisfaction. "So if it's possible to send something through this wormhole, then I don't know about everyone else, but my worst case scenario is that whoever we're dealing with either has sent something through it, or is *going* to."

Everyone sat quietly, contemplating Stevas' suggestion. After a long moment, Langford spoke up.

"Well, if this is a tunnel of some kind, it would certainly explain how someone was able to step onto one of our ships out of thin air." He motioned to the screen. "Dr. Harding, is it possible that what Clay saw on the Pathfinder was a small person-size wormhole?"

"It's possible," he said, shaking his head again, "but it is very hard to believe. I mean the amount of technical advancement to do what we are talking about, *if* someone was even able to create this ring, then presumably a very small tunnel wouldn't be very difficult. But, we are making a *lot* of assumptions here."

"Anyone have any other ideas or explanations?" Langford asked.

Borger shrugged. "Nothing else that matches the circumstances."

"What do you mean?"

"I mean, it seems to fit. The power involved, the complexity, time to build. Why it would appear to be hidden underwater. The energy and magnetic field distortion. It seems to be the most reasonable idea. I also agree with Dr. Harding that if someone is able to build a big wormhole, they certainly would not have trouble making a small one. I think the important thing to consider here is what we may already be thinking. We may be dealing with someone vastly smarter than we are."

Miller leaned forward and covered his face with his hands. "I was afraid someone was going to say that. Dr.

Wong," he said, turning back to the screen. "You are our resident expert on astrobiology. I presume you have been able to review the pictures and video of this Palin person?"

Professor Wong's image filled the screen as he spoke. In his early fifties, with glasses and very little gray hair, Wong's reputation in the astronomical field was well known. "Yes, I have."

"What is your opinion?"

"Meaning?" asked Wong.

"Meaning…" said Miller, "are we even talking about humans anymore?"

Wong frowned. "Well…while it's *feasible* that this ring may be a portal of some kind, I doubt this man Palin is an alien, if that's what we're asking. Judging from his anatomy, including the patient x-rays from Dr. Kanna on the Pathfinder, they look far too human."

"What do you mean 'too human'?" asked Bullman, the Army chief.

"Well, let's make some rather broad assumptions here. Say we were dealing with an alien race that built this wormhole, and they are able to power it from somewhere else, potentially far away. Their anatomy is simply not different enough," Wong explained. "The bottom line is that any life form developing on a different planet would have its own evolutionary path. Another planet, for instance, would have wildly different environmental variables than Earth. Maybe it's smaller than Earth, maybe it's hotter, maybe the days are shorter, maybe there is less water. The fact is that with millions of small, even tiny, differences between our environments, there would be an infinite number of variations of physical form for them to evolve into. So, with an almost limitless amount of diversity, the odds of another race developing into near identical beings is…well, a mathematical impossibility."

"An impossibility?"

Wong nodded. "Damn near."

Miller leaned back and sighed. He then raised his hand

to rub his eyes. "Okay. So, let me get this straight. We think we have a wormhole under the ocean, going somewhere we don't know, requiring more energy that we can ever hope to produce, built by someone a lot smarter than us, and they are *not* alien." He looked around the room and then at the screen. "Have I missed anything?"

No one replied.

"Admiral Langford," Miller suddenly leaned forward in his chair. "We need more information and I'd like your team to get it."

"Yes, sir," Langford responded.

"We have an interrogator due to arrive at your location shortly. Let's see what we can find out from this captive, Palin. But, we need to be careful here. Dare I say that taking any action prematurely could be very dangerous?" Miller looked around the room. "Let's reconvene in the morning when we hopefully know more. Thank you, everyone." With that, he reached for the remote control on his conference room table and his window blinked out.

"Thank you, gentlemen," Langford said. "We'll be in touch." He reached for his own controller and closed all of the calls except for Borger and Caesare. Langford and Foster both stood up.

"Clay," said Langford, "head back to the main base and get some sleep. " He turned to Foster. "Do you have a plane he can use?"

"We'll find one."

"Thanks," he turned back to Clay. "In the morning, I want you in the air."

"Yes, sir," answered Clay.

"You two," he said to Borger and Caesare. "Keep on that video. See if there is anything else you can find out."

"Yes, sir," they answered in unison.

Both Langford and Foster left the room.

Clay watched the door close behind them. He then turned to the large monitor, where Borger and Caesare were still on screen. "Well, *that* was interesting."

23

ALISON WATCHED AS the harness holding Dirk
slowly swung over the aquarium's glass tank and then
stopped. It then began to descend until it gently touched
the water. It continued down until Dirk was a few feet
below the water line. At this point, a small rope was pulled
which released a large clasp allowing the harness to unfold
and fall away. Dirk wriggled out and swam excitedly
around the tank several times. He then headed to the large
glass wall, where Sally was watching the children press
their hands and noses against the glass and waving at them.
After a few moments, Dirk turned, swimming under and
away from Sally and the children. When he reached the far
end of the tank, he sped back directly toward the glass,
suddenly twisting around and around to perform several
barrel rolls through the bright blue water. The children
went crazy.

Alison was always struck at how much Dirk and Sally
loved children. Many mornings, the dolphins were waiting
at the glass wall when the doors of the aquarium opened
and the children came streaming through. They clearly
had a connection with each other, and she never tired of
watching them. She walked back to her lab at the other
end of the tank, leaving the lobby and the laughing
children. When she reached the metal door, she slid her
card through the small slot and waited for the door to
unlock with a loud click. She pulled the door open and
stepped into the green carpeted room of their lab.

She walked up behind Lee Kenwood and looked over

his shoulder. "How are things looking?"

"Fine," he said. "All systems are good. In fact, IMIS picked up a few more words while we were gone."

"Our vocabulary list is getting long," she noted, looking at his monitor.

Lee nodded. He finished typing and closed a window on his screen. He opened another window, a new program that Alison had not seen before. Lee slid his chair to the side and looked up at her. "I have a surprise for you."

She looked at him with a puzzled expression, expecting him to finish the sentence. He just sat smiling at her.

"What?" she finally asked. She looked back to his screen. The new program showed a large black circle with a thin green line through it. She looked back to Lee wondering what she was supposed to be looking at.

"Lean in," Lee said.

Alison leaned closer to his desk. She still had no idea.

"Now talk," he whispered.

She still looked puzzled.

He whispered again. "Say 'hi'."

She frowned and looked at his screen again. "Hi."

The thin green line danced when she spoke, then went flat again. A moment later, she heard IMIS translate the short word into the tank.

Dirk and Sally turned around and swam over to the lab. *Hi Alison*, they replied.

Alison's eyes widened. "Did IMIS actually hear me?"

Lee smiled. "Voice recognition. No more typing." He reached out and slid the keyboard away from them. "Just talk into the microphone and IMIS will automatically translate."

Alison watched Lee as she spoke again. Again, the green line danced at the sound of her voice. "How are you today?" she asked.

We good, said Dirk. *How you?*

"Lee," she cried, "you are amazing!"

He smiled. "Pretty cool, huh?"

Alison picked a banana out of her bag. She peeled it and walked over to the tank where Dirk and Sally were floating on the other side, watching her. She took a small bite, reached out, and put her hand on the glass. Dirk floated forward and touched his nose to the other side. Sally remained where she was and continued watching Alison. She peeled more of the banana and took another bite.

What eat Alison? asked Sally.

Surprised, Alison looked at Sally. After a moment, she turned from the glass and walked back over to Lee's desk. She took the mouse and opened the window listing IMIS' current vocabulary list. She scanned the list, trying to decide on the best word to use.

Alison leaned in close to the microphone. "I am eating a plant." As an afterthought, she walked back to the glass and held the banana up for Sally to see. Very slowly, Sally drifted forward to examine the fruit.

You like plant? asked Sally.

Before Alison could answer, Lee rolled his desk a little closer so the microphone could pick her voice up from where she was standing.

Alison nodded. "I like many plants." She grabbed her bag and pulled out an apple. After taking a small bite, she held it up for Sally to see.

Sally examined it. *No eat plants.*

"I know," Alison smiled. "But I love plants."

Sally wiggled her tail excitedly. *Me love Dirk.*

Alison chuckled this time. "I love Dirk too."

A sound burst out through Sally's blowhole that Alison's team took to be laughter.

"Why did you laugh?" Alison asked.

Sally wiggled her tail again. *You no love Dirk. Me love Dirk.*

Alison looked curiously at Sally. She turned slightly and glanced at Lee's reflection in the glass, which now had

Chris standing behind him. Both men were watching.

"You love Dirk?"

Me love Dirk, she said again. *Dirk love me.*

Alison looked back at Chris. "You don't think?"

Chris raised an eyebrow. "I think so."

"Is Dirk your mate, Sally?" Alison asked.

Yes. He my mate. I him mate. Me love Dirk.

"Oh my goodness." Alison said, turning back to Chris and Lee. She made a cutting motion across her neck, signaling Lee to stop the microphone. He quickly clicked the 'pause' button. "They love each other."

Chris picked up on her excitement. "Are we surprised?" he asked.

"Well, no," she replied. "I mean, there has always been an assumption that animals experience levels of affection, but it sounds like Sally is describing something deeper." Alison suddenly gasped and covered her mouth. "Oh my god. Do you think…is it possible that they don't just love each other, but are *in* love?"

Both Chris and Lee looked at each other, speechless.

We go back Alison? asked Dirk, who had joined Sally at the glass.

Lee turned the microphone back on as Alison spoke. "Go back? Go back where, Dirk?"

Outside.

Alison's mood changed instantly. She took a deep breath. She was expecting this. Dirk and Sally had lived at the aquarium since they were ten years old. It had never occurred to Alison that they would be back in the ocean. But, now it was downright inevitable after taking them out to help John Clay.

She opened her mouth to reply when Dirk spoke again.

How long stay?

Alison closed her eyes. The question was like a dagger through her heart. "Do you like it here?" she asked.

Yes like here, Dirk said. *Much food.* He broke away excitedly, swam a small circle and returned. *When food?*

Alison forced a smile. Dirk was getting fed more often now that he could actually ask for food. "You just ate, Dirk."

Sally was still floating and watching Alison. *You sad.*

"They read human emotions so easily," Chris said, stepping up to the glass. He placed his hand gently on her shoulder. "While we can barely tell when Dirk is hungry."

Alison shook her head at Lee, who paused the microphone again. "We're going to lose them Chris. All because of that damn trip to help out the Navy." She was suddenly overwhelmed with frustration. "It's all Frank's fault! Why the hell did he have to agree to that?! He has totally screwed us, Chris! We're going to lose Dirk and Sally, and that's going to be end of this whole thing!"

"That's not true, Alison, and you know it. Frank could have said 'no', but that could have brought an end to our project even faster. We both knew this was a risk." She tried to act innocent, but Chris shook his head. "No, don't give me that. I know you've thought about it too. We both have. We set out to be the first humans to actually talk to another species and we have, and it's huge! But, neither one of us ever thought for a second that Dirk and Sally *liked* being in captivity. Oh, sure, they have a good life, free food that they don't have to hop through rings for, constant medical attention, no environmental dangers. But, being safe doesn't mean being *happy*." He looked back through the glass and sighed. "The level of communication we've achieved with IMIS is beyond our wildest dreams, Ali. And now we find out that Dirk and Sally don't like living in a cage; that's not a big surprise to either one of us. Sad? Yes. But, we can't blame Frank for that, and we can't blame the Navy either."

Alison began to tear up and quickly wiped it away. Chris was right, but it did not make her feel any better. They had done something amazing and now she was going to lose them as a result.

Your friend here, said Sally.

136

Alison forced a smile. "Yes, my friends are here."

No other friend, Sally replied. *From metal.*

"Oh." Alison realized that Sally was talking about John Clay. "No, friend not here."

Sally laughed.

Chris squeezed Alison's shoulder and walked back over to Lee's desk. He picked up his cup of coffee and looked back. "You never know, maybe if we let them go they would come back."

Alison frowned.

"Well, maybe once in a while," Chris shrugged.

Me like talk Alison, Sally said.

Alison looked at Sally through red eyes. "I like talking to you too, Sally."

Why you wait long?

Alison laughed. Why did it take so long for humans to talk to them? She had to be kidding. "We had to build a metal to help us."

An error could be heard from Lee's monitor. Something did not translate correctly. It didn't matter.

We no talk very long time.

Alison gave a confused look. "We haven't talked in a long time?"

No.

"You and me?" Alison asked.

No. People.

Alison's jaw dropped. Did she hear Sally right? She turned to Chris. "Did she just say what I think she said?"

Chris was also frozen, holding his cup just inches from his lips.

She must have meant something else. Alison suddenly jumped when someone behind her said "Hello".

She whirled around to find John Clay standing at the back of the room, near the rear exit. He looked around and realized that he had either startled them or interrupted something important, or both.

"Sorry," he motioned toward the lobby. "The women

at the front recommended I come in this way." He looked at Alison. "Is everything okay?"

"Yes," she said. She looked away and checked to make sure her eyes were dry. "Just a morning full of excitement." She looked at Clay and saw that he looked tired.

He crossed the room and gave a short wave to Chris and Lee. "I'm sorry to interrupt. I'm also sorry for all the drama aboard the ship. Things got a little…interesting."

"I bet," she replied, walking toward him. "Is everything okay?"

"Yes. I wish I could explain, but-"

"That's okay," she said. "I understand." Alison motioned to Chris and Lee. "We all appreciate you bringing Dirk and Sally back quickly."

Clay smiled. "Well, it was the least we could do after all the trouble you went to bringing them out to help us."

He didn't know the half of it, thought Alison.

Clay looked curiously at Sally, who seemed to be staring at all of them. Dirk was swimming small circles around the near end of the tank.

"So, are you here on pleasure or business?" Alison asked. "I hope you don't expect a free pass to the aquarium." His hair seemed thicker and wavier than she remembered.

"Both," Clay replied. "I was also hoping to talk to your dolphins. We never had a chance to ask them about our submersible."

"Sure," she waved him over to the tank by Lee's desk. She called into the microphone for Dirk. He swam back and stopped near Sally, who was still moving gently to keep in place. "Did you find the metal bubble?" she asked them.

Yes, Dirk answered.

"Do you remember where it is?"

Yes. Dirk paused, as if thinking or trying to articulate. *South. East.* After a moment, IMIS combined the words to *Southeast*.

"How far?" asked Alison, with a glance at Clay.

After a longer pause, Dirk replied. *Very far. Many clicks.*

She frowned. "What is a click?"

Click is go.

Alison shook her head. She was going to have to approach this from a different angle. "How far is a click, Dirk?"

Dirk turned to look at the other end of the tank. He darted off, swimming to the far end, then back to the glass in front of Alison and Clay. *Click.*

"That was a click?"

Yes.

"How many clicks to the metal bubble, Dirk?"

Dirk was silent for a long moment. Finally, he replied. *Hundred. Eight.* Again, IMIS changed the words. Dirk's reply became *Eight hundred.*

Alison and Clay looked over at the sound of Chris dropping his cup. He was staring at Dirk. Clay looked down at the spilt coffee at Chris' feet and then back at Alison. "What happened?"

Alison looked like she had seen a ghost. "They can *count.*"

Clay raised his eyebrows in surprise. "Wow."

"They can count," Alison said, again to herself. "I've got to sit down." She backed up and lowered herself onto the edge of a nearby table.

"This is big," said Chris. "I mean really, really big."

"I know," nodded Alison. The ability to count had far reaching implications. It indicated a depth of understanding far removed from simple hellos, and questions about feeding time. Just the indication that they understood the difference between words and numbers was staggering. In fact, just their understanding of *words* would have been incredible. Alison was beginning to feel completely unprepared for the kind of information that Dirk and Sally were revealing to them.

Clay smiled. "It seems I'm amazed every time I come here."

Alison was not listening.

Clay leaned toward her. "Not to spoil the mood, but can we ask them how deep our sub was?"

Twenty, replied Dirk.

Clay was startled. "They can understand me too?"

Alison smirked. "Evidently."

Clay turned back to Dirk. "Twenty clicks deep, Dirk?"

Yes.

"Thank you," Clay nodded. He looked at Dirk and Sally for a long time before turning around to the team. "Well, I'd better-"

Near them city.

Clay suddenly stopped. He turned back. "What?"

Near them city.

Alison quickly stood up again. "Did you say a *city*?"

Yes.

Alison looked at Clay nervously. She wasn't sure she wanted the next answer. "Who's city?"

Them. Others.

Clay stepped closer to the glass. "Have you been to the city, Dirk?"

Yes.

"What does it look like?"

Beautiful.

Alison, Chris, and Lee looked thoroughly confused. They had no idea what the dolphins were talking about. Clay did. "How many live in the beautiful city?" he asked.

No know.

Clay thought for a moment, then pulled the silver brick out of his pocket. He took another step closer. "Dirk, Sally, do you know what this is?" He held it up high.

No.

No.

Clay took a deep breath. "Do you know why the other people are here?"

Dirk's answer was unmistakable. *Water.*

Clay put the brick down on the table and reached for his cell phone. It had no signal. He looked at Alison. "I need to use your phone."

24

PALIN SAT ALONE in the middle of a large, white room in a small metal chair, his hands cuffed behind his back. The only exit was a single door on the far wall. Two security cameras were perched in either corner of the ceiling. Next to the door, a large one-way mirror served as an observation room. He looked around the room curiously and looked up when the door opened and broke the deafening silence.

In walked a lean man, with glasses and short red hair. He eased the door closed and then turned to Palin. Walking across the room, the man sat down in the opposite chair, facing him. After a moment, he spoke in a calm voice.

"Hello, Palin. My name is Albert Keister."

Palin did not answer.

Keister nodded, unsurprised. "I work for the Navy and I'm here to ask you some questions." When Palin remained silent, he continued. "I know you speak English. I've read the report on what happened aboard our ship. Something out of the ordinary, to say the least." Still nothing. "We obviously would like to know who you are and how you did that."

Palin still had not moved, but looked at him, unblinking. Keister studied Palin for a long time. This, he thought, was going to be difficult.

*****

As soon as the Humvee stopped, Clay jumped out of the passenger's seat and ran to the nondescript building, where the door was held open for him. This time, he was quickly escorted through the security checkpoint. He went down the elevator to the conference room where they had their group video call less than twelve hours before. As Clay walked in, he was surprised to see Defense Secretary Miller and Security Advisor Stevas in person. They were seated with Langford and Foster, and instinctively stood up when he entered.

Clay stopped and saluted.

Miller quickly returned the gesture and motioned to a chair at the end of the long table. "Have a seat, Clay."

Clay quickly sat down.

"Clay, I'd like you to tell me again exactly what you said to this Palin person and what he said to you," Miller said.

Clay repeated the exchange while the Secretary listened intently. When he was done, Miller gave a short nod and put his hands together, thinking. Finally, he looked at Clay. "I am aware of your security clearance, but nevertheless, I want to stress that nothing leaves this room."

Clay nodded. "Of course."

"To begin with," he started, "our friend does not appear to be very talkative. Albert Keister is one of our very best interrogators and he couldn't get a word out of him." Miller shrugged. "Now we obviously need to be careful here, so we are not about to get aggressive with him. But judging from Keister's visit, we had better do something or we could be waiting here a very long time."

"Yes, sir," Clay responded.

"He has already talked to you," Miller continued, "so to make this short and sweet, we'd like you to try talking to

142

him."

"Me, sir?" Clay replied, with surprise. "I'm not really qualified-"

"These are unusual circumstances which require unusual tactics. Besides, some of us are concerned that whatever it is we are dealing with may have the means of being weaponized." It was clear that Miller was referring to Stevas. Miller looked intently at Clay. "I know you're not an interrogation expert, but we're not talking about waterboarding here. You're a smart guy and, like I said, you have already established at least a limited level of communication with him. We need some answers and we need them quickly."

Clay nodded again. "I'll do my best sir."

"Good," Miller said. "Now, what is it about these dolphins that you wanted to share?"

Clay looked uneasily around the table. "Sir, it appears that the dolphins have made contact with whoever these people are." He paused at their initial reaction of surprise. "And there may be a large number of them involved here; enough for the dolphins to refer to a *city*."

Their surprise moved instantly to shock. Stevas almost coughed his reply. "What do you mean a city?!"

"I mean an establishment underwater, near the ring. Maybe large enough to house hundreds."

Miller held up his hand, cutting Stevas off. "Are you positive about this?"

"Not positive, sir. I repeatedly asked the dolphins, and in multiple ways. I always got the same answer."

"Wait just a damn minute!" shot Stevas. "You're telling us this revelation came from a computer that may or may *not* be talking to some dolphins? Are you kidding?!" He looked at Langford. "Please tell me this is not your top guy!"

Langford's eyes narrowed, but Clay replied quickly. "Sir, I believe this communication to be real. And that system they built is damn impressive."

"I'm not going to base security decisions off of a fish. We need some real intelligence here," Stevas folded his arms and leaned back, "not messages from a computerized magic eight ball. Jesus, Clay."

Miller looked at Stevas and then back to Clay. "I'm inclined to agree. I will say that I think I believe you on this system, but we need something much more concrete."

Langford turned to Clay. "Did you find out where the Triton is?"

"I believe so." Clay considered correcting Stevas' derogatory reference to the dolphins, but decided against it.

"Okay, we'll arrange for whatever you need to go get it. We need to know what that camera has on it."

"Yes, sir," Clay replied. He looked around the table. "There is something else I need to tell you." Everyone at the table looked at him expectantly. "I asked the dolphins if they knew why these people were here." He took a deep breath. "They said 'water'."

"Water?" Miller's eyes narrowed. "What does that mean?"

"I'm not sure. I wasn't able to get much more context," replied Clay. "It may be that water is somehow critical to them or what they are doing. Perhaps the ring is using the hydrogen from our water to power itself, or some other need that we don't know about."

Stevas frowned. "You're saying this is what is powering that thing?"

"Perhaps," Clay answered. "I spoke to Borger about it. It's certainly feasible. Hydrogen atoms hold a lot of potential energy."

Miller opened his mouth, but he was cut off by Stevas. "That sounds like a stretch to me," he said, shaking his head. "This is all from these fish again, I'm assuming." The tone Stevas used every time he said 'fish' was very derogatory.

Clay nodded somewhat reluctantly. "They evidently

didn't get that exact."

"So, you're telling us," Stevas continued, "that there is a city on the bottom of the ocean and the people living in it need our water for some reason."

"I believe-" Clay started, but was also cut off by Stevas.

"Let me tell you what I believe," Stevas said, clearly frustrated. "In case you have forgotten, in the last twenty-four hours, we have established that this is a portal, which is probably designed as a delivery mechanism for some kind of weapon that's probably more advanced than anything we could build for a long time." Stevas' voice grew louder as his words became more impassioned. "And we don't know whether that something has come through it yet! We could be on the brink of warfare and only finding out about it now! And," he said, rolling his eyes, "you come to us with *they might need the water for something*? You know what I say to that? Who gives a goddamn?!" He turned and looked at Miller. "We need to be planning defensive steps now, before it's too late, rather than talking to these damn fish!"

Miller sat quietly, considering what Stevas had said. Finally, he said, "I'm beginning to agree that we need to take a defensive position here. We just don't know anything about this thing." He looked at Clay. "Even if your dolphins are right, unless it presents itself as some sort of priority, we need to focus on defense here." Miller glanced at Stevas. "However, that doesn't mean we should ignore it completely. Clay, please continue your investigation. If you and Borger find something more on this that warrants further discussion, let us know. But first, have a talk with our Palin friend."

"Yes, sir," Clay said. "Is there anything else sir?"

Miller looked to the others before shaking his head. "No, that will be all. Mr. Keister is waiting for you outside. He will brief you, and together you can take another crack."

Clay nodded and stood up. He promptly turned and walked to the door.

Stevas watched the door close slowly behind him before looking at Miller. "We better do something and we better do it fast."

"I agree," Foster finally spoke up from across the table.

"And what exactly would we do?" Miller asked. "We don't even know definitively what this thing is. Do you?! Hell, for all I know it could be an enormous illusion." He looked hard at Stevas. "Do you know something that I don't? Because if not, I'd like to know just what kind of *action* you have in mind based on the same lack of factual intelligence that I'm facing."

Stevas hit the table with his hand. "I'm not approaching this from an intelligence perspective. I'm thinking that whatever this thing is built to do, it may already have done it. We don't know how long this ring has been down there. All the data gathering in the world is not going to make a damn bit of difference if we wake up tomorrow under attack! If this means you want to label me as shooting first and asking questions later, I don't give a damn. What scares the hell out of me right now is that we might not be here later to ask questions!"

*****

Clay followed Keister into the large white room and felt a pang of sympathy when he spotted Palin. He was not sure what arrangement he would find him in, but was somewhat regretful that he was dressed and bound like an inmate from a maximum security prison. He noticed the video cameras as they walked across the white polished floor. Looking at the walls, he guessed them to be soundproof. He suspected this room was used often.

Palin watched them approach from his forced posture. A look of acceptance could be seen in his eyes for he did not struggle. In fact, Clay thought, his body did not seem to move in the slightest.

Both men took a seat in front of Palin, with Clay sitting slightly off to his right. He was surprised to see Palin looking at him rather than Keister.

Keister noticed this and gave a slight nod to Clay, giving him permission to start with the questions and tactics he had outlined. Questions were one thing, but the correct phrasing, context and words used were critical.

Clay leaned forward and cleared his throat. "Are you alright?" he asked.

Palin looked at Clay for a long moment. His expression seemed to soften slightly. "Uncomfortable," he said slowly, "but not unexpected."

"Is there anything we can get you?" Clay asked.

Palin slowly shook his head.

Keister wrote something onto a pad of paper and showed it to Clay. It read *start with name*. Before Clay could speak Palin said, "My name is Palin." Both Clay and Keister looked at each other.

Just Palin. Okay. Clay turned back to him and asked, "How did you get on board our ship?"

Again, Palin did not answer right away. "A doorway was created," he finally said, slowly.

Clay waited for more information, but did not get it. Palin merely sat calmly, staring at him. "What kind of a doorway?"

"An energy doorway."

Clay smirked at the short answers. Why did he think that Palin would deliver some great monologue? "An energy doorway," he repeated. "An energy doorway to where?"

"From," he corrected.

"*From* where?" Clay said.

"The doorway was created from our settlement."

"And where is your settlement?" asked Clay.

Palin gave Clay a look of vague amusement. He cocked his head slightly, as one might do when asking someone else if they were serious. "You already know the answer to this question, yes?"

"The bottom of the ocean?"

Palin nodded.

"Are you human?" Clay asked.

"Yes."

Clay looked at Keister and then down to his notebook. He had no more messages for Clay written on it. Instead, he continued watching Palin intently. No doubt for the more subtle body movements. Clay wondered how much body language Keister could get when Palin was handcuffed with both arms behind his back. "So," he continued, "you are human but you are using a technology which appears to be beyond anyone else's capabilities."

"Anyone else?" Palin questioned.

Clay raised his eyebrows and shrugged. "Countries, governments, anyone else on the planet. No one to our knowledge is capable of doing what you did. What nationality are you?"

Another trace of amusement curled the side of Palin's mouth. "None."

"No nationality," Clay repeated. He thought a moment. "How many people are in this settlement of yours?"

"Twelve hundred."

Clay shot Keister another glance. "Twelve hundred. That does not sound like a large settlement."

"It is not," Palin replied. After some hesitancy, he added, "That is all that is left."

Clay frowned in confusion. "What do you mean 'all that is left'?"

Palin inhaled deeply. He appeared conflicted over what he was sharing, and Clay wondered why he was choosing to reveal this information at all. He didn't think it was fear. Palin had to know that they were not about to harm him.

Palin spoke carefully. "We are all that remains of a

very old group."

"What group is that?" asked Clay. "Do you mean a lineage?" Clay suddenly thought how bizarre this was beginning to sound.

"We are an old group but have not been here very long."

These answers were becoming increasingly cryptic. Clay sat watching Palin. After several moments, Keister looked over to see if he was going to continue. Clay abruptly asked, "What is the ring for?"

Palin breathed in again. "It is a very large doorway."

"Another doorway," Clay mused. "And where does this very large door go? What is on the other side?"

"Home."

"Where is home?"

Palin hesitated, but gave in. "A nearby planet."

Clay could not believe what he was hearing. If this were true, an awful lot of science theory was about to become science fact. "Your home is a nearby planet?" he asked.

"Yes."

"But you are human," Clay said, pointing out the contradiction. Clearly, he could not be human if he were from another planet. He remembered Wong pointing out on the video call that the odds of an extraterrestrial evolving into the same human form were effectively zero.

"I am human."

Clay frowned. "I have it on good authority that humans are exclusive to Earth," he said, with a touch of sarcasm.

Palin's smirk returned. "And who's authority would that be?"

An expert, Clay thought. *Actually, a supposed expert that I met less than twenty-four hours ago on a giant monitor.* He decided against a debate.

"How long have you been here?"

"Sixty years."

"Sixty years? And doing what?"

Palin did not respond.

Clay made a mental note to relax and leaned back slightly. "So you are human but from a different planet?"

Palin nodded.

Keister spoke up. "How can you be human *and* an alien?"

Palin looked at Keister, almost politely, but slowly turned back to Clay. "There is more to evolution than you have yet learned, especially that which is carbon based."

Clay leaned forward again. "Are you saying that the human form is a common result of evolution?"

"Carbon based evolution," Palin corrected.

"So," Keister said, "planets with carbon life eventually develop human beings?"

Palin looked curiously at Keister. He nodded his head. "Carbon DNA contains characteristics that affect common, but not precise, evolutionary outcomes; generally things like four limbs, two eyes, internal respiratory systems, five senses, and in some cases, larger brains. Survivability is always the priority." Palin looked back to Clay.

"Why are you here?" he asked.

"We are visiting."

Clay smiled on the inside. He was certain that Palin had just lied to him. "Visiting for what, exactly?"

Palin gave an almost imperceptible shrug. The most he could manage with his hands bound, Clay suspected. "We are observers." Palin's tone seemed to shorten.

"What was your man doing on our ship?" Keister asked.

Palin gave Keister an expressionless answer. "Observing."

Clay was watching Palin closely. They were losing him. He was going to have to be more direct. "What is the ring for?"

"It is how we came here."

150

Clay nodded. "It's awfully big." Again, Palin remained quiet. His body language, at least what Clay could detect, was changing. He was quickly becoming uncomfortable. He locked his eyes on Palin's. "It looks large enough to bring something else through, something very big."

Palin stared at Clay. After a long silence, he suddenly pushed his chair back, signaling that he was done with the conversation.

25

KATHRYN LOKKE SAT in the C130 airplane, bundled tightly in her thick parka. Her hood was raised up, barely fitting over the bulky headphones which allowed her to talk to the flight crew. A quick shiver ran down from her shoulders. She counted back the years since she had been in this kind of weather and temperature. Peering down through the side window, she watched the white surface of Antarctica speed beneath them as the plane headed for the main base at McMurdo.

The plane slowly pitched forward as the pilots began their descent. As the plane sank closer to the ground, Kathryn could see four giant supply tanks on the far end of the base, beyond the hundred or so buildings surrounding the three airfields. In the far distance, she could make out the distant harbor with two big supply ships which sat motionless in the dark grey water. Even further still was a thin line extending into the distance, the McMurdo road to the South Pole.

The plane came in low over the white runway and

gently touched down.   Kathryn and the thirty-four researchers behind her sat forward and began gathering their things. The plane taxied off the runway and stopped in front of a small terminal building. Bags were grabbed and the passengers shuffled out and down the stairs. Several large vans were waiting to receive them and everyone scattered to the nearest vehicle, throwing their bag up into the roof rack and quickly jumping inside the heated interiors.

Once loaded, all of the vehicles headed out in a single file line, driving half a mile to a tall nondescript hangar. A large door opened as they approached. All seven vehicles drove inside and parked. The door was quickly closed behind them.

Kathryn climbed out of the lead van and stepped down onto the building's smooth concrete floor.

"Dr. Lokke?" asked a man approaching from the center of the hangar. His accent was distinctly New Zealand. "I'm Steven Anderson," he said, extending his hand.

Kathryn slipped off her glove and shook it. "Hi, Steven. We meet at last," she replied with a smile. "Thanks for all your team's help on this."

"Ah, our pleasure," Anderson nodded. "That ice quake scared the daylights out of us too. Besides," he turned his head, motioning behind him, "it's nice to have the company."

She turned and waved her staff over.

"Well, the good news," Anderson said, "is that you've got the best weather possible. Should have clear skies for the next six or seven days. Probably get all the way up to minus 5 or 6 degrees Fahrenheit."

"What a relief," moaned Jason Haines, walking up behind Kathryn. Jason was one of the newest and youngest geologists to join the USGS. He had been there just thirteen months, yet was one of the first to volunteer for the trip.

She introduced the two and waited for the others. His team had assembled the two dozen snowmobiles and arranged for the transport planes that would drop the researchers, and all of their supplies, at the Ronne Ice Shelf. Anderson's team would act as their guides.

Anderson went over the plan, explaining how Kathryn and her team would split up into ten groups. They would then try to cover the length of the massive slide in five days, getting as much information as possible. At the end of the five days, they would have exact measurements on the extent of the slide, strata samplings for subsurface composition and density, any signs of lateral slide, and a host of other pieces of data. If all went well, it would arm Kathryn with enough hard data to show the White House just how dangerous this situation was.

Jason Haines, still standing next to Kathryn, raised his hand with a question. Anderson nodded and Haines spoke up. "How often are we to be in contact?"

Anderson spoke up to make sure he was heard by everyone. "Communication will be constant." He motioned to several of his team members standing behind him. "As you know, each team of three will be accompanied by a guide. My men know the area well and are as comfortable in these conditions as anyone can be, if you want to call it *comfortable*." Anderson's accent projected a friendly tone. But he, and all of the men, had a hardened look that was all business. "A small supply outpost will be located on the shelf in a central location. Your guides will be talking to them every fifteen minutes with coordinates and a team status. It does not take long out here to freeze to death, so *do not* get lost. If any team is not heard from for more than twenty minutes, a reconnaissance crew will be dispatched immediately, and they will begin trying to reestablish contact while in transit." Anderson paused for just a moment to make sure everyone was listening. He reminded Kathryn of a sergeant explaining a detailed exercise to his unit. "As soon as they reestablish contact, they will turn around and head back to the outpost. If they do not reestablish contact, they will be to you within 30 minutes. If you see us coming across the ice, stop and wave your arms as high as you can. It can be very hard to see, even with a very small amount of haze." He looked over the small group. "Next question?"

Another of Kathryn's team raised their hand, a woman named Ruppa Tadri, one of her best seismologists. She looked around shyly. "What if we need some...*privacy*?"

Anderson smiled. "This is the Antarctic. If you get lost and fall down a hole, you may be dead before we find the hole. Believe me, you *do not* want privacy!" A nervous laugh ran through the group. "Don't be shy, ladies and gentlemen. You may feel a little embarrassed at first, but it is far more important that we can see you at all times." He paused again before continuing. "The good news is that we have excellent weather this week. If the wind is calm, we will provide a small round tent for anyone feeling particularly self-conscious. And let me answer what is likely your next question. Dig a deep hole and bury it. You can use this." Anderson held up a small mountain climbing pick. "You will all have one of these and we will give you some basic instructions. I guarantee you will find this to be your best friend during your time on the Shelf." Anderson smiled again. "Next question?"

After another twenty minutes of questions and answers, Anderson led the team out the side of the hangar to another building a couple hundred yards away. The mess hall was anything but a mess hall. The dining area was over twenty thousand square feet and held dozens of comfortable chairs and tables. On the far side of the room was a large viewing area with four satellite televisions, surrounded by almost as many couches. Half of the room was a giant sunroom decorated with many different kinds of plants from all over the world. If Kathryn's team was surprised at the dining area, they were stunned by the meals that came out of the kitchen. They included salads loaded with fresh greens and vegetables, all grown locally in one of the McMurdo's large hydroponic gardens. There was even fresh fruit from hydroponic citrus trees. This was clearly the hub of the station.

Tadri approached Kathryn with an empty plate. She was on her way back to the kitchen for seconds. "Kathryn, aren't you going to eat anything?"

"Huh? Oh right," Kathryn replied absently. She realized that she had been thinking so much about the next several days that she was still standing in the same place, holding her plate.

"Are you alright?" Tadri asked.

"Oh...yes. Thanks. I'm just thinking about everything."

Tadri smiled. "Well, try to take a break. We have to be up at four a.m."

She was right. Kathryn had to find a way to stop obsessing. They were barely going to get enough sleep as it was before an early morning breakfast and airlift. The last thing she needed was to be up half the night before heading into one of the toughest weeks she would have in years.

She patted Tadri on the arm and followed her into the kitchen.

*****

The next morning after a large breakfast, Kathryn's team assembled and boarded three of the same C130 aircraft they had arrived on. Each plane had been packed with three teams and their supplies. The last plane, which Kathryn was on, held a fourth team. Thirty minutes after boarding, the planes were airborne and headed for the ice shelf. The team members huddled together for warmth next to their bags and supplies, which sat in front of eight large snowmobiles. Through the window, the sun was slowly rising from the horizon, where it remained during the night, low yet always in daylight during Antarctica's summer months.

Kathryn looked around at the faces of her team. She was surprised to see an edge on their faces that they did not have the day before. Probably the acceptance that they were here now and there was no turning back. She felt a sense of pride that many of her researchers had volunteered to come when they heard the White House's, or more specifically, the National Security Advisor Stevas' response to her warning.

After a long two hours, she felt the familiar dip of the plane's nose signaling a descent. The other two planes banked in opposite directions, heading west and east to drop their teams further along the wide fissure.

Kathryn's plane landed with a hard thud on the ice shelf which was flatter than the area closer to the crack. They came to a stop and the propellers slowed to an idling speed. Anderson's men threw open the door and rolled a ladder outward for the exiting team. At the rear of the fuselage, they unlocked and opened a large custom door, which allowed them to slide the snowmobiles out and down a steep ramp. Next, were the food, bags, and fuel, which also slid down the ramp with a hard thud. Kathryn's guide was a large man named Andrew with light hair who, judging from his tattoos, appeared to be ex-military. He jumped out and helped pull the equipment out. Andrew gave a thumbs-up to the other crewmembers onboard and pulled the large sled of equipment toward one of the snowmobiles. Kathryn, Tadri, and their third member, Pierre, climbed down the metal folding ladder. Once their feet touched the ice, the ladder was quickly retracted back up into the open door behind them. They ran to Andrew who had clipped the supplies to the back of one of the snowmobiles with a large metal clasp.

Andrew climbed on and motioned to Kathryn, who got on behind him. Pierre and Tadri climbed on the second snowmobile and both men started the engines. As Andrew led them away, the doors on the plane were closed. Less than a minute later, the engines roared back to life and the C130 began rolling forward.

As they sped toward the edge of the ice shelf, Kathryn looked back over her shoulder at Pierre and Tadri, then at the plane in the distance, which had just lifted back up into the air. From the time it touched down, the entire drop-off had taken less than ten minutes. She hoped the others would go as smoothly.

26

PRESIDENT CARR STOOD in the White House conference room, facing the large monitor with his arms folded across his chest. He watched the video of Keister and Clay speaking with Palin. Behind him, around the large table, sat Stevas, Miller, Langford, Clay, Keister and his military chiefs. The video ended with Palin scooting his chair back. The screen came to an abrupt end, frozen on the last frame of the video. Carr remained staring at the picture as the room fell silent. He slowly began shaking his head. "What in the hell are we dealing with here?" he said, turning around. Carr leaned forward, putting his hands on the table. "I mean, Jesus," he raised his voice, "do we even know whether this man is a friend or not?!" He looked around the table. "Well?!"

Stevas spoke up. "We need to assume *not*." He continued when the President looked at him. "We cannot be sure of anything, which means we have to assume the worst. This ring is huge, far larger than they would need to bring just a thousand people through. I don't believe for a minute that they have been here long. I think they came through and got caught before they could bring whatever comes through next!"

"So you're saying what then?" asked the President.

"I'm saying we need to take action while we still can."

"And what kind of action are we talking about?"

Stevas glanced around the room. "We destroy the damn thing."

Clay looked at Langford, who managed to remain completely still.

"Destroy the ring?" asked Miller, sitting across from him.

Stevas nodded. "Shut down the portal. Destroy it and by doing so, we cut them off."

Clay could not believe his ears. He looked at the military brass at the end of the table, and they seemed as un-phased as Langford. Was Clay the only one who thought Stevas had just gone off the deep end?

"Just like that?" replied Miller.

"That's right," Stevas said, looking back to the President. "Look, we have to be preemptive here. If we do it right, we close down any possibility they have to attack us and, with luck, we trap them here as leverage." The President did not answer. He was considering Stevas' point. "At the very least that buys us time."

Miller frowned. "Time for what?"

"To prepare, in case they come back. A defense, for Christ sake!"

Miller remained skeptical. "Wait a minute, how do they come back if we destroy this thing on our end?"

Stevas looked surprised by the question. He clearly did not have an answer. In fact, Clay wondered if he had even considered that. How could the President be listening to this man? Clay cleared his throat and everyone in the room turned to him.

"Excuse me," he said slowly. "But I think we may be

overlooking some things here." Stevas gave him a cold stare, but Clay ignored him and asked the question anyway. "Surely we don't believe they would be incapable of returning if we destroyed the ring. After all, they got here before without a ring on this side. We don't know how they would, but if they did come back, shouldn't we expect them to be a little…upset?"

Stevas' stare grew even colder.

"And shouldn't we be concerned at the ramifications of destroying this portal?"

Stevas looked hard at Clay when he replied. "Our experts don't think there will be any negative side effects. We're just pulling the plug."

Miller broke in. "Who? Who doesn't think so?"

Stevas turned to Miller with a slow and deliberate reply. "Experts."

Langford looked at Stevas. "And how are you envisioning we destroy this ring?"

The Naval chief, Bruce Bishop, leaned forward at the other end of the table. "Subs." Everyone turned to Bishop. "We can have the ring surrounded with two dozen Trident submarines inside of twenty-four hours."

Clay's heart sank. This sounded like something that had already been planned out, and they were now just trying to sound objective for formality.

"They probably have some kind of defense, so launching a large number of torpedoes gives us the best chance of getting through. The intent is to do just enough damage to stop it from spinning."

Everyone turned to the President who had remained quiet. He looked down, thinking, and finally raised his head. "Any other opinions?"

Clay had to keep himself from jumping out of his chair. "Uh…yes, sir," he said, raising his hand. "How about *not* doing that?" It was not meant to be funny, but Clay could see Langford's smirk out of the corner of his eye. Clay looked at the others. "I don't understand. We know virtually nothing about this man, or these people, yet we are willing to start a war because we *think* they are going to attack us?"

"Tell me, Mr. Clay," said the President as he straightened, "how would you explain yourself to the country, to the world, if you are wrong? How would you explain it to them if we are attacked and you did nothing with what little time you had available?"

In his mind, the chance of an imminent attack was low, and based on virtually no information. In fact, the information Stevas chose to cite was handpicked from everything else they knew. He denied the claim on how long they had been here, but he happily accepted as fact that the portal was from another planet. He would not accept the idea that they were here for a more benign reason, but he certainly accepted that there was a small number of them. He was choosing specific items to make his case and throwing out the rest, all while using everyone's fear of the small chance he was right. Clay suspected he simply wanted to attack, but why?

"Mr. President," Langford interrupted, putting a cautious hand on the table next to Clay's. "I think what John is getting at here is to remind us that we make the best decisions when we have the most accurate information. In this case, we have very little information, which means any decision we make now could easily be a bad one."

"Sir," Clay continued, "a lot of our information to date suggests there may be other possibilities here, and not all necessarily dangerous."

"Which means what?" Stevas chided from across the table. "We give them the benefit of the doubt?"

Neither Langford nor Clay even bothered to look at Stevas. Instead, they kept their attention on the President. "Not the benefit of the doubt, sir, just time to gather more information and make the best decision possible."

"Alright," said the President. "Then get me some more

information."

"Yes, sir," Langford replied.

"I presume you're referring to this remote sub of yours?" he asked.

Langford nodded. "We think it may hold significantly more information on it."

"Do we know where it is?" the President asked.

Langford looked at Clay, who nodded. "Yes, sir."

The President leaned forward again onto the table, leveling his gaze directly at Clay. "Then go get it!"

27

THE K-955 SUBMERSIBLE was the smallest and fastest submarine in the Navy. Designed primarily for research and recovery, the small craft housed a maximum of four people, which left two empty seats behind Clay and Caesare. Together inside, they ran through a complete systems check. The water from outside sloshed up over the forward window while they bobbed back and forth on the surface of the Caribbean Sea.

Several miles from where they were hoping to find the Triton II was as far as Captain Emerson was willing to get with the Pathfinder. He could not believe it when he read his instructions from the Pentagon that Clay and Caesare were headed back out. Emerson and his crew barely had time to accept the transfer of the K-955 from a sister ship before the helicopter dropped the two men back onto his foredeck. He greeted them by simply shaking his head.

Navy SEALs, including ex-SEALs, had a reputation for being a little crazy. Clay expected they had just that reputation in Emerson's mind. He looked to his right, where Caesare was holding a manual, and verifying the locations of the various instruments. "How does your side look?"

Caesare shrugged. "Good. Pretty straight forward, actually." He looked to the left side. "How about you?"

Clay nodded. "Not bad." He gripped the control stick in front of him. "Stick will take a little getting used to."

"We've got," Caesare looked back over his shoulder at a digital read-out behind them, "a full charge, which should give us about a twenty to thirty mile range." He looked forward again. "We also have full oxygen which should last well beyond that, especially without two more sets of lungs behind us. I think we're about ready."

Clay reached up and tested the hatch seal by trying to turn the large metal wheel. He then moved the microphone on his headset closer to his mouth. "Pathfinder, this is 'Saint Bernard.'"

"Go ahead, Saint Bernard," came Tay's voice through their headphones.

"We are checked out and ready to launch," Clay said.

"Roger that. Release at will."

With a quick nod, Clay reached up to a large red handle above them and wrapped his hand through. "Releasing now," he said, and pulled down hard. There was only a slight dip when the sub detached from the arm, since it was already floating on the surface under its own buoyancy. The sub began to roll to the right just as Caesare engaged the main motor, giving it instant propulsion and causing the roll to correct itself. As the small sub surged forward, the waves that were lapping across the front, bubbled window suddenly rushed up and over the top, causing the front to dip slightly. Clay kept his right hand on the stick and slowly inched it forward, increasing their speed. He then lowered the small flaps on the tail, which increased their dive angle, and the K-955 smoothly slipped below the surface.

"Feels good," remarked Clay.

"Good," said Caesare, looking down as his notebook. "We need a heading of 131 degrees."

Clay turned until the directional indicator matched.

"At this rate," continued Caesare, "we should reach the bottom in about eight minutes."

The bottom of the Caribbean Sea, or at least this part of it, was rather boring. As many of the coral reefs passed beneath them, so did vast stretches of white fields of sand. Past ninety feet deep, Caesare activated the ultra-bright LEDs, ringing the front of the sub so they could see further in front of them. The K-955 skimmed over several shelves, which dropped below into patches of dark coral and more of the large fields of sand.

Thirty minutes later, something appeared on the small green screen in front of Caesare. "Looks like we have a large object a few degrees off to port. About three hundred yards ahead."

Clay gave a gentle turn and inched off the throttle, allowing the sub to slow. He continued forward at a reduced speed, and eased up completely as the object got closer and closer to the center of Caesare's screen.

"Just about on it…" he said slowly. "Okay, reverse throttle and stop."

The tiny sub slowed to a gentle stop. Both men looked forward through the small bubble, peering closely at the sandy bottom. Several patches of green plant life poked up and were scattered randomly around them. They slowly waved back and forth in the ocean's gentle current. Clay gave the stick a tiny tap and inched the craft forward.

Caesare stretched to look out to the side. "We should be *right* on top of it."

"I see something," said Clay. "He dipped the front forward and pushed a button, which forced a strong burst of current out from just beneath the sub's belly. The current pushed a large amount of sand and soil away, but caused a cloud to temporarily envelop the area. They waited patiently as it dispersed. Just below them was a very large and rusted metal anchor."

"Crap." Caesare leaned back in his seat. "We're oh for four."

"Well, on the bright side, at least the Triton should be easy to spot," Clay said. "Even if it drove itself head first into the sand, it should still be sticking out like a sore thumb."

"What a relief," Caesare said sarcastically, as he wiped off some condensation from the window in front of him. "You know-" he was suddenly cut off when their sub rocked from side to side. "What was that?"

Clay shook his head. "I don't know." He leaned forward and looked out the window at the brightly lit sand.

"Are we in a cross current?"

Clay frowned. "At this depth, I doubt it." Outside the sub, the sand remained still. The small cloud created by the sub a few minutes earlier had almost completely settled. Their sub rocked again, harder.

"Whoa!" Caesare said, bracing himself against the side window and ceiling of the sub. He and Clay looked at each other. "Are you sure?"

Clay was puzzled. He grabbed the handle of the forward exterior light and rotated it around in front of them. He spotted some coral ahead, and inched the sub forward. The sub glided to within fifty feet of coral reef, covered by a variety of plant life, some of which were long tendril shaped flutes jutting up from the rock base. "Look."

Caesare followed his gaze through the front window and out to the plants beyond. "They're barely moving."

"Exactly."

"Strange." Caesare looked out the side window and back behind them. Maybe we're in some kind of channel. He turned back around when the small green screen beeped again. Another object was showing on the radar-like screen. "Got another one. Could this be lucky number five?"

They sped up and glided over the coral, then down the other side and across another patch of sand.

"A few degrees north," Caesare said.

Ahead, a larger ridge of coral rose above the sand, which Clay skirted and angled away to starboard. Something in the distance reflected the sub's bright light, which prompted Clay to ease up on the stick. "This one isn't buried," he said. As they neared, the object became brighter, indicating a highly reflective material or a relatively clean surface.

"Looks about the right size."

"It sure does." Clay let off the stick again to let the water slow the sub's speed to a crawl. After several more seconds, the unmistakable shape of the Triton II materialized in front of them, with its nose deep in the sand.

"Thar she blows!" declared Caesare.

Clay nodded. "Thank god. I was beginning to have my doubts." Something occurred to him and he turned to Caesare. "You know what this means, don't you?"

"Yeah, we'll be headed back tonight!"

"No," Clay said, "the dolphins were right. We found it…" He looked at the GPS coordinates, "And it's not more than a quarter mile from where they said it was. This validates the team's translation system."

"That's true," Caesare nodded. "Wait," he said, with a raised eyebrow. "Did somebody claim it didn't work?"

"I forgot to tell you that part." Clay inched up to the Triton and pulled back on the stick to stop them completely. "Stevas tried pretty hard to discredit them. It seems their information didn't necessarily mesh with his *larger view*."

"You're kidding. What did he say?"

"Unfortunately, I can't repeat the conversation. Let's just say that he is *aggressively* considering our options."

Caesare shook his head. "How did that guy ever make it to that position? Makes me really doubt the system sometimes." He turned on another set of lights, flooding the area directly below, and grabbed the handle of their craft's articulating arm. He gave Clay a smile. "Shall we make our pickup?"

Slowly, from underneath the submersible, a long articulating arm unfolded and extended outward. Caesare controlled it from inside the sub, his fingers wrapped around and through the complex handle. The thin metal arm stretched out in front of the window, reaching for the Triton sitting silently in the sand.

"Easy does it," Caesare mumbled to himself.

Clay kept his hand steady on the stick, trying to maintain perfect buoyancy and keep the sub as still as possible.

The long, crab-shaped claw on the end of the arm approached the rear end of the Triton. Caesare slowly twisted his handle, which caused the claw to twist in the same direction. He pushed it forward again and tried to loop the larger half of the claw under the Triton's propeller. After several attempts, he finally managed to wrap the claw up through a small gap near the rear-stabilizing fin. Tightening his grip caused the claw to close and grab the Triton's tail. Very slowly, he pulled on the handle, simultaneously retracting the metal arm. The Triton did not move. Caesare pulled harder, careful not to loosen his grip. The Triton still did not move.

Clay continued watching his instruments and tried to keep the K-955 still.

"Damn," said Caesare, "this thing really managed to burrow itself in." He pulled harder and finally the sand surrounding the buried end of Triton began to move. More of the sand fell away and the Triton came free. The rest of the sand slowly fell away as it slid out.

"Nice," said Clay. "Now bring it in and we-" suddenly, their sub shook violently and a powerful surge sent them and the sub smashing into the mound of sand. "What the hell?!" Clay struggled to regain control. He pulled back on the stick, reversing the motor, but the craft was dragging backward. Clay looked out and then up through a small window on top. "What the hell is wrong with our buoyancy?" He looked at the instruments. "Are we taking in water?" Clay was referring to the K-955's buoyancy tanks, which filled with water to increase the sub's underwater weight and allow it to descend. To rise, the pilot would inject high-pressure air into the tanks, forcing some of the heavy water out and increasing the craft's buoyancy. Neutral buoyancy was a combination of air and water that provided the perfect weight and allowed the craft to remain at a desired level. Clay had suddenly lost control of it. He could barely move the sub, which now felt stuck to the sandy bottom. He pushed a button above the control stick, increasing the air and decreasing their weight. The hiss of the high-pressure air could be heard from below, and outside the cockpit.

Caesare quickly shifted from side to side as they hit the ground and rolled sideways. He tried to brace himself with his only free hand, the other still on the articulating arm's handle. He was trying desperately not to lose his grip on the Triton, which was bobbing back and forth like a huge fish trying to escape his clutch. His forearm tightened while he squeezed as hard as he could.

Clay jammed the control stick back and forth, trying to keep the craft from dragging. They were becoming more buoyant, but it was too slow. Something above caught Clay's eye. He looked up into the darkened water, the sunlight from above now only a dull pinpoint far above them. He kept looking until he saw it again. "This isn't a current," he said to Caesare. "I think we have company."

"What?!" Caesare twisted his head, trying unsuccessfully to look through the small window above. "What is it?!"

"I don't know," said Clay. Again, they were suddenly

slammed back against the ocean bottom. The K-955 groaned under the impact, with a loud metal reverberation behind them. He looked up again just as a giant shadow passed above them. "Whatever it is, it's big."

"We've got to get out of here." Caesare looked at Clay. "Do we drop the Triton?"

"No way." Clay's eyes narrowed. "I'm not going down for this thing again. Hold on!" He pushed the stick forward and slammed his other hand down on the button, pushing more water out of the tanks in a loud rush of pressurized air. Almost immediately, the sub bounced up from the sand. The motor whirled at full throttle sending up a cloud behind them. The K-955 zipped forward, its nose pointed to the surface.

Something hit the sub, this time, causing it to roll hard to one side. Clay quickly rolled against it to compensate and managed to level them back out, his hand still jamming the stick as far forward as possible.

"Oh my god," said Caesare, looking out the side window. "It's a sperm whale!"

"Here? Are you kidding?"

"Not kidding," Caesare said, with a pause. "And there are two of them!"

Clay practically leaned on the stick, trying to get every last ounce of speed from the sub's motors.

"They're coming at us!" yelled Caesare.

Suddenly, the K-955 was slammed sideways, causing it to roll completely over. Clay tried to counter the movement, but realized that the roll had too much momentum. He instead moved the stick back, allowing them to roll with the impact. As they came around, he compensated again and managed to keep them on an upward course.

"Clay," Caesare said quietly.

"You don't have to whisper, Steve. They're not going to hear you," Clay replied, looking at their depth gauge. They were still almost eighty feet from the surface.

"Clay," Caesare said, again.

Clay looked at Caesare, who was staring at him. He turned to show Clay the side window. Clay's eyes opened wide when he saw the huge dent in the side of the hull. What was far more critical, however, was the crack in the window, with water streaming down the inside wall. It was a major leak that would scare anyone, even at a shallow depth. The strength of the hull was seriously compromised, and the thick Plexiglas window was ruptured. If it collapsed entirely, their inside pressure would be lost and the torrent of incoming sea water would drown them within seconds. Clay and Caesare both knew their only hope was in that tiny window holding together. They also knew that they would not survive another impact.

Clay looked back at Caesare. "Blow the tanks."

Caesare flipped up a clear cover and slammed his fist against the large emergency button labeled 'Emergency Discharge'. The sub shook violently as four charges exploded, and the large buoyancy tanks instantly jettisoned from the hull, falling outward. Losing the extra weight of the tanks, along with the upward force of the charges accelerated the sub's ascent again and they rose toward the surface. The explosion caused the leak in the window to open wider, sending in a much larger flood of water. It quickly inched up past their shins. Caesare looked down, quickly switching hands to maintain his grip on the Triton. "We'd better hurry."

Clay was glancing back and forth between their depth gauge and the bright blue water above. The large shadow of Emerson's Pathfinder could be seen overhead. The sub quickly passed fifty feet and continued to race toward the surface.

Caesare looked repeatedly through the remaining windows. "I can't see them!" He tried to look through the broken window but could not make out anything through the distortion. "No idea where they are."

Clay stared at the gauge and noticed their ascent beginning to slow.

Caesare saw something was wrong. "What is it?"

"We're slowing," Clay said. "The incoming water is increasing our weight again."

Caesare unbuckled himself and slid out of his seat, still maintaining a grip on the handle in front of him. He twisted past Clay and reached into the rear of the cockpit. He felt back and forth below the water. "No oxygen tanks." He knew they could not open the top hatch until they reached the surface since the ocean water would make it far too heavy to push up. Hell, even if they could, they would drown under the massive deluge of water which would make the cracked window look like a trickle.

The sub's upward momentum continued to slow as it passed forty feet and the incoming water reached their laps.

*****

Above them, in the communications room of the Pathfinder, Captain Emerson and several of his crew were huddled around a large sonar display. The speakerphone was on, transmitting everything Clay and Caesare were saying.

"They're slowing," Tay said. He was sitting in the chair in front of Emerson.

"How fast are they moving?"

"About ten feet per minute, but slowing fast."

"Anything else they can jettison?" Emerson asked.

Tay shook his head. "Not from the inside."

Another crewmember stood to the side, urgently searching through the K-955's heavy manual.

Emerson stood up and turned to Lightfoot, who was standing just behind him. "We have to do something."

Lightfoot stared at the captain who motioned outside. "Yes, sir!" With that, they both quickly darted out of the room and ran toward the back of the ship.

*****

The water inside the sub was at chest level and rising fast, as the increasing amount of water filled the quickly shrinking space in the cockpit.

Tay's voice crackled over the speaker. "Guys, it looks like there should be spare breathers built into a side panel of your seats!" Tay leaned over and looked at the manual being held by his crewmember. "On the right side."

Caesare switched hands again on the large handle and reached around to examine his seat. Only able to feel the tip, he slid his hand up and down beneath the water, feeling for a clasp. He found a lip in the metal and quickly pulled it up. The panel flipped only partially open, due to the volume of the water around it. Caesare reached back, yanked it off, and felt inside. He gripped the small metal canister and wiggled it out. The small pony tank was approximately twelve inches long and had a green rubber mouthpiece on top. Caesare handed it to Clay and quickly extracted the second bottle from Clay's seat.

"Where are the whales?"

Caesare looked out through the two windows still above the waterline. "Can't see them over here." He looked at Clay. "What's the plan?"

Clay frowned. He desperately pushed a few times on the stick. There was nothing left. The twin motors were at maximum propulsion, trying to push them forward against the increasing weight of the sub. "We're barely moving. This is as far as we're going to get." He looked at the gauge. "Twenty-one feet." Clay looked up through the top window. The huge shadow of the Pathfinder loomed over them. He looked at Caesare and held up his tiny oxygen tank. "Well, these should give us," he shrugged, "ten minutes? If we wait for the water to fill the cockpit and equalize the pressure, we should be able to get the hatch open and make a swim for it."

Caesare's chin dipped into the water when he nodded. "That was the only thing I could think of. You go out firs-" He suddenly stopped talking when he noticed Clay staring at something over his shoulder. He turned and looked out through what was left of the side window. Two large shapes were approaching. At that moment, they felt a sensation and looked up at the depth gauge. The weight of the sub had overcome the strength of the propellers. The K-955 began sliding back down. The gauge increased to twenty-two feet, then twenty-three, and twenty-four. It was quickly falling downward.

Caesare looked back out the window. The whales were getting closer. "What in the hell is their problem?!"

They both knew that they could not open the hatch unless the entire cockpit was filled with water. With the water rising quickly, that would not take long, but the whales would reach them first. Even if they could survive another impact, the sub was now descending fast enough that by the time they were able to get outside, they would be too far down to make it to the surface. That is, unless they wanted a fatal case of the bends.

Clay looked at his friend. "This may be it."

Caesare gave a silent nod. They both tilted their faces up and away from the rising water, then reached out to the sides to get a strong hold, readying for the impact.

Both of the men turned unexpectedly when they heard a sound from outside, a loud clunk. The sound of metal dragged against the front of the hull.

"What was that?" First Clay, then Caesare, dunked their heads beneath the water and pressed their faces to the large bubble window. A blurry shadow could be seen through the glass, a human figure.

*****

Emerson, Tay and two other crewmen stood on the

large flat platform of the Pathfinder's stern. With two on each side of the platform, they tried to maintain their balance over the ship's rocking while each fed a large cable into the blue water. End over end, their hands moved deftly to keep the cables from becoming taut. On one side, Emerson and Tay fed a thick black oxygen line while the men across the platform fed a large steel cable from a giant wheel behind them.

Beneath the water, Lightfoot was dressed in nothing but his boxer shorts, a mask, and fins, holding onto the front of the K-955 sub which he could feel sinking beneath him. Lightfoot worked to attach the thick cable to the sub without getting his oxygen line wrapped up in it. He wore a full mask which covered his entire face and gave him excellent visibility, but as he desperately tried to pull himself up and over the top of the sub, his heavy breathing was beginning to fog the glass. The benefit of the full face mask was that it provided an undistorted view and allowed the person to speak while working, but Lightfoot was putting out a great deal of carbon dioxide and overwhelming the gentle flow of oxygen which kept it clear.

As Lightfoot scampered on top, he saw the large steel loops used by the winch to lower it from the ship. He grabbed one and pulled himself closer, careful not to lose his grip on the cable. He pulled hard on the cable and managed to get it a foot closer. It was getting tighter as the sub continued to fall back into the depths faster than Emerson and his team could feed it down. Lightfoot pulled himself closer and passed over the small window on top of the sub. Glancing down, Lightfoot could make out the interior lights, which were very dim and now completely submerged below the water inside. The silhouettes of Clay and Caesare were both staring back at him, each breathing through a small air canister.

Inside, Clay raised his head and grabbed the controls again. *He needs some slack!* He pulled the stick all the way back, tilting the craft up with what little power they still had.

As the K-955 inched higher, Lightfoot pulled hard again on the cable and got just enough slack to run through one of the giant loops. He grimaced as he struggled to push the end through, but with one last effort, he managed to clip the large hook up and back onto itself. He pressed his mask closer to verify it was secure, then pushed a large button on the side of his mask.

"She's hooked!" he yelled.

His voice was broadcast up and over the ship's external speakers. When Tay heard Lightfoot's voice, he ran across the platform and wrapped his hand around a chrome colored lever. He forced it up several notches to engage the motor at full power. The huge platform on the stern suddenly dipped deeply into the water, as it counteracted the inertia of the sub's descent. They all stumbled and turned when the motor let out a terrible screech. It eventually began to turn, pulling in the cable.

Below them, Lightfoot was sliding off the top when the sub jerked upward. He quickly grabbed hold of the thick rubber oxygen line. Above him, on deck, Emerson's two extra crewmen jumped to the other side of the platform to help pull the oxygen line back in, hand over hand.

They ignored the churning of the motor as it continued to reel in the cable, turning faster and faster.

As they pulled him up, Lightfoot kicked his feet hard to try to catch the sub. Once on the surface, he needed to get the sub's hatch open as quickly as possible. Clay and Caesare had been completely submerged inside for several minutes, which meant their canisters would soon be out of usable air. Lightfoot got close enough to grasp the hatch handle and hung on, riding the sub as it rose to the surface.

"Fifteen feet," said Harris, over the loud speakers.

Emerson looked up at the announcement, then back to his men. "Okay, get to the edge and hold on. She's coming up hard!"

The four men held onto something near the end of the platform to steady themselves. The wheel behind them was turning now at top speed. This was going to be rough as there was no chance to bleed off any momentum before the sub breached the surface, which meant it was going to overshoot. And since the cable was fed directly over the side of the stern, rather than from the large extended winch, the sub was most likely going to come up hard *under* the Pathfinder.

"Ten feet!" called Harris' voice.

Moments later, the sub smashed into the underside of the Pathfinder's stern platform. All four men were lifted completely off the deck and into the air, along with everything else that was not nailed down. Equipment and tools flew everywhere, and they all came down hard together. One of Emerson's junior crewmen lost his grip and slipped overboard, hitting the K-955's now exposed tail and disappeared into the waves.

"Man overboard!" yelled Emerson. The other junior crewman nodded and searched for his shipmate. Once spotted, he grabbed a float ring and jumped in after him, barely avoiding the sub as it pitched and rolled out from under the Pathfinder. A deafening shriek of metal on metal filled the air as the port side of the sub scraped along the bottom of the platform before finally freeing itself. As it rotated freely, Lightfoot popped up out of the white swell, still holding onto the hatch. He ripped off his mask and turned toward the circular door, straddling his legs across the top. He shook the water off of his face and gripped the handle hard, turning it with everything he had. The wheel relented and slowly began to turn. Lightfoot kept working it and then, with a heave, pulled it open. Instantly, hundreds of gallons of water came flooding out along with two large dark figures.

As the water poured out, the weight of the sub quickly changed. It began to roll backwards, taking the hatch opening back beneath the water. Lightfoot scrambled against the hull's rotation, staying upright as it turned. Less than thirty feet away, the heads of Emerson's two junior crewmen popped up, unharmed. Now all eyes were on the area of water in front of the twisting sub.

After several seconds, both Clay and Caesare surfaced and looked around. They spotted Emerson and Tay and pointed back to the sub. "Get the Triton!" they yelled.

Everyone looked to the K-955 and spotted the small Triton, flopping back and forth, miraculously still clasped in the sub's retractable claw. Lightfoot scrambled down to the tiny rover and unhooked it. He then pulled it behind him as he slid down the side of the K-955's belly and into the water, with the Triton in tow.

All five men slowly made their way to the ship's platform. Emerson and Tay reached over the side and pulled them up one by one. They grabbed Lightfoot and the Triton last, hefting it up over the heads of the others. All of them slouched forward, feet hanging over the end, trying to catch their breath. Emerson and Tay set the Triton down and joined the rest of the men, sitting down behind them.

After a long silence, Emerson reached over and put his hand on Clay's shoulder. He gave him a broad smile. "I was afraid we might just lose you two."

Clay looked at Emerson and returned the smile, his chest still heaving. His soaked hair hung down, pasted against his forehead with water streaming down over his face. "The thought crossed our minds once or twice."

Emerson turned to his crewman. "Whitey, Ballmer, you guys alright?"

Whitey, the larger of the two, nodded his head. "Yep." Next to him, Ballmer merely held up his hand and gave a thumbs-up.

Emerson turned to Caesare. "Caesare?"

Caesare put his hands behind him and leaned back on them. "I'm okay."

Emerson took a deep breath and looked at the K-955 rolling back and forth in the rising swells. The sub had deep scrapes covering most of its side but remained on the surface. It was still tethered to the Pathfinder by the large steel cable which was slack, yet still visible below the surface of the water. "Anyone else really starting to hate this place?"

28

KATHRYN LOKKE REACHED up and rubbed the sleep out of her eyes before opening them. She looked at her watch and then peered around the tent. It was 5:00 a.m., and only Andrew's sleeping bag was empty. Pierre and Tadri remained completely buried inside their own bags, neither leaving any skin exposed. Kathryn looked at the thin layer of ice which formed around the base of the triple layered, insulated tent. She thought about how even the most modern materials still could not keep you from freezing your butt off. At least you still *felt* like you were freezing it off. She was sure that, in reality, these advanced materials provided some serious protection, in spite of the attention they paid to the cold that still managed to get through.

Kathryn turned onto her back and closed her eyes for several minutes, trying to gauge her chances of getting back to sleep. Eventually, she frowned and turned back over. She grabbed her thick knit cap and put it back on her head, then pulled the sides down over her ears. She quietly pulled herself out of her bag and sat up, putting her thick jacket on, followed by her insulated pants and Gore-

Tex boots. She managed to unzip the vinyl zipper without waking Pierre or Tadri and poked her head out.

The sun was low on the horizon which was white in every direction. Kathryn glanced at the second tent and could see an orange-blue glow from the small flickering flame inside. She pulled the large door flap open and stepped out, quickly re-zipping it from the outside. Even without the wind, the early morning air felt like it penetrated through her clothes immediately. She ran across the twenty feet of frozen ground and flung open the tent flap as fast as she could. Without a second's delay, she jumped inside.

Andrew looked up from his aluminum coffee mug. "Morning," he said, in a low voice.

"Good morning." She zipped the door closed and turned to sit down on one of the small lightweight collapsing chairs on the other side of the burner. She leaned in close to the flame which was keeping the coffee hot and the tent warm. She picked up a mug, scraped some ice out, and poured herself a cup.

Kathryn really did not care for coffee but decided three days ago that she was not going to look a gift horse in the mouth. Taking a sip, she frowned at the bitterness and wrapped her hands around the warm metal cup. She looked absently around the tent. Most of their geological gear lined the far wall, including two laptops and a satellite phone.

"Things are going well, eh?" asked Andrew, in this thick New Zealand accent.

"Touch wood," she said, with a grin, which was the Kiwi equivalent of the same American phrase. She looked around for a piece of wood to tap. Both looked around the tent and laughed quietly when they realized that everything around them was made with lightweight metals and fabrics.

Andrew finished his coffee and reached down for the small Teflon coated frying pan. "So," he said, "I know the official reason for you all being here. But it doesn't seem to wash out." He lit a match off the burner and used it to ignite a second. "If you already knew the extent of the Shelf slide, why come back with so many in such a mad rush?"

Kathryn looked at him and then quietly glanced down at the flame in front of her. "Pride." She kept gazing and then shrugged and looked back at him. "And a little arrogance, I guess."

He put the pan on the flame, dug into the food chest, then retrieve some eggs and a strip of bacon. "Your pride or theirs?" he asked, with a knowing grin.

"Mine."

"Ah," Andrew nodded. "So, your pride and *their* arrogance, eh?"

She smiled behind her cup. "How'd you know?"

"Politics aren't limited by country. We've got our own share of dramas down here." He cracked open two eggs into the pan. "In fact, I got a mate working in one of our government branches. The things he tells me leave me in no hurry to get back."

"How did you wind up out here? I can't tell if you're a researcher or a soldier."

Andrew laughed. "Ah, I'm a soldier, but I do a little research too. Have to. Not to mention that conditions out here are rough enough that you tend to want to help out a bit just to get things wrapped up quicker." The eggs started to bubble and he reached for the plastic spatula. "You want these over easy again?"

"Please." Kathryn watched him flip the eggs. He was not a bad cook. In fact, after factoring in the environment, she decided he was an excellent cook. "Do you lead people out here a lot?"

"Ah, yeah," he said, dragging his words. "Few years ago, a team from China was out and they got lost in a snow storm. Only two of the five made it back, and the ones that did were in pretty bad shape. We had offered to go out with them until they acclimated and all, but they refused. After that, we started going out with everyone, no exceptions."

"Better safe than sorry," She nodded. "I'm afraid to think of how we might fare if the weather turned bad on us."

"Nah," he smiled again. "You'd be alright with us." He flipped the eggs onto the small metal plate and slid the bacon on top. He handed it to Kathryn and reached back into the chest. "If we leave early, I'll be able to make us all a big farewell breakfast."

Like Kathryn and her four person team, the rest of the teams also landed without incident, except for one failed snowmobile on the last drop. Thankfully, it was the three man team, and they were still able to manage with one machine. The rest of the project had so far gone fairly smoothly, and with over half of their work done, they were expected to leave a full two days early. Something *everyone* was happy about.

The teams had already placed most of the seismographs along the fault line. The new models were solar powered and connected via a direct satellite link. About the size of a large shoebox, they would be able to measure any changes on the Shelf up to fractions of an inch in any direction. The majority of work in the next two days would be primarily measurements and sample gathering.

Kathryn turned around when she heard the unzipping of the tent door behind her. In stepped Tadri, who seemed to zip it back up even faster than she did. "Did I hear someone talking about breakfast?"

"Yeah, you sure did," Andrew replied, "have a seat and I'll fix ya right up."

"Bless you." Tadri sat down next to Lokke and drained some coffee from the percolator. She let out a gentle groan with her first sip. "Coffee has never tasted so good in all my life."

Andrew smiled. "Yeah, the Antarctic will do that. Everything hot tastes better, and everything cold tastes a little worse."

"Must be why we all started crying over your stew last night," Kathryn said, and they all laughed.

Tadri looked at Kathryn. "How many more of the SatQuake units do we have to place?"

"Just three more. The rest of the trip should be mostly data collection."

"Any problems with the other teams?" Tadri had turned in early the night before, before Kathryn had made her rounds checking in with the other teams over satellite phone.

Kathryn shook her head. "Not really. A few hardware units that don't seem to want to work, couple of small injuries from tripping, and a lot of complaints about the food." She smiled at Andrew, waiting for a reaction.

"Heeey," he said, as he handed a plate of eggs to Tadri. "Can I help it if the other gents can't cook like me?"

"All in all, it's been pretty smooth." Kathryn continued. "We really lucked out with this weather and everyone is eager to leave early."

"You know," Tadri said to Kathryn. "There were a lot of unhappy people when you told us what we were going to be doing. A lot of people complaining that this was just a political axe to grind for you. But, I think this has been good for everyone. Most of us had not just gotten soft, but I think some of our skills had gotten a little rusty too. I know a lot of people are probably still pissing and moaning on the outside, but I think everyone will be better for this."

"Thank you." Kathryn gave a gentle raise of her eyebrows. "To be honest, I thought I was going to get a wave of resignations over this."

Tadri winked. "Well, you might still get a few."

"Just hope they are the right ones," Andrew grinned.

Kathryn and Tadri looked at each other as if Andrew

somehow knew who the problem members of the department were. They both burst out laughing.

*****

Kathryn's four person group was out on the ridgeline by 7:00 a.m. Two hours later, Pierre was positioning one of the seismographs while Kathryn and Tadri measured the width, depth, and horizontal shift of the fissure caused by the quake. Andrew walked ahead examining the ground for signs of cracks or weakness in the ice. A few falls from the other teams had resulted in only minor injuries. However, a collapse under foot could easily result in something much worse, ranging from a broken ankle or compound fracture, to a cave in from which it would take too long to get someone out, if at all. Ironically, the vast majority of deaths in the remote regions of the Antarctic were caused by smaller injuries that prevented the victims from getting out of the elements in time. This was a lesson that all of the guides explained to Kathryn's people on the first day and repeated frequently.

The two women approached the edge of the large crevice and looked down at one of the deepest gaps they had seen. They guessed it was close to fifty feet deep and tip toed carefully along the edge, knowing that the edge was often still unstable. Tadri knelt down and positioned her small laser unit for what felt like the ten thousandth time. She turned it on and looked at the bright red line extending across the gap. Then she turned the small wheel along the bottom, slowly dropping the angle of the laser, until the bright spot appeared on the lip of the opposite wall. Tadri read the figure on the display. "Forty three feet, seven and three eighths inches."

Kathryn stood behind her and entered the measurement on a large handheld device, which automatically locked in their GPS location.

Tadri then turned a second laser downward, focusing

on the bottom of the crevice. "Fifty three feet, three inches and one sixteenth."

Kathryn entered the numbers and frowned. She hit a button and displayed all of the measurements in a spreadsheet view. Running down the list, she noticed something. "Hmm."

Tadri stood up and turned around. "What's up?"

"Have you noticed a trend here as we move south?"

Tadri thought a minute. "It's getting deeper isn't it?"

Kathryn nodded.

"That's not good," Tadri said. "If it's getting deeper, the further in we go that makes it very unlikely it's a surface fracture and —"

"And it extends *through* the Shelf," finished Kathryn.

A few hundred yards away, Pierre secured the last leg of his SatQuake. He stood up and dusted the ice off his knees. He looked south at the rest of the group and started to turn when something caught his eye. He turned and looked back down at the seismograph below him. The red light on top was lit. Pierre stared at the bright LED bulb for a moment and then reached down and hit the reset button. The light went off. He nodded and picked up his pack. He turned and took a few steps before stopping again. He turned back to the SatQuake. The red light was on again.

Pierre grabbed the walkie-talkie from his hip and held it up to his mouth. He pressed down the transmit button. "Hey, Kathryn, you there?"

Kathryn heard Pierre's voice on her own hip and grabbed her walkie-talkie. She looked back at Pierre, who she could see clearly, but was well out of earshot. "Go ahead, Pierre."

"I think we have a bad SatQuake unit here." he said.

"What's wrong with it?"

"The alert light keeps coming on." He looked around, doing a three hundred and sixty degree scan. "It's either not working right or the sensor is too sensitive. There's no other noise around to pick up."

"Did you try the reset?"

"Yep," Pierre answered. He pressed the reset again and watched the light go off. After several seconds, it came on again. "Just tried it again. Still comes back on." He looked back the way they came. "Didn't have this problem on any of the others."

"Is it syncing with the satellite alright?" asked Kathryn.

"Seems to be. Both battery and satellite lights are green."

"That's strange," said Kathryn. "I wonder what the problem is."

"Beat's me. What do you want me to do?"

"Just leave it. I'll note that it's having issues. Grab the snowmobile and come on over."

"Will do. Gonna grab a snack. See ya in a few." He replaced the walkie-talkie on his hip and knelt down to dig through his pack for an energy bar.

Kathryn watched Pierre in the distance, rummaging through his bag. She looked down at Tadri, who was folding up the laser. "Looks like we have a bad seismograph."

"Well, I guess it was bound to happen." Tadri collapsed the small legs on the unit and slid it back into a thick duffel bag.

"Guess so. They're pretty reliable though. I can't remember the last time we had a bad-"

Tadri turned around to see why Kathryn had stopped talking and found her gazing at Pierre in the distance. She looked back at Tadri and slowly pulled the walkie-talkie back from her hip. She held it to her mouth and slowly pushed the button again.

"Pierre. Can you hear me?" Kathryn shot Tadri a worried look as she waited for a reply. Tadri's eyes suddenly opened wide.

"Yeah, Kathryn. Go ahead," came Pierre's voice.

"Pierre, get away from the ridge."

"What?"

Kathryn squeezed the small transmitter in her hand. "Get *away* from the edge!"

"What for?" he asked.

Kathryn looked at Tadri and pressed the transmit button down again. "That unit may not be broken."

Pierre heard her voice and turned south to look at them. Before he could reply, the ice below them began to shake.

Kathryn's eyes widened. She looked at the ground then back to Tadri. The shaking intensified, causing them to stumble and grab each other for support. "RUN!" she shouted.

Tadri was thrown to the ground and quickly rolled over, continuing forward on her hands and knees as Kathryn looked for Pierre. He had disappeared behind the thick wall of white mist rising from the fractures splitting the frozen ground. Kathryn raised the walkie-talkie to her mouth, trying desperately to stay on her feet. "Pierre?!" she shouted. She tried to peer through the thick mist. "Pierre!" The sound of the quake thundered all around them, and she held the small unit up against her ear. There was no reply. She held the button down again and screamed as loud as she could. "PIERRE!"

Suddenly, a pair of strong hands squeezed the back of her parka like a vice. Kathryn fell to the ground, looking up to find Andrew dragging her behind him, away from the widening crack in the surface. He trudged forward, stumbling from side to side, struggling to stay on his feet, through the violent shaking. After thirty or forty feet, he finally lost his balance and fell to the ground, but continued scrambling forward, pulling Kathryn behind him.

The world suddenly felt in slow motion as Kathryn kicked at the icy ground, trying to help further their distance. She could see large pieces where they were just standing suddenly crack and fall into what now looked like a chasm, inching its way toward them. She twisted her body to the outside, then onto her hands and knees, in a desperate attempt to get further away from the edge. She followed Andrew towards Tadri, who was also on her hands and knees ahead of them. Kathryn noticed something that she would not process until later. During their mad scramble, Andrew's face seemed oddly composed as he kept scanning the area around them and looking backward. How in the world could he remain so focused?

Finally, the rumbling subsided and the ground gradually became still again. They were left on the ground panting, surrounded in a white fog created by the breaking of massive amounts of ice shelf. The crack in the earth was barely visible in front of them through the thick white curtain, but it looked frighteningly wide. Kathryn was staring at what little she could see of the gigantic crack when she realized that Andrew was patting her down and turning her body from side to side. When he was confident that she had sustained no injuries, he quickly made his way to Tadri and repeated the process.

He returned to Kathryn moments later and pulled the walkie-talkie from her hand. Pressing down on the large button, he called out for Pierre. "Pierre, mate, are you there?" He moved the device away from his mouth and listened. After a long pause, he shook his head. With a jerk, he ripped a whistle and cord from around of his neck, and dropped it into her lap. "Wait here," he said, peering into the thick fog. Without another word, he pulled a small digital compass from a jacket pocket, held it up for a moment, and disappeared into nothingness.

Kathryn and Tadri sat motionless, listening to Andrew's footsteps moving away from them. After a long moment, Tadri scooted next to her and snaked her arm inside Kathryn's. They huddled together. Their immediate worry was for Pierre, but Kathryn's thoughts quickly began to spread to the rest of the team. There were a lot of people out here because of her and any one of them may have been caught in that quake. Jesus, all of them could have been. Her chest suddenly began to feel heavy, and her fear grew into a paralyzing mix of guilt and terror.

Tadri felt Kathryn's body begin to shake through their linked arms and turned to her. "Kathryn? Are you okay?"

Kathryn looked at Tadri with a helpless stare. She slowly shook her head. "The others." She trailed off, looking back at the fog, trying desperately to peer beyond.

Tadri grabbed her gloved hand and squeezed it. "I'm sure everybody's fine, Kathryn! I'm sure everyone got away just like we did." Kathryn looked back at her. "Including Pierre."

Kathryn was not so sure. She thought about how quickly and easily those edges fell away. She had to find out. She turned and looked for her large pack which had the long-range radio on it, but the thick white mist had already moved past them and enveloped the entire area. Kathryn started to turn when Tadri gripped her tightly.

"What are you doing?"

"I have to get to my pack and call the other teams."

Tadri turned around. "Do you *see* your pack?"

Kathryn smirked and pointed. "It's right over there about forty feet away.

"Are you sure?" Tadri asked.

Kathryn nodded impatiently. "Yes!" Tadri remained silent staring at her. Kathryn took the hint and looked around. They were completely enveloped now and could not see anything. "Well, I'm pretty sure it's right over there."

Tadri kept a firm grip on her arm. "Do you even know which direction you're facing? I don't!"

Kathryn looked again, thinking about the question. "No." She sighed, slouching back down to the ground.

Tadri looked up. Even the sky was white. "I say we

wait until Andrew gets back, or until we can actually see something."

They both sat waiting for what seemed like hours. Finally, they heard the distant crunching of footsteps and stood up excitedly. It took almost a full minute for Andrew to appear out of the wall of mist. They smiled at him but realized he was not smiling back. He stopped in front of them and swung something large around his shoulders dropping it at their feet. It was Pierre's bag.

Kathryn's eyes opened wide, fearful of what was coming.

"I can't find him."

She immediately felt like she had been hit in the chest with a hammer.

"I reckon he fell in. He was pretty close when it started." Andrew knelt down and unzipped the bag. He dug through it, taking a quick inventory.

"Wha-what do we do?" she asked.

"We get our bags and go back to look for him. I didn't hear anything when I called out for him, but I'm not ready to give up. Get your bags," he looked at his compass. "They're just a few meters that way." As he pointed, Kathryn noted that it was not the direction she was about to head earlier. "We need our equipment and as much rope as we can find. We have some on the other snowmobile. Hopefully, we have enough between the two."

Both women took a tentative step in the direction that Andrew had indicated, but turned back with an uncertain look. He nodded his head, still squatting down looking in the bag. "Just follow the sound back to me, you'll be fine."

Andrew led the way back on foot, with Kathryn and Tadri riding their snowmobile slowly behind him. The visibility was improving, and they were able to make out the outline of the other snowmobile at almost thirty feet when they arrived. Part of the front skids hung over the edge of the steep drop, but amazingly had not fallen in. Andrew quickly tied a rope back to back on the snowmobiles. Kathryn slowly eased the throttle, pulling the second vehicle to safety.

Andrew stood carefully on the edge and peered into the deep white chasm. He could make out the tips of large ice chunks below, but could not see anything else further down. "Pieeerre!" he called aloud and listened. "Pieeeeeeerre!" They heard only silence around them.

Andrew changed the lines on the snowmobiles, so each now had their own individual length of rope attached to its rear rack. He pulled hard on each to make sure the machines did not budge.

"What are you doing?" Kathryn asked.

"I'm going down."

"What? You don't even know how far down it is!"

He shot her an impatient look. "Look...Kathryn, he's probably buried, which means we don't have long. It's probably already too late. But it's now or never." He pointed to the snowmobiles. "I need you two to sit on those to make sure they don't go anywhere."

Both women nodded and planted themselves on the seat, facing backwards. Kathryn grabbed her pack and pulled out her radio.

"Don't!"

She looked at Andrew. "What? We have to find out if everyone is okay. They may need help too!"

"If they do, then my teammates are doing exactly as I am. Besides, we don't want to make any noise if Pierre is trying to call for help under a meter of snow." He ran the ropes through his belt and got ready to descend. He planted his feet against the edge and looked back at them. "I'll be right back."

189

29

CLAY WOKE TO the sound of his phone. He opened one eye and peered at the bright screen. After taking a moment to push the fog from his head, he accepted the call. "Borger. How goes it?"

"Hey, Clay, I wake you up?"

"No," he said, before thinking about the question. "Actually, yes, but go ahead."

"Clay, we're gonna need to get everybody on a call."

Clay rubbed his hand across his face and sat up on the bed. "Talk to me."

Borger paused on the other end. "It's not what we thought, Clay."

"What do you mean?"

"It's worse," Borger sighed. "I don't think we should say too much on your cell. We're gonna need a secure line. Maybe start with Langford."

Clay nodded. "Okay, hold tight. I'll find him and Caesare." He hung up the phone and stared at it for a minute. He raised his eyes and looked around the darkened room. When he had first woken, it took him a few seconds to remember where he was. He and Caesare, along with a couple of Emerson's men, had been airlifted back to NAS JAX last night, where they quickly unloaded the Triton. After getting it into a lab, they removed the hard drive and attached it to a computer so they could transfer the data to Borger. It took a couple hours, but once Borger had the data, he suggested they all get some rest and give him some time to go over it. That was all the prompting they needed. They procured some quarters reserved for civilian visitors, and hit the sack. That was a little over four hours ago. Now it was four thirty a.m., and he needed to find Langford for a conference call. Finding Caesare was easy. He could hear him snoring through the wall next door.

Fifteen minutes later, Langford was the last of the four men to dial into the call. He wasted no time. "What do you have, Will?"

"Well, sir, I just got off the phone with Dr. Harding at MIT. We've spent the last two hours going over the hard drive data that Clay and Caesare sent over. The Triton captured twelve hours and fifty two minutes of video after losing contact with the ship, and slowly spiraled downward in large concentric circles until hitting the bottom. Most of the video is not useful, as it captured things above the submersible, such as views of the surface or the ship above."

"Okay, so what are we here to talk about?" Langford interrupted.

"Sir, most of the video was pointing up, but the segments of video pointing *below* the craft are why I asked Clay to get you guys on a call." He hesitated a moment before continuing. "The camera on the Triton is an ultrahigh definition camera which records much more detail than what it transfers over its wireless connection, which is what we saw before. With this new data, we can more clearly see the ring. The physical characteristics are more advanced than we had previously believed. For example, the width is thicker than I thought, and I believe it is moving faster than what we had calculated."

"And what does that change?" asked Langford.

"Well, those observations do not change much of our previous assumptions. If anything, they just tell us that the ring probably requires more power than we thought. But, it's the inside of the ring that changes things."

"Inside the ring?"

"Yes, sir," Borger continued. "We can observe details

within the ring's interior, which gives us some inference; as in a *direction*."

Clay spoke up. "What does that mean?"

"I believe the assertion on our video call the other day was that these...*people* are planning to bring something through the ring."

Clay and Caesare looked at each other across the table. That was not their assertion. It was Stevas' assertion. They were sure Langford was thinking the same thing when his voice came over the phone line. "That is correct."

"Sir, I think we have this backwards. Instead of bringing something through, it...it looks like they may be sending something *out*."

There was a long silence before Langford replied. "Alright, give me some time to wake everyone up."

*****

Secretary of Defense Miller, Chief of Staff Mason, and National Security Advisor Stevas appeared on the video screen within thirty minutes. A few moments later, a video feed from a Pentagon war room with the four Joint Chiefs appeared. In the bottom right hand corner were Langford and Borger's video windows which were already online along with Clay and Caesare. They were broadcasting from the NAS JAX conference room. Professors Harding and Wong appeared just as Langford began speaking.

"Gentlemen, we have some news, an update from the information recovered from the Triton submersible. Data which has been verified by both Mr. Borger, as well as Professor Harding and his team at MIT. The video taken below the surface is very clear and has given us new information about the ring." He broke just for a moment. "We may have a larger problem on our hands."

"Larger than a global invasion?" Stevas asked, sarcastically.

"I'll let you decide," Langford replied. "I will turn this over to Mr. Borger in a moment to speak to the details, but the bottom line is that it looks like we had the direction of the portal backwards. The issue is not about what the ring is bringing in. It's about what it is sending out."

"Sending out?" Miller's eyes narrowed. "What do you mean *out*?"

"We think this is a one way tunnel," said Borger. "And the direction is clearly outbound, not inbound."

Miller looked at Mason and Stevas sitting next to him, and turned back to the screen. "And what exactly is that?"

"Water," replied Borger. "It appears to be water."

"Excuse me?"

Borger took a deep breath. "The camera on the submersible is very high quality and I am confident in what it shows, which is a massive inflow of water into the ring." Borger considered his words before speaking the next line. "I think the dolphins were right, it's about the water, as in *taking* our water."

For a split second, Clay thought the live video feeds had malfunctioned as everyone appeared to be frozen. But, when Stevas leaned forward he realized there was nothing wrong with their video transmissions, everyone had simply had the same reaction.

"Are you telling us that the purpose of this ring is in fact, to steal our water?"

Borger carefully considered Stevas' question. "Well, there is still a lot more we do not know...but it definitely looks like the direction of the portal is one way."

"Mr. Harding," Miller said, "is this your assessment as well?"

Harding nodded into his camera. "I'm afraid so."

"Is there any possibility that we are wrong?"

"Yes, it is possible. As I said, there is still much we don't know. But what we know so far, and have been able to verify...we are pretty sure of." The screen was suddenly filled with a high definition video picture of the ring, being shared from Borger's computer. He played it in slow motion as he explained. "A strong current of water, even within the ocean, creates a visual distortion which can be measured. We can then make some calculations on this distortion." Borger then highlighted several areas within the video picture with red circles. "There are other indicators as well, such as the movement patterns of the surrounding plant life and sediment, and the direction of flow within the ring. There are more subtle optical cues as well, all of which are measurable with a relatively high degree of accuracy."

"How much water are we talking about?" Miller asked.

"We're not sure. Professor Harding and his team are working on that, but our preliminary estimate... is a hell of a lot."

"This just gets better and better," Miller said, shaking his head. "And we don't know where this is going?"

Borger frowned. "Probably off planet."

Miller was still shaking his head. "And if we are losing a 'hell of a lot of water' why didn't anyone notice this out of the tens of thousands of scientists around the world, except for a couple of dolphins?"

No one answered.

Miller looked directly across his table and stared at Stevas. "Or maybe someone *did* notice."

Stevas stared back but said nothing.

"Okay," Miller said, turning back to everyone on screen. "Mr. Mason will wake the President and Vice President." He looked at his watch. "Everyone meet at JAX." Miller looked again at Stevas. "Looks like you were right, Clay. Now, before you start gloating, go find Keister."

30

KATHRYN SAT ON the ground, her knees raised to her chest with her head between them. The large handheld radio lay on its side in the ice next to her, silent. Tadri sat next to her, with an arm wrapped around. Kathryn raised her head just long enough to wipe more tears away. She was devastated. Pierre was gone. Andrew searched for over an hour, but could find no trace of him...sight nor sound. Judging from the depth of the chasm, he was now likely buried beneath twenty feet of ice, if not more.

Even worse was the news from the other teams. Upon Andrew's return, they found that six others had fallen in and been lost as well. Just as he had said, all of the other guides went down after them, but only two were brought back up alive. Three bodies were recovered. Four could not be found, including Pierre.

It could not have been worse, Kathryn thought to herself. It was all her fault. Seven people were dead because of her. She brought them all, practically forced them to come, and for what? All so she could show those bastards in Washington!

Andrew finished tying their gear to the snowmobiles and walked over to her and Tadri. "We're ready."

She stared at him silently, saying nothing. She reached for his hand and he pulled her up.

A voice came across the radio. Andrew reached down to pick it up. The three of them listened in on a short conversation. "Base, this is Team Nine. We are moving out and headed for the rendezvous. Over."

The reply was immediate. "Roger that, Nine. Estimated touchdown at your location in approximately two hours twenty minutes." Kathryn recognized the second voice as Steve Anderson, Andrew's commanding officer and the head of the small New Zealand research team stationed at McMurdo.

After Andrew had returned from his search for Pierre, it was Steve Anderson to whom he reported the grim news. Their other guides did the same, and as each report of a fatality was heard over the radio, Kathryn's heart sank deeper and deeper.

"Are you ready?" Andrew asked her and Tadri.

She gave a painful nod, and he raised the radio to his mouth. "Team Ten ready to head out."

"Roger that, Team Ten. We should be at your rendezvous in approximately three hours."

"Copy. Ten out." Andrew lowered the radio and clipped it to his thick nylon belt. He scanned the area again and then turned back to the women, following their gaze back to the monstrous crack in the ice. Most of the white haze had cleared and the enormity of the second quake was breathtaking. More than that, it was painful knowing that one of their group would remain there entombed. He walked over to the lead snowmobile and waited.

Kathryn stared for a long time at the place where she had last seen Pierre. The longer she stared, the harder it was to turn away. This was it. This was ground zero of her decision and people had paid with their lives. They were not coming home, ever, because of her.

She felt Tadri's hand on her shoulder and turned to look at her. Neither said anything. They simply turned around together and walked back to the snowmobiles. Kathryn climbed silently aboard behind Andrew, while Tadri got onto the second machine. They started both engines and slowly pulled away.

*****

The trip to the rendezvous location was over thirty miles away, over flat icy terrain. The quake had been so great that they were still detecting aftershocks on the seismic sensors. Even though Anderson and his pilots were airborne minutes after the reports began coming in, without knowing how deep the crack now was, the last thing they needed to do was to land a few loud, giant airplanes close by. Instead, ten different sites were identified that each of the teams were able to reach based on their remaining personnel, supplies and fuel levels. The risks were low, but Anderson's team was not about to take any chances.

*****

The ground was challenging, but their progress was steady. Andrew and the two women carefully navigated several depressions and gaps in the ice without much danger. They reached their destination almost forty five minutes before their pick up. Andrew opened a pack and offered Kathryn and Tadri something to eat while they waited, but neither accepted. Instead, they sat near the warm engine of his snowmobile and tried to shield themselves from the increasing wind. Not long after, he dropped down next to them. They all sat silently for the hour it took to finally hear the sound of the plane in the distance.

The silver glint of the familiar C130 aircraft became visible in the bright sky from several miles away. Andrew reached into his pack and retrieved a landing flare. Walking away, he ignited the small tube and let it spew a thick red smoke, blowing away from him along with the cold breeze. When he reached the flat area identified as their makeshift landing strip, he threw the flare as far as he could out onto the ice. He turned and walked back to Kathryn and Tadri. Together, they watched the large plane bank slightly toward the smoke signal. The pitch of the engines slowed as it began dropping in altitude. The landing gear followed, slowly unfolding out from under its belly like a massive bird stretching its legs.

With a couple hundred feet left, the plane leveled out and passed overhead, giving the pilot a chance to assess the surface of the frozen ground. A moment later, Anderson's voice came over the radio. "Landing site appears acceptable. Stand by for touch down."

The aircraft made a wide circle and approached again from the same direction, which was against the wind. The engines slowed even more, and it dropped steadily until reaching just ten feet above the ground. Finally, less than a half mile out, it gently fell and bounced onto the ice. The engines suddenly screamed as their thrust was redirected forward to slow the plane. It bounced and shuddered several times as the wheels hit uneven ground until it slowed to a halt.

Andrew and the two women mounted the snowmobiles and started forward. They headed for the beginning of the strip while the large plane slowly turned around and followed them. Andrew brought them around in a large arc. He waited to see where the tail of the C130 would line up after turning, yet again into the wind and readying itself for takeoff. When the aircraft stopped, the specially modified tail folded down. A large hydraulic ramp extended over the tail section and then down to the ground. Andrew pulled them forward slowly and motioned Kathryn to dismount behind him. After her, he swung his leg over and left the engine idling.

Steven Anderson and Kyle Bassen, the guide of Team Eight, descended the ramp and approached. Anderson raised his eyebrows slightly at Andrew who nodded and then motioned to the two women. Anderson understood and walked directly to Kathryn.

"How ya going there, Ms. Lokke?" he asked.

She struggled as she felt her emotions suddenly well up inside. She only managed a nod.

Anderson frowned after reading her face. He waited a few moments, giving her a chance to compose herself, fighting his instinct to reach out. She was under a great deal of stress and likely very cognizant of how she appeared in front of her team, some of whom were now watching her through the opening in the rear of the plane. When he continued, he spoke a little more slowly. "The rest of your team is headed back to McMurdo, aside from those inside. We also have one of the recovered bodies aboard." There was no easy way to say that, but she appeared to take it well enough. "Are you okay?" he asked.

Kathryn's gaze strengthened, and yet she answered with surprising honesty. "No. Not really."

Anderson nodded and motioned to Kyle, standing next to him. "Can we help you aboard?"

Her answer was exactly what he expected. "No." With that, she walked past them, followed by Tadri, and climbed the slippery ramp in short controlled steps. When she got to the top, she looked into the fuselage of the plane to find teams Seven through Nine. They were huddled together at the far end, with all eyes on her. The other snowmobiles and packs had been secured to the sides of the hull, leaving a tight path through to the other end.

She and Tadri slowly navigated through, toward the others. As she passed some of the gear, she suddenly saw the shape of the wrapped body and froze. She knew from the reports that it was Jason, the youngest and newest addition to her team. Kathryn could hear Tadri behind her, and she forced herself forward again.

When she reached the front of the plane, the others squeezed closer together to make room on the narrow bench seat. They were all bundled in their parkas for warmth. Kathryn looked at the others; their gazes were a mix of sympathy, contempt, and sheer disbelief that any of this had happened to them. She looked at the faces of Leo Torbin and Gale Preece, the two researchers who were onsite at the Halley research station when the first major quake hit. Gale was leaning gently against Leo. What Kathryn did not know was that Leo had saved her, grabbing Gale and keeping her from falling under the collapsing ice as some of the others had.

After the last of their gear was loaded, Anderson and the others re-boarded and closed the tail section. He gave the thumbs up to the pilots who were looking back through the cockpit door. Moments later, the engines roared back to life, drowning out everything else inside. The plane shuddered and picked up speed and the ride progressed from bumpy to almost violent as the aircraft jumped and plowed through the uneven terrain. Inside, Kathryn and her team instinctively held onto one another until the pounding disappeared, and the plane was airborne.

After several minutes, they leveled out and Anderson came forward. He motioned for Kathryn to join him. She stood and shuffled back to where he was standing, looking over his shoulder at Jason's body bag again. She leaned next to Anderson, against two big bags of gear.

"There is something I didn't get a chance to tell you outside," he said, in a lowered voice.

She leaned in expectantly.

He looked at the others and lowered his voice even more. "We're not heading back to McMurdo."

She raised her eyebrows, surprised. "Where *are* we heading?"

"It sounds like someone pretty high up in my government got a call from someone in yours," he said, with a slight frown. "We have been asked to return you directly back to the Falklands."

"You were asked?"

He shrugged. "Let's say asked firmly."

"This is probably going to sound like a dumb question, but can this plane make it that far with all of this equipment on board?"

"Barely."

"Well," she said, looking back at the other team members. "I don't think anyone is going to object. It just gets us back to civilization that much faster."

He nodded. "Right. I just thought you should know. Apparently, there will be another aircraft waiting for you when we land."

"I guess someone really wants to get us home in a hurry."

Anderson shook his head. "No, the plane isn't waiting for everyone. It's waiting for you, specifically."

*****

Kathryn woke up when she felt the plane bank hard to the right. She looked out the window and could see land beneath them. Some of the others looked even more excited than she was to see brown land, instead of white. Kathryn watched as the plane passed over nearly a hundred small lakes before lining up for its approach. The sky was dark blue, with the sun just sinking below the western horizon. One of Anderson's men, sitting nearby, reminded everyone to fasten their harnesses and prepare for landing. Hopefully, a much smoother landing this time.

The touchdown was uneventful, and the C130 slowed as it taxied down one of the long runways of Britain's Royal Air Force station. The area was a focal point in 1982 during the war over the Falkland archipelago between Argentina and the United Kingdom. The war lasted just two months, but cost the lives of over nine hundred Argentinian and British soldiers. After the victory, the British greatly reinforced the defense of the islands, particularly on the East Falkland Island where they had just landed.

The plane came to a stop, and all of Kathryn's team

eagerly unbuckled and stood up. The air that rushed in when the side door opened was noticeably warmer. She waited for everyone to exit before following them down the ladder. As they walked toward a large waiting bus, Kathryn looked around and spotted the two other planes which had picked up the rest of her team. She reasoned that everyone must already be inside, which gave her some solace. It was over, at least for them.

"Dr. Lokke?" a British officer standing nearby asked.

"Yes."

He reached out to shake her hand. "I'm Captain Dyson. Welcome."

Kathryn watched the bus close its doors and slowly pull away. Tadri stared at her through the window with a confused look on her face. She gave a small wave and turned back. "Thank you," Kathryn said.

"We have a plane waiting to take you to the U.S. I trust you were briefed."

"Yes," she said. "I was briefed."

"Very good. The flight back will be faster, but I'm afraid the accommodations are rather tight. I recommend that you take a few minutes to stretch and perhaps use the loo before you leave. Can I get you anything? Maybe something to eat?"

Kathryn nodded. "Yes, thank you. That would be fine. I mean the stretch and a trip to the ladies' room. I'm not really hungry."

"I understand. If you would be so kind as to follow me, I can escort you." Dyson led her to a small SUV and opened the door for her. "If you do get hungry, I would recommend you not drink anything. There is no toilet on this plane."

"Good tip." She closed the door and leaned her seat back.

*****

The plane waiting for her was a surprise. Even with her limited knowledge of the military, she recognized the famed SR71 Blackbird as they approached in the car. The Blackbird was a result of the cold war and the need for the U.S. to have a faster spy plane, after an earlier model was shot down over the Soviet Union. The SR71's shape was unmistakable. Most U.S. citizens had seen several pictures of it over the years.

"Um, didn't I read that these planes were officially decommissioned not too long ago?"

Dyson smiled. "Well, you may have read that."

He opened the back lift gate of the SUV and pulled out a pressurized pilot suit, in her size.

"I have to wear that?" Kathryn asked, surprised.

"I'm afraid so. The good news is that this plane is very fast and the flight will not be long. The bad news is that you will be traveling above the speed of sound, and you will need this suit for protection."

"Okay, this is ridiculous. Who the hell wants me back so fast that I need to wear protection *inside* the plane?"

Dyson shook his head helplessly. "I'm afraid I don't know, ma'am."

"Fine!" She removed her parka and flung it into the car. Next, she removed her boots, put a hand on Dyson's shoulder for balance, and slid a leg into the suit.

31

EVERYONE WAS STANDING when President Carr entered the underground conference room at JAX, twelve hours later. Vice President Edward Bailey followed him in. Bailey's stockiness, at five foot eight inches, stood out in contrast to Carr's taller slender frame. Both were in their mid-fifties, but while Carr had a long established political career, Bailey's spanned less than half of Carr's.

Carr walked to the head of the table, and Bailey stood to his right. "Gentlemen, please have a seat." He remained standing and continued. "Thank you for getting here quickly. I have just gotten off a call with several heads of state: Russia, China, Britain, and several others. I have informed them of some of our developments here, and I'm sure you can imagine that they were all rather surprised. I will say, however, that I have not provided all of the details yet as we are obviously still trying to piece things together ourselves. I will also tell you that the United Nations is putting together a team of their top people, and plan to have them here within a couple days. What this means is this situation is about to get very political and very messy."

"Secretary Miller has briefed me on the latest developments which we are all here to discuss. You might also be curious why it took us twelve hours to convene. The reason is that we have added a couple people to the invite. The first is Mr. Lawrence." Carr motioned to the man sitting across from Langford. "Mr. Lawrence heads the research department of the Department of Energy. He is fully up to speed." Carr glanced at his watch. "The second person has just arrived and is being escorted to our room. As soon as we have everyone here, I would like to do a formal round of introductions so everyone knows who is who. I would also-"

Carr was suddenly interrupted by the conference room door opening and one of the guards ushering in Kathryn Lokke, who looked disheveled to put it mildly. She walked into a room and looked around, surprised at the large attendance. "Ah, Ms. Lokke," Carr greeted her. "Please do come in." Mason got up and offered her his seat. "Let me first apologize for the urgency involved in getting you here. I know you have had a very rough couple of days. Do you feel alright and can we get you anything?"

Kathryn was exhausted and not happy about being thrown into what appeared to be some kind of national security meeting with very little sleep in the last forty-eight hours. She was also now starving, had a growing headache, and had the displeasure of sitting next to Stevas, a man that she had come to loathe.

"No thank you, I'm fine." Kathryn replied.

Carr nodded sympathetically. "I know you have just returned from a terrible ordeal. I am very sorry to put you on the spot here, but judging from what has been relayed to me about you and your team, I think you will agree that time is of the essence."

Kathryn was reserved. "I would."

"Unfortunately, most of the men in this room are not up to date on our last meeting or what has transpired since then. Do you feel you have the energy to give us a detailed summary?"

"Gladly." Kathryn replied, and slowly stood back up.

President Carr quickly went around the table introducing Langford, Clay, Caesare, and Borger from Naval Investigations. He also introduced doctors Harding and Wong, as well as Lawrence from The Energy Department. The rest of the men - Miller, Stevas, Mason, Bullman, and Bishop - she had met before at the White House.

Kathryn looked around the room and exhaled. She had had a long time to think on her way back. People that she knew and respected died because of game playing between her and others in this room. That was why she had barely slept in two days. She could not stop thinking about them, and their families. Had any of these men lost any sleep over them?

She lowered her head and took a deep breath. "I'm Kathryn Lokke, and I am the Director of the United States Geological Survey. Late last evening, seven of my colleagues died during a sudden earthquake along the top of the Ronne Ice Shelf in Antarctica. We were assessing the aftermath of an earlier quake, which runs the length of the shelf and threatens to dislodge a giant glacier. If this glacier breaks from the shelf and falls into the ocean, there is little doubt that it would create a tsunami like we have never seen. It would likely wipe out most life along both sides of the Atlantic seaboard."

Clay and Caesare looked at each other quietly.

Kathryn looked sternly at the men on Stevas' side of the table. "The reason that my team was on the shelf is because when I presented this information to some of you at the White House, you ignored my warning, preferring to portray me as non-credible. Well, now we are in far more danger, and frankly I don't give a damn what you think of me." Now Carr's team looked at each other. "The next quake came much sooner that even I had feared, and was much worse. Not only have good people died, but the time we have left to deal with this is greatly shortened. Let me put it in a way many of you will understand," she said, sarcastically, "we are now staring down the barrel of a gun." She looked around the room and stopped on Stevas, giving him an icy glare. "I don't care what you do to me. I don't care what you do to my reputation, and I don't care what you do to my career. Fire me if you want. Arrest me. Do whatever you like, but I am not going to cower to politicians who would rather be *jackasses* than to do the right thing!" She finally took her eyes off Stevas and looked at the door. "You can find someone else to be your puppet! But when this nightmare happens, I'm going to tell anyone that will listen that some of you simply didn't give a shit!"

Kathryn pushed her chair out of the way and walked toward the door. She yanked it open and stepped through when she heard "STOP!" She turned around to see Carr standing again at the head of the table.

"Okay," he said. "Okay. We deserved that. You're

right, we didn't listen. And I am truly sorry for your colleagues. But we're listening *now*." Carr gestured to her chair. "Please." He gestured again. "Please stay."

Kathryn stood in the doorway, wondering if she were in shock. Partly for realizing what she had just said to the President of the United States, and partly for hearing him actually apologize. When was the last time that happened? She was so angry. She wanted to leave. But if she was right about the Ronne, then they had very little time. She could not just walk away. She had to do something. She tried to get a handle on her emotions and to calm her breathing. Hate was not going to help anything. She let the door close slowly behind her and walked back to her chair.

Carr nodded his thanks and then sat down. Kathryn sighed and remained standing again. "If the shelf itself collapsed," she started, "it would be a small issue. Ice breaks off all the time and ice floats. The glacier, however, is very large. It's one of the largest solid land masses in the Antarctic. If that detaches from the ice which holds it in place and collapses, it goes straight down. And when it does, it will displace an enormous amount of water and energy. We know that these things have happened in the distant past, and we know that they have been absolutely devastating."

Clay raised his hand.

"Yes?" she asked.

"Any ideas on what is causing this?"

Kathryn took a deep breath. "Some will tell you that it is part of the larger Global Warming trend. The ice is melting at both poles. With the Ronne Shelf being so large, the underlying ice floating on the ocean surface is melting away, losing strength and the ability to hold the glacier in place." She straightened up and put her hands on her hips. "However, I think it's something different. My belief is that while the ice is indeed melting, it is not happening as quickly as others claim, and instead the actual volume of water is decreasing which is what is exerting pressure and causing the shelf to separate."

"What do you mean the 'water volume is decreasing'?" asked Miller.

She shrugged. "To put it simply, there is less water under the ice than there used to be."

"And what happened to the water?" he asked.

"That I don't know. But I believe it is a global phenomenon. I have put forth a scientific paper with my calculations, however, in all honesty, no one believes me."

"So," said President Carr, "what should we do?"

Kathryn leaned forward, putting her hands on the table, and looked up from her tussled hair. "We blow it up."

More looks were exchanged around the table. "We blow what up?" asked the Vice President.

"We blow up the shelf, preemptively." She walked over to a large whiteboard on the wall. Picking up a pen, she drew a rough horseshoe shape of the ice shelf. She then added a large oval to the inside ridge where the glacier was located. "Here is the glacier. And this line," she drew a squiggly line around the inside, "is where the crack is, created by the earthquake, also called an ice quake." She switched colors and drew another line further out from the crack. "If we can intentionally break the shelf closer to the water, we should be able to alleviate enough pressure and weight currently pulling against the glacier."

The room was silent, with all eyes on her drawing. "And how much would we have to *blow up*?" Carr asked.

Kathryn shook her head as she thought it over. "I don't know. We would have to run some computer simulations. I would guess at least fifty miles worth."

"Has anything like this been done before?" Miller asked.

"No," she replied. "Not by a long shot."

"And how long would it take to set this up?" Carr followed.

"I don't know," she said, with an inquisitive look at Carr. "It depends on what kind of resources we are given."

"Fair enough." He looked around the room. "Okay, thank you, Ms. Lokke. I would like to ask that you stay on base as we all figure this out."

"Fine." She nodded. "But what happens to my team?"

Miller leaned forward. "At the moment, they should be quite comfortable on base in the Falklands. I think we would all agree that we need to keep things quiet until we figure out exactly what our game plan is. Unfortunately, bringing your team back too soon could severely compromise things. Ms. Lokke, is there information or data to be compiled from your expedition?"

"Yes. A lot of data."

Miller looked at the President. "I suggest keeping them where they are and giving them an interim project. Compiling their data seems logical and then Ms. Lokke can bring them into the next phase as needed."

Carr looked at Kathryn. "Any objections, Ms. Lokke?"

"No. As long as they are safe."

"They should have access to anything they need," Miller said. "Of course, you do understand that we will need to apply some level of lockdown when it comes to communications. For example, to family and friends."

"I understand." She replied. "But I want to be honest with them. They deserve that. They're responsible adults. After what we just went through, they can appreciate the danger and risk involved with how this is handled."

"Fine." Carr nodded. "Let's just make sure that we're in agreement with what you communicate to them. In the meantime, you deserve some rest. We have accommodations arranged for you, and the sergeant outside will provide anything you need. Including a good meal, which I'm guessing is probably long overdue."

Kathryn adjusted her shirt and brushed some hair behind her ear. "It is."

Clay noticed that Lokke seemed to visibly relax. She also suddenly looked very tired.

As she walked toward the door, everyone in the room stood up.

"Thank you," was all she said before opening the door and stepping through.

They remained standing quietly as the door clicked shut. President Carr sighed and leaned forward onto the table. "I haven't been dressed down like that in a long time." Some of the men let a small grin slip out. The President motioned to the others and sat back down. "As you were."

As everyone sat back down, Caesare leaned toward Clay. "I like her," he whispered.

"So do I."

"Thoughts?" asked the President.

Langford cleared his throat. "Well, I think we may know where all of her water has disappeared to."

Carr raised his eyebrows and frowned. "Indeed." He leaned slightly back in his chair. "Let's hear from our science experts. Mr. Borger?"

"Yes, sir?"

"So, tell us, is this in fact some kind of portal?"

"I believe so." He looked across the table to Harding. "From everything we can measure, the direction of water flow is one way, into the ring. What happens to it from there, we don't know, but the most logical conclusion is off planet."

"Mr. Harding? Do you concur?"

Harding looked at the President. "Yes, sir."

Bill Mason, Carr's Chief of Staff, who had been noticeably silent throughout, spoke up. "We're going to have to stop the water flow one way or another."

"I agree," Stevas quickly added.

There were several nods around the room.

"So what happens if we destroy this thing?" Carr asked. "Is there any danger of collateral damage here?"

Doctor Lawrence, from the Department of Energy, shook his head and adjusted his glasses. "Not that we can see. If we destroy the ring or damage it enough, we shut it down."

Borger looked at Lawrence and then gave a worried glance to Clay. "Um…how exactly do we know that?"

Lawrence looked condescendingly at Borger. "Energy is our business, son." He turned back to Carr. "Mr. President, we've already run several scenarios based on the data. There does not appear to be energy emanating outward, which means the system, whatever it is, is self-contained. Furthermore, the depth provides a heavy blanket of protection through oceanic pressure, which means that even should the ring break apart the density and weight of the sea water around it would contain any explosive action. In fact, given the inward direction of the water flow, any major damage would more likely be inward than outward. We've looked at this from all angles."

Clay looked back at Borger. He wondered if these were the 'experts' that Stevas referred to before.

Langford spoke up. "It sounds like we're making decisions on some pretty large assumptions here."

Lawrence glared at Langford. His large frame and posture indicated that intimidation seemed to be a specialty. "Our assumptions are based on *your* data. Unless your data is bad, we are confident in our findings. Are you saying that you have given us bad data?"

Langford took the insult in stride, but did not look away. "Given the holes in what we have had time to find out, our data is as sound as we're going to get."

Lawrence frowned and looked back at the President.

"If we don't destroy the ring," Miller said, "then we risk a glacial collapse that creates a tsunami capable of destroying everything and everyone within driving distance of the Atlantic Ocean. And if we do destroy the ring, we risk a war with an enemy that we know nothing about, how many they number, or where they are."

"He said there were 1,200 in their settlement." Clay reminded them.

"That's right," said Miller, "but we obviously can't take that as gospel now, can we?"

The President sighed. "We need more options. The two we have are not good."

"There's always diplomacy," replied Clay.

Carr thought about it and nodded. "Talk them out of it?"

Clay shrugged. "Maybe. We still don't know why they're after the water. I think we should find out as much as we can before deciding what options we have."

"I agree," said Carr.

Miller looked at him. "I trust you found Keister."

Clay nodded. "Yes, sir."

"Then go talk to him again."

Stevas held up a hand. "Before we go in there waving a white flag and trying to negotiate, I think we might want to consider another possibility...that they say *no*." He shrugged. "Say whatever they are doing, they simply don't stop, can't stop, or refuse to. Then what? If it comes to us having to destroy that thing, then we need to be ready."

"You're suggesting the subs?" asked the President.

"Yes. We send out the Tridents." He looked around the room. "We get our subs either in place, or damn close. If nothing else, it shows them we are serious."

Clay thought about his meeting with Stevas at the White House. Stevas had wanted to destroy the ring, before they even knew what it was. Now that they did know, he was even more eager.

"Admiral Bishop?" Carr said, turning to the Naval Chief. "You said previously that we had a couple dozen Trident submarines that could be in the Caribbean within twenty four hours. Is that correct?"

Bishop folded his hands on the table when he

answered. "Yes, sir. Of course, the element of surprise will be lost, but we would be in position to act swiftly."

"And it will give us more leverage," added Stevas.

"Perhaps. Or, we incite something even worse." Carr thought it over. What were the risks of actually starting an incident by parking some nuclear submarines nearby? If they did need to destroy the ring, what would be the catalyst? Waiting for something else to happen first in the Antarctic would be like closing the barn doors after the animals had fled. They could not wait until a tsunami was already headed north.

President Carr turned back to Bishop. "Admiral, launch the Tridents. But I want them at a safe distance. As far from the ring as we can be, but still able to act quickly, if needed."

Bishop nodded. "Yes sir."

Carr tapped the table with this finger for emphasis. "And, NO action or engagement without my orders! Understood?"

"Yes, sir."

"Alright, Mr. Clay," he said. "Go have another chat with our friend."

*****

Keister and Clay approached the holding cell underground. With every step, their shoes clicked on the clean floor and echoed down the hallway. As they approached the two armed marines outside the room, Clay looked at their M16 assault rifles and noticed their safeties were off. He glanced at the gear they wore, including their armor, boots, and helmet types. It was one of the habits from his time spent in the Navy SEALs.

The first guard looked them over and turned to his left. He withdrew a security card with this left hand and swiped it through a small vertical slot. The light blinked green and the lock on the inside of the door clicked loudly. The guard did not open the door. Instead, he stepped clear, put his second hand back on the rifle, and watched Keister and Clay carefully.

Keister grabbed the door handle and twisted. The thick metal door swung inward and they both stepped through. Palin was on a small portable cot near the corner. He lay on his side with his back to them, un-cuffed. Clay noted a small food table with a food tray and the remains of his dinner. Interestingly, everything looked eaten except the meat and cheese, which was moved to the side of the tray.

Palin slowly turned over and looked at them. Upon seeing Clay, he turned and sat up on the bed, then stood and walked to his only chair. He planted himself smoothly, waiting as they both pulled their chairs over to him. He did not look tired to Clay, but he did need a shave.

Clay sat down in front of him and wasted no time. "Where are you from?"

"I have told you-"

"No," Clay interrupted. "*Where* are you from?"

Palin nodded. He took a deep breath. "Our sun…is a neighboring star to your own. It is called Lalande. Your planet is the third in your solar system, ours is the second." He stopped but then added. "You cannot see it yet with your technology."

Clay leaned forward. "And why are you here?"

Palin did not answer.

"You're not visiting," Clay said.

Palin shook his head. "No."

"So why are you here?"

Palin furrowed his brow. "You wish to know whether we intend to harm you."

Clay nodded.

Palin sighed. "You are a lucky race. Luckier than you know." He tilted his head and asked Clay a question. "Do you know how planets are formed?"

Clay shook his head.

"They are formed by the slow accumulation of dust-like matter in a solar system, very large amounts of matter. Some of that matter is ice, which then turns to water as the planet forms and begins to warm."

Clay remained quiet. He wondered where this was going.

"You see, a planet with water is not rare. But a planet almost entirely covered with water, like yours, is."

"Our amount of water is rare?"

"Yes," Palin said, "very rare."

Clay gave him a hard look. "Why are you taking our water?"

Palin was taken aback. After a long pause, he continued, "You have no idea how fortunate you are. So much water provides such incredible resilience for life. And you take it for granted. You have so much, that you pollute on an unimaginable scale with barely a second thought." He shook his head in pity. "Your pollution runs much deeper than you know. Much deeper than you will understand for a long time." He took another deep breath. "A level of pollution that we could not afford."

Clay looked at Keister, who continued to scribble notes. "What does that mean?"

"Our planet developed with water as well, but far less. It is precious, the single most important element for all forms of evolution."

"And yet you had enough to evolve too."

Palin shrugged. "Until now."

"What does that mean?"

Palin looked at Clay. "Our planet is dying. We have suffered a cataclysmic event which has vaporized most of our only two oceans. We have had to turn underground for what little water is left. But our ecosystem is near extinction, as are we. The portal that you have seen may be our last technological achievement. We have exhausted many of our remaining resources to build it, and to come here."

"Are you telling me that you're trying to save your planet?" Clay asked.

"We are trying to save our planet *and* our race."

Clay leaned back in his chair. Keister told him that one of the first rules was to not appear surprised at anything. Clay was having a very difficult time appearing calm, when almost every time Palin spoke, he dropped a bomb. They were not here to destroy us. They were here to save themselves as part of some last ditch effort. Of course, it was possible he was lying, but so far, everything seemed to fit. All he could think about was Stevas almost foaming at the mouth to blow them up.

"So," he said, "you're just taking our water...and that doesn't strike you as *problematic*."

Palin shook his head. "You have more than you need. More than you will ever need. Besides, your polar ice caps are now melting to compensate."

"Don't be so sure," Clay replied. This time, Palin looked confused. "You're taking too much water, too fast. And if you're relying on the melting of our caps to compensate, then we are all in serious trouble." Not surprisingly, Palin was not following. Clay continued. "We have had several quakes in our south pole which has destabilized large areas of an ice shelf. The water level has dropped enough to cause a shift in pressure, which is about to result in a tsunami that will kill millions of people."

Palin considered what he said. He thought about it for a long time before answering. "We're not stealing your water."

Clay smirked. "Then what do you call it?"

Palin gave him an almost puzzled look. "If you have more than enough, should you not give it?"

Clay opened his eyes wide with disbelief. "Not at the cost of millions of lives."

"This tsunami will not kill everyone. Most will survive,

will they not?"

"Yes but-"

"Is it not better to save both races than let one perish?" Palin asked.

Clay shook his head incredulously. "This is not a business transaction."

"History, for both of our worlds, is filled with millions and millions of meaningless deaths. Wars over lands or resources that later meant nothing. The worst, over religious beliefs, which were nothing more than emotional ideas being systematically forced onto others. Humans, both of us, have given much less thought and value to life than my people are doing now."

Palin's reference to humans struck Clay oddly. "You said humans, as in both of us. I still don't understand. How can you be human yet from a different planet?"

Palin sighed. "Do you remember when I told you about the cycles within carbon?"

"Yes."

"The process of evolution is not random. Everything is determined by certain limits or preferences, and evolution is no different. Carbon, like all elements, has its own characteristics, which means that it will react uniquely to a force placed upon it. When the force is evolution, carbon has tendencies, call them 'paths of least resistance'. This means that, over time, those tendencies within carbon will lean toward certain types of biological structures and designs which prove practical. Again, things like hands and feet, eyes and ears, brains, muscles, and fingers, are all practical assets to furthering the process. This is one reason we look alike."

"Just one reason?" Clay asked.

Palin smiled. "Yes. The second reason, and perhaps the most important, is where the elements came from that created us, our solar systems, our planets, even our soil and air. These elements are all released when a star explodes, resulting in the end of the fusion process within that star. My point is that when the star explodes, it scatters these elements over a great distance, including the same amino acids. You see, the reason we are so similar is because it was a giant explosion that fertilized both of our solar systems with the same elements. We were created by the same atomic building blocks. This, along with carbon's natural tendencies during evolution, is why we are so very similar." Palin leaned forward in his chair. "Mr. Clay, we are your evolutionary *brothers and sisters*."

Clay's mouth suddenly fell open, and Keister dropped his notebook. They were both speechless.

"You see," Palin continued, "letting one of us perish is like allowing your only true relative in the universe to disappear."

32

CLAY SAT STARING out of the window as the Gulfstream III neared Andrews Air Force Base. It was late afternoon and the sun was casting an eastern shadow across the Virginia landscape. As the aircraft banked right, Clay could see Washington D.C. in the distance. His favorite landmark from the air, the Washington Monument, was easy to see. Even though few passengers did, Clay reached over and buckled his seatbelt as they began to descend. Gulfsteams were small and comfortable commercial jets used by the military, and passengers never bothered with most of the safety precautions. However, after having run training maneuvers through many different types, most SEALs were intimately familiar with all aspects of an aircraft. They knew where the strongest parts of the structure were, the weakest, which areas failed first during impact, and a host of other details. Most Special Forces graduates he knew were sticklers for safety, especially while riding in things over which they had no control.

Clay lay back against the headrest. *Chaotic* was the best word he could think of to describe the last several hours since he had spoken with Palin. When they returned to the conference room, things had changed drastically. The President and his cabinet were in private meetings for over three hours. When finished, Clay noticed that several high ranking Generals had joined them. Langford had already sent Caesare and Borger back to D.C. to continue analyzing the data. Both doctors were gone and only Lawrence, the man from the DOE, remained. Finally, after a short discussion, Langford sent him back too.

After landing, Clay had a car issued to him and headed west on Suitland Parkway. The sun was close to setting and the drive was slow, as everyone headed home in rush hour traffic. Crossing the bridge to South Capitol Street, the traffic lightened a little. At 395, it slowed again. He made his way over the 14th Street Bridge and pulled into the emptying parking lot of the Pentagon. He had barely landed when Caesare called and asked if he could swing by Borger's office before heading home. Clay walked briskly through an entrance and down a flight of stairs.

When he walked in, Caesare and Borger were both sitting in the middle of the room talking to each other.

"Hi, Clay!" Uncharacteristically, Borger jumped up from the chair and ushered Clay in. He motioned to a chair for Clay, while he shut the door behind him. "Thanks for coming."

Clay nodded and sat down heavily. "Everything okay?" Caesare asked.

Clay shrugged. "I guess it depends on your definition of okay." He ran his fingers through his hair. "Things got interesting when I got back upstairs."

"Yeah," Caesare said, "we got shipped out of there in a hurry. Must have been some conversation you had with ole' Palin."

"You could say that." He looked at Borger, who was examining the walls. "What's with him?"

"I don't know." Caesare said, looking back at him. "He just scanned the room for bugs. He wants to talk to us about something important, but wanted to wait for you."

Clay watched Borger curiously. After he was finished, he came back and sat in front of Clay and Caesare. "Okay, we're clean," he said, adjusting himself in the chair. He began immediately. "Look, I need to talk to you guys about something."

They both nodded.

"I think we have a problem, a very big problem." Clay could not remember seeing Borger this excited. "I think that guy Lawrence, in our meeting at JAX, is wrong. And I mean *really* wrong. When the President asked if there was any downside to destroying the ring and he said 'no', well, I think there is. You see, we know this ring is a portal, and if it is operating on the same fundamental theories as we believe it would operate-"

"We?" Clay interrupted.

Borger shook his head. "Not we as in *us*, we as in our physicists. Anyway, if it works the same way, which I believe it does, then the other end of that tunnel is literally bound to this end. They are both exactly the same size, they're turning at the same speed, and powered by the same energy…which means that space and time would see them as *one* gateway."

"So…" Caesare said, slowly, "if you destroyed one…"

"Then you would destroy them both!" Borger replied excitedly. "Why that guy would say the ring was self-contained makes no sense. How on earth could he believe that? Either he is seriously incompetent, or he is lying for some reason that makes no sense."

Caesare cleared his throat. "Well, I wouldn't rule out the incompetent part. After all, he does work for the government."

Clay squinted and looked at Caesare. "You work for the government."

Caesare raised his hands and shrugged. "Need I say more?"

Clay turned back to Borger. "So what happens if they destroy the ring, if they are bound to each other?"

"Well this is where it gets theoretical. But the physics involved are solid. And remember that the amount of energy involved here is pretty much unimaginable, given today's standards." Borger stopped and exhaled, trying to slow down. "Destroying these rings, with the energy involved, could be really bad."

Clay and Caesare both leaned forward. "How bad?"

Borger nodded, but spoke carefully. "Like really *really* bad, for both planets."

"Oh, boy," mumbled Caesare.

"This is serious!" cried Borger. "It's why I wanted to talk to you both right away."

Clay sat, thinking. "How sure are you? I mean, what kind of chances are we talking about?"

"I don't know." Borger said, shaking his head. He wheeled himself backward and tapped his keyboard, displaying a screen full of complex mathematical calculations. "Only a physicist could talk to you about the odds. I don't know what the exact numbers are, but they're real. In fact, it almost doesn't matter what the odds are."

"What do you mean?"

"Look, I'm a history buff. Remember the atomic bomb we dropped on Hiroshima? Did you know that the physicists who created it, led by Robert Oppenheimer, actually calculated and acknowledged that there was a *one in three million* chance that the fission process might not stop when it was supposed to and could go on to melt down the entire Earth?"

"Is that true?" Clay asked.

"Yes, it is." Borger scooted his chair back to Clay and Caesare. "My point is, they *knew* there was a one in three million chance of destroying the entire planet, and they tested it anyway! Obviously, that didn't happen, but they still took the chance. They put everyone's life on the line on the presumption that they were right." He looked back at the screen. "I don't know what the odds are with destroying those rings, but I can tell you they are a whole hell of a lot lower than that! This time I would guess the odds are somewhere around one in five. And this time, it's possible that we could destroy two planets!"

"Jesus Christ," Caesare said, putting his hands over his face. "This just gets better and better."

"You don't know the half of it," Clay said.

Caesare dropped his hands and looked forlornly at Clay. "What?"

Clay sighed and proceeded to tell them about his conversation with Palin. When he was done, they both had the same reaction as he and Keister had. He waited for them to digest it before continuing. "And it gets worse. Langford was in on those closed-door meetings afterwards. When he came out, he pulled me aside and explained that they had been discussing two things. First and foremost were the details of the submarine attack, which we all know about. The rest of the meeting however, was about Plan B."

"Plan B?" Borger asked.

Caesare frowned. "There is always a Plan B. The backup plan. In fact, there is probably a backup plan to the backup plan. Let me guess. Stevas?"

Clay nodded. "Stevas is no dummy. He's an ass and a war monger, but he is not stupid. He knows that there must be a backup plan, and that's what they were working out."

Caesare studied Clay. "So do you know what this backup plan is?"

"Langford told me that if the sub attack fails, then they plan to nuke it."

"Jesus." Caesare moaned and put his hand over his face again. "Those subs have all the nukes they could need."

"No." Clay shook his head. "That's not how they plan to do it. That was the original idea, but they have another angle. They plan to send it in...on the back of one of those dolphins."

"The talking dolphins?" Borger asked.

"Yes," Clay answered. "Apparently, Stevas is now a believer. They know where the ring is, they've been there before, and if Palin's people are looking at the subs, they probably aren't going to be looking too closely at the fish swimming in and out." Clay looked back and forth at them. "Remote detonation."

The room was silent. No one spoke.

"And that's not all." Clay finally said.

Caesare moaned again. "For the love of God!"

Clay spoke deliberately. "Langford wants us to do it."

They both looked confused. "He wants us to do what?"

"He wants us to steal the dolphins and the equipment."

33

KATHRYN LEANED HER seat back and tried to get comfortable as they pulled away from the gate. This plane was large and comfortable compared to the last two she had been on. It was amazing what a little heat and lack of a pressurized flight suit could do to improve someone's experience. She felt like a new person after being fed and getting a few undisturbed hours of sleep.

She closed her eyes and thought about what lay ahead of her, the flight back to the Falklands, the explanation to her team, and a frantic attempt to prevent a catastrophe. The long flight was the least of her worries. If anything, it was a blessing, giving her time to figure out how to tell her team that some of them had to go back.

She thought back to the meeting with the President and his cabinet. At least they listened to her this time, although it may have had something to do with her essentially telling them all to go to hell. But it also got a commitment from the President to give her whatever resources she needed, so maybe it was not all bad. In addition to the money, he ordered his Chief of Staff Mason to make available whoever Kathryn needed, with no exceptions. Her first order of business was to contact a number of international experts that she would need in addition to her own team. The second priority was to locate some of the best demolition teams in the country. Something Mason and his staff were working on. Next, was to procure the supplies needed. And finally, they had to do it all quietly. *Yes*, she thought, *she had a lot to work through*. A long flight was just what she needed.

She opened a backpack and retrieved a laptop computer provided by one of the administrative assistants at JAX. She placed it on the table in front of her and turned it on. As she leaned her seat forward again, the door behind her opened, and a steward approached with a phone in his hand.

"Ms. Lokke?" he asked.

"Yes?"

He handed her the phone. "You have a call."

She gave him a surprised look and glanced through the window at the dark tarmac passing under them. "Now?"

He simply nodded and left.

She held the phone to her ear. "Hello?"

"Is this Ms. Lokke?"

"Speaking."

"Ms. Lokke, my name is John Clay. I don't know if you remember me, but we met this morning in the conference room."

"I remember you," she replied. "Weren't you the one that asked me the causality question?"

She could not hear Clay smile on the other end. "Yes, I did. You have a very good memory. Listen, Ms. Lokke, I know this may not be an ideal time, but I have something important to ask you."

"Okay."

"This is going to sound like a strange question," Clay said, "but could other outside factors contribute to a collapse of the ice shelf?"

She frowned. "What kind of outside factors?"

"Say, for example, vibrations or shock waves?"

Kathryn thought for a moment. "I suppose it would have to depend on what kind of shock waves and how strong they were."

"Well, as you probably know, the government sometimes conducts underwater detonations of weapons for testing purposes," Clay said.

"Shock waves or vibrations do travel well underwater, but I suspect those kinds of detonations would be too small to have much of an effect. The ice shelf is very far away. Unless, of course, one of your tests were carried out very close to it."

"I see," said Clay. "And what if the magnitude were much greater, say a nuclear detonation?"

Kathryn's eyes opened wide. "Are you telling me that you have a nuclear test planned? Where?!"

"The mid-Atlantic," answered Clay.

"Yes! That would be very dangerous. It's a straight shot down the Atlantic, directly to the Ronne!"

"I was afraid of that."

"Mr. Clay, listen to me." Kathryn pressed the phone to her ear, as the plane's engines grew louder in preparation for takeoff. "If you guys are planning a nuclear test in the Atlantic, you must stop immediately! Do you understand?"

"Yes, ma'am. I do."

Clay thanked Kathryn and ended the call. He was quiet for a long moment before turning to Caesare and Borger, who were listening, "So...how bad do you guys want your pensions?"

Caesare shrugged. "Well, if there ends up being no place to spend it..."

They both looked at Borger, who shook his head. "Don't look at me, I'm a contractor."

Clay walked forward and sat down in front of them. He sat, thinking, then turned to Borger. "Will, do you have any hacking skills?"

He nodded. "In my last job, I was a White Hat."

"What's a White Hat?" Caesare asked.

"People that hack computers for nefarious purposes are called Black Hats." He grinned. "White Hats are the guys who catch them."

34

THE SMALL AIRFIELD in Homerville, Georgia looked like something out of an old Hollywood movie. The runway looked nearly abandoned and barely usable. A row of two dozen hangars lined the west side of the field near the entrance, most of which were empty collecting dust and leaves. Not far away stood what was left of a small café, boarded up with a crooked sign hanging precariously from the roof that read "Dolly's Café".

Standing alone, near the south end of the field, was a small building. It was the only sign of life left from what appeared to be a popular stop-through decades before. Its sign was still intact and read "Homerville Rotorheads". It just grazed Steve Caesare's head when he walked under it. Caesare turned the doorknob, noting the peeling paint, and heard the familiar jingle of a bell hitting the other side of the door as it swung open. He looked around the room and came back to the small desk in the middle. Loaded with papers, it was the only thing that looked to be recently used.

"One sec!" someone called from the back.

Caesare nodded and turned to a small rack on the wall. He picked out one of the brochures on chartering. Most of the others looked about as old as Dolly's Café.

An old man appeared through the doorway behind the desk. He was dressed in an old flannel shirt and blue jeans. His hair was completely white, matching his mustache, and combed neatly. "You must be the fella that called earlier," he said. "Steve, right?"

"Yes, sir." Caesare replied, reaching out to shake his hand.

"My name's Charlie." His chair squeaked loudly when he sat down. "So what do you want to rent my helicopter for?"

"I work for a movie production company and we're scouting the area for locations," Caesare answered.

Charlie wrinkled his nose and looked out through the window. "What kind of movie you making out here?"

"Uh, an action movie. Military type. I'm one of the consultants."

"I never really cared for those action flicks. Two hours of someone shooting everything in sight." Charlie said. "You military?"

Caesare nodded. "I'm retired."

Charlie looked him over. "You know how to fly a helicopter?"

"Yes, sir."

"Got a license?"

"Yes, sir." Caesare answered. He handed Charlie a picture of him standing in front of a large Seahawk helicopter with his helmet tucked under his arm.

Charlie looked at the photo and then handed it back. "Eh, you're fine." He stood up and walked around the desk. "Let me show her to you."

As Caesare followed him back out the front door, he asked, "How long you been here, Charlie?"

Charlie chuckled. "Hell, I don't think I can count that high anymore. Feels like forever." He led him around the corner of the building. "Let's see, I opened this place up in '64, so I guess we're well over fifty years now. Wife died nine years ago, and I just ain't got all that much else to do. And the rent's cheap." He laughed at his own joke and led Caesare around a small group of trees. When they rounded the trees, Caesare's smile disappeared.

Charlie nodded to the small chopper on an old, cracked concrete pad. "Only one I got that's worth a damn."

Caesare stood looking at it. It was a small two-seater, but what he was not expecting was the long bar extending out almost ten feet beneath the skids. "A crop duster?"

*****

Clay walked calmly down the hall approaching Palin's interrogation room. He glanced at his watch as he neared the door. He nodded at the first guard, who looked him over. "No Keister?" the guard asked.

Clay shook his head. "Just me tonight."

The guard grunted and reached for his access card. As he turned toward the door, Clay was instantly on him. In one move, he wrapped his left hand around the guard's mouth and kicked his supporting foot out from under him, pulling him off balance. In a panic, the guard fired several rounds into the ceiling as he fell back against Clay, unable to breathe or get his footing. In the same movement, using his right hand, Clay pulled a stun gun from behind him and fired two electrified prongs into the right leg of the second guard. The second guard screamed in pain, dropped his rifle and fell to the ground. The ten thousand volts ravaged his muscular system, causing him to convulse wildly. The first guard dropped his gun and tried desperately to right himself and regain his balance, but Clay kept taking steps backward, knowing the human body's instinctual reaction is to avoid falling as its first priority. The guard, still struggling and reaching behind him for something to grab, inhaled the mixture soaked into the cloth glove on Clay's left hand. The chloroform was already beginning to confuse his senses.

Clay continued moving backward to keep the guard stumbling, but then made a quick turn in the hallway and began walking backward toward the second guard. The guard on the floor was trying desperately to fight the seizures and reach his gun with his shaking hands. Just as he got close, Clay dropped the larger, sagging guard on top of him and kicked the rifle out of reach. The second guard, now beneath the first, tried to get free, but instantly felt Clay's cloth glove over his own mouth. Less than a minute later, they were both unconscious.

Clay pulled out some handcuffs and rags. He quickly bound and gagged both men. Stepping over the first guard, Clay yanked the access card free. He looked up and down the long quiet hallway, swiped the card, and opened the door.

Clay stepped into the room and paused. Looking up at the cameras, he hoped Borger had done his thing with the video feed. Not hearing any alarms, he moved across the room to Palin, who was already sitting up after hearing the disturbance outside.

Clay removed a pair of cutters from his pocket and looked Palin over, but he was not bound. "We have to go."

Palin looked concerned. "What is wrong?"

"Your people and the ring are in danger." Clay said, pulling Palin to his feet. "Are you injured?"

"No," Palin said. "What do you mean 'in danger'?"

"My government is going to launch a submarine strike to destroy the ring."

Palin's face looked surprisingly calm. "It's okay."

"What?"

"It's okay," Palin repeated, "we have anticipated this."

Clay shook his head. "Well, if it doesn't work, they are going to strap a nuclear weapon to a dolphin and send it in that way. Have you anticipated that?"

Palin's eyes opened wide. "No."

"I didn't think so." Clay looked at his watch again. "And, by the way, when that bomb goes off, if we're even still here, the shock wave may be strong enough to reach the South Pole and trigger the tsunami all by itself."

"I must get back!" Palin had a look of panic in his eyes.

"You don't say," Clay said sarcastically. "We have to get out of here. Can you move?"

"Yes!" Palin was suddenly eager.

"Can you *run*?" Clay asked.

"I can!"

"Good." Clay grabbed his shoulder and started moving for the door. He suddenly stopped as the door opened from the other side. Slowly the barrel of a gun crept in, and was pointed at them. The deadly face of a marine appeared behind it.

Clay did not move. He watched the marine take a single step into the room. Both men stood frozen, staring at each other.

The marine spoke. "Clay."

Clay kept his eyes on him. "Munn."

Munn lowered his rifle and looked slowly around the room, and then to Palin. "Interesting timing," he smirked. "Almost everyone is on the other side of the base getting ready for some big UN delegation due to land any minute."

"No kidding," Clay replied.

Munn looked behind him at the two guards on the floor. "Are they dead?"

Clay shook his head. "No. But the one on the bottom is probably going to limp for a while."

Munn looked back down at the guard and shrugged. "He's an ass anyway."

Someone behind Munn passed something forward. Munn grabbed it and tossed it into the room. It was a large duffle bag. He looked at Clay. "It won't be long before these two are found. You'd better hurry."

Clay nodded and led Palin toward the bag.

Munn gave Clay a farewell gesture and disappeared. He suddenly popped his head back in. "By the way, we're now even." And he was gone.

Clay quickly unzipped the back and pulled out a dark jumpsuit for Palin. "Get this on, quickly!"

While Palin dressed, Clay withdrew an AR-15 and ammunition belt loaded with several high capacity magazines. He also clipped a holster onto his side and dropped a .40 caliber Springfield into it. No sooner had Palin zipped up the jumpsuit, when Clay grabbed him and shoved him through the door.

They ran back down the hall and up three flights of stairs. When they reached the first large set of doors, Clay tried the guard's access card. The slot buzzed and flashed a red light. He tried it again. The loud buzz sounded again. Clay turned around and looked up at the ceiling mounted camera.

Will Borger was watching Clay and Palin on his monitor. He quickly typed some keys on his keyboard, and the door behind Clay unlocked with a green light.

Clay put his hand on the handle and motioned Palin to back up.

In one motion, he jerked the door open and trained his rifle through the other side, finger near the trigger. The bright entryway was empty. They proceeded quietly, as Clay kept his muzzle trained on the steel door at the end of the hall. As they neared the end of the hall, Clay looked over his shoulder, checking for Palin.

At the steel door, Clay tried his card again. No dice. He waited for Borger. After ten seconds of silence, he began to grow concerned, but the electronic lock finally clicked. Clay slowly pushed the door open and looked outside. It looked empty. He closed his eyes and listened. Nothing. He grabbed Palin and broke into a run, headed for two vehicles on the far side of the open, graveled area. Palin ran quickly behind him as Clay swept his gun back and forth.

They made it halfway to the first vehicle, a small white Humvee, when the alarm went off. A screeching siren from the building behind them, along with a bright red rotating light, alerted nearly the entire base.

"Crap!" He looked at Palin. "Any chance you can teleport us out of here?"

"I need the brick."

"What brick?" Clay asked.

Palin made a small rectangle with his hands. "The small silver device you took on the ship."

Clay suddenly remembered the object. He looked around absently, trying to remember where he left it. "Damn it!" he said, when he thought of where it was. "I don't have it."

They watched as a searchlight from a tower in the distance pointed toward them. They could hear yelling coming from multiple locations and two pair of headlights crested a small hill.

Clay looked back to the building. "Plan B."

They ran back to the door, still ajar, then ran back

down the entryway. They reached the stairs and heard faint voices below. Clay knew there would be men responding from the lower levels. They were lucky if they had two minutes.

They ran up two flights of stairs and stopped at another door. Clay looked away and fired three rounds through the lock. With a hard thrust, he kicked the door open, and he and Palin burst out onto the roof.

It was a large roof. He could clearly see more headlights in the distance. Over a dozen men ran towards them on foot. Bullets suddenly flew overhead and hit the wall of the stairwell behind them.

"Get down!" Clay pushed Palin down onto the cold roof, and staying low, ran back to the stairs. He listened to the voices getting louder. They were coming fast. More bullets hit the outside wall. One made it through, scattering pieces of plaster and sheetrock all over the top stair. Clay looked around the dark roof, where Palin was lying quietly.

The pounding of footsteps grew louder up the stairs. Clay knelt down and closed the door with only the barrel of his gun visible, pointing downward. More bullets impacted the wall. He waited patiently until he saw lights approaching in the stairwell. He pointed his gun down to the corner where the stairwell made its last turn before ascending to the roof. The reflection of the lights grew brighter from around the corner. Finally, when the pounding grew loud enough and the lights reached full brightness, he knew they were close. He fired three shots into the wall on that last corner. The footsteps stopped instantly. The bright lights that were reflecting off the walls suddenly went out.

Clay knew they would take the last flight of stairs slowly now. Being shot at had that effect. Clay fired one more bullet into the wall and then backed up and let the door shut. Staying low, he ran back to Palin. "You okay?"

Palin nodded. "Yes. Although our situation does not

look good."

"I know, I know," agreed Clay. This is exactly where he did not want to be. He slowly slid down onto his belly and got into position, propping up onto his elbows with his gun pointed at the stairs. He was thankful for the raised edge around the roof, making it difficult to be seen from the ground, and for the men approaching the building. Clay leveled his eye with the rifle sights and locked in on the dark shape of the roof's exit door.

Finally, the door slowly started to open. Inside, it was pitch black, which made it hard to discern who or what was being used to open the door. When it reached a fully open position, Clay could see something move toward the bottom hinge, something to prop it open. Just as a muzzle began to poke out, Clay heard something. It was the sound of an engine.

Suddenly, the dark shape of a helicopter rose up and over the far corner of the building and swept over the roof. As it passed over the stairwell, a huge deluge of liquid was released from the skids, smashing through the opening and knocking the men inside backwards, slipping and tumbling back down the stairs.

The small helicopter banked hard to the right, as sparks flew off from bullets fired from the ground. Caesare quickly dipped back down and circled, slowing at the far edge for safety.

"Run!" Clay yelled, pulling Palin to his feet and pushing him forward. They ran low, as quickly as they could, to the waiting chopper floating just a few feet above the roofline. As they reached the edge, Clay pushed Palin into the small oval opening of the passenger's seat. There was no room for a third person. Bullets ricocheted again off the side of the helicopter, as marines covered in a slippery liquid came tumbling out of the stairwell. Clay looked at Caesare sitting in the pilot's seat. He gave a quick nod and then motioned over his shoulder. Caesare nodded back.

Caesare opened the engine wide and tilted away from

the building. In one motion, Clay turned and emptied the rest of his magazine just over the heads of the marines. He continued his turn, stepping onto the edge of the roof, dropping his rifle, and dove head first off the side of the building.

*****

Borger switched the view on his monitor to one of the security cameras at the airstrip. He started shutting down the sirens as quickly as he could, but men were already running out of the buildings. They headed for the other side of the base in armored vehicles. Several ran out onto the nearby tarmac where four UH-60 Black Hawk helicopters sat waiting. The pilots climbed in, quickly powering up the systems and starting the engines. The cockpits lit up as all the instruments came to life, and the rotors slowly began turning overhead. The pilots strapped themselves in and turned their computerized helmets on, waiting for the weapons system to sync with their digitized face plates.

"Uh oh," Borger said. He cut all of the lighting to the runway and tarmac, but it was too late. The cockpit navigation systems on the helicopters were now fully functional. They could fly with no outside lights or visibility at all. The rotors increased in speed as they neared the point of lift.

Suddenly, a bright blue wave of light passed over the buildings and across the tarmac. It passed the choppers and disappeared. The Black Hawk's lights and cockpit instruments went out, and the engines died leaving only the sound of the rotors spinning and winding back down. The pilots inside looked at each other, confused and tried to power back up. The aircrafts were all dead.

Borger's eyes widened. "What the hell was that?"

35

ALISON SHAW OPENED her apartment door and walked through, trying not to spill the large stack of mail in her hands before the door tried to close on her. She stepped out of the way just in time for it to sweep past, closing loudly behind her. She tossed the mail onto her kitchen counter and put the keys down next to it. She then dropped her large shoulder bag onto the carpet. She looked at the microwave clock and sighed.

She retrieved a wine glass from the cabinet and a bottle of chardonnay from the fridge. She poured herself a glass, and with a sigh, plopped down onto the couch. How, she thought, did she ever think things would slow down after IMIS was left to do its thing? She was busier now than she was before. Of course, then it was mostly prep work. Now it was execution. The project was more successful than she had dared dream. The system worked, real communication was established, and they were learning more than they ever expected. Over the last several days, things had really become exciting. Finding that Dirk and Sally could not only identify a number, but actually *count*, was a huge discovery. It opened the door for much deeper cognitive ability and abstract thinking. What she did not expect was where that would lead. Dirk and Sally had started asking questions.

No longer were they just asking how she was or what she was eating. Now, they were trying to form sentences and concepts that seemed even beyond the limits of IMIS. But, even with their existing vocabulary, the dolphins were asking Alison questions that she struggled to answer. It started with why humans wore clothes, which was hard enough. But it was when they asked *why people dirty ocean?*

that she really had trouble. They wanted to know why humans were polluting the oceans, or the world, for that matter. This not only showed a deeper awareness of the world around them, but the ability to understand the relationship between humans and their changing world. The dolphins also seemed curious why the deeper their question, the longer it took for the humans to answer them. Many earlier studies of the mammals suggested that they had cognitive abilities similar to very small children, which was clearly an enormous underestimation. This suggested to Alison that our human ability to even *test* the intelligence of other animals was more limited than we knew.

She took another sip of wine and leaned back, putting a foot up on the edge of her coffee table. She stared at a Wyland portrait hanging on the wall. What an incredible world it was, a wonderful world on so many levels. And, a world that she wanted to share with someone.

She suddenly frowned at that thought. She thought about her last two relationships. Both failed, and the last one bordered on abusive. She realized now that it was after that relationship that she had really thrown herself into work. It was her way to escape from a terrible time in her life. And she had come to love Dirk and Sally so much, it gave her an excuse to avoid the possibility of ending up in another bad relationship. She had been hiding for a long time, and now it had hardened her into someone she didn't like. Alison wiped a tear from her eye before it could fall. She didn't want to hide anymore.

Unexpectedly, Alison found herself thinking of John Clay. He was intelligent and interesting, and even had a sense of humor hiding in there somewhere. She wondered if she was going to see him again. She hoped she would. Who was she kidding? She probably wasn't even his type. He was worldly, experienced, and handsome.

Alison wondered where he was. She wondered what he was doing. Probably something fun, somewhere exciting, and with multiple women on his arm.

*****

John Clay clung to the bottom of the helicopter, desperately trying to hang on as Caesare maneuvered through the tree lines as close to the ground as possible to avoid radar. Jumping off the roof, Clay collided with the metal skids hard and felt his shoulder dislocate badly. He felt a searing pain in his left arm as he held on with everything he had. The constant slapping into treetops prevented him from getting a better hold, or swinging his leg up with Caesare's zigging and zagging in almost complete darkness.

Clay shifted to give his left arm a break, hanging more from the right side. He tried again to get his leg over the bar used for crop dusting, but it was covered with liquid insecticide and too slippery to get any kind of grip on. A large tree limb suddenly hit him in the chest and nearly knocked him off the rail. His right arm started to shake. He was not sure how much longer he could hold on. Clay knew that if he fell at this speed he would not survive.

Inside the cockpit, Caesare had no idea whether John had been able to grab hold in time. He could not see the right side of the skids and the darkness was not helping. Palin was grabbing the edge of the open door tightly. He could see no sign of Clay either. Caesare hoped he was there but had to assume he wasn't. He popped up over a group of tall trees and dove back down again. It was now up to him to get Palin home.

Almost thirty minutes later, Caesare spotted the clearing he was looking for. The glow lights on the ground gave enough light to confirm the location, but not enough to see the landing area in any detail. He came in low and circled the small clearing looking for anything out of the ordinary. Seeing nothing, he slowed their descent and came down in the center. With a slight pause just above the ground, he fell the last couple feet and bumped gently on the thick grass. He turned down the engine and looked at Palin.

"You okay?"

Palin was a little shaken but nodded back.

As the rotor slowed, Caesare jumped out with a nervous knot in his stomach. He bent down and looked under the frame of the helicopter. On the other side, he spotted a large shape lying horizontally. He quickly ran around the front, passing Palin who was stepping carefully down. Clay was on the ground, clutching his left shoulder and groaning.

"Clay!" Caesare yelled excitedly. "You crazy bastard. Are you okay?" Caesare rolled him onto his back and saw that Clay's left shoulder was much higher than his right. He gently felt the area, front and back. "It doesn't feel broken. Probably dislocated."

Clay nodded but did not speak.

"I'll set it for you," Caesare said.

"Wait, wait." Clay protested through clenched teeth. "Just give me a minute."

Palin arrived and, together, they sat him up.

Clay looked up at him. "Are you okay?"

Palin nodded. Together, he and Caesare helped Clay back down onto the cool grass.

"Ready?" Caesare reached under his shoulder.

Clay winced, but nodded. With a sudden motion, Caesare moved the joint, dropping it back into place. Clay let out a loud groan and rolled back onto his side. He laid there for a few long minutes, trying to regain his breath. "Did you have to hit every tree?!"

"Hey, you were the one who wanted to do this in the dark."

"That's true." Clay forced himself into a sitting position. He searched for his right pocket and noticed the pistol still in its holster. "How in the world did that not fall out?"

"See, it couldn't have been that bad" Caesare joked.

Clay found the pocket and ripped the Velcro open. He pulled out a small padded package, unrolling it until his disposable cell phone fell out. He turned it on and dialed a number.

A similar phone rang on Borger's desk. He answered immediately. "Clay?"

"Hey, Will." Clay gritted his teeth again as the other two helped him onto his feet. "How did we do?"

"Not too bad," said Borger, "you were gone before most of them showed up." He moved the phone to his other ear and reached for his mouse. "The darkness helped, and so did the big welcoming party on the other side of the base. Caesare did pop up high enough a few times to show up on radar, and they are coming after you. Fortunately, I was able to change the radar's algorithm, so it reported you moving in the wrong direction. They are currently pursuing you to the north, so that should give you some time."

"Okay, they coming in choppers?" Clay asked.

"Actually no, they are primarily on wheels."

"What? No aircraft?"

"No," answered Borger. "We got a little help on that front."

Clay did not know what that meant, and frankly didn't care. Whatever luck he had going for them he was not about to question. "Okay, we've got to head out. Anything else?"

"Yeah." Borger said, switching windows on his computer screen. He typed a couple of commands and looked again at the response. "It looks like our twelve Trident subs are approaching Bimini."

"Already? That was fast."

"Well maybe not," Borger said. "Clay...the orders were issued three days ago."

Clay thought for a moment. "But that would be before

the President ordered them out."

"Exactly. So either we were being played by everyone in that room, or-"

"Or someone *else* had already given the order," Clay finished.

"Or both."

Clay looked at Caesare, who was examining the tail of the small helicopter. Some of the film was peeling off from hitting the trees, revealing the chopper's real call letters. "Anything else?" Clay asked Borger.

"Not for the moment. We should get off the line."

"See ya later." Clay nodded and ended the call.

"What's up?" Caesare asked, pressing the torn film back into place.

"I'll explain on the way."

*****

Hank Stevas watched the large group of United Nations delegates and scientists flood the reception area from behind a glass wall. He shook his head. This was turning into a circus.

Bill Mason stood behind him on his cell phone. After a few minutes, he hung up. "That alarm was from our building on the west side. Palin is gone."

Stevas' eyes narrowed and his face grew red. "Clay!"

"Why would Clay take him?"

"Because he's a goddamn boy scout!" Stevas spat. "And now he knows everything." He shook his head angrily. "I *told* Langford not to tell him! I told him I would take care of it, but he wouldn't listen."

"So what do we do?" Mason asked.

Stevas looked back at the people continuing to pour into the larger room, smiling and shaking hands. "Clay knows exactly what we have planned, and even if he didn't, these people are going to turn this into a political nightmare. After a week of talking, they'll form a scientific

241

commission." The disgust almost dripped from his lips. "Democracy is such a poison."

"When Clay gets Palin home, we're sunk," said Mason.

Stevas looked at him. "If we're going to do something, we have to do it now. We're losing control." Stevas pulled out his phone and dialed a number. He spoke slowly. "This is Stevas. Do it."

There was a pause while someone on the other end spoke. "That's right. I am speaking with the full authority of the President."

He hung up. "If he won't do anything, we will."

"So where is Clay headed?"

Stevas thought it over. "He's headed South."

36

ALISON SUDDENLY AWOKE to someone pounding on her front door. Trying to get her bearings, she sat up and grabbed her robe off the back of the door. She shuffled quickly down the dark hallway, flipping on the kitchen light, before she reached the door and looked through the peephole. In one motion, she unlocked the deadbolt and stepped back, swinging the door open. Chris Ramirez was on the other side, covered in sweat and out of breath.

"Chris what are you-"

"It's gone! It's all gone, Alison!"

She looked confused. "What are you talking about?"

"Everything! Everything is gone! The servers, IMIS, and the *dolphins,* Alison! Dirk and Sally are gone too!"

Alison was in shock. Her mouth opened, but nothing

came out. She tried to form words, but could only shake her head in disbelief.

*****

The lab was empty. Cleared out. Alison could not believe it. Wiring and parts of the computers were strewn all over the floor. One of the desks was overturned, and dozens of books scattered around it. The racks of servers and all of their data, the heart of IMIS, were gone. The entire wall where they had once stood looked eerily blank. And the worst part was the tank; filled with nothing but water. Dirk and Sally were gone.

Alison felt nauseous, grabbing the corner of a table for support. She felt like she was going to be sick. Across the room, Lee Kenwood picked through what was left on the floor. He kicked over books and pieces of metal left from the server racks. Chris stood next to Alison, silently.

Alison simply could not speak. She could not find any words. Her chest felt tight, as if on the verge of a heart attack. Her face was flushed, and she was doing all she could to keep from bursting into tears.

Behind her, Frank Dubois burst into the room. "What in the hell...," he said shaking his head. "What...what happened?" he asked to no one in particular.

Alison's nausea suddenly turned to anger. It welled up inside her uncontrollably. She turned and almost screamed at him.

"Are you happy, Frank?! Are you happy now?! Everything we worked for, *everything is gone!*" She looked at him with disdain. "You just had to do it, didn't you?! You just took their money! You just sold out to anyone who would give it to you! You make me sick!"

Dubois was stunned. He looked around, confused. "What are you talking about? What...what happened? Who did this?"

"Who did this?" she screamed. "Who the hell do you

243

think?! The government! I told you they wanted this from the beginning. Did you think they were just going to let us tinker the whole time?!"

"Government?" he said, shaking his head. "The government as in who?"

"The Navy!" she replied disgustedly. "They knew what we were doing from the very beginning!"

"The Navy?"

"Yes, the Navy!" she cried. "And I'll tell you exactly who…John Clay!" Alison could not believe she ever liked that bastard. She felt so angry and hurt at the same time. "He's such a liar!" she growled. Everybody stood looking at her.

"Well, then, I say we hang him!" a voice said behind her.

She whirled around to see Clay standing behind them along with Caesare and Palin. They all looked exhausted. Clay looked like he had been in a bar room brawl, and lost.

Alison's eyes opened wide with rage. She ran at him and slapped at his face. "You did this!"

Clay caught her hand a few inches from his cheek. "Easy, Alison."

"Don't call me Alison!" she barked. "You-"

"I didn't do this," he said calmly.

Alison was taken aback. She just stared at him, frozen. She suddenly was not sure what to say. She shook her head disbelievingly.

Clay looked at her calmly. "If I had done this, why would I be here now?" He turned and looked at Caesare and Palin. "Why would we be here?"

Alison stumbled for words. Why indeed? "If it wasn't you, then who was it?"

He gave a slight shake of his head. "I'm not sure."

Everyone stood looking each other over. Finally, Caesare dropped a giant duffle bag on the floor. "Well, that was a hell of a greeting."

Alison put her hands on her hips. "Well, if you didn't

do this, why *are* you here?"

"I need something. Something I accidentally left when I was here last." Clay said. "It's that small silver object about the size of a deck of cards." He made an approximation with his hands.

"What's it for?" she asked.

"It's a long story, but it's important."

She folded her arms. "I'll give it to you when you tell me what the hell is going on."

Clay sighed and looked at Caesare and Palin. They both shrugged. "It's complicated," he began. "When I was here last...Dirk talked about a city under the water."

"I remember."

"Well this is Palin," he said, motioning backward. "He's from that city. Our government wants to destroy it, and their power plant, which could have some really nasty side effects."

"Why?"

Clay exhaled. "Basically, because they're idiots."

Alison's eyes narrowed. "Okay, I'm inclined to agree with that."

*****

Will Borger reached for his cup and took another sip of coffee. He watched his monitor carefully and noticed a call originate from Stevas' cell phone. He leaned in closer and started typing on his keyboard to reveal the number it was placed to. He traced the second number through the system. It belonged to the cell phone of Bruce Bishop, the Navy Chief. Borger continued watching as another call was then placed from Bishop's phone. With a bit more work, Borger found that Bishop's call was to a Naval Operations Center.

Borger brought up another window and watched the screen of data scroll by. He stopped it midway through, zeroing in on multiple outbound messages beginning with the word "Alert". It was an encrypted message which meant that Borger could not read it. He stared at it for a long time, then had an idea. The message was encrypted, but perhaps the log file that generated and sent it was not. It took him about fifteen minutes to locate the correct server, log in, and find the log file itself. Matching the time of the Alert messages and the log file entries, he found the generating code. It was not encrypted. Borger quickly reassembled the bits and the message reappeared.

Oh no. He thought to himself. The message was a command to the subs. He suddenly thought about the ring and realized what had been eluding him all this time. "The Alabama!" He quickly turned to a second monitor and brought up another window. He found the data logs that Clay had given him from the Alabama and frantically searched through pages of diagnostic information. Finding the first piece he needed, Borger printed it out and kept searching. A few moments later, he found the second and printed again. He grabbed both pieces of paper and placed them next to each other. He started scribbling calculations in the margins. After a few minutes, he had it. Borger grabbed the cell phone and dialed as fast as he could.

*****

Clay was in the middle of a sentence when the cell phone rang in his pocket. He held up a hand apologetically, and flipped it open. "Go ahead, Will."

"Clay!" Borger nearly shouted. "We've got a problem! Actually, a couple of 'em."

"What is it?" He calmly looked at Alison and her team.

"The subs have just been ordered to fire on the ring! But that's not the worst part.," Borger said in a rush. "I think this is going to end badly, for us. Remember the Alabama?"

"Of course I do."

"Well, their mission was cancelled because they had a computer malfunction when identifying their location. Clay, there *was no* malfunction!"

Clay's eyebrows rose. "What do you mean, no malfunction?"

"Remember that the Alabama's systems suddenly put it fifteen miles off course, which was thought to be a computer glitch. But the computers were right! They were always right. The Alabama got too close to the ring, Clay. It got too close to the ring and was instantly transported to the other side. Granted, their angle was a little off, but that's why the computers said they were suddenly somewhere else. *Because they were.*"

Clay rolled his eyes. Of course! Now it all made sense. The sudden GPS change, the clocks that were still in sync, even the sound that the sonar operator heard just before it happened. But then, he looked puzzled. "So why is that a problem?"

"Clay, those subs are about to fire a bunch of armed torpedoes at the ring. I think the same thing is going to happen. What if those torpedoes come out the other side?"

"Jesus," Clay said. "Is there time to warn them?"

Borger's voice became grim. "I don't think so."

Clay gave Caesare and Palin a look that matched Borger's tone.

"Clay, there's something else." Borger said softly.

"Of course there is," he replied sarcastically.

"When this fails, I'm sure they are going to try sending in the nuke, using the dolphins. But there is something we haven't considered." Borger looked down at his calculations. "Remember we asked Ms. Lokke about a nuclear blast under water, and its shock waves reaching the South Pole? Well, what we didn't ask is what happens when billions of tons of water get vaporized in that blast."

Clay thought about it. "It's going to create a vacuum."

"Of course. That water is going to disappear instantly,

creating a massive surge which rushes in to fill it, a surge that will include water flowing away from the ice shelf at a rapid pace."

Clay closed his eyes and shook his head. "Will, I'm really beginning to hate talking to you on the phone."

"Clay," Borger said. "We *have* to stop that nuke."

Clay looked at Alison and her team. "I'm working on that."

Caesare looked at Clay as he hung up. "What now?"

"The Tridents are engaging, and that nuke is going to cause a whole hell of a lot of damage."

Lee Kenwood spoke up. "Is this about the city?"

Clay nodded. "And about your dolphins." He turned back to Alison. "Alison, your dolphins were taken because they know where the city is. They've been there. They were taken because our government is going to use them to nuke Palin and his people. They plan on strapping an atomic warhead to your dolphins' backs and sending them in. And they're going to do it soon."

Alison gasped. "No!"

"Those sons of bitches!" Chris growled.

"Where is this city?" she asked.

"Not far. Off the coast of Bimini."

Alison nodded, silently, and then walked over to one of the tables. She bent down and picked up her backpack. Reaching inside, she retrieved Palin's cube. "I assume this is yours." She handed it directly to Palin. She was certainly not going to admit to anyone that she kept it as a reason to call Clay.

Palin smiled and took it gently from her hand. At the same time, Caesare dropped down and unzipped his bag. He pulled out more rifles and magazines of ammo, handing some to Clay.

Clay looked at Alison. "We need to get your team somewhere safe. After that, we need to borrow your boat."

They looked at each other, suddenly concerned.

"Why?" Alison asked.

"Because now that you've talked to us, you are no longer safe." Clay shrugged. "We also kinda busted out of jail."

"You did?!" she said with surprise.

They all turned to Caesare.

Caesare looked aggravated. "Why the hell does everyone always think I'm the one that's been in jail?!"

Clay checked the magazine in his gun and slapped it back in. "Anyone here have a safe place to hide? A vacation home, friend's cabin, anything like that?"

Alison frowned. "Apparently, you're not familiar with how grant funding works."

"You've got me there. Are there any other ways out of here other than the service hallway and the main entrance?"

"Yes," answered Dubois. "There is a maintenance corridor back there." He pointed to a dark corner near the end of the tank. "It's not used often, but it will get us outside."

"Good," said Clay. "What I want you to do-" He suddenly stopped. Alison started to say something, but he cut her off with a raised hand. He listened carefully.

Caesare was also listening. They both looked up, then back to the dark hallway. "We've got company."

Just then, a bullet zipped past Clay and hit Dubois in the chest, ripping a hole through him. He was dead by the time he hit the ground.

"Get down!" Clay instantly jumped on top of Alison and reached out to pull Chris down with them.

Caesare was also moving. He zipped around, grabbed Palin, and used the momentum to throw him into Lee Kenwood, knocking them both over like bowling pins. He opened fire immediately, showering the hallway with bullets. Caesare's return fire bought them a few seconds of delay, as they all hit the ground and scurried behind a row of large, heavy desks.

Clay quickly crawled forward, grabbing and pushing Palin, Alison, Chris, and Lee, ahead of him. He motioned for them all to lie down on the ground and become as small a target as possible. While Caesare shot back, Clay grabbed a long table behind him and tipped it over. He pushed it forward against the back of the desks to add a second layer of protection. The monitor on the desk above them suddenly exploded. Three slugs could be heard hitting the thick metal on the other side of the desk. Clay had the others scoot forward and stay behind the upturned table. He then took a defensive position and fired back.

A loud grunt could be heard from the hallway, and one of the silhouettes fell to the floor. Clay and Caesare came back down, knelt behind the desks, replacing their magazines without looking. More shots came from the hallway. Caesare looked at Clay. "You hear that?"

Clay nodded. "They're coming closer." Two bullets skipped off the top of the desk and over Clay's head, impacting the giant tank behind them. The bullets were stopped dead in the glass. Clay looked up at the tank and then over to Alison. "How thick is that glass?"

Alison was cringing at the sound of the gunfire. She tried to think. "Six inches…it's six inches."

"Good," Clay said. He looked around at what he could see of the room. Caesare unloaded another magazine and reached for a replacement. "Where is that corridor?" Clay asked her.

She took one of her hands away from her ears and pointed to the corner of the room behind her. Clay followed her pointing hand and could see the subtle lines of a small door, close to where the tank met the building. It was almost a clear shot to the door along the back side of the desks, but there was about ten feet of open space between the last table and the door. When he heard a short lull from the other side, he quickly rose and fired three rounds into the hallway. He looked at Caesare, pointed down the line of furniture, and then pointed to the wall where the small door was.

Caesare squinted toward the door and then nodded his head. He grabbed another magazine and looked up at the ceiling. He turned to Clay, covered his eyes for a moment, and then made some kind of flashing sign with his hands. Clay looked up and then nodded back. Four more rounds hit the top of the desk and lodged themselves into the tank's glass, next to the others. He reached over and grabbed Alison, pulling her close.

He whispered loudly in her ear. "We have to get you three out of here!" Behind him, Caesare unloaded another magazine. "We're going to take out the lights. That should give you time to make it to the door. When you get outside, look before you run. If it's clear, you run like hell. Find some place safe. Don't worry about us."

Alison nodded and looked back to Chris and Lee. She turned around and whispered to them. Clay watched them. None seemed frozen or in panic, which meant they were at least thinking. Scared to death but thinking. That was a hell of a lot better than freezing like a deer in headlights.

Clay turned back and got Caesare's attention. Steve nodded and reached into his bag to withdraw a large light. He grabbed the cord and plugged it into the nearest power strip. Caesare nodded again. With that Clay quickly turned back and mouthed the words to Alison. "Get ready." She nodded back, putting her hands on the floor, ready to move.

Clay and Caesare changed their locations behind the desks. Then simultaneously, they both rose up over the top. Caesare fired at their attackers, while Clay aimed carefully at the ceiling, destroying all four of the overhead lights and plunging the huge room into darkness. "Go!" he whispered loudly. He heard the sound of them quickly crawling away.

The firing stopped briefly. On the floor, Caesare

grabbed the top of his light and placed it atop the desk. Neither of them moved. Instead, they counted. They knew that it normally took five to ten seconds for an expert to transition to a pair of night vision goggles. It was a normal part of tactical training, which allowed a soldier to continue even in pitch black. By magnifying what little light there was by fifty thousand times, night vision goggles provided more than enough vision to continue the fight. The drawback of course was that it magnified all light by fifty thousand times.

Caesare got to *seven* and flipped the switch on the two million candle mega-lamp. It instantly flooded the entire room like a search light, blinding the five men who had expected Clay and Caesare to be donning their own goggles. Instead, the intense magnification of the search light rendered them unable to see anything at all. At that moment, Alison and the others ran into the open, toward the door. Clay and Caesare came up over the desks and opened fire, dropping all five of them.

They both sat down quickly and reloaded. They could hear the small door click shut in the distance.

"Any more?" Clay asked.

"Don't know." Caesare turned and scanned again. Then just as he swung to the right, he saw something out of the corner of his eye. A muzzle flashed from the second hallway leading to the main entrance. With less cover from that direction, the bullet ripped through a stack of binders and hit Caesare in the right shoulder. He yelled and fell backward, emptying the rest of this magazine in the new direction. More flashes were seen, as several more silhouettes spread and took up positions. Clay came over the top of Caesare and fired everything he had. He quickly pulled the end of the last desk down in front of them, but it was too late. Even as several more bullets hit the other side of the desk, Caesare rolled onto his side grabbing his shoulder.

"How bad?" cried Clay over the gunfire and papers

flying all around them.

Caesare gritted his teeth. "I can make it."

Suddenly, Palin spoke from behind them. "John?"

Thunk thunk thunk. More bullets hit the front of the desk. Clay looked at Palin to find him staring back with a calm expression. Clay waited for him to say something else, but then lowered his gaze to see the bright red circle spreading across Palin's chest. It was a direct hit.

"John." he said again, starting to fade off. His eyes started to close as his head tilted back.

"Palin!" Clay grabbed Palin and tried to shake him awake. "Palin!! Stay with me!"

Suddenly, a brilliant blue flash of light filled the room from behind them, adding to the bright search light. Clay looked up to see the air split in half and open into a large hole in the shape of an oval. He looked at Palin, who was unconscious. A glow was coming from his coat pocket. It was the cube.

Clay looked back to Caesare, who was reloading his gun. "Get him out of here, Clay!"

Caesare gave him his best smile. "Don't worry, I'll be okay." Clay stared at him for a long moment. They both knew it was a lie. Caesare had limited use of his shooting arm, and more shadows could be seen entering from the main hallway. The two friends stared at each other. They knew this was it.

"Get him out of here!" Caesare yelled again. So many bullets were hitting the other side of the desk that it was beginning to move, pushing in on Caesare. "Give me your gun," he said, "and go stop that nuke!"

Clay hesitated for only a second. He then replaced the magazine, flipped his rifle around, and handed it over. He then turned and kicked one of the desks to the side outwards, making a small path. He grabbed Palin and laid him flat on his back, making it easier to pick him up. He looked at Caesare and nodded. Again, they moved together. Caesare came up over the desk, shooting with both guns giving the cover needed for Clay to pick Palin and throw him over his shoulder. With his dislocated shoulder screaming in pain, Clay got to his feet and ran.

Behind him, Caesare got hit twice in the chest and fell backward onto the floor. Clay ran as hard as he could, with every step propelling him toward the glowing portal. Palin was heavy but at just several feet away Clay pushed off with everything he had, throwing them both forward. They flew through the air and into the center of the dark oval. It was then that Clay and a large bullet entered the portal at the same instant.

37

RED LIGHTS REPLACED the interior ones on each of the twelve submarine bridges, and commands were called down for all levels to "man battle stations". The Tridents had received their orders and were preparing to fire. They had strategically positioned themselves with six on one side of the giant ring and six coming around the far side, to reduce risk. Each submarine also remained nearly five hundred yards apart from each other. The commanders had no idea what kind of strike Palin's people might retaliate with, so it was lunacy to have all of the ships together, providing a singular target.

At nearly the same time on each Trident, the torpedoes were armed and loaded into both forward tubes. The communications officer onboard the lead sub, the Montana, sat glued to his instruments. He waited for any word or change in orders that might signal aborting the attack. The Montana's commander, Captain Hallgren, waited patiently, knowing the other subs were also loading and arming. With no radio communication, they had to do this the old-fashioned way. He kept checking the red LED clock on the wall.

After another minute, he looked at his communications officer, who looked back at him and shook his head. Hallgren turned to his Operational Commander. "All hands...stand by."

His Operational Commander repeated the message into the microphone. Hallgren took a deep breath and watched the digital clock hit its mark. "Fire!"

The Operational Commander immediately passed the order. "Shoot two one! Shoot two one!"

Less than a second later, two torpedoes burst from their tubes on either side of the Trident's bow, as they did on the other subs simultaneously. The torpedoes raced forward, their target less than two thousand yards away. The men on board waited, listening for the sound of a direct hit. Their hearts began to beat faster.

"One thousand yards..." called the Helmsman.

"Eight hundred yards..."

"Six hundred yards..."

"Four hund-" The Helmsman stopped. He pressed his headset harder against his ears. "Sir! I've lost them."

"What?!" said Hallgren. "What do you mean *lost* them?"

"I don't know, sir. I just...wait!" Suddenly, a piercing alarm sounded behind them. His eyes opened wide. "Sir! Torpedoes are CLOSING!"

"Closing?!" Hallgren yelled. "Closing on who?"

"Closing on *US*, sir!" replied the Helmsman. "Ten...NO, twelve torpedoes in the water at eight hundred yards bearing 192, bearing 183, bearing 166..."

"Evasive maneuvers! Get us turned around!" He looked at his helmsman. "Are they ours?!"

"No, sir!" he said, shaking his head. He turned to Hallgren. "I think they're from the other subs."

"That's impossible! They're over fifteen miles away!" Hallgren shouted.

With full power, the Montana began to turn. At that moment, the other eleven subs were all doing the same thing.

"Five hundred yards and closing!"

"Blow the tanks," growled Hallgren.

Still turning, the Montana opened its tanks and forced a hundred thousand gallons of water out as an emergency measure. The exiting water was replaced with air quickly, increasing its buoyancy. The Montana slowly started to rise. Beneath the water, the sounds of all the subs pressurizing their tanks could be heard for miles.

"Three hundred yards!"

The Montana's crew held tight and, like the others, desperately willed the monstrous ship up through the dark waters. Their ascent was agonizingly slow.

"A hundred and fifty yards!" called the Helmsman.

"Launch the decoys!" yelled Hallgren.

Several large canisters shot from the rear tubes and began to descend. They instantly began releasing bubbles and noise to confuse the detection systems of the torpedoes. Several torpedoes suddenly changed course and smashed into the decoys exploding prematurely, but the others did not. One by one, the rest found their mark, slamming into the submarines with powerful blasts. Their hulls were instantly destroyed, causing them to implode under water. The Montana, still clawing for the surface, was the last to be hit. Like the others, its hull shuddered under the impact and collapsed in on itself. Slowly, the shock waves subsided. What was left of the twelve nuclear submarines stopped their ascent and slowly began the lifeless slide into the dark waters below.

38

THE SMALL METAL door opened slowly with a creaking sound. Alison tilted her head out just far enough to get a look around. Beyond the grass that surrounded the back of the building was the secondary parking lot, and it appeared empty. She looked slowly to the right, the direction back to the main entrance, and saw nothing but the familiar dark trees and shrubs. She leaned just a little outside, looking around the door's edge to the left. The large grassy area, littered with picnic tables, sat silently. Further and around the left side of the building was the exterior of the giant tank. It had no entrance into the aquarium except from the large deck which was high above and inaccessible from the ground.

"What do you see?" Chris stood nervously behind her.

"Nothing. Shhh!" she snapped. She tried to concentrate over the sound of gunfire inside the building. She could not hear anything outside. Alison looked at the waist high hedge that bordered the far end of the parking lot. Beyond that, were trees, and further still was a faint outline of a sloped roof. She turned around. "It looks clear. I think if we can make it to the hedge, we can stay out of sight until we get to the larger trees. From there, we should be able to get to the maintenance shed.

They both pushed their heads through for a look.

"That looks awfully far," said Chris.

"Not if we're fast." Alison looked at Chris who was wearing a white t-shirt. She quickly pulled her green sweatshirt over her head. "Take off your shirt and wear this." She straightened the dark shirt she was wearing underneath.

With shaking hands, Chris pulled off his shirt and put

the tiny sweatshirt on. It was at least two sizes too small and barely covered his skin, but was better than wearing a white shirt, acting as a beacon. They both looked at Kenwood's red shirt.

"Hey, at least it's not white."

"Okay." Alison looked at them. "Ready?"

The other two nodded. Suddenly, back down the hall they heard the gunfire stop. That was all the incentive they needed. "Stay low!" Alison whispered over her shoulder and ran toward the hedge. All three stayed close, and reaching the hedge, they dropped to the ground behind it. They slowly peered up over it, seeing more of the parking lot and the road to the main lot. Still no sign of movement.

"C'mon!" Alison ran, bending down as far as she could to stay below the top of the hedge. Chris and Lee followed behind.

Less than ten seconds later, they were ducking behind one of the larger trees in the aquarium's outdoor area. Still seeing no one behind them, they ran for the dark structure near the edge of the property. The large shed, hidden behind the trees, was used by the gardeners and various grounds people who maintained the exterior of the property. They quickly tried the main door, which was locked. They spread out and circled it. Both windows on each side were also locked. Alison looked around for another place to run, when she suddenly heard the smashing of one of the windows. She turned around to see Lee holding a large rock. He held a finger over his lips and proceeded to clear the rest of the glass by running the rock around the inside edge of the frame. Alison looked around and ran a few feet to a small banana tree. She pulled off two of its thick leaves and draped them over the window edge. Using them for protection, Chris and Lee lifted her up and in through the window. Moments later, Lee followed her in and Chris tumbled in last. As an afterthought, Alison kicked the broken glass out of view and leaned a few long handled tools up against the open window.

A few minutes later, two of the soldiers burst out through the maintenance corridor looking for them. They slowly scanned the grounds, spreading out with their guns up, pressed into their shoulders. One headed past the outside tank and toward the other end of the building. The other silently trotted across the small parking lot to a long hedge. He jumped over and panned his rifle across the picnic area. He followed the hedge, looking left and right, until he came to the end. To his right, a small road led back to the main entrance and split in two after passing a small walkway. It ran up to the same double doors and hallway that his other team members had charged through earlier. He turned back and looked at a group of large trees. Behind it, he could see the edge of a low hanging roof.

He moved quietly through the trees and found the large shed which the roof was attached to. He very carefully stepped around each corner, ready to fire at any moment. When he found no one hiding around the outside, he tried the door. He then peered back around the left corner, noticing a broken window on the west side. Unable to see anything inside, he flipped on the LED light at the end of his barrel, bathing the entire inside of the shed with the bright beam.

He scanned back and forth, seeing a wall of tools, along with dozens of sacks of fertilizers and compost on the back wall. A giant lawnmower sat on the opposite side. Behind the lawnmower were a couple small rusted gasoline tanks, and in the middle countless buckets and hoses, all stacked neatly in place. Suddenly, a voice sounded over the headset wrapped tightly around his ear. "No, no sign of them yet," he said, stepping back from the window to listen. "I think they made a run for it. They can't be more than a half mile away. We can still get 'em." He listened again and nodded. "Okay, heading back." The soldier took one last look at the window and, not seeing any glass on the floor and the tools leaning against it, decided it had been broken for a while. He turned and quickly ran back toward the building. When he got close, the rest of the team emerged and all ran smoothly toward the beach. After two trips to retrieve the bodies of their team members, they pulled three black zodiac boats out of the bushes and dragged them back down the sand, and into the water. Within seconds, they had the engines started, their gear aboard, and had disappeared into the darkness.

*****

It was over thirty minutes before Alison peeked out from under one of the heavy compost sacks. Her face smeared with dirt, she looked slowly out and toward the window. A small amount of light shone through from the tiny gibbous moon overhead, creating a silhouette around the trees and bushes rustling outside in the wind. She half slid, half pulled herself out from the small gap left between the bags and the wall, and looked around quietly. They had not heard anything since what sounded like boats speeding off in the ocean, but they were afraid that one or two might have stayed back, in hopes of flushing them out.

Alison peered out of the window and then walked to the other side, looking through the dirty glass. "I think they're gone," she whispered to Chris and Lee. A few seconds later, they both wiggled out, covered in dirt themselves.

They looked through the windows to double check. Alison was shaking. "Oh my god! They killed them! They killed them all!"

Lee tried to calm her. "We don't know that for sure, Alison."

"No?" She yelled under her breath. "What the hell do

you call it when everyone goes in, but only one side comes back out?! My god, they killed them - Clay, Caesare, and their friend." She suddenly gasped. "They killed Frank!"

Chris was looking out the window and then ran back to the other side. "We've got to do something!"

Alison grew quiet. Her eyes welled up as she absorbed the full weight of what had happened. "They died for us," she said, looking at Chris, then Lee. Her voice began to tremble. "Clay and the others died, so we could get out."

All three of them sat in the shed, thinking about what she had just said.

Chris sighed and slumped back into the seat of the lawnmower. "I think we'd better call the police."

"I don't know," Alison said, suddenly shaking her head. "Is it just me or did those guys look like *government*?"

Lee nodded. "Looked like it to me."

"Then can the police even protect us?" Alison asked them. "What if we call the police and they've been told 'shoot to kill', or something? I mean, we saw the whole thing in there!"

"Are you kidding?" Chris exclaimed. "The cops are the only chance we have."

Alison and Lee looked at each other but remained silent.

"What the hell is wrong with you guys? Everyone in there is dead, including Frank! We could be in there lying right next to him!"

Alison raised her voice slowly. "Well, that doesn't mean we want to give them a reason to come back either."

"Oh, okay, great," whined Chris, "let's just hide out here then! You know, put in a change of address-"

"Knock it off!" Alison snapped, cutting him off.

"I don't think they're going to let us live," said Lee, quietly. He looked at both of them. "Alison's right. We *did* see everything. We also know why they took Dirk and Sally. We know about the city, or ring, or whatever it is. And now we're witnesses. We know too much and they have to cover it up. That's how they do it."

Alison nodded. "And for whatever reason, they had to leave quickly, but it doesn't mean they won't be back. Maybe they let things die down and wait for us to come home." She sat quietly. "Unless," she said, suddenly looking up.

"Unless what?"

"Unless we stop Dirk and Sally," she said.

"Stop them?" Chris asked.

"Stop them from delivering the bomb," Alison said, standing up. "That's why John said they had come here. They were trying to stop it."

"Yeah," Lee agreed. "I say we stop it and then call the press and tell them everything."

Chris folded his arms. "And how do you propose we stop them? In case you've forgotten, there's nothing left. They took everything, the equipment, our notes, everything."

Alison had stood up but now slumped back down thinking.

"Uh," Lee raised his hand. "I have backups."

"What?"

Lee grinned. "I have backups."

Chris looked confused. "What do you mean? The backup tapes were in the servers, and they took them all."

"I back up the servers every night," Lee said. "And I replace those tapes every week. Most of the tapes are shipped to a storage facility, but the last two weeks have not been sent yet."

"So…where exactly are those tapes?" Alison asked.

"Downstairs in the storage closet."

Alison and Chris looked at each other, but he shook his head. "It doesn't matter. The tapes don't help without the servers."

Alison saw that Lee was grinning again. "What?" she asked again, with a cautious look.

"We have a server. We have two. The small servers

we took on board the Pathfinder. Captain Emerson had them shipped back to me about a week ago."

"Any chance those servers are in the storage closet downstairs too?"

"Yes, they are."

Alison smiled broadly with excitement. "Lee Kenwood, I could just-" She suddenly changed her mind and just lunged at him, giving him a giant kiss. "You are amazing!"

"I know," he joked.

"Could we install it on the boat?"

"What?!" Chris said, jumping to his feet. "We're taking the boat?"

The boat was a thirty-year old, forty foot Bayliner diesel powerboat. It was donated to the aquarium years ago, and primarily used for small trips out on the ocean for local research groups, or students on a field trip.

"We're not taking the boat, Chris. *I'm* taking the boat."

"What are you talking about?"

"I'm doing this…alone," she said, calmly. "It's dangerous. I'm not going to risk two more lives over this. There's something big going on here, and I'm not going to let us all die over it."

Chris just stared at her, silently constructing his argument. Finally he said "Alison, don't you think we should leave this to the pros? My mom has a friend who's a cop. I'm sure we can trust him."

Alison frowned at Chris. "We may not have time. And I really don't know who we can trust, Chris. To tell you the truth, I can't let anything happen to Dirk and Sally, or anybody else out there. I love those dolphins. You know that."

"I know," Chris said, with a sigh. "But they mean a lot to us too. You know that!"

She put her hand on his arm. "Then help me."

He sighed again, defeated. "Fine." Chris looked over at Lee. "What do we have to do, Lee?"

Lee ran through the list of things they would need. They slowly climbed back out of the window, and made sure there was no movement other than the trees. Cautiously, they made their way back toward the building. When they reached the edge, they pulled open the double doors. Quietly, the three snuck down the main hallway, back toward the lab. It was completely black, for which Alison was glad. It meant they could walk around the edge of the wall to the stairs without having to see any of the bodies. She felt sick thinking that Clay, Dubois, Caesare, and their friend Palin, were lying lifeless somewhere in the darkness. As they made their way through the lab, their shoes crunched on broken glass and pieces of plaster from the walls. When they reached the stairs, Lee led the way down with his left hand on the railing. They reached the storage room and found the electricity to the building was still on. Inside the closet, Lee grabbed one of the servers. Chris carried a monitor, while Alison followed them out with the backup tapes, a keyboard, and a number of other items that she did not recognize.

They made their way back outside, out to the water where a small dock led to the boat, sitting and bobbing contently in the gentle swells. They quietly climbed aboard, putting their equipment down inside the cabin. Alison quickly closed all the curtains and turned on one small light so Lee could see.

"Chris," he said, "I need you to find some straps or rope to hold this stuff down. If you can, grab a toolbox too."

Chris nodded and disappeared outside.

"What should I do? asked Alison.

"Where's your phone?"

She gave a puzzled look and patted down her clothes. "I don't know." She thought for a minute. "I think I left it in Chris' car."

"Go get it. And grab the charger too."

While the other two were gone, Lee pieced together the

server components. He fired up the engine and kept it idling as quietly as possible, while he powered up the server and began restoring the data from the tapes. He let the data restore run, and proceeded to rewire the boat's existing speakers and microphone into the server.

Alison arrived with her phone and handed it to Lee. He duct-taped it to the dashboard, above the boat's steering wheel, and plugged the charger in. A few moments later, Chris returned with the straps and toolbox. Together, they wrapped the straps around the server and monitor, then tugged on them to be sure the systems would stay upright against the back and forth motion of the boat. It took another thirty minutes to restore the data onto the server and a few more still to test it. All in all, it took them less than an hour and a half.

Lee finally finished typing. "I think we're about ready." He looked at Alison. "Okay, let me walk you through this. I was able to restore IMIS' information all the way up to last week. However, you are limited only to the vocabulary up to that point. This does not include the bulk of the raw data, which means you cannot learn new words. But you should have more than enough translation capability to find Dirk and Sally, and warn them. Now," he said, pointing to the server on the floor, "the server uses a lot of power, which means you must be running the engine for it to operate. I attached a small battery backup though. If the engine is turned off, you can probably still use it for ten minutes, but that's it. Oh, and the server is sensitive to any significant motion, so do your best to keep the boat steady."

Next, he pointed to her cell phone. "I've turned on the GPS navigation on your cell phone and plugged in the coordinates for Bimini. You shouldn't have any problem finding it. Basically, it's about seventy miles, due east. I also disabled your cellular signal so they can't track you. You also have," he looked at the gauge, "about half of tank of fuel, which should be more than enough to get you there and back. Any questions?"

She shook her head. "I don't think so."

"Okay-" Lee suddenly stopped and looked around. Where's Chris?"

"I don't know."

Outside, they heard someone hop onboard. A few seconds later, the door opened with Chris panting. His arms were filled with junk food from the vending machine inside. "Here, take this," he said, dropping everything into a seat next to them. "Wait!" Chris shouted, quickly pulling an orange life vest from under the same seat. He wrapped it around Alison and clipped it in front.

She smiled at him reassuringly and gave him a tight hug. She then turned and hugged Lee.

"I'll be fine," she said, wondering if that sounded more like a question than a statement. She looked at Chris. "Chris, take Lee and find your mom's police friend. It won't be long before the cleaning crew comes in, and then all hell is going to break loose. We need to make sure we're in front of this and already explaining things to somebody."

"And what if they ask where you are?"

She shrugged. "Tell them you don't know. Tell them we got separated after the shooting. By the time they start to suspect anything, I should already be back with Dirk and Sally."

They both nodded sullenly. They opened the door and backed out.

"Find them, Alison," were Lee's last words before they shut the door and stepped off, back onto the dock. Together, they untied the dock lines and threw them aboard, waiting for her to pull away. She peered through the side window and waved. She then pushed forward on the throttle and the engines revved louder, pushing the boat forward through the small waves.

When Alison was close to a mile out, she opened the engine up and sped forward. The sea was relatively calm as the boat's bow cut smoothly through the waves. She reached down and typed a simple message as a test; *Sally Dirk Stop Danger*. She hit the return key and the screen read, "Translating…"

Satisfied, she looked back up and gripped the wheel with both hands. She stared intently through the glass, as she could see very little in the dark ocean in front of her.

Alison thought about the one potential problem with her plan, something she was hoping neither Chris nor Lee would bring up. *If by some miracle she did find and stop them, what on earth was she going to do with a nuclear bomb?*

39

"WHAT?!" STEVAS SCREAMED into his phone. He was in disbelief. "All of them?! Every single one?" He listened in anger and his face turned dark red.

"God dammit!" He turned and looked across the table to Mason, who was watching apprehensively. Stevas closed his eyes and ran his hand through his hair in frustration. "They did it!' he said. "By god they did it! They hit us first! I *knew* we should have moved faster."

He ended the call and looked at Mason. "The bastards destroyed every one of our subs. Every one." He looked at the wall still shaking his head. "This is Miller's fault. He kept dragging his damn feet."

Mason sighed from across the table. "It didn't help having to bring the Tridents in slowly. They could see that coming from a mile away."

Stevas turned and pointed at him. "That's right!" He started pacing. "If they had done things like I wanted to do, like *we* wanted to do, that ring would be a giant pile of junk right now. Goddamn bureaucracy! And those damn panty waists, Miller and Langford. We had the President thinking straight before they turned everything around." He put his hands on his hips. "Dammit!"

"They're not going to listen, you know." Mason said. "Miller and Langford are just going to see this attack as them being provoked."

"I know." Stevas said, continuing to pace. "And if we think this is bad, just wait until all of these U.N. idiots get involved."

"Game over."

"Not if I can help it." Stevas held up his phone and began dialing.

*****

The tank was smaller than their old tank and the building was dark, making it hard to see. Dirk and Sally hovered near the glass wall watching all the men walk back and forth, quickly piecing the last of the many servers together. One man, tall and lanky with dark hair, was sitting in front of the tank typing on a computer. His face reflected an eerie glow from the monitor in front of him. They both wondered where Alison and the others were.

After what seemed like a long time, the man finished typing and looked up at them. A short pause later, the words *Hello Dirk and Sally* came through the underwater speakers.

Dirk swam past the speaker, excited. *Hello*, he answered.

Sally swam close to the microphone. *Where Alison? Where Chris? Where Lee?*

The man forced a smile and typed back. *They will come soon. We are friends.* IMIS translated, and Dirk swam excitedly again. The man noticed that Sally continued to watch him very carefully. *We need help.* He typed.

268

Dirk answered quickly. *Yes help. Dirk like help.*
We want to give gift to people. He said. *People in the city.*

Dirk rolled to the top of the tank and came back down. *Dirk take gift. People nice.*

Thank you Dirk. The man at the computer replied. *Must go fast.*

Two scuba divers descended from the top of the tank holding a thick harness. In the middle of the harness was a large lump, hiding a compact nuclear warhead. It was preprogrammed for the ring's depth and location. As soon as it got within a quarter mile of any part of the ring, it would instantly detonate.

The harness was gently fitted onto Dirk's back and fastened underneath. When they were done, he wagged his tail eagerly and swam around the small tank. Sally stayed close, swimming next to him.

The man behind the computer was now standing at the end of the tank watching, when someone walked up behind him. "We ready, Jared?" The young man turned to see Naval Chief Bruce Bishop.

"Yes, sir."

"Any problems?" Bishop asked.

"None at all sir. They seem to be adjusting quickly."

Bishop shrugged. "Good, though it's not going to matter much longer." He peered at Dirk and Sally through the glass alongside Jared. "If they're ready, let's send them out."

Jared nodded and picked up a phone on his desk. "Open the doors." He put the phone down and typed a message out. *Please take gift fast Dirk. Hurry.*

Dirk swim fast, Dirk replied. A few minutes later, behind the dolphins, two large doors began to open slowly. The ocean water on the other side rushed through and mixed with the tank water, creating a tiny vortex. Using their powerful tails, both dolphins waited for the surge to subside, then quickly darted into the open ocean and were gone.

40

FOR THE SECOND time in less than two weeks, an exhausted Kathryn Lokke saw the McMurdo base station in Antarctica appear on the horizon. Her plane was much larger this time but only slightly more comfortable. Even so, she was really going to miss it when they had to transfer to the smaller and much colder C130s.

She turned and looked at the rows of people behind her. The effort had come together faster than she could have hoped. True to his word, President Carr delivered everyone and everything she needed. International experts were brought in almost overnight, and when she explained to her own team what they were up against, almost all of them volunteered to go back. She had never felt so proud and humbled at the same time.

There was also no question in her mind, telling them the whole truth was the right thing to do. When they learned how grave the situation was, partly after compiling their own results, they were ready to get to work immediately. Nearly all of the remaining members became part of the project planning effort to 'blow up' the Ronne Ice Shelf and prevent a modern catastrophe. Her team worked relentlessly. By the time the demolition teams had landed, many of the largest logistical problems and details had been worked out. Now the entire group, along with their equipment, was back.

At over 500 feet thick, the Ronne Ice Shelf presented a number of challenges. First and foremost was the depth of the wells required to ensure the greatest level of explosive effect. And the required mobile drill rigs were huge. They were also slow. In fact, as she found out, it was not the size of the drilling vehicle that was the challenge, but the amount of the drill string piping needed for each vehicle. With at least three hundred feet of piping per drill, they took up most of the storage capacity on the plane.

Next was the food and supplies. Anderson's New Zealand team would again serve as guides, but the project was expected to last for months, which meant the food and supplies were substantial. The compact snowplow would be essential in creating airstrips smooth enough to land on, in order for the planes to safely drop off more supplies. Satellite pictures and deep level scans would help identify the best areas. Although in the end, it would be up to those on the ground to decide where to plow.

Due to the urgency involved in getting the project underway, it was decided that it would be carried out in a staggered approach. This meant that with the essentials addressed, Kathryn would then be onsite to continue the planning from their base on the ice. Thanks to some innovative inflatable building structures from Norway, they were able to bring a relatively permanent form of shelter with them. Made out of an expandable material that strengthened as it was exposed to oxygen, the small outbuildings would be fully insulated and capable of housing up to five people each. Best of all, they were heavy but still mobile. As the drills moved, so could the camp.

The explosives were expected to be approximately a mile apart. It was just enough, according to their computer simulations, to create the vibration and stress needed on the inner shelf to effectively allow it to break itself off, and relieve stress at the core. Finally, due to the energy required for the mobile drills, explosives and fuel would be delivered on an almost constant basis. And while her team would be measuring and assessing the surface for the drills, the best news Kathryn could give her team would be that they would sleep warmly at night. That fact alone made them smile.

It only took four hours to land and transfer their equipment to the waiting C130 planes. They were the best aircraft for transport to the ice shelf. They were more durable and had a much better strength and carrying capacity, when factoring in the length required for a landing field. Kathryn had hoped her body had adjusted, at least a little, to the extreme cold, but the deep chill on board her C130 told her otherwise.

The planes finally landed and began unloading. The long sunlit nights allowed them to begin setting up immediately, and within just a few hours, they had most of the inflatable houses up and operational. The inside temperatures were increasing and expected to reach a balmy sixty degrees Fahrenheit. The drill teams prepped their three mobile drillers and readied them for the next morning. They estimated that each mobile drill could create one two-hundred foot hole per day, which meant that they were expecting a rate of progress of two or three miles a day, for a total of sixty to seventy miles per month. Therefore, their best case scenario would allow them to detonate in six to eight weeks.

Kathryn hoped they had enough time.

41

THE SWELLS WERE getting taller the further Alison got from land, and the morning sun was finally beginning to crest over the horizon. The straps that the guys installed were keeping the server relatively stable. She kept her hand on the equipment when she could, to help counter the rocking motion of the boat. The increasing swells and the sensitivity of the server kept her limited to a relatively slow speed. After more than two hours, she was not even half the distance to Bimini. Alison also realized that to transmit a clear signal, she had to stop and turn off the engine. This kept the engine noise from impairing the broadcast from the speakers, something she remembered from their trip on the Pathfinder. Unfortunately, every time she turned off the engine, the battery backup device would sound an audible alarm indicating that it had lost power from its source. She wished Lee had remembered to disable that. The benefit, though, was that she had a digital display of exactly how much more time she had left before the battery went dead.

Alison throttled down again and let the boat coast to a stop. Most of the boat's rolling motion disappeared, and she let go of the server to reach over and turn off the ignition. She turned on the monitor and typed the command again. *Dirk Sally Stop Danger.* A moment later, she heard the sound come out from the speakers under the boat. She waited patiently for a couple minutes and tried again. While she waited, she wondered how far the sound from those speakers could travel in the open ocean. She knew that sound traveled better underwater, but she had not thought to ask Lee what the distance was. It also occurred to her that she didn't know exactly which direction Dirk and Sally might be coming from. They assumed it would be a similarly straight line from Miami, but if not, then the range of the speakers was even more critical. The other unknown was when Dirk and Sally would be coming. John Clay indicated it was going to happen soon, but the more she thought about the statement, the less sure she was. Did he mean 'soon' as in now, or 'soon' as in a couple of weeks? In the end, she didn't know. She just had to go with her gut.

Alison was beginning to feel the exhaustion setting in. She sat down and reached for a couple more packs of Oreo cookies. The previous dose had perked her up, and she was hoping they would again as she tore the wrapper open. She slowly chewed the cookies, thinking how much less enjoyable junk food was when it was your only option.

Alison sent one last message before starting up the engine again. When the engine rumbled to life, the alert on the battery shut off and the system went back to charging. She eased the throttle forward again, verifying her location on the GPS, as the boat resumed her drive forward through the small waves.

After the third hour, she began stopping the boat more frequently and sending more broadcasts. Sitting on the seat waiting, she watched the server nervously as it rocked more from side to side under the influence of the swells rolling under the boat. She looked at the digital screen on the backup battery. She had three minutes of power left. At two minutes, she turned the engine back on and continued forward. Alison was getting increasingly nervous.

After each stop, Alison's anxiety grew until she was well within sight of Bimini Island's south cay. She did not know where this underwater city was, but she couldn't be very far from it. It probably would not be long until she was right on top of it which meant she might not be able to reach Dirk and Sally until it was too late. Her heart began beating faster at the sudden prospect of now being too close to what was about to happen.

Alison quickly stood up and decided to head back away from the island. She turned the key to start the engine and listened to the battery alert, waiting to hear it go off. In a moment of confusion, she looked down at her hand thinking something did not seem right. The battery alert was still sounding, but she realized the key had already been turned. She was not sure what she did wrong, but she tried it again, twisting it back to its original position and turning the key again. Again, nothing happened. She looked at the battery and the alarm was still ringing. The display on the battery read five minutes and forty-eight seconds, but what caused Alison to panic was that the display did not indicate that it was charging again.

She quickly examined the ignition area, thinking she hit something or flipped a switch, accidentally turning something off. She could not find anything. Every piece seemed firmly in place or downright immovable. She tried to start the engine again, this time a little more forcibly. All she heard was a mechanical "click" somewhere inside. She instantly felt a feeling of dread come over her and stop right in the middle of her stomach, as though she was going to be sick. "Oh god," she said, trying the key one more time. Still nothing.

"Oh god! Please, please start!" she moaned. She kicked the area beneath the steering wheel, very nearly breaking her foot. She was now in a full panic. She looked at the battery display which read five minutes and twenty-one seconds left. Alison suddenly realized that if she could not start the engine, this was all she had left on the server. She desperately hit the return key sending out another broadcast. The battery continued to count down. "No! No! NO!!" She checked the gas gauge and found the tank still a quarter full. She tried an interior light, which showed the electrical was working.

As the battery kept counting down, a dark realization swept over her like a terrible nightmare. Not only was she about to lose power and the ability to call out to Dirk and Sally...but without the ability to start the engine, she couldn't *leave*. She was stuck and probably well within range of being killed instantly when the bomb went off. She was trapped.

"God, please no!' Screaming, she hit the keyboard over and over in desperation. Below her, the sound from the speakers could be heard broadcasting the same familiar clicks in rapid succession. She stood watching helplessly as the battery display counted down past the five-minute mark.

*****

Sally followed close behind an excited Dirk, who swam quickly through the emerald blue waters. Both were happy to be in the open ocean again. She stayed close to Dirk easily as the large gift on his back slowed him down. She could now detect the distant hum of the giant ring almost twenty miles away. It was then that she heard something else, a faint sound coming from another direction. Sally slowed, listening, as Dirk began to pull away. The sound was familiar. She watched Dirk, intent on helping his friends, slowly fade ahead into the glimmering blue veil of the underwater sunlight.

*****

Alison kept hitting the keyboard, sending out the message again and again. The display was down to two minutes and thirty-two seconds. She was desperately digging through the storage compartments, looking for a manual to the boat. Of course, it was pointless. She did not know the first thing about boats or mechanics, but she looked anyway. She simply could not think of anything else to do. She had every cushion seat turned over and finally pulled up the last storage compartment lid. She felt a glimmer of hope, spotting a large toolbox and pulling it out. Alison flipped the cover over and dug through the tools as quickly as she could. No manual. Her heart sank.

She looked at the battery. It read one minute and forty-five seconds. She hit the keyboard again and collapsed down onto the floor crying. She felt so utterly stupid. She hardly knew anything about what was happening, and here she was running to the rescue.

Except there was no rescue. Instead, she had condemned herself to die as she sat helplessly in the middle of the ocean. She even tried turning her phone's cellular back on but there was no signal. It was hopeless.

She was crying so hard now that she did not hear IMIS relay a message. *Alison.* She tried to catch her breath, and looked at the battery display which was now nothing more than torture. It was almost down to one minute. IMIS broadcasted again and Alison's heart stopped. *Alison.*

Alison almost couldn't move. Half frozen, she forced herself to the side of the cabin and looked outside. Sally was next to her, with her head sticking out of the water. "Oh my god!" she ran for the door. "Wait!" She suddenly stopped when her hand grabbed the handle and turned around. The display said forty-seven seconds. In a flash, she rushed back to the keyboard and typed as fast as she could. *Sally danger. Must leave fast. Get Dirk.* She hit the enter key and waited what felt like an eternity for Sally's reply.

Dirk far now. Has gift.

"No! No!!" Alison moaned. She quickly typed again. *Must leave. Gift much much danger.*

She hit the enter key and looked at the display. It passed ten seconds. She could hear the server making noise, preparing to shut down. "Nooooo!" Alison yelled.

And then it was off. The screen went blank. All of the lights on the server disappeared.

"Dammit!" she shouted. She turned and burst through the door into the open air. Sally was watching her, making a series of clicks and whistles, but Alison no longer had any idea what she was saying. She looked out over the water, then to the dark flat line on the horizon which was Bimini. How far ahead was Dirk? How close was the ring? Her hands were shaking. The explosion could come any second.

Alison looked off to the south and could see the tiny island of North Cat Cay, a few miles away. She then looked down at Sally. In desperation, she jumped from the side of the boat and into the water. She passed Sally and began swimming in the direction of North Cat, but she did not get more than ten feet before Sally bumped her from behind.

Alison shook her head. "We have to leave, Sally!" Sally remained quiet, watching her. Alison gave her an exasperated look. Frustrated at her inability to communicate, she started swimming again. But she knew it was futile. Even an Olympic athlete could not swim that far in time. It was all she could think of.

Sally bumped her again from the back, momentarily pushing her underwater. Alison sputtered, coughing water out of her mouth, and then continued swimming. Again, Sally bumped her. "We have to GO!" She spit more water out.

She turned away again and felt another bump, this time harder. Alison realized she was not moving. Instead she felt Sally's nose and mouth dig into her back, grab the life jacket strap, and rip it free. The life jacket suddenly came loose around her neck and she scrambled to keep it on. Sally then bit the jacket around Alison's neck and pulled it off.

"What are you doing?!" Alison screamed, trying to tread water.

Sally gave another series of clicks and whistles. She then flipped the jacket around, keeping the neck area in her teeth. Alison stared at her, trying to understand. She looked at the white nylon straps hanging on either side of Sally.

Suddenly Alison's eyes opened wide. She quickly swam up behind Sally and wrapped her arms around Sally's thick neck. She gave her a kiss on the back of the head and then reached for the straps, wrapping them around her wrists. "Go Sally!" she yelled.

At once, Sally bolted forward with Alison hanging on behind her. Her powerful tail pumped hard behind them and the water surged past. Alison laid her head against Sally's neck and closed her eyes, trying to keep as much water out of her face as possible. She felt Sally's whole body move back and forth, soon reaching a smooth rhythm powering through the water.

*****

Dirk did not know where Sally went, but he could now see the distant bright blue glow from the ring. He pushed forward excitedly and descended deeper and deeper toward the bottom.

*****

Alison was struggling to keep from choking on all the water. She tried to lift her head for air. They were getting closer to North Cat. Suddenly, Sally accelerated. Alison began to slide side to side from the motion and fought to stay on. The pressure on her wrists was cutting off her circulation. She could barely feel her hands, now white and losing blood. Alison lifted her head and could see something ahead. It looked like... rocks. Did Sally see them? Were they going to come all this way just to smash themselves onto the rocks by accident? Sally's pace suddenly quickened even more.

Alison looked up again. It was a breakwater! And it was made up of thousands of giant boulders.

"Sally, stop!" Alison yelled, but Sally seemed to move even faster. "Sally, rocks!"

At that instant, behind them and deep underwater, the nuclear material inside the bomb fused and the atomic detonation was unleashed. In a fraction of a second, billions of tons of water were instantly vaporized. The explosion lifted a massive amount of water over twenty feet above sea level before falling back down again into the giant vacuum created in the center. The shock wave was enormous and traveled out in every direction, hitting Bimini first. Trees, cars, and buildings, were instantly flattened as Bimini's two islands absorbed much of the impact headed westward. The rest of the shock wave quickly rippled outward into the Atlantic, to the northeast and southeast.

After climbing over Bimini's islands, the wall of energy approached North Cat Cay at over two hundred miles per hour. Sally was now upon the breakwater and, with all of her might, she jumped as high into the air as she could, with Alison desperately holding on. In what felt like slow motion, they traveled over the breakwater rocks and hit the water on the other side, just as the shock wave smashed into the north side of the island.

42

PRESIDENT CARR WALKED into his oval office and slammed the door behind him. He turned to the men waiting for him, as angry as anyone had ever seen him.

"Who did it?!" he yelled.

Miller, Mason, Stevas, Langford, Bishop, and Bullman, all stood before him quietly.

"I said, who did it?!" Carr pointed at them angrily. "We all know that I'm going to find out soon, and the longer I have to wait, the more I will want someone in jail!"

The men all looked at each other. Clearly, some of them had no idea what he was talking about. Some, however, did. Stevas stepped forward and came out swinging.

"I did," he said, in a low growl. "I did what you wouldn't do! I did what you *couldn't* do."

Carr was not the least bit surprised. "You set off a nuclear bomb less than a hundred miles outside of a major metropolitan city. And you did it against my direct orders!"

"I did what had to be done." Stevas spat back. "Our country, our entire world, was on the brink of annihilation. The U.N. was bringing in the mother of all bureaucracies, and our time to control the situation was almost up. If we hadn't done it then, we wouldn't have been able to do it at all!"

"I gave you a direct order!" the President growled.

Stevas stepped towards him in defiance. "And I did what had to be done! I stopped it, and I stopped *them*! If you want to arrest me for saving this planet, then go ahead. I'll gladly sit by while I type out the whole story, explaining that our President didn't have the guts to act when it was clear that we were under attack!"

"Under attack?" The President looked at Stevas with disdain.

"That's right!" Stevas sneered. He looked at Miller. "What's wrong? Didn't your servant here tell you that those bastards destroyed all twelve of our subs? Every single one! And if you want to stand here and act like we still had time for some kind of diplomacy, then you go right ahead. I know what happened, and in the end, I did what you should have done!"

The President remained still, glaring at the smaller Stevas with a look that said he was contemplating punching him out. The room fell silent with both men staring at each other, chests heaving.

"And you didn't care," the President said, trying to control himself, "what the risk of blowing up that ring was to us or them."

Stevas shook his head. "Lawrence was confident there was no threat." He paused for effect. "And guess what, we're *still here.*"

Kathryn Lokke sat inside the small inflatable habitat, sitting at a small desk with her laptop computer. She was surprised at how well it worked at retaining the heat and giving them all some semblance of normality, considering the accommodations during their last stay. In one brisk movement, she closed her laptop, then stood up and put her parka and gloves back on.

The day was off to a good start, she thought, as she stepped outside. Not far away, one of her teams was examining the ice, making deep holes and testing for density. The area had to be strong enough to support the weight of the drilling machines, but not so hard that it would impede their drilling speed. Her other two teams were one and then two miles ahead of them, also looking for ideal areas for those holes.

One of the big mobile drilling machines rolled past Kathryn on its way to meet up with one of the forward teams. The tiny ice crystals kicking up behind the machine stung her face momentarily before she turned away. After it passed, she walked behind it and crossed the small working area. Steve Anderson, the head of the New Zealand team, was standing next to her old pal, Andrew, the guide who virtually saved her the last time here. They both looked up when she approached.

"G'day, Ms. Lokke." They said, almost in unison.

"I told you, it's Kathryn."

"Roight." they said, in their Kiwi accent.

"How are my charges coming?" she asked, referring to the explosives that would be placed at the bottom of the drilled lines.

"They should be here any minute," Steve confirmed. "Just spoke with the crew a couple minutes ago." He nodded past Kathryn's shoulder and she turned around.

"The airstrip is ready."

She could see Manly coming back toward them in his big red plow, bumping up and down inside his cab. He had one of the toughest jobs. After this job, he was headed forward to the end of the line, where he would have to plow yet another strip next to where they would camp for the night. Between gas, food, the explosives, additional people, and equipment, they would be getting a drop off nearly every morning for the next two weeks. Fortunately, next week would bring another plow and one of Manly's partners, which would make it easier and provide some backup.

Kathryn looked back when she heard the sound of the plane. It took her some time to find it in the bright sky, even though she had now seen more of these C130's then she ever wanted to. As the plane grew closer, lowering its landing gear, she and the two others began walking toward the strip.

The two men were talking about where they planned to put the supplies, when Kathryn stopped to tie her right boot which had come loose. She bent down and pulled the lace taught again and began to tie the knot, but stopped when she saw something appear next to her boot. It was a tiny crack. She looked at it curiously, without moving. A few seconds later, another crack appeared, this one slightly bigger. Was she standing on a weak spot?

Kathryn slowly stood up and looked around. Small cracks were appearing everywhere. She turned back to Steve and Andrew, who were still walking toward the plane that was now less than fifty feet above the ground.

"Hey." she said, but neither of the men heard her. "HEY!" she called out, louder.

Steven and Andrew turned and looked back at Kathryn. She was standing still, looking at the ground. "Yeah?"

"Look!" she yelled.

"Look at what?" Steve answered.

"Look at the ICE!" Her voice was trembling.

Both men looked around them and saw the tiny cracks forming all around. They looked back at Kathryn and their eyes opened wide when they saw what was behind her. Kathryn turned to see a giant crack forming and pieces of ice shooting up from the ground. Farther in, over the ice shelf, she could see many more pieces exploding into the air.

She looked at the two men in front of her. "Run!" she shouted. "RUN!" The people working behind her, including Manly who was just getting out of the truck, turned and looked at her curiously. "RUN!" Kathryn yelled again, waving them toward her. She looked further on, to the group of inflated structures serving as sleeping quarters. There were at least several more people inside. She felt sick as she realized they were too far way to hear her over the noise.

She turned back and saw the large plane rolling past them a few hundred yards away. She pointed to the aircraft and starting running. Steve and Andrew were already ahead of her. They were all running and yelling to anyone else they could see. They all stopped and called to the others again. "RUN!"

When she turned around, she saw her four-man team, who had just been measuring the ice, now running as fast as they could toward her. Far off in the background, she could see the familiar white fog rising into the air, but this time it was much, much bigger. In the far distance, she could see mud slides beginning against the base of the giant glacier. It was happening! The glacier was collapsing!

Now, Manly was running toward her with his arm behind one of the drillers. Kathryn turned to Steve and Andrew and shouted, pointing at the plane. "Don't let the plane stop!" They both nodded and ran after it.

The shaking began under her feet. She kept waving the others towards her and looked for anyone else. Tadri was one of the team members running to her. She stopped to pick up someone who had fallen and helped her to her feet. Kathryn kept looking at the living quarter huts, praying that they would come out. She looked back at the plane, watching Steven and Andrew jump up through the rear door as it slowed to a stop. A moment later, the engines, which were winding down, suddenly roared back to life. The plane quickly began to turn around to face the other direction.

The others finally caught up to Kathryn, and they all ran for the plane together. She looked over her shoulder and finally saw the others coming out of the living quarters. They looked around, then saw Kathryn and the rest running toward the plane. At that moment, a wide crack appeared, spreading in a long jagged line between Kathryn and the camp. It was too late.

The shaking was growing stronger and everyone tried to keep from stumbling sideways. They covered the distance to the strip, as the plane was slowly passing them. Stumbling back and forth, they rounded the back of the plane and chased after the side door. Both men were waiting, and holding onto each side of the door. They grabbed Tadri's hand, pulling her off her feet and inside. They reached out for the driller, and then for Manly and the rest. Finally, they grabbed Kathryn and hauled her in.

The engines roared again and the plane accelerated. Everyone in the back looked out the side windows as the ice sped past. They watched the cracks grow larger and larger. The wheels of the plane hit a big crack and everyone flew up, hitting the metal ceiling then fell back down. They all looked at one another rubbing their heads.

The plane was really moving. Outside, most of the ice became a blur, but all of the supplies were still onboard and with the added weight of its new passengers, the plane was struggling to take off. *Boom.* They felt another impact against the wheels that sent everyone into the air, fumbling for a better hold after they crashed back to the floor again.

Kathryn looked out one of the side windows. The glacier was barely visible and had turned dark brown from all the slides. The plane suddenly became smooth as it lifted off the ice, just as she watched the glacier collapse in the distance under its own weight.

At that moment, several billion tons of rock and ice separated and slid beneath the shelf. The collapse displaced an unimaginable amount of water, forcing it out and up into a massive tsunami. As the tsunami rose, it forced the entire ice shelf up with it, rising hundreds of feet within seconds.

Kathryn's team on the plane watched the ice shelf rise up, pushed skyward by the force of the tsunami. Their eyes grew wide and their breathing increased with every foot the shelf rose under them. As it climbed higher and higher, everyone instinctively tightened their grip, waiting for the land mass they had all just been standing on to smash into the bottom of the airplane.

The plane climbed as quickly as it could, but the speed of the rising shelf was much faster. No one in the back heard the pilots shouting in the cockpit and giving the engines everything they could. It was at that moment Kathryn remembered all of the drilling explosives that were still onboard. The ice below looked like it was now just inches away. Several of them closed their eyes and waited for the impact, but it never came.

*****

President Carr was glaring at Stevas when the phone on his desk beeped three times. He left the men standing in front of him and walked across the room and around his desk, pushing the speaker button on his handset. The voice of one of Mason's female assistants came on. "Mr. President, I have an urgent message for you from a Ms. Lokke."

Carr looked at the phone and squinted curiously. He

looked at the other men and replied. "Put her through."
There was a short click and the President spoke up loudly.
"Hello, Ms. Lokke, what do I-"

"It's happening!" Kathryn screamed frantically through
the phone. "It's collapsing right now!"

Panic filled the room as Carr looked at the others.
"The Shelf?"

"The glacier! The glacier has collapsed and destroyed
the shelf!"

"Oh, god." the President tried to think as he lowered
himself close to the phone. "Is it as bad as you thought?"

"Yes!" Kathryn answered immediately. The sound of
the plane's engines in the background drowned out her
voice. "The tsunami is enormous and it's headed north!"

"How fast?" Carr asked, as the other men quickly
crowded around his desk. "How much time do we have?"

"I don't know." She yelled over the background noise.
"Probably three or four hundred miles an hour which
means it would hit Florida in," she paused, "something like
twelve hours. But it will hit South America long before
that!"

Carr closed his eyes and hung his head. "What are our
options, Ms. Lokke?"

"I told you there were no options. We can't stop this.
The only thing we can do is evacuate!"

"Hold on." The President muted the line. He looked
at the men around him. "Jesus Christ. Is that even
possible?"

"Evacuate the entire Atlantic seaboard, in both North
and South America?" Miller said, shaking his head. "No,
not in twelve hours."

"But some would be able to get out right?" Carr said.

"Not necessarily," replied Langford. "We'd start a
panic of biblical proportions. It would likely be nothing
but a mob scene until the tsunami arrived."

"Mr. President?" asked Kathryn.

Carr quickly took her off mute. "Yes, Ms. Lokke, we're

here."

"You stopped the nuclear test right?!"

He raised his eyebrows and looked at the phone. "Nuclear test? What nuclear test?"

"The one that John Clay told me about."

Carr looked up again at the group surrounding his desk. "What exactly did John Clay tell you, Ms. Lokke?"

Kathryn was still yelling over the engines. "He called and asked me whether the shock wave from a nuclear test you were planning could accidentally trigger the glacier collapse. He was going to stop it." She paused for a moment when she realized what had just happened. "My god, you didn't stop it did you?! *That's* what caused the collapse! Tell me you stopped it."

The President muted his microphone again and looked directly at Stevas. It all became clear. "Clay knew what was going to happen, and he was trying to stop your attack." The President raised his voice. "Your nuclear explosion just triggered a global tsunami!"

Stevas' face went white. He shook his head, utterly speechless.

The President looked like he was going to come over the desk at him. Instinctively, the other men stepped back. "You did what you had to do! That's what you said, and now tens of millions of people are going to die because of YOU!"

"I-I was just doing what…" Stevas stammered, looking at Mason for help. "I didn't know. It was the ring we were worried about…I didn't know it would trigger anything."

"Look at me, Hank." The President growled as he leaned forward. "*Where* is John Clay?"

Stevas did not answer. His mind was struggling to understand exactly how everything had just turned so horribly wrong.

"I said," the President repeated, "where is John Clay?!"

Stevas looked down at the floor. "I-I sent a Delta

team." He looked up sheepishly. "They killed him."

Langford's eyes suddenly filled with rage, and he leapt at Stevas. "You son of a bitch!" He grabbed Stevas by the collar and hit him with a right punch, knocking him over a small table and onto the floor. Without missing a beat, Langford jumped over the table and reached for Stevas again before Miller and Bullman grabbed his arms and pulled him back.

"Mr. President?" Kathryn called out. "Are you there?"

"Yes, Ms. Lokke, I'm still here. Please hold on a minute." He looked at Stevas who was trying to stand up. "We're working through something here." The President watched Stevas regain his balance and back away from everyone in the room. The President was about to walk around his desk when his phone beeped again three times. He slowly reached down and hit the second line. "Yes?"

"Mr. President," a man's voice said, "this is Agent Rubke, downstairs. There's uh…someone here to see you."

"Someone to see me?" Carr asked. "Who the hell is it?"

"He says his name is John Clay."

43

THE SECRET SERVICE agent walked into the room and held the door open, waiting for Clay to enter. Everyone was surprised to see Palin follow Clay into the room. Clay stopped and scanned the room. When he got to Stevas, his eyes locked on him. "That's him," he said to Palin.

Palin stood still, staring at Stevas. For the first time, Clay saw genuine fear in Stevas' eyes and watched as he backed up still further into the wall. If he could have become the wall, he would have.

"I'm sorry, sir," the agent said to the President. "We don't know how they got past the gate."

"It's alright. You can leave us."

The agent hesitated until Carr looked at him again. He finally stepped past them and joined the other two agents waiting outside. The door closed quietly behind Clay and Palin.

"Well, well, Mr. Clay. We've been looking for you." The President stepped forward, glancing at Stevas. "In fact, we thought something had happened to you."

"Something did." Clay followed Carr's look back to Stevas and then looked over at Langford. "They killed Caesare."

Langford's jaw tightened in anger, but he remained silent, glaring at Stevas.

"I'm sorry, Clay. It seems some of us thought you may have been on the wrong side. Something that just got corrected a few minutes ago. I think I can speak for everyone here when I say we are relieved that you are alright. Both you and Mr. Palin." He gestured toward the phone. "Ms. Lokke has informed us that you were evidently trying to stop the nuclear blast."

"That's right." Clay stated simply.

"Well, now we have a serious problem on our hands. That nuclear explosion apparently triggered the collapse in the Ronne Ice Shelf just a few minutes ago. We now have a tsunami headed north that we cannot stop."

Clay pointed to the phone. "Is she still on the line?"

The President reached down and pushed the button for the first line. "Ms. Lokke, are you still there?"

After a moment, her voice came out of the speaker. The engines sounded lower. "Yes, sir. We have to head back to McMurdo though as we won't have enough fuel. I have lost sight of the tsunami."

Carr quickly motioned to Mason, his Chief of Staff. "Get us a video feed! However you have to do it."

Mason nodded, walked to the far side of the room, and pulled his cell phone from his jacket.

Clay looked at the President who nodded and moved back, giving him the phone. Clay walked across the large rug and sat slowly down in the seat. Palin followed and stood next to him. Clay exhaled slowly and spoke into the phone.

"Ms. Lokke, this is John Clay. We spoke a few days ago."

"I remember. You said you were going to stop the explosion. What the hell happened?"

"Well," Clay said, "some people had other plans." He softly put a hand to his chest and scooted forward in his chair. His wound was still extremely painful. "Ms. Lokke, I understand this cannot be stopped by conventional means...but there are other islands that are also at risk of a massive collapse, correct?"

"Yes," she replied quickly.

"Isn't Tristan Island one of those high risk locations?"

"Uh, yeah," she said, with a touch of sarcasm, "although Tristan is medium risk. There are dozens of them around the world."

"Ms. Lokke," Clay continued slowly. "Isn't Tristan's slide zone on the south side of the island?"

"Well, yes." Kathryn suddenly gasped. "Oh my god! Yes it is!"

"Is this possible?" Clay asked her.

"Yes!" She almost yelled into her headset. "Yes, it's possible! We'd have to check some things, but it might work." She paused. "But we would need something to start it."

Everyone seemed to close in around Clay and Palin at the desk. "What?" said the President. "What might work?!"

Clay turned to Carr. "These land mass collapses have happened throughout history and are very infrequent, but as we know, the effects are devastating. Tristan is a large island in the South Atlantic and is one of the locations where part of the land mass is slowly separating. It's not due for a very long time but we may be able to help it happen, and create a tidal wave traveling in the opposite direction." He looked at everyone as he spoke. "If we can't stop the tsunami headed this way, perhaps we can block it."

Everyone looked eager. "Ms. Lokke?" Carr asked.

"We need to verify our data," she said, "Most waves pass through each other but it is possible for some to collide, given the right circumstances. Something called constructive interference. It's not as common but there's still a chance of reducing the size of the wave traveling north. It may mean the difference between thousands of lives instead of millions."

Carr looked back to Clay. "And how would we start it?"

"It would take something big," he said, "like a nuclear impact."

The President shook his head. "Wait a minute. We're talking about *another* nuclear bomb?"

The irony was not wasted on Clay, or the President, for that matter. Without the first nuke, they would not have needed the second. But, more importantly, this would be the first time a nuclear explosion was used to save lives. The President stepped back, shaking his head. *How on earth was he going to explain two nuclear explosions?*

Langford placed his hand gently on Clay's shoulder. "How did you know that, John?"

Clay shrugged innocently. "I read up on Ms. Lokke and her work after we met her at JAX."

Miller looked at the President. "Sir, we are going to require launch codes for this. And the Vice President."

*****

"Mr. President, we have a visual on the tsunami." Mason turned on a large monitor on the wall. "It's a live satellite." The picture in the monitor showed a wide angle view of the South Atlantic Ocean. When Mason zoomed in, a small, almost faint line could be seen moving up the picture.

"It looks smaller than I thought."

"Tsunamis cannot be seen in deep water," answered Clay. "They grow when they reach the shore."

The phone rang and Carr answered immediately. "Go ahead."

Kathryn's voice came over the speaker. "Mr. President, we've just gone over the data with some colleagues in D.C. We think this is our best option."

Carr sighed. "And what happens if we unleash another wave in the wrong direction?"

"Mr. President," came Kathryn's voice over the loud engines. "I honestly don't think we can make this situation worse."

He looked at Mason. "Get the Chinese and the Russians on the phone. We better make damn sure they know what this is when it shows up on their radars." Mason nodded and ran for the door. He opened it just as Miller and Vice President Bailey were coming in. Miller was carrying the infamous briefcase called 'the football', which carried the country's nuclear launch codes. He placed it on the table in front of the President.

Carr skipped to his second phone line. When the female voice answered, he said, "Get me NORAD." He then moved to the metal briefcase, turning the tumblers to the correct combination and then pressing the buttons in to release the locks. The lid popped open quietly.

"NORAD is on, sir," replied the female voice. A moment later, it was replaced by a deep voice. "This is

293

General Schmidt."

The Vice President stepped to his side as Carr leaned into the microphone. "This is President Jonathan Scott Carr. Prepare to verify."

The sky was overcast over most of central Georgia. The trees were dark green, and the forest seemed to go on forever. The rolling forested hills were only interrupted periodically by patches of open space, covered with bright green grass waving gently under the cool breeze. One large patch of open space was nearly hidden among the oaks and pines, surrounded by a large steel chain link fence. The old painted sign on the entrance to the area read 'No Trespassing - Department of Agriculture'. Inside the fence was a large metal shed with a dome on top of the roof. A tall antenna tower stood next to it.

Suddenly, the silence was split when a deafening siren sounded and the dome lit up with a bright orange spinning light. On the ground, a large section of grass rumbled sideways, revealing a silo beneath it. As the silo was revealed, so was the tip of a large missile. No sooner had the door slid fully open, the silo instantly filled with smoke and fire. In less than a second, the missile shot from the ground, climbed quickly through the air and disappeared into the gray clouds above.

44

FIRST SIGHTED IN 1506, the island of Tristan Da Cunha was the largest island in the most remote archipelago in the Atlantic Ocean, lying over 1,700 miles from the nearest major land mass. Annexed by the United Kingdom in 1816 to prevent it being used as a staging ground to rescue Napoleon Bonaparte on Saint Helena, the island was home to just over two hundred sixty residents. With only one small town called "The Settlement", the local families were far removed from modern conveniences, and problems.

Eleven-year-old, Neri Repetto, had finished school and was climbing the hill to his secret place along the island's only waterfall. The days were long this time of year and he still had plenty of time to finish his chores. Today, he hoped to surprise his mother and younger brother with fish for dinner. He had been hoping the same thing every day for almost two weeks, but Neri was not one to give up.

As he climbed the side of the mountain, he spotted a goat behind a large tree and contemplated whether he should take it back to Mrs. Hagan. He decided to take it home on his way back. The afternoon was warm. In tattered shoes, Neri jumped from rock to rock as he continued to climb. It was not long before he could hear the sound of the waterfall beyond the large trees. With long strides, Neri quickened his pace and headed into the shade beneath the trees.

Neri froze. He stood, still staring, trying to figure out what it was that he was looking at. He slowly looked around. Seeing no one else, he took a few steps forward. It did not look like anything he had ever seen. He crept a little closer. It was wavering slightly, and the bright blue light formed a large oval that was a little higher than his head. The center looked dark, but not quite black. He studied the object carefully. He looked at the ground in front of the strange oval. There appeared to be footprints in the wet grass.

"Mama! Mama!" Neri ran yelling into the small house.

"Neri!" His mother snapped at him, looking up from

her wood stove. "Your brother is asleep!"

"Mama!" he said quietly. "You have to come see!"

She wiped her hands on her apron. "Come see what, Neri? Did one of those goats run off again?"

"Yes, yes, but that's not what I want to show you." He grabbed her hand and pulled her reluctantly out the door.

His mother stepped outside, looking around. None of the red roofs of The Settlement appeared to be on fire and there was no sound coming from the main street. "What is it? I don't see anything."

"No," he said, "it's up there." Neri pointed to the trail that ran up the mountainside. "Up by the waterfall."

His mother squinted her eyes. "I still don't see anything."

"You can't see it from here. You have to come up." He insisted, still pulling on her arm.

"Please, Neri," she sighed. "I can't very well leave your brother here alone."

Neri was still breathing hard from his run back to town. "It's...a light. A bright blue light, just standing on the grass."

She eyed Neri with a raised eyebrow. "Have you been eating the mushrooms?"

"No!" he complained. "I was on my way to fish. It's up there next to my spot. It's...incredible."

"I'm sure it is," his mother said, shaking her apron out. She really could not imagine what he was talking about. She turned to walk back into the house when something caught her eye. She turned around and looked up along the hill. There was something in the sky, something moving very quickly and leaving a white trail behind it, like the big airplanes did. "What is that?"

Neri looked up and saw it too.

His mother watched it carefully and then suddenly opened her eyes wide. She did not know what it was but it looked like it was headed towards them. "Neri!" she screamed, grabbing him by the arm. "Get inside!" She threw him through the door ahead of her. As she began to close the door, she paused just for a moment. *Why is the sky so blue?* She thought to herself that she had never seen anything like that before. She blinked and looked at the other buildings around her. Everything looked blue.

*****

The President and his cabinet watched as the giant wave moved up through the Atlantic ocean at a speed of over three hundred miles per hour. The island of Tristan Da Cunha with its small archipelago was just below the latitude of Africa's Cape of Good Hope. Everyone could see clearly from the satellite that if it could not be stopped there, the damage would start almost immediately when it hit Africa's southwestern coast. I would begin with the first large metropolitan city of Cape Town and its population of over three million. The next city to be devastated was Buenos Aires, on the South American coast and the other side of the Atlantic.

Kathryn had landed just minutes ago at McMurdo where she and her team now watched from a large conference room. The room was deathly silent as they watched the massive wave.

The dark line in the ocean approached a small uninhabited island, two hundred miles southeast of Tristan. This island would provide the best measurement of the tsunami's energy. It would be the first island hit full force, and give a visual estimation for what was to come.

Kathryn and her team knew that if a counter wave could not be generated before the tsunami passed much farther beyond this first island, the wave would not be able to travel far enough from Tristan to provide the effect they needed, or spread wide enough across the ocean.

As the tsunami reached the first island, it quickly grew much larger on the monitor as the island's rising mass beneath the ocean forced the full size of the tsunami up to the surface.   Kathryn and her team gasped.   It was *enormous*.

In one smooth movement, the wave struck and quickly wrapped itself around, enveloping the entire island. Part of the island's southern facing cliffs could be seen crumbling into giant pieces, before the water engulfed everything. The total shock, however, felt both from the White House and McMurdo, came when the island completely disappeared from view. Over twenty five square miles of solid rock reaching hundreds of feet high, was completely destroyed in less than a minute. It was as if the top of the island had been simply wiped way.

"Oh my god!" Kathryn Lokke gasped. It was so much bigger than any of them were expecting. Her hopes of stopping this thing, even with a counter tsunami, began to melt.

In the White House, President Carr's face, as well as the others, went completely white.

The incredible wave of destruction continued its relentless push north.

*****

A blue dome covered The Settlement as the intercontinental ballistic missile approached Tristan at over 3,000 miles per hour. Its coordinates were exact. The missile dove and detonated less than 300 feet above the south end of the island. Even with the island's peak blocking some of the impact, the entire sky turned bright white, as the incredible force of the nuclear reaction was unleashed. Much of the rocky slope instantly turned to glass and the downward impact against the mountain caused the structure beneath the island to shift and then buckle altogether. A line formed and cut its way across the southern slope, breaking the glass and rock into millions of fragments and sending them upward in every direction. A deep rumbling followed, shaking the entire island violently.

Then in one giant motion, a third of the island slid away from the mountain and off its underwater base, plunging straight into the ocean. The energy released in the warhead was just a fraction of that released when the slide displaced an enormous mass of water, pushing it forward into a second gigantic wave.

*****

The wave raced southward, almost instantly washing over the smaller islands of the archipelago, taking every bit of loose soil or life form with it.

Everyone watched as two waves of unimaginable power sped towards each other. It took less than ten minutes for them to cover the distance. When they reached each other, the impact was easily visible as the dark lines on the satellite suddenly turned white. The white line of impact became thick and began to grow wider and wider, becoming a mile wide, then five miles, then ten. The pressure pushed the water into the air, forming a giant white wall which began to ripple out almost half way across the Atlantic. The wall of water grew taller and taller reaching nearly three hundred feet above the surface before it began to slow. The rising water finally began to slow, and then stopped, dropping back toward the ocean. When it hit the surface, the impact created a huge depression, which was quickly covered by the incoming surge on both sides. Both sides of the surge smashed into one another, created another wall, which itself eventually dropped down to make another depression, followed by one final surge.

At hundreds of miles per hour, each successive surge followed the ripple outward in both directions, as the tails from both waves finally impacted each other.

*****

From the satellite, they could see the thick line of water begin to disperse and eventually return to its normal blue color. The faint lines from each wave could be seen continuing further away, having passed through each other, but with virtually none of their energy left.

Everyone at McMurdo screamed and jumped up and down, hugging each other. Kathryn stood motionless, feeling the energy drain from her body. At the same time, her eyes filled up with tears. She couldn't believe it. She simply could not believe it. It worked. It actually worked.

In Washington, the President fell back into his chair exhausted. The rest of the men clapped wildly and Stevas, still off to the side, clapped harder than anyone. They all stared at the monitor, watching the water swirl and blend back in with the rest of the ocean. Carr covered his face with his hands and just shook his head. He had no words. No words at all.

45

CLAY STEPPED OUT of the portal, behind Palin, and into a large blue room. He looked around and realized that they were standing in a large sphere surrounded by water. The portal blinked out behind them and the room darkened, allowing his eyes to adjust. He looked at the nearby wall and walked to it. The water appeared to somehow be part of the room. Incredulous, he turned and looked back at Palin, who merely smiled. Clay reached out and touched the wall. His finger went straight through into the cold water on the other side. He drew his hand back and looked at his wet finger. He tasted it. Saltwater.

He looked further through the water and could see the distorted shape of the ring, giant and still. He turned back to Palin. "This is the city. Your settlement."

"Yes."

"We were here before, right?" Clay examined the room.

Palin made a humorous expression. "Yes, but we were unconscious then."

Clay smiled and nodded his head. He looked through the wall on the other side and could see hundreds of similar spheres. Something caught his eye and he turned to see a moving object headed their way. It looked like a tunnel forming from another sphere to theirs. In the tunnel were several people, all walking toward them.

The tunnel connected to their room and a small group entered, led by a woman dressed in a deep colored blue robe. On her head was a band with stones embedded in it. She walked smoothly toward him and stopped a few steps away.

"Hello, Mr. Clay," she said, with a smile. "My name is Laana." She reached out her hand and he took it gently.

"Laana." Clay bowed slightly.

She continued to smile as she watched him. "I want to thank you. You have helped us greatly. Without you, I'm afraid we would not have survived."

"Well, with all due respect, I think I was also part of the problem."

Her blue eyes softened at the edges. "I suppose so, but there *were* others. Yet in the end, you were our salvation. You returned Palin in time for us to protect ourselves, and the ring. Without you, both rings would have been destroyed and neither of our people would have survived."

He accepted the compliment. "It was my pleasure."

A loud sound reverberated behind them. Clay turned around to see the ring slowly begin turning again.

"What now?" he asked.

She motioned to the others behind her. "Now we go

home." She answered his next question before he could ask it. "We have enough water now to maintain and grow again." Behind her, Clay noticed some of the distant spheres begin to move. They seemed to detach from the rest and float inward, toward the ring. Others also began to detach until dozens were following. Clay realized that she was still holding his hand. She gave it a warm squeeze. "We are thankful that Palin found a good man to trust."

"I have questions," he said. "A lot of them, actually."

She smiled. "I'm sure you do."

"Why did you tell us everything?" He looked over her shoulder at Palin. "Why reveal everything to us so easily?"

Laana tilted her head. "Palin agreed to tell you. He was in your debt. You see, the man you allowed him to save aboard your vessel…was his son."

Clay's eyes widened. "I had no idea."

She smiled. "Besides, we knew we could not remain undetected for long."

Clay contemplated his next question. He was afraid of what she would say. He took a deep breath. "Is there-" he began, when Laana held up her hand and stopped him.

"As for your other questions," she said, "your people will need to discover the answers for themselves. It is unwise for a race to gain knowledge too quickly. Trust me."

With that, she let his hand slip from hers and took a step back. The others behind her, in similar robes, all nodded to him and turned away smoothly. One by one, they left as the tunnel reappeared and traveled back in the opposite direction.

Only Palin remained. The tunnel stayed open, waiting for him. He approached Clay and put out his hand.

"Thank you, John Clay."

"You're welcome, Palin." Clay looked at him and smiled. "Brothers?"

Palin squeezed his hand. "Brothers."

46

ALISON SAT IN what was left of her large research room. The aquarium was officially shut down for three weeks. The carpet was gone and dozens of workers were repairing the walls. On the far side, some of the carpet had already been replaced, and the servers were being reinstalled with the help of Lee and Chris. New desks were being carried in through the large hallway and stacked to the side until the floor was ready. Now, the workers were slowly beginning to file out for the evening.

She looked at the tank. The bullets had been removed from the glass, and the holes patched and refinished. Inside, Sally slowly swam in place, healing from the deep wounds that covered her body. Alison had fared even worse. Her right arm was in a cast and lacerations covered most of her face. Her legs had been very badly injured, but fortunately, the wheelchair she sat in was temporary.

The place felt like an opened tomb. She thought of the people who had died. She thought of Dirk, who had innocently swam right into the middle of it all, thinking he was helping. Dolphins were so much more beautiful than humans, she thought. They deserved to be here more than we did.

She lowered her head. Dirk and Sally felt like her children, and losing Dirk hurt her heart more than she ever thought possible.

Suddenly, there was a bright flash. Alison looked up and around the room. After exchanging curious looks with Chris and Lee, she looked back and froze when her eyes fell on the tank. There in the water, next to Sally, was

Dirk, slowly moving his tail back and forth. Sally burst with excitement, circling him over and over, wounds and all. Dirk nudged her affectionately as she passed. After several moments, he turned his attention to Alison and swam to the edge of the tank. He opened his mouth and said something, but without IMIS, it would go unheard.

He looked at her curiously, unsure why she was shaking. It would be some time before she could explain human crying to him.

And it would be almost a full year before Alison would learn what had even happened.

*****

President Carr stepped up to the lectern. He looked like he had aged rapidly in the last week. With his normal prose, he smiled and began the press conference.

"My fellow Americans, I am both troubled and proud to report to you the extraordinary efforts of our men and women in uniform in stopping not just one, but two nuclear terrorist attacks. As you know, avoiding a nuclear strike on American soil is our upmost priority, and today we have done precisely that. Two airplanes, one coming from the Middle East and one coming from Africa, were both identified, and destroyed, before they could reach our shores. And while we can be glad that they were stopped, the bombs were, in fact, armed and detonated on impact. Fortunately, the lives lost were minimal. We believe these two warheads were stolen from Russia's stockpile, which we will…"

Clay watched the President from his barstool at the end of the counter. The spin was better than he expected. He reached for his beer, which had hardly been touched. Governments lie, he thought. They always have and they always will. He raised the glass to his lips, but stopped short and put it back down. He sighed and stood up slowly, holding his side. It was going to be a long recovery.

He pulled a bill from his wallet and dropped it onto the counter.

*****

Out on the street, he decided to go for a walk and headed toward Constitution Avenue. Within a few blocks, he could see the tip of the Washington Monument over the rest of the buildings. At the park, he found and sat down on a bench, admiring the monuments to our forefathers.

"Next time you have one of your bright ideas," a voice said behind him, "you can count me out."

Startled, Clay whirled around to see Steve Caesare standing behind him. He blinked several times. "What...how?" He stood up without turning around, wondering if he were hallucinating.

Caesare, with a load of bandages under his clothes, stood smiling at Clay.

"I don't understand," Clay said, walking toward him.

He shrugged. "Back in the lab, when you went through that portal thing, I managed to crawl through before it closed. I don't really remember much after that."

Clay simply stood there, shaking his head. His eyes began to well up.

"Aw," Caesare said. "I hope you're not gonna cry right here in front of everybody."

Clay smiled and wiped the tears away. He walked forward to Caesare and hugged him, causing both of them to groan in pain.

"Hey," Caesare said, stepping back. "Did you hear about Stevas?"

Clay shook his head. "No."

"Nobody's seen him. Sounds like his wife called in a missing person's report and nobody can find him. What a shame, huh?"

"Carr probably threw him in jail."

"From what I hear they don't know where he is either."

The two exchanged a puzzled look. After a long moment, a grin began to spread across both their faces. They turned and began walking away from the park. "So what now?" asked Caesare. "I still get my pension right?"

Clay stopped and frowned at him. "Man, I'm sorry, I told Borger he could have it."

Caesare laughed. "Damn, John, I wasn't even cold yet."

Clay smiled at him and looked up at the setting sun. "Actually, I thought I might take a drive south to Miami. Maybe check out the aquarium. I hear they're doing some interesting things down there."

LEAP

Chapter 1

"I THINK YOU'D better get down here. We've got company."

Her eyes opened wide with the phone receiver still gripped tightly in her hand. She immediately hung up and jumped out of her chair, rounding the desk and running for the door. After flinging it open and sprinting down the carpeted hallway, she approached the wide stairs and descended as quickly as she could without tripping.

The layout of the new building was strikingly similar to the old one, but here the air conditioning system was barely able to stave off Puerto Rico's brutal humidity. By the time she'd made it to the large double doors, the familiar flush through her body told her that her sweat glands were kicking into gear. She lowered her head and leaned into the doors, pushing them both open.

The familiar computerized voice sounded almost immediately. *Hello Alison.*

Alison smiled broadly toward the giant seawater tank. "Hello, Sally," she replied, partially out of breath. "You're back."

Sally wiggled her tail happily. *We back.*

Alison raised an eyebrow, scanning the rest of the tank's bright blue water. "Where's Dirk?"

Before she could answer, Dirk plunged into the top of the tank with a giant splash and performed a barrel roll as he skirted past Sally.

Alison laughed. He loved making a grand entrance. Of course, they really needed to change the part of the tank that allowed him to do that.

Dirk continued to the bottom where he swung up and around before coasting in next to Sally. *Hello Alison. Hello Chris.*

Alison smirked and tilted her head slightly. "Hello, Dirk."

We happy see you.

"We're happy to see you too." Chris Ramirez joined Alison in front of the tank, holding his perpetual cup of coffee. How he could drink coffee all day in this heat, she would never know.

Their new facility was smaller than the aquarium in Miami, but this one was strictly a research center, which meant fewer unplanned distractions. Gutted from an old cannery, the building was refurbished and expanded to include a large indoor-outdoor tank for Dirk and Sally. Now they could come and go as they pleased. No more bars.

It was, of course, the least she and the team could do after what they'd all been through. And true to their word, the dolphins returned regularly. It also helped that Dirk was fed like a king.

Behind Alison and Chris, and against the far wall, stood an immense computer system with hundreds of blinking lights. IMIS, short for Inter Mammal Interpretive System, was the same system that made their first communications with Dirk and Sally possible. But now IMIS was over twice its original size. After her team relocated to Puerto Rico and closer to the dolphins' natural breeding ground, the IMIS system had gone through a major upgrade. It was almost quaint to think about its abilities before, compared to its computing power now. It made Lee Kenwood, their head of technology, absolutely giddy. In fact, Alison and Chris had both joked to Lee that it looked as though he were trying to show up the engineers at NASA.

Alison didn't fully understand the specifications of the newly upgraded IMIS, but she did know it had a lot to do with what Lee called *teraflops*. But to her, it was simply bigger and faster. And even though it had doubled in size, Lee claimed it was almost eight times more powerful. The amount of data that IMIS could process before in a day, it could now do in a couple hours.

Sally swam close to the underwater microphone. *How you Alison?*

"I am very well," she smiled. "How are you?"

We good. You ready now.

"Not yet, but soon."

Smiling, Chris took a sip from his cup. "I guess we have some calls to make."

"We sure do."

Food now.

Alison glanced back at Dirk as he thrust his tail up and down, excitedly. She folded her arms in front and shook her head.

If the world had been surprised at their breakthrough before, this time they were going to be absolutely stunned.

2

"THE CRADLE OF Naval Aviation" was the unofficial name of the Naval Air Base near Pensacola, Florida. It was built as the country's first Naval Air Station and remained so even well into the First World War. In present day, it was known for being the primary training facility for all Navy, Marine, and Coast Guard aviators and flight officers. It was also home to the Blue Angels, the Navy's famed flight demonstration squadron.

Spanning an area of well over eight thousand acres, the Pensacola Naval Complex employed twenty-three thousand military and seventy-four hundred civilians. Not surprisingly, it was a major hub for modern hi-tech naval research and testing.

It was also where Commanders John Clay and Steve Caesare, from Naval Investigations, had been living for the past two weeks.

Both men briskly made their way down the long, polished hallway of the Naval Education and Training Command building's third floor. When they reached the end, the pair stopped before a large white door. John Clay knocked and the door was promptly opened from the inside. Stepping into the room, Clay and Caesare recognized Rear Admiral David Einhorn, the commander of the NETC. Einhorn was sitting behind his desk with his Force Master Chief standing next to him, both of whom ceased their conversation and looked up expectantly when Clay and Caesare entered. Almost unnoticed, the lieutenant who had opened the door then silently stepped out behind them and closed it again.

Einhorn nodded. "Gentlemen, I understand you have something for me."

"Yes, sir," replied Clay. They both approached the desk, but Clay took an extra step forward and handed Admiral Einhorn a thin folder. "We've finished the investigation, sir. Here is the signed report."

Einhorn took the folder and flipped it open, glancing over the first page. "A power failure? Are you kidding?"

Clay shook his head. "No, sir."

"How the hell does a power failure cause a drone to go rogue?"

They'd been expecting this reaction, especially from Einhorn. After all, they'd already uploaded their report online and forwarded copies to both Einhorn and their own boss, Admiral Langford, a half hour ago. Their hand delivered copy was merely a formality. Judging from his reaction, Einhorn had read the online version already.

Einhorn hadn't wanted them there from the beginning. The failure with the drone was a fluke as far as he was concerned. Hell, as far as his entire staff was concerned. But it did happen. A new drone lost connection with its remote pilot for twelve seconds. It may not have seemed like a big deal to everyone else, especially since the connection was reestablished successfully, but it required an investigation. Not because the Navy necessarily worried about the connection, but because of what might have happened during those twelve seconds.

A few years before, a Predator Drone had been captured in Iran by blocking the aircraft's satellite connection back to its remote pilot in Arizona. Worse, Iran never had to hack the drone. They only had to keep the connection blocked long enough to force it into an emergency mode, which compelled the drone to get itself to the ground safely. It was a bug in the software: a mistake.

Nevertheless, having the world watch their televisions and see Iranian soldiers dancing up and down on one of the Unites States' four million dollar secret weapons was not something the Pentagon was willing to endure again.

Clay cleared his throat and answered Einhorn. "Well, sir, the failure was caused by a power fluctuation on one of the drone's motherboards. It's the same board that controls the transceivers and antennas. We think it's a design flaw with the hardware since we've been able to reproduce the problem several times."

Einhorn dropped the file on his desk and leaned back in his chair, clearly irritated. "So, was it hacked?"

"No, sir."

"I didn't think so," the Admiral scoffed. "I told them they were sending you boys out for nothing."

This time Clay and Caesare looked at each other. "Well," replied Caesare, "it doesn't necessarily mean that it *couldn't* be hacked…sir."

Einhorn furrowed his brow at Caesare. He didn't care for either one of them. He had a department to run, one of the most important in the Navy, and he didn't like these guys from investigations poking their noses wherever they liked. Yet, while Einhorn was not happy, he certainly wasn't stupid either.

It wasn't clear why, but he knew both of the commanders standing before him reported directly to Admiral Langford, the President's new Chairman of the Joint Chiefs of Staff. Langford had replaced General Griffith, who moved to fill the role of National Security Advisor after that position was unexpectedly vacated. Now Langford had the President's ear, so Einhorn wasn't about to do or say anything stupid.

"So, what's your recommendation then?" asked Einhorn, with heavy sarcasm.

Clay paid no attention to the Admiral's tone. "A full analysis, which includes an audit of the hardware design and software computer code."

"And how long will that take?"

"I'm not sure, sir. It would depend on the resources available." Clay knew Einhorn wasn't going to like any estimate he offered, so he simply left it at that.

Einhorn grunted and picked up the folder again. "Well, I trust Langford will let us know how to proceed. I suppose that's all, gentlemen. Thank you for your time."

Clay and Caesare both gave slight nods and spun around. They walked back to the door and exited without a sound.

After Caesare pulled the door closed behind him, he looked at Clay. "Have we ever discussed how thankless this job is?"

"Almost weekly," smiled Clay. He turned to fall into step with Caesare when his cell phone rang. Stopping, he pulled it out of his pocket and looked at the displayed number. "It's Langford."

He held the phone to his ear. "This is Clay." After a long pause, he replied with a simple, "Yes, sir."

Caesare raised his eyebrows, curiously. "That was quick."

"We need to find a conference room."

*****

Truth be told, Admiral Langford never wanted the chairman job. But in the end, he was an officer and the President asked him to do it. And frankly, he was leery of who else would have been asked had he declined. Although he originally had his doubts, Langford decided that Carr actually had the fortitude and ethics to be a solid President. And that was something most military leaders longed for.

Langford's weathered face appeared on the video screen in front of Clay and Caesare. "I see you've uploaded your report on the drone. Have you talked to Einhorn yet?"

"Yes, sir," Clay nodded. "We just dropped off the signed hard copy."

"How'd he take it?"

Caesare smiled. "He loved it!"

"I bet." Langford couldn't decide whether to scoff or roll his eyes. "I guess as long as he didn't physically throw you out of his office, we can consider it a success. You're probably aware that he's not a big fan of Investigations."

"We picked up on that."

"Good," Langford continued, glancing at his watch. "I'm sure I'll be hearing from him shortly." He looked back into the camera. "In the meantime, I'm sending a plane for you. I need you on it ASAP."

"Where are we going?"

"Brazil. We have a bit of a situation. Call it a

surprise."

"I hate surprises," Caesare chortled.

Clay looked at Caesare. "That's true, sir. His second marriage was largely a surprise."

The corner of Langford's lip curled at the joke. "Relax. It's not an engagement party. It appears we are the proud owners of a new sub."

Clay and Caesare peered with anticipation at the screen.

"Last night the Brazilian Navy captured a submarine off the coast of French Giana. It's Russian. November class."

Both men's expressions changed from curious to confused. "November class? I thought those were decommissioned."

"So did we." The admiral leaned forward onto his elbows. "It appears at least one was not. It was first detected three days ago and a Brazilian Tikuna was dispatched."

"And they *captured* it?" Clay asked. A single submarine catching another was quite a feat.

Langford smiled, reading Clay's face. "Well, they asked for a little help. We had two of our boats behind the Tikuna. Unofficially, of course."

"What's a November doing in Brazilian waters?" asked Caesare. "Something that old wouldn't simply be out on patrol."

"No, it wouldn't. Unfortunately, we don't know why. The crew isn't talking. All twenty-seven of them."

"Twenty-seven?"

"A skeleton crew," confirmed Langford.

Caesare raised an eyebrow. "Is that even possible?"

"Evidently."

"What did the Russians say?"

"We haven't asked them yet," Langford replied, with a smile.

"You're not suggesting *we* talk to the crew, sir?"

"No, I want you two to get down there and take a look

at that Russian sub. The pictures we got back suggest it has something important on board, and we want to know what it is."

3

LEE KENWOOD WAS thrilled with their new lab. Finally able to separate their systems from the main observation area, it gave him some much needed elbow room to work on the hardware for their next project. And it was a doozy.

He also appreciated the extra help from Juan Diaz, a Puerto Rican native and computer engineer, just a few years out of college. He was a fast study and incredibly sharp.

Lee and Juan both looked up from a large table they were standing over as Alison opened the door, letting in a loud roar from the yelling children behind her.

"Hi, Ali," they said, in tandem. Lee punched a button on his keyboard and watched the results appear across the screen. Juan was carefully holding still a large device with a thin computer cable attached.

"Hello." Alison let the door close behind her and crossed the room. "How are things looking?"

"Pretty good. We've got most of it uploaded and tested. I think we should be ready by Thursday morning." He looked up from his screen. "I take it Dirk and Sally are back?"

"How can you tell?"

"Sounds like a zoo out there."

The 'zoo' was approximately forty screaming, very

excited children. During their big move to Puerto Rico, Alison and her team somehow managed to become local celebrities with all of the press. Earlier in the year, her team had officially revealed the amazing breakthrough of their IMIS translation system in a demonstration for several news crews. Not surprisingly, the news went global and people from everywhere quickly descended upon the aquarium to see for themselves. Their communications with the dolphins was deemed the 'Achievement of a Lifetime' by several magazines, and for the next two months, she and her staff were invited on hundreds of television and radio interviews. It was overwhelming, but it initially provided a welcome change of pace after what they'd been through. However, in the end, the attention and visits never seemed to let up, so their move off the mainland wasn't just for their research; it was also for their sanity.

Of course, no matter where they went, they were going to garner a lot of attention, and Puerto Rico was no different. In fact, the entire island went wild when they found out that one of their old buildings on the south side of the island, just outside of Ponce, would be converted into a new research center for the famous 'Dirk and Sally.' What *was* a surprise was the reaction of the kids in Puerto Rico.

In the States, during their early stages of research, Alison and her team played host to countless children on field trips, coming to visit the dolphins. Many of the kids were genuinely excited, but many others were not. Instead, they sat off to the side, glued to their cell phone screens. Alison had thought it odd at first, but after seeing the same thing class after class, it became downright depressing.

However, she did remember a very special fifth grade class from Hedrick Elementary in Lewisville, Texas, and the Puerto Rican children reminded her of them a lot. In Puerto Rico, all the children were absolutely *thrilled* to come. Every face remained pressed against the thick glass the entire time. They couldn't get enough, and, as a result, it couldn't help but bring back some of that early excitement for Alison and her team. So, in exchange, they decided to do something special for the kids.

Alison had an idea one day and talked to Lee and Juan about it. It took a while, but they managed to set up a smaller translation server for visitors. It had a much shorter vocabulary than the giant IMIS system and couldn't translate new words, but it allowed the children to do something astounding: actually stand in front of the tank and talk with a real-life dolphin.

Alison remembered watching the children type on the keyboard for the first time, thinking some of the kids might actually pop from the excitement. It was contagious. She had never seen Dirk and Sally so excited either. They would stay and talk to the children for hours until the very last one had left.

Of course, Dirk and Sally were free now and they came and went as they pleased. So, when they did arrive, Alison and her team would promptly call the nearby schools to arrange some visits. And neither the children, nor Dirk and Sally, ever showed any signs of tiring. It was indeed a 'zoo' and she loved it.

"By the way," Lee interrupted, standing behind her. "Did DeeAnn find you? She was looking for you earlier. Something about helping with her research this afternoon."

"No. I'll head over."

Lee nodded and turned back to Juan, who was showing him something on his monitor. As Alison turned to leave, her phone rang. She looked at the screen and answered immediately.

"Hey there," she said, smiling sheepishly.

"Hi," replied a deep voice on the other end.

"How are *you*?"

She instinctively turned away from Lee and Juan, who

both chuckled at her. Lee playfully cupped his hands over his mouth. "Tell him we said, 'hi.'"

She made a shushing gesture with her hand and turned further around. "Sorry."

John Clay chuckled himself. "I'm fine. How are you?"

"Oh, pretty good. I was just standing here giving Lee and Juan some tips on computers."

Clay laughed. "I bet that's some advice."

"Hey," she said, half pretending to be hurt. "I have a toaster. I know how this stuff works! So, where are you?"

"Um, I'm on a plane."

Alison glanced at her watch. "Already? I thought your flight wasn't until this evening."

"Yeah, about that...unfortunately, something's come up and I'm not going to be able to make it."

Alison looked dejected. "That's too bad. I was looking forward to seeing you."

"I know. I'm sorry. So was I. Hopefully, it won't be too long."

"Where are you going?"

"Brazil," Clay answered. "Not too far. Just on the other side of you."

"Can you say what for?"

"I'm afraid I can't. Let's just pretend I'm scouting romantic vacation spots."

"You know it's going to be one year pretty soon."

"Yes, I know."

Of course he did, she thought. The man didn't forget anything. He had a mind like a steel trap. He was actually kind of amazing that way. He not only knew how to *listen*, but he actually remembered what she said for more than ten seconds.

Alison had to admit, he was nothing like she had expected when they first met. He worked for the Navy, a branch of the military she loathed. Of course, to be truthful, she hated all military branches. But as it turned out, John Clay wasn't just some Marine jarhead. In fact, he was not only a man; he was a bona fide anomaly. He was smart, considerate, and devastatingly handsome. And those shoulders!

"I'm really sorry, Alison." Clay swayed side to side in his seat as his plane turned and bounced onto the runway. "I'll call you in the next day or two, okay?"

"Okay," Alison said, still wearing a trace of a frown. "Be safe."

"Always."

"Bye." She ended the call and remained staring at the phone.

"I take it he's not coming," Lee said behind her.

She sighed and dropped her hand, sliding the phone back into her pocket. "No."

*****

The plane was a C-20 Gulfstream III, which had arrived less than thirty minutes after their video call with Langford. Clay powered off his phone and closed his eyes, pressing his head gently into the leather headrest. He regretted hearing the disappointment in Alison's voice.

After a long moment and from the table between them, Clay picked up the folder containing his copy of the report on the Russian sub and flipped it open again. He remained quiet, thinking.

"So, what I can't figure out," Caesare said, speaking first, "is what the hell kind of interest Brazil would hold for a Russian sub, and an old one at that?"

"I've been wondering the same thing. Russia has a pretty good relationship with Brazil, so why the secrecy?"

"Because that's what you do when you're *hiding*."

"But what were they hiding from?" Clay pondered. "And why a fifty-year-old submarine everyone else in the world thought had been decommissioned?"

"Maybe it was *because* everyone thought it had been decommissioned," Caesare said, with a touch of sarcasm.

He raised his bottle of beer and took a swig. "But if I was Russia and wanted to go stealth, I sure as hell wouldn't do it in a November class sub. They're noisy."

Clay tilted his head back and absently examined the ceiling. "Brazil has the second largest navy in the Americas. Their entire fleet and infrastructure are well known. What could the Russians be trying to find out?"

"It's also odd that they haven't said anything."

"Agreed. If there really was some secret to hide, wouldn't they want to get their crew out quickly?"

"Unless speaking up makes it worse." Caesare tilted his bottle, examining it. "Even if it did, why not just make up some PR story or misdirection? Governments do that all the time."

"True. But it means we're still asking the same question. What do they want to know about Brazil?"

Caesare placed the bottle in a cup holder and leaned his seat back. "Maybe there's a simpler explanation."

Clay raised an eyebrow, waiting.

"Maybe their navigator's just an idiot."

Clay laughed. Outside, the dual engines of the Gulfstream reached maximum thrust, and the plane abruptly began to roll forward as the pilot released the brakes. The aircraft sped down the runway, building speed until it lifted smoothly into the air.

As he watched the ground quickly fall away, Clay tried to relax, but couldn't seem to dismiss something. It was a nagging question that should have been answered in the report, but wasn't.

LEAP

Answers will be revealed…
And history will be made…again.

ABOUT THE AUTHOR

Michael Grumley lives in Northern California with his wife and two young daughters. His email address is michael@michaelgrumley.com, and his website is www.michaelgrumley.com where you can also find a supplemental Q&A page to the story.

MESSAGE FROM THE AUTHOR

Thank you for reading my debut novel "Breakthrough". I hope you enjoyed it. If you would be so kind as to take a moment and add a review, I would be very grateful. Unfortunately, reviews and referrals are the only real ways for a new, self-published author to compete with the big name writers, and it sure would be nice to make it out of the dark and dusty aisles of Amazon.

If you do write a review, please email me at the address above and I will forward you a special version of the book's last page, revealing a hidden subplot that some readers may have missed. I thought it would be a fun way to say "Thank You".

Made in the USA
San Bernardino, CA
19 July 2018